Twist of Fate

Twist of Fate

Bil Holton

Liberty Publishing Group
Durham, North Carolina

Requests for permission, as well as to schedule Bil Holton for speaking engagements, may be addressed to:

Liberty Publishing Group
Attn: Author, Bil Holton
1405 Autumn Ridge Drive
Durham, NC 27712

ISBN: 978-1-893095-93-9
Library of Congress Control Number: 2016912343

Dedicated to the most beautiful and one of the most spiritual, strongest, intuitive, and compassionate women I know—my wife, Cher, my soulmate and bringer of joy.

PROLOGUE

"Ladies and gentlemen, welcome to the second half of the United States Ten Dance Championship Final. The six finalists are the best of the best. Hold onto your seats because you are about to witness some of the best Latin dancing in the world."

The emcee was interrupted by thunderous applause from the largest audience ever assembled in the championship ballroom.

Signaling the audience for silence, he continued, "Our competitors are ready! Are *you* ready?"

The excited audience responded with shouts, applause, and foot stomps. Their enthusiasm filled the arena. Strobe lights bathed the dance floor with multicolored flashes of light as the competitors paraded onto the freshly-swept parquet floor.

"In numerical order, here they are! Each couple will dance a sixty-second exhibition as their number is introduced. From Toronto, Canada, couple number 211, Alex Bensalen and Suzanne Heroux."

Each succeeding couple teased the audience with their amazing athleticism and attitude as they performed to the music selected for their brief introduction.

When Jim and Kim Sanborn's number was called, the audience leapt to their feet, giving the defending champions a standing ovation. After they completed their short number, the Sanborns joined the other competitors on the sidelines while the last couple danced their introduction. Then the emcee called the six couples back onto the dance floor.

"Here they are, ladies and gentlemen. Let's have one more round of applause for our six finalists. Aren't they remarkable?"

Electricity filled the air as the audience sent their adulation to the performers, who took their positions on the dance floor. Spectators shouted the names of their favorite couples and whistled their delight, anticipating the start of the ten dance final.

"Music, please," the emcee announced, sending the dancers into their choreographed routines. The competitors pranced and strutted to the sounds of the cha-cha, rumba and mambo, sending the audience into fanatical outbursts of praise.

"Who's your favorite couple?" the emcee teased as he waved the microphone toward the audience.

"270!" someone shouted above the din.

"216," another followed.

"285."

"270! Come on, Jim and Kim."

"Let's show all of our contestants how much we appreciate them," the emcee replied, prompting the audience to renew their applause for the enterprising competitors.

Jim promenaded Kim across the dance floor to a spot adjacent to the judges. Dressed in her sensuous purple Spandex costume, Kim strutted proudly beside her husband and assumed an exotic position a few feet away from him, to prepare for the fourth dance in the set.

"The next dance," announced the emcee, "is the famed Paso Doble. The man is the matador and the woman represents his cape. Of all the Latin dances, the Paso Doble places incredible physical demands on the competitors. Notice how the music's well-timed crescendos compel the dancers to strike enthusiastic poses, and perform flamboyant leaps and spins. The competitors will dance to the music, *Spanish Gypsy Dance*. The music, please."

As the music began, all eyes moved to the couple who performed the Paso Doble better than anyone else. Jim, the brave matador, elevated himself above Kim and glided into the exquisitely-timed choreography that had made the couple unbeatable. The couple's precision was phenomenal; their style and attitude impeccable. By its very nature, the Paso Doble is an exhibitionist dance, and the Sanborns executed the required steps, leaps, and spins better than anyone else. Perfectly syncopated with the music's demands, the couple made it difficult for the spectators to watch any of the other competitors for long. Even the steely-eyed judges who lined the perimeter of the ballroom floor found themselves magnetized by the Sanborn's spectacular athleticism and grace.

As the music prepared the dancers for the last crescendo, the audience collectively shifted forward slightly in their seats, anticipating the final majestic poses of the competitors. The energy in the ballroom was at a fever pitch as the dance ended and the finale's theatrics sent the spectators to their feet in thunderous applause.

The Sanborns were the last couple to break character as they rose to enjoy the extended standing ovation in their behalf. They bowed respectfully to the audience and then readied themselves for the last Latin dance of the competition, the Jive.

Jim made eye contact with Kim.

"How's your stamina, babe?"

"I'm good to go," she replied confidently. "My shoulder hasn't given me any trouble."

"Great! I've got plenty of juice left, too! Let's hit this one with all the gusto we've got."

"Are we starting with the vertical back flip?"

"And ending with it, to show our stamina. After all, we're the Millennium Couple."

Kim arched her eyebrows and smiled as the dance was announced by the emcee.

By the time the music began, the Sanborns were already into their choreographed opening. Their routine was a carefully homogenized sequence of vaudevillian jazz, rock and roll, ragtime, hustle and swing combinations. Their enthusiastic performance was filled with unbelievable energy. Spectators and judges alike were mesmerized at their explosiveness.

The Sanborns hit their marks, and their moves were crisp and energetic. When Kim nailed her vertical back flip, the audience showed its appreciation by giving them a spirited standing ovation.

All of the competitors had danced superbly, but the Sanborns had shown once again why they were the defending national champions. The buzz of the spectators followed the competitors as they processed off the floor. By the time they stepped off the parquet floor at the far end of the dance area, there seemed to be a general feeling among spectators and competitors alike that the Sanborns had raised the bar again.

As they accepted their competitor's precursory announcement congratulations, the Sanborns continued to move toward the back of the staging area behind the judges' tables. Jim escorted Kim to a secluded corner and kissed her fully on the lips.

"You were fantastic tonight, babe."

"You weren't so bad yourself. I've never seen you have so much energy at the end of a competition. Your stamina is amazing."

"It takes two, babe. You were on, too. If we don't win this again this year, something's wrong. We sizzled."

Kim nodded proudly and then repositioned one of her shoulder straps.

"Oh, look, I broke a nail," she pouted, holding up her left hand for his assessment.

Jim let out a quick sympathetic sigh, which turned into a counterfeit frown.

"Stop that. Stop making fun of me. At least it held out till we finished our sets."

"That's right. And it's not like you haven't broken a nail before," Jim teased.

"I know. It just makes my hand look so awful."

Jim took his wife's hand and kissed the jagged nail tip.

"There. Does that championship finger feel better now?"

Kim smiled joyfully.

"Does it hurt?" Jim asked.

"No. Not at all. I don't even know when I did it."

Both of them straightened when the call for the six finalists came over the PA system. Jim grabbed a quick swig of water from the water bottle he always kept handy, then escorted his wife onto the dance floor.

The announcer began with the introduction and awards presentation of the sixth place winners, a couple from Canada. The couple from Germany was next and the fourth place couple was from England. Finishing third was a beautiful couple from Japan.

The Sanborns embraced the couple standing next to them as the emcee waited for the applause to settle. Both of the remaining couples, the Sanborns and the couple standing beside them, Ben Dare and Irene Anunnaki, were from the United States. That meant both the gold and silver medals in the Ten Dance Championship belonged to Americans. When the emcee announced that both couples were from the same dance studio in Raleigh, North Carolina, the audience erupted again.

When the Dare-Anunnaki pair heard their name announced as runners-up, the auditorium erupted again with applause and respectful whistles and shouts.

"Well, neighbors. You've just won back-to-back championships. Congratulations," Ben addressed the Sanborns.

"Thanks," Kim replied as she accepted his kiss on her cheek.

"This is the first time in DanceSport history for two business partners to place first and second in a national ten dance final, you know," Jim exclaimed as he embraced Ben. "You two danced phenomenally well. Just think, our studio took top national honors here."

Irene smiled and then perfunctorily submitted to congratulations from the couple that had kept them from gold two years in a row.

"When are you two retiring?" Ben teased, as he pulled Irene with him toward the judges' podium.

"You wish," Jim countered. "Get on over there and accept your prize money."

Both couples laughed as Ben and Irene tactfully hurried over to the awards area.

"He took it pretty well, didn't he?" Jim whispered to Kim.

"Better than I thought he would. But I know Irene is upset," Kim replied as she waved at an admiring fan and then straightened in response to a subtle tug on her waist by Jim, who was looking directly at the judges' podium.

"And now, ladies and gentlemen, This year's United States Ten Dance Champions, placing first in Cha-Cha, Mambo, Rumba, Paso Doble and second in Jive. Number 270, Jim and Kim Sanborn."

Jim whispered something to Kim as he led her to the center of the floor to bow to the cheering crowd, but the roar of the crowd muted his comment. As the Sanborns turned and walked toward the podium, accepted their trophy and prize money, and received congratulations from the other competitors, the emcee announced the names of all of the contributing sponsors.

The couples lined up in the order of their finish and posed for the customary photographs before leaving the floor. However, the Sanborns were corralled by the tournament's organizer before they could leave the floor and ushered over to the TV booth for congratulatory interviews.

"You've done it again," Ron Muntz praised, as his co-host, Sandy Dunlap beamed beside him.

The Sanborn's smiled as they greeted the celebrities.

"How does it feel to win back-to-back titles?" Sandy asked.

"Wonderful! Very gratifying. We've worked very hard this year," Jim exclaimed as he gave Kim a celebratory hug.

"You had some tough competition this year," Ron added.

"And it's getting tougher every year," Kim agreed.

"But we know that going into it," Jim explained as he wiped the perspiration off his forehead. "We don't take any of our competitions for granted. It's ours to lose and we don't intend losing because of our lack of preparation."

"You were so well choreographed in all of your routines. You even added a few more moves in both your Cha-Cha and Rumba performances, didn't you?" Ron said.

"Yes, thanks for noticing," Jim replied quickly. "We wanted to step-up our performances and show the judges we're working toward constant improvement."

"And challenge," Kim added, glancing at Jim for approval.

"You've certainly done that," Sandy exclaimed. "You two are a joy to watch. This is my first year co-hosting with Ron, and I can tell you, I've never had a more enjoyable evening."

"I enjoyed it, too," Ron agreed as he glanced at the film producer nearby, who was holding up a card indicating thirty seconds to commercial. "Well, Jim and Kim Sanford, are you coming back next year?"

"A three-peat sounds nice," Jim said, smiling broadly at Kim, who nodded her agreement.

"Of course we've got the Ohio Star Ball and Blackpool competitions to prepare for. But, yes, we'll be back."

"Wonderful," Sandy praised as Ron motioned for the Sanborns to exit to his left. "From the stately Fontainebleau Hotel in Miami, Florida, we were proud to bring you the United States DanceSport Championships. On behalf of Ron Muntz and myself and the USDSC, thank you for tuning in. Goodnight."

Delaying their retreat long enough to spend the next forty-five minutes greeting well-wishers from the audience and signing autographs, the Sanborns finally made a dignified exit to adjourn to their hotel suite. As soon as Jim closed the door behind them, he reached for Kim and held her face in his palms.

"We did it!"

Kim stood still while he kissed her and then she placed her hands over his.

"And it feels wonderful!" she replied happily.

"The Ohio Star Ball is next. And then Blackpool," Jim said enthusiastically.

"Oh, honey, stop that. Let's enjoy this championship before you think ahead."

"You're right," he agreed as he gently released her. A quick tug at this bow tie produced his next comment. "Let's enjoy our second national championship."

Kim sent him an approving glance as she sauntered through the sitting room. Jim caught up to her and waited patiently while she unhooked the rhinestone clasp on her cape before he eased if off her shoulders. Retracing his steps, he dutifully hung it on one of the hotel hangers before he pulled his shoes off.

"Ah, that feels good," he said, enjoying his own foot rub.

By the time Jim began to massage his other foot, Kim was knocking at the adjoining door between their suite and her parents, who had traveled with them to baby-sit their four-year-old son, Graham.

Her father opened the door and smiled sleepily.

"Hi, Dad! How's our little one?" Kim whispered.

"He's sleeping," came his instant reply. "He's been a joy to watch."

Kim stepped into her parent's room with Jim close behind.

"He stayed up until midnight," her mother reported quietly from the king-sized bed next to her grandson. "But the little dear just couldn't hold out any longer."

"Jerry," Jim addressed Kim's father, "you look like it's past your bedtime, too."

"Pauline's as well," Kim's father confirmed, vouching for his wife. "But it was great watching you two repeat your championship."

"You were wonderful," Pauline chorused.

"Thank you two for watching him for us," Kim said as she tip-toed over to her son.

"Graham is so mature for a four-year-old," Pauline announced softly. "He knew when he was tired and asked to come up to the room."

The others smiled at her announcement and focused their attention on the sleeping child.

"Why don't you leave him with us tonight?" Pauline asked. "He'll be all right."

"Are you sure?" Kim countered coyly.

"Of course, we're sure," her father volunteered. "No use disturbing him now. You two enjoy your championship night. Party hardy if you want to join the others downstairs. We'll see you in the morning."

"You're sure," Jim whispered, reaching for Kim's hand.

"Go. Go you two," Pauline ordered.

"Good night," Jerry insisted as he gently pushed his daughter and son-in-law through the adjoining door and closed it.

Jim pulled Kim to him and planted an affectionate kiss on her forehead.

"Congratulations, Mrs. Sanborn, You wanted to enjoy this championship. We've just been given the green light."

Kim smiled joyfully.

"Let's just stay here," she said thoughtfully and sat on the bed to emphasize her fatigue.

"Oh?" came Jim's playful rebuttal as he sat beside her.

"I'm all peopled out. Can we just stay here?"

"Of course. You're okay, aren't you?"

Kim nodded and then reached for his hand.

"I feel wonderful, wonderfully tired. I feel wonderfully wonderful! I want to be selfish with the rest of the night. All I want is us."

Jim pulled her to him and leaned his forehead against hers.

"What do you say we get out of these sweaty dance clothes and relax?"

"A nice hot bath sounds wonderful," Kim added.

"Works for me," Jim agreed. "I'll draw your water first."

"*My* water? Can't we tub it together," teased Kim.

"Why Mrs. Sanborn, that sounds like an invitation."

"I want to talk to you about Christmas," Kim said, batting her eyelashes.

"You want to discuss Christmas in the bathtub?" he teased.

"Can you think of a better place to talk about giving and receiving?" Kim countered, trailing her fingers across his chest.

Jim winked and pulled Kim closer.

"Giving and receiving sound perfect. Why don't I get the wine. You start the tub water."

He kissed her and nudged her gently toward the bathroom.

"I love you," Kim said as she slid her hand down his arm and squeezed his hand. "I don't know what I'd do without you."

Jim smiled. "I love you, too, and I expect to be around a long time. So, you're stuck with me for at least the next sixty or seventy years."

"Promise?"

"I promise," Jim said, crossing his fingers over his heart.

CHAPTER ONE

K im eased herself through the front door, carrying the packages she'd accumulated from her last-minute Christmas shopping spree at the mall. She was particularly pleased with one of her purchases, a brass statue of two ballroom dancers she had bought for the vacant pedestal in the bedroom.

He'll be so surprised, she smiled to herself as she placed the packages on the low-backed sofa in the living room. Her purse followed the avalanche of packages as she allowed its strap to slide off her shoulder.

Kim freed her phone from its cozy perch in her purse pocket to check for messages, but halted her advance to take an approving look at the mound of gifts she had spent her hard-earned money on.

I'm getting as frivolous as Jim, she sighed happily. *He's always buying too many gifts at Christmas.* She extended her smile slightly when she thought about her husband's penchant for philanthropy.

"He specializes in just-because gifts," she confessed aloud. "That's one of the things I love about that man."

That last statement carried her to the phone perched atop an antique oak stand. Nestled next to the phone were the customary writing pad and gold pen. Adjacent to the writing materials was the family photo taken by Kim's father to capture his grandson's first cabaret dance number at last year's ballroom dance competition with his parents. It was her favorite picture of the three of them.

She smiled as she took her purple leather gloves off, exposing soft hands and well-manicured long fingernails. After stuffing the gloves in her coat pocket, she quickly unbuttoned her coat and prompted the security app on the phone. Then she tilted her left shoulder enough to start her coat's migration off her shoulder. The coat slid easily off her and onto the carpet as she checked the phone messages logged electronically in the phone. There were three new messages.

The first call was a hang-up, which she deleted quickly. The next one was from her Mother:

"Hello, dear. We've got a fresh turkey from Hannaford's and plenty of sauerkraut for Jim. Oh, thank him for the firewood. Tell him we'll give him the honor of lighting the Christmas Day fire when he gets here.

"Give those two men of yours a hug for us. We'll see you tomorrow. Oh—will you bring some unsweetened almond milk and egg nog with you? Your dad forgot to buy some and I don't want to have to go back out. Got healthy turkey trimmings and no-sugar added desserts for our meals tomorrow. You two people eat much too healthy. Love ya. Bye."

The curve of Kim's smile lingered as she thought, *Life is good.* She had never been so happy. She had a husband who loved her. Her son was a bright, loving and healthy child. Their dance studio was one of three featured in a nationally syndicated column, and as a professional couple they were still enjoying the celebrity status as the United States Professional Ten Dance Sport Champions. She glanced at the family photo again as she quickly tapped for the third message.

The third call was from Jim:

"Hi, honey. I'm running a little late. I've already picked up Graham and now I'm headed to the grocery store to pick up a few things. Oh, I noticed several of the outdoor tree lights are burned out, so I'll get a couple of replacements while I'm out.

"Gotta stop by the service station, too, to feed the car and check the tire pressure. We'll see you soon. Probably around six-thirty. Love ya."

Kim looked at her watch.

"Twenty after six already," she whispered to herself. She pushed the phone's off button, retrieved her coat, and retraced her steps to the sofa.

"I hate to run Jim back out tonight after milk and nog," she lamented aloud. "It's going to cost me." She smiled, remembering fondly the compensation-for-favors game he always played with her anytime she asked him to do something beyond-the-call-of-duty. Payment would generally take the form of meals at her expense, back rubs, special desserts, or lovemaking. Every payment was C.O.D.—compensation on delivery—and she enjoyed the deliveries as much as Jim.

§   §   §   §   §   §

By the time Jim buckled his four-year-old son's seat belt, it was too late. The opportunistic thug rushed up to the car and wedged a .38 caliber pistol into Jim's left temple.

"Do as I say or I'll blow your rich head off," slurred the assailant.

"What the ... ?" Jim said, wincing as the carjacker pushed the barrel against his temple.

"Into the car! Move! Now!" shouted the attacker, as he pressed the revolver hammer back with this thumb. "I ain't got time to fool with you."

The cold metal barrel dug into the side of Jim's head, leaving a circular indention the size of the gun barrel on his temple.

"Please don't shoot. I've got a child in the car," he pleaded, reeling from the pressure of the cold steel projectile.

Sitting wide-eyed, frozen to his safety seat in the back of the car, Graham watched his father grimace as the carjacker took pleasure in inflicting pain on his victim.

"Please don't hurt my son," Jim pleaded once again, trying his best to remain composed.

"Shut up!" the attacker demanded as he shoved Jim into the front seat.

Then the assailant slithered into the back seat immediately behind Jim. As he settled in next to Graham, the youngster began to cry.

"Shut up, kid," he yelled, as he pulled the rear door closed.

"He's only four years old," Jim said angrily. "He won't hurt ... "

"I told you to shut the hell up!" screamed the thug as he smacked Jim with his open palm on the back of the head and poked the barrel of the handgun into the back of Jim's neck for emphasis.

He leaned against the back of the front seat and put his mouth near Jim's ear. Jim felt the ruffian's stale breath on the back of his neck as the uninvited guest barked his next demand.

"Close the door, ass hole, you're lettin' the cold air in. And shut this kid up."

Jim turned his head slightly to the right to say something, but thought better of it. A quick glance at the petrified expression on his son's face censored his impulse to grab the barrel of the revolver, which was repositioned now behind his right earlobe.

"Graham, it's okay, honey. This man's not going to hurt us. He's just broke and wants a little money He's ... "

"I told you to shut the boy up—not, not wind him up. Now close the door and drive outta here."

As he leaned to his left to close the car door, Jim hesitated. His fear had morphed into outrage. He knew if he closed the door he was sealing their fate. His mind flashed back to the self-defense course he and Kim had taken the year before. The instructors had stressed the importance of staying out of the car. His thoughts jumped quickly to their warnings: "Shout fire," they said. "Scream. Throw your money one way and run in the opposite direction. Take your chances on becoming a moving target. But never allow yourself to be forced into the car. Your chances of survival are zero as hostages. The car will become your tomb," they had stressed.

But it's all happened so fast, he reminded himself. *Graham is already seat-belted. What can I do?*

The gunman sensed Jim's hesitancy.

"Go ahead. Try it. I'll shoot you right here," he growled as he tauntingly leveled the gun at Graham's head. "And him, too," he smiled, glancing menacingly at the speechless child.

"No! No, don't do that. No, please. You don't have to do that." Jim countered. His combat etiquette for this sort of thing was rusty. He knew he would have to use all of his negotiation skills. He'd been a highly paid mediation consultant for ten years before he switched careers and became a writer, so he and Kim could pursue their professional dance career. But he had never faced this kind of threat. He would have to be at his confrontational best. He had a son to protect. Their lives depended upon his ability to compromise the intentions of the animal crouched in the back seat.

Jim pulled the door shut and then glanced into the rearview mirror at the malefactor. *Lord, help us,* he whispered to himself.

"That's better. You're still havin' trouble warmin' up to me, ain't ya?" the carjacker teased. "Start the damn car. I ain't got all day."

Jim lowered his eyebrows, but remained facing the windshield. He managed to steal a glance in the mirror at Graham, who started to cry again.

"Shut him up. Shut him to hell up," growled the attacker, as he brandished the gun at the youngster.

"He's frightened. What do you expect?"

"I 'spect him to shut up or I'll shut him up."

"Take it easy, okay? I'll try to calm my son down."

Jim slowly turned toward Graham, but flinched when the carjacker poked the gun against his right cheek. He hoped his nervousness wouldn't add to Graham's fright.

"Graham, honey, it's all right. I love you. Try not to cry, okay? This man doesn't want you to cry. He needs to take some money from me and then he'll go."

Graham's sobs turned into nods as he obediently listened to his father. Jim forced a smile in Graham's direction, then he made eye contact with the arrogant abductor.

"It would help if you'd lower your voice and put that gun down. I'm not going to jeopardize my son's life by trying anything foolish," Jim petitioned calmly. "There's no reason to threaten us like that. You've got the gun. That means you're in charge."

The assailant looked past Jim and peered through the windshield, forcing Jim to turn in that direction himself. A plump middle-aged woman carrying a bag of groceries was fumbling for change in her purse. She stopped in front of one of the red pots the Salvation Army always makes available at Christmas and dropped in a donation. Then she headed toward the car parked next to Jim's BMW. The carjacker became edgy as the woman approached.

"Okay, Yeah. Right. I'm in charge. Start the car now or I'll pop all three of ya," he hissed, tilting his head toward the approaching woman, who was oblivious to the drama unfolding in the car parked next to her weathered station wagon.

Jim pulled slowly out of the vertical parking space. He hoped the woman would see their predicament. But she didn't. Her attention was focused on extricating her car keys from her purse. She didn't even look up as they pulled slowly past her.

Jim's heart sank. His bickering thoughts competed with his escalating nervousness.

How many more opportunities will there be for rescue? What does this heathen want? If it's money, will he be satisfied with the contents of my wallet? My credit cards— the sixty or seventy dollars in bills? Will he find the pair of Franklins stashed in the hidden compartment? Does he want the car?

Jim's anxious thoughts fast-forwarded to more disquieting possibilities.

If he wants the Beamer, why doesn't he just force us out of it? Is he waiting for a more secluded place to ditch us and the car? Maybe he wants to guarantee himself more get-away time. Yes, that's it! He'll rob me and take the car after he's sure we can't get to a phone or summon help easily.

He glanced at Graham's reflection in his rear-view mirror. His son was sitting, hands crossed in his lap, looking trance-like at the fidgety carjacker. Jim saw the silvery ribbons of tear tracks glisten on his son's face. Graham looked like a despondent little Tiny Tim, dressed in his royal blue winter waist coat and new jeans. But this wasn't a Charles Dickens story. They were in serious trouble. And the man in the back seat was more like a deranged Grinch than Ebenezer Scrooge.

"Your bank far from here?" the carjacker growled.

Jim shot him a look in the mirror and gripped the steering wheel tightly to control his shaking hands.

"I said ... "

"I heard you." Jim cut him off, and then hesitated. He wondered if he should lead the dark-haired thug on a wild-goose chase to buy time to devise an escape plan. "It's across town."

A demonic laugh sprang from the assailant's lips.

"That kinda crap's gonna get you killed, hot shot. What do you take me for?" he asked indignantly, using his free hand to slap Jim on the back of the head again. "I was born at night, but it weren't last night. People buy groceries and do their bankin' close to home, so don't feed me that shit."

He poked the butt of the gun into the top of the plastic grocery bag beside him. "You got milk and ice cream in here. You ain't drivin' across town with stuff that melts."

"No, you're right." Jim confessed diplomatically. "I apologize for misleading you. I shouldn't have tried that."

"You're damn right you shouldna."

"I won't do that again. You can't blame me for trying, can you? What would you do if you were me?" Jim asked, trying to gain some sort of psychological advantage.

"There ain't gonna be no you if you try pullin' somethin' like that again, 'cause I'll shoot you right here."

"You don't have to threaten me," Jim interrupted. "I told you it won't happen again."

Jim glanced at Graham. The little fellow was biting his lip.

"The bank, man," cajoled the carjacker. "We're gonna make a sizable withdrawal." He shoved the barrel behind Jim's ear again. "Is that all right with you? You're my personal banker—how's that?"

Jim defiantly used the back of his head to push slightly against the ever-present revolver.

"I'm afraid you've got me confused with someone else. I'm not rich. And you don't have to keep pushing that piece into my head," he snapped.

"I'll leave it where I want it."

"Our bank is just a few blocks from here," Jim said, changing the subject.

"Payday," chimed the assailant.

"It's Christmas Eve, for heaven sakes," Jim reminded him. "If you need money or the car, take them. Just don't hurt us. Let us celebrate Christmas with our family. My wife is expecting. I ... she... "

"Shut up! You think talkin' to me like that is gonna soften me. I told you I wasn't born yesterday."

"Please let my son go. I promise I won't tell anyone if you'll just get out and leave us alone. No one's been hurt. We can all still walk away from this. You a little richer, me a little ... "

"I told you to shut up," growled the carjacker as he hit the back of Jim's seat with his fist.

Jim bit his lip so hard that it bled. He would have to out-think this assailant. And fast. He sensed things were only going to get worse.

"Pull up to the drive-in window. You're gonna give me a cash present. It's your Christmas Eve gift to little ole me," he taunted. Then he looked menacingly at Graham. "You've already got enough presents. Ain't that right, boy?"

CHAPTER TWO

K im had just finished wrapping the brass statue when she realized what time it was. "Six forty-five" she said aloud. "I've got to get moving."

She quickly added the gifts she just bought to the previously-wrapped Christmas presents stacked on the floor beside her. Ribboned and papered with brightly-colored wrappings, the gifts resembled miniature mountains of frugality and excess.

"New gifts and used wrapping paper," Kim acknowledged to herself aloud. "No use spending money on paper when you can use last year's paper for this year's gifts."

There were five gifts for Jim's family. Her parents' half dozen or so gifts were nestled next to the small hide-a-bed. The gift for Pamela, her best friend and next door neighbor, was still on the wrapping table. The gifts for Pamela's sister, Karen, and their grandparents, George and Constance Lee, were all assigned to the floor space next to the front of the bed.

Shortly after Graham's bedtime, she thought joyfully to herself, the packages will all be bowed and placed under the tree.

She eyed the packages she had bought for Jim and Graham and let out a playfully guilty sigh.

"One, two, three, four," she counted aloud, ticking each number off on her fingers for added emphasis. "Five, six, seven, eight." She shook her head, confirming their holiday extravagance. Her eyes landed on the giant stuffed giraffe loitering nonchalantly in the corner. Jim had won it for Graham at last year's state fair.

"We've bought too many gifts again," she addressed the stuffed animal. "It's usually Jim's fault, but I got the buying bug this year," she admitted as she walked over to the orange tower of stuffed pile.

She laughed, running her fingers along its furry neck. "We have the Heritage Comp coming up in February. I should have spent less at Christmas and saved for the dance competition. But, Christmas ... Well, Christmas is ... Christmas. And this will be the best Christmas yet."

The stuffed orange and white animal just stood there, staring at her indifferently through expertly painted glass eyes.

Kim wasn't going to let the giraffe's apathy stifle her enthusiasm, so she picked up a red felt Santa's hat from the oak dresser nearby and placed it on the mummified toy's head.

"There," she cooed. "Now you're officially one of Santa's helpers. That means you'll have to stick your neck out and have some fun."

Another look at her watch arched her eyebrows.

"Six-fifty," Kim said aloud as her sigh turned to a frown. "They'll be here any minute and I haven't even started dinner yet."

On her way out of the room she affectionately caressed a framed photo on the dresser. It was the one of the three of them at Disney World two summers before. Her eye caught the birthmark on Graham's right knee. It was a perfect five-pointed star the size of a pea. Birthmarks were common in Jim's family. His parents' God-given tattoos were located in unexposed areas, while Jim's birthmark, a perfectly-shaped oval, spotted the top of his left hand.

Graham's was the most prominent and well-defined, winning him a special place in the family's freckled lineage.

§ § § § § §

"You did real good," the thief said as they pulled away from the bank. "No surprises. No bawling." He looked at Graham. "And no bullshit," he continued, as he poked Jim in the back of the neck again with the gun barrel.

Graham started to whimper but a menacing look from the heathen beside him aborted any sobs that might have started.

When they were less than half a block away from the bank, the thug spoke. "Gimme your wallet," he demanded, and spitefully poked Jim again.

Jim hesitated long enough to show his resentment, then reached into his sport coat pocket to lift his wallet. As he clasped the wallet, he felt his hand brush against something else stowed in the pocket. The mini-recorder! His razor-sharp mind seized upon its importance. He'd used it earlier to interview Rick Chrystler, the owner of the Fred Astaire Dance Studio in North Raleigh, as research for a scene in his next novel. He pulled out his wallet and handed it over his shoulder to the carjacker. Then he eased his hand back into his coat pocket and pushed the rewind button on the recorder.

Please, God, he prayed silently, *keep the recorder quiet.*

"You can take everything else, but please leave the pictures," Jim petitioned as he quickly checked the intruder's whereabouts in the mirror.

The ruffian only grunted.

"They're of our family. One of them in particular can't be replaced because there is no negative. They're all special photographs ... "

"You still can't keep your mouth shut, can you?" the thief retorted as he rifled through Jim's wallet.

"Ooh, ain't she a purty thing now," he teased when he got to Kim's picture.

Jim tightened his lips, seething at the thief's filthy implication.

The pillager took everything but the pictures and threw the wallet back at Jim. "Keep your silly pictures. They don't do nothin' for me."

Jim tried unsuccessfully to grab the wallet before it slipped off the seat. His resentment heightened. Somehow, he reasoned, *I've got to get this creep out of the car.*

Seeing Graham's frightened reflection in the mirror, Jim chanced giving him a quick wink in an effort to soothe the child's fears. "It's going to be all right, Graham. Our hitch-hiker will want us to drop him off soon," he explained, attempting to force his own agenda on the recalcitrant thief.

The mugger busied himself adding the money he stole from the wallet to his stash from the bank account.

It's now or never, Jim assured himself. He slowly reached into his vest pocket and pushed the record button on the recorder. *Gotcha,* he triumphed silently. *You won't get away with this. Anything you say,* he smiled to himself, *everything you say will be caught on tape. You'll incriminate yourself.*

Jim's thoughts switched from manufacturing evidence to self-preservation. *Please God,* he prayed silently, *deliver us from this evil. What have we done to attract this evil? God Almighty, hear my prayer. If you must take one of us, take me. Protect our son. Surround him with white light. Keep him safe. Oh, Kim, honey, I'm so sorry I got us into this. You must be worried sick about us by now.*

The thought of his wife's concern accelerated his thinking. His thoughts centered on outsmarting the thug in the back seat.

"You know my name, but I don't know yours," Jim badgered the felon. "Do you mind telling me who's separating us from our money?"

"Do you mind shuttin' up?" the thief hissed. "Jus' keep driving and stay on your side of the road."

Jim jerked the steering wheel to his right, realizing he had crossed the center line.

Graham's whimpers turned into full-fledged wails as he reacted to the commotion.

"Here we go again. So help me I'm gonna ... "

"That's what I'm trying to do, help you," Jim raised his voice. "I've told you to put the gun away and stop shouting. My son's not used to being around loud people who threaten people with guns."

The felon gritted his teeth, but didn't say anything.

"How old are you? Eighteen? Nineteen?" Jim quizzed cautiously.

"I'm old enough," grunted the crook.

"Well, you don't look quite twenty." Jim glanced in the mirror. "Maybe twenty-one."

"You're talkin' too much," snapped the assailant.

"Look, James or Mike or Latrell or whatever your name is ... "

"Buster," the thug squealed.

"What?"

"Buster," he repeated. "My name's Buster Matthe ... " he sliced into his own sentence. "I ain't telling you my name. You think I'm stupid or somethin'?"

"Buster. I thought I should at least be on a first name basis with the six foot, two hundred pound gunman in the back seat of my car. You from around here?"

"Turn here. Slow down, man. Turn here," Buster interrupted.

"Oh, you mean left on Blue Ridge Road?" Jim clarified.

"Yeah, that's right." The assailant shot Jim a suspicious look. "Why are you sayin' things like that ?"

"Things like what, Buster?"

"Things like repeatin' me, callin' my name, tryin' to be friendly when you know your ass is in trouble."

"I'm trying to treat you like a human being, Buster. I hope you'll return the favor."

Buster glanced at Graham, who was looking fretfully at him.

"Whatcha lookin' at, boy?" he growled, causing the youngster to cry. "There you go again," Buster moaned indignantly.

"He'll be all right," Jim interceded. "Graham, honey, it's okay. We'll be all right." Jim turned slightly toward the back seat, causing Buster to strike his arm with the butt of the pistol.

"Turn around and keep your eyes on the road. The kid'll be all right. Go straight through the next intersection."

"You mean where Blue Ridge turns into Ebenezer Church Road?"

"Shut up and keep drivin'."

"I'm just trying to clarify your orders," Jim patronized. "I want to do as you say, Buster. You've got my money. Now let us go. I promise you, I won't report this to the police if you let us go. How about it? I'll consider this just one of those unpleasant detours in life. Our lives mean more to me than the money ... or this car. You want the car?" He glanced at Buster in the mirror. "Seriously, take the car. Tie us up and take the Beamer. I'll report the money and car stolen tomorrow. That'll give you plenty of time to get away. What do you say?"

"What's in the black bag?"

"What?" Jim asked.

"The bag on the floorboard back here."

"That's daddy's dance shoes, Graham announced innocently. "Do you want them, too?"

"What would I want with them?" snarled Buster.

"You can dance in them," Graham countered softly.

"Dance in them?" jeered Buster. "Dance in them."

He poked Jim in the back of the head again.

"You a dancer, boy?"

Jim pretended he didn't hear him.

Buster leaned toward Graham again.

"You wanna see your daddy dance?"

Graham sensed he should not react to the felon's arrogance.

Buster allowed a slippery grin to crease his face as he leaned closer to Jim again.

"I'm gonna make you dance, hot shot. You wait and see."

"Let us go unharmed. You can take the car. If you want more assurance, let's stop here at Aztec Drive and let Graham out. You can hold me hostage long enough to get away."

"Got it all planned out, do you?"

"I'm only trying to make this a win-win situation for everyone. You get the money and transportation and we get to spend Christmas with our family. What do you say, Buster?"

Jim was feeling very uneasy. He didn't like where this was going. Buster seemed preoccupied and was checking his watch every couple of minutes. Jim used his left hand to wipe the perspiration from his brow.

"Turn here," Buster instructed, ignoring Jim's last comment.

"Buster, Let us go now. We're far enough out of town."

"I can't let you go. You know that."

"Of course you can. It's up to you. I told you I won't ..."

"It's not up to me," Buster interrupted.

Jim lowered his eyebrows and threw Buster a puzzled look in the mirror.

"What do you mean it's not up to you?"

"Slow down," Buster replied quickly.

"You've got your whole life ahead of you. You don't want to do this. Don't ruin the rest of your life by doing something you'll regret."

Jim was pleading now. He wanted to find some speck of decency in Buster. He wanted to protect Graham. He wanted to live.

"Pull over behind that car—the green one."

"You mean into Sun Circle? Buster, you're wearing a nice dark brown leather jacket. Is that a Fort Bragg paratrooper's patch on it?" Jim amped up his taped description of the man who sat defiantly in the back seat. Realizing he didn't have much time, Jim asked, "Who do you hate, Buster? You've got the initials H.A.T.E. tattooed on your left knuckles. You must hate somebody."

Jim's desperation heightened. Buster's sudden muteness sent chills up his spine.

"Are you meeting someone here," Jim asked. "You're going to tie us up here, right?"

"Stop right here." Buster spoke calmly. Too calmly.

"Buster, please! Let my son go. Please. He can't hurt you and he's too young to identify you." Jim wanted to scream. His bargaining had turned to pleading. He felt another sudden urge to grab Buster's revolver.

It might go off, he thought quickly. *I can't take the chance of hurting Graham. Damn it, I've got to do something—and quickly.*

"Turn the key off," Buster ordered.

Jim glanced into the rearview mirror. Buster was still directly behind him, but positioned too far back to chance a scuffle.

"What are you going to do? We're parked behind the mint green Camaro." Jim nervously filled the awkward silence. He hoped the cassette tape was still recording their conversation.

If the worst happens, Jim thought, *the police will at least have the animal's description. Please, God, surround us with white light. Damn it. I'm parked too close to see the license plate. That was stupid!*

"Don't move." The order fell maliciously from Buster's lips.

Jim felt deathly cold metal on the back of his neck again. His eyes widened as he held his breath. His eyes darted rapidly as he listened nervously for the click of the hammer to signal the weapon's readiness.

"Give me the keys."

"Please, Buster. Let us go," Jim pleaded, hoping for a miracle.

"Give 'em to me—now!"

Jim slowly removed the keys from the ignition. He squeezed the keys tightly and took a deep breath, before handing them to Buster.

Jim heard the rear car door open and felt the barrel lift from the back of his neck. He let out a nervous sigh and followed Buster's movements as the creep stood outside the car.

When Buster slammed the back car door, both father and son jumped.

Buster took a few steps toward the front of the BMW and halted his advance. Jim's car keys were in one of Buster's gloved hands. The .38 was in the other.

When did he put those on? Jim asked himself. *He doesn't want to leave prints.* Jim gasped. *My God, he's going to kill us.*

Jim spoke quickly, hoping his voice was loud enough for the recorder. "He's wearing expensive boots, black and gold design, pointed toes with brass tips, I think. He has brown eyes and is wearing a gold earring in his left ear."

Jim shivered violently. He looked wide-eyed at Graham, who was staring blankly at him.

"Graham, can you unbuckle your seat belt?"

Graham nodded and struggled with the belt buckle.

"Push the button down, honey, push it with your thumb."

Jim looked nervously at Buster who was walking toward the Camaro.

"Have you unlocked it yet?"

"No."

"Graham, honey, try harder. You've got to unlock it! Please hurry!"

"I can't."

"Yes, you can. You must!"

Jim did a proper job on his own harness and glanced at Buster again.

"Graham, honey ... "

"I did it. I did it, Daddy!"

"Good, son, that's terrific. Now when I tell you, I want you to open the door and run. I want you to run into the woods as far as you can. See the woods over there?"

Graham nodded.

When he comes back to the car, Jim calculated coldly, *I'll open the car door quickly and slam it into him, if he's close enough to it. Lord, please help my timing to be right.*

Jim tilted his head toward Graham but kept his eyes slanted at Buster. The goon was speaking to someone in the Camaro and then he straightened and inspected the neighborhood.

Jim's heart skipped a couple of beats.

"I don't like this," Jim whispered. "He's talking to someone in the Camaro," Jim reported for the benefit of the recording. "I can't make out who it is. It looks like a woman. But I'm not sure about that. It's ... no ... yes! It is a woman! She's talking on a cell phone." Jim quickly turned to Graham.

"Graham, Graham, honey."

Graham's eyes widened, but his lips remained closed.

"Graham, honey, remember, when I tell you, I want you to open the car door and run. Do you understand?"

Graham nodded. "I'm scared, Daddy."

"I know, honey. So am I. But it's okay. Don't worry. I'll be right behind you. Okay?"

"Okay, Daddy."

"I love you, Graham."

Graham's lips formed a tight smile.

"Don't wait for me. If you beat me out of the car, I'll catch up to you, okay? Then I'll carry you piggy back through the woods over there."

Jim nodded toward the cluster of trees blanketed in darkness at the side of the road. He censored his own instructions when he saw Graham's facial expression change. His son was looking past him.

Jim wheeled around in his seat and was startled by Buster's presence.

The felon was standing just outside the driver's side window. His .38 was pointed directly at Jim.

"Oh my God! Buster please! No!"

"Merry Christmas, ass hole. Tell baby Jesus I said happy birthday."

Bang! Bang! Bang!

CHAPTER THREE

I don't know where he is, Mother and I'm getting worried," Kim confessed. "It's not like Jim to be this late."

"He hasn't called?" asked Pauline.

"Yes, an hour ago. He was picking up a few things, and expected to be home long before now."

"Oh, well, he's probably caught in traffic. How's my little grandson doing? I bet he's excited about Christmas!"

"Mother, Graham is with Jim."

"I thought you picked Graham up."

"No, not today. I had last minute shopping to do, so Jim said he'd swing by the daycare on his way to the grocery store," Kim responded, trying to conceal her agitation at her mother's well-meaning inquisition.

"Wasn't Jim in Greenville today?"

"No, mother. He was in Raleigh. He said his last stop was the gas station to service the car," Kim remembered.

There was a pause the length of two heartbeats before her mother spoke again.

"You mean the Texaco on Falls of the Neuse?"

"Yes, And before you ask, I've already called. Jim hasn't been there yet. And that's why I'm a little worried."

"I'm sure he'll be home any minute, dear. The traffic is horrendous these days. Try not to get upset."

"I'm already upset. It's not like Jim to be this late. And the spaghetti's been sitting on the stove for over forty minutes now."

Pauline's sigh slid through the phone connection.

"And the garlic bread is hard and cold," Kim lamented.

Pauline censored her criticism and chose instead to address her daughter's uneasiness.

"Kim, honey. Everything's going to be all right. I'm sure there's a perfectly good explanation for his being late," Pauline answered, waving off her husband's inquisitive looks. He was just coming downstairs from his jigsaw puzzle board and caught the middle of their conversation.

"Jerry," Pauline put her hand over the receiver, "everything's fine. I'll catch you up on our conversation in a minute. Jim's not home yet and we're trying to determine whether we should be worried or not."

"I'm going to call Hannaford's. Jody is working one of the registers today and if he's been there, she will have seen him." Kim tried not to exaggerate her concern, but this kind of delay was uncharacteristic of Jim.

"All right, dear," her mother replied. "Please call me as soon as you hear from Jim."

"Yes, of course, mother." Kim gritted her teeth. "I'll have Jim call as soon as ..." She interrupted herself when she heard two short bursts from the doorbell. "They're back, mother. I'll call you later."

Without giving her mother a chance to reply, Kim quickly tapped the "off" button on her cell phone and laid it on the kitchen counter.

She paused briefly to give the spaghetti a perfunctory stir and then hurriedly stepped into the dining room.

"Hello. Glad you two are back," she called out her enthusiastic greeting a few paces into the dining room. Then a thought hit her. *Why would he ring the doorbell? He has a key.*

She accelerated her advance through the archway separating the dining room from the living room and walked hurriedly toward the front door.

"He's probably got his hands full of groceries," she said aloud, as she wiped her hands on her apron.

"I'll be right there, honey" Kim shouted, as her reply competed with another ring from the doorbell.

"Okay, okay," she laughed, "give me a chance."

When she opened the front door, her smile faded and the bright lights which danced in her emerald eyes disappeared.

Two policemen in full uniform were standing, stone-faced, on her front porch.

Kim's heart sank.

"What can I do for you, officers?" Kim forced a nervous smile.

"Are you Mrs. Sanborn?" the older officer asked mechanically.

Kim nodded.

"May we come in?" the same officer spoke again.

Kim raised her eyebrows and nodded, backing politely away from the doorway.

Both officers wiped their shoes on the mat outside and followed her into the vaulted living room.

"I'm Lt. McCauley and this is Officer Wells."

Kim could tell something was amiss.

"Is there anything wrong, officers?" Kim asked, trying to make her voice come out natural. Her emotional antenna set off an internal alarm, making her ears ring.

"Is your husband's name James Sanborn?" Lt. McCauley asked in his most investigative tone.

"Yes. What's wrong? Oh God, have they been in an accident?" Kim asked hurriedly.

"I'm afraid we have some bad news for you," Lt. McCauley announced in the heavy language of distressing news.

Kim recoiled. She was already subconsciously retreating from the searing report she knew he was about to give.

"Oh, my God, they've been hurt, haven't they?" she prophesied. Her eyes were riveted onto him, needing his confirmation but not wanting it.

The officers exchanged wary glances.

"Where are they? Please! Tell me they're ... no, oh no," she faltered. Goose flesh rose on her arms.

"Mrs. Sanborn," Lt. McCauley began slowly. His voice tightened as he pushed out the words. "Your husband has been killed. He ..."

Kim's hands flew over her mouth. The scream she knew was there stayed frozen in her throat. Then she reeled backward as if she had been struck. She stutter stepped over the carpet until she tripped over her own feet, losing one of her shoes in the process.

Officer Wells caught her by the arm before Kim hit the floor and gently lowered her onto the cushioned arm of the couch.

"He was shot in his car at close range," the lieutenant reported, speaking quietly and empathetically. "Looks like it was robbery, although there was no sign of a struggle."

Kim gasped. Her quivering lips began to go numb and the color evaporated from her face. Her throat felt heavy and thick and dry. But she was able to whisper the words out.

"And my son? Where's Graham? Where's my son?" Then her voice picked up speed and volume. "Is my son all right? My son was in the car. Is ... is my son, is he ...?"

Before either officer could respond, Kim bolted past them like she had been shot out of a cannon and headed toward the front door.

"You've got him in your car, right?" she screamed as she jerked unsuccessfully at the front door knob.

Lt. McCauley reached her first, and as he tried to restrain her, she flung his arm away and renewed her struggle with the front door.

"Mrs. Sanborn," Lt. McCauley entreated. He tried to steady her, but Kim's forcefulness caused him to slip on the marble tile at the front entrance.

"Are you saying your son was with your husband?" he asked, once he gained his footing.

Her staccatoed screams filled the room as she began to shake convulsively. "Yes! Yes! He ... Graham's . . ." She continued to resist him as she forced the door open. "My son's not outside in your police car?"

She started to pull away from him again, but he held her tightly.

Lt. McCauley squinted his eyes and shook his head, unable to look directly into her frightened eyes. "We didn't realize there was a passenger. We don't know where your son is. There were no signs of a child being in the car."

"What about the car seat?" she asked indignantly.

The officer frowned, then shrugged innocently. "There was no car seat in the car."

Kim screamed at the top of her lungs and withered in his arms. Her weight caught him off balance causing him to brace her against the front door. Officer Wells came to both of their rescue.

The officers gently pried Kim from the front door and escorted her back to the couch.

Smothered by despair, she forced herself to speak.

"Jim picked Graham up from daycare about a quarter after five today," she whispered, struggling to regain her composure. She used her trembling hand to brush her waist-length hair off her face.

"Are you sure your son was in the car with your husband tonight?"

"Yes, I'm sure. Do you think I'm the kind of mother who doesn't know where my child is? He was in the car with my husband," she shouted.

"Okay. Okay," Officer Wells proxied for both of the policemen.

She closed her tear-filled eyes and hesitated only momentarily before she launched another impassioned attack at the officers.

"He's just a baby. My baby's out there somewhere. You've got to find him. You'd better find him, do you hear me?" Her anger brought Kim to her feet.

Lt. McCauley turned to Officer Wells.

"Call out to the scene and get hold of Novakovich. Make sure they comb the area for the boy. Check with the local residents. And search the woods in the Ebenezer Church Road vicinity. The boy may be ..." he blunted his own sentence as he looked at the distraught mother beside him. "The child may have gotten away and run into the woods," he recovered. "Alert them there may be a youngster out in the cold."

Officer Wells started toward the front door. The Lieutenant motioned for him to standby for a moment, then turned to Kim, who had just buried her face in her hands.

"Mrs. Sanborn."

Kim raised her head slowly, bringing her eyes above her fingertips, but her palms still covered her mouth. The red polish on her long fingernails made her face appear even more ashen.

"May we have a recent picture of your son?" He looked at her sympathetically. "It'll help us ..."

Her nod made the rest of his explanation unnecessary. Kim started to move, but couldn't find her legs, so she pointed to a cluster of pictures on the mantel above the fireplace.

"Take the one," she gulped, trying to form her lips into a coherent sentence, "take the one lying on the mantelpiece. We haven't framed it yet."

Her attempt to blink back the tears only produced more, as her gaze followed Officer Wells' movement across the living room. When he picked up the picture, she let out a gut-wrenching sob. It was as if another precious piece of her family was being taken away. She allowed the lieutenant to assist her onto the couch.

"He's wearing a navy blue waist coat, white knit hat and jeans," she whispered. Sighing heavily, she continued, "And he's four years old. Just four years old."

"I'll be out in just a minute," Lt. McCauley notified the other officer, who tipped his hat at Kim and eased himself through the front door.

The lieutenant approached Kim and lowered himself in a squatting position directly in front of her. *Such a beautiful woman,* he thought. *Too nice to have such a catastrophic thing happen to her, especially on Christmas Eve.*

He rested his elbows on his thighs and nervously fingered his hat with both hands.

"You all right?" His eyes came to rest on hers.

Kim followed her nod with a whispered reply. "No. I'm not all right! I'll never be all right! My God, do you hear yourself? My husband is ... and my son ... please, you've got to find him."

"We're going to do our best. Officer Wells is mobilizing a search for him now."

Kim forced a weak smile. "Yes," she whispered. "I know, and I'm going with you."

"Mrs. Sanborn, I don't think that's a ..."

"My son's out there somewhere. I'm going to find him."

The lieutenant offered token resistance, until she stood facing him.

"Mrs. Sanborn..."

"We're wasting time. I've got to find my baby."

"Okay. But there are a few questions I need to ask you."

"Questions? Damn you. I want answers. My ... my husband is dead ... and my son is missing."

"We want to find him, too. Help me do my job."

Kim glared at him.

"Okay. You can ask me on the way. I've got to find my son."

"We'll ... we'll need you to identify the ..." he cut into his own sentence, "to identify your husband's body at some point." He met her fixed stare. "Would you be able to come downtown tomorrow?"

Kim wiped her eyes with the back of her hand and then accepted the tissue Lt. McCauley provided.

"No," she vetoed emphatically as she rose, attempting to step around him. Her maneuver forced the officer to follow her quickly across the room. "I'll go tonight—after I've found my son."

"Mrs. Sanborn." Lt. McCauley was momentarily caught off guard. "I don't think ..."

"I'm joining you in your search for my son tonight. There's no way I'm going to leave my baby out there alone. I'm not going to settle down until we find him. Do you understand?"

Lt. McCauley threw his hands up in mock surrender. "Okay. Okay. If that's the way you want it," he surrendered. He caught the determined gleam in her mascara-smeared eyes. "I can't stop you, can I?"

"That's right. You can't stop me. You don't even want to try."

Kim slanted herself around the end of the couch and walked quickly toward her purple all-weather coat.

"I'll get it for you," he offered, moving politely in front of her to retrieve it.

Kim stood in dignified silence while he helped her into her coat. A brittle smile creased her lips as the officer thoughtfully remembered her purse and fetched it for her. She had her coat buttoned and purse over her shoulder by the time she got to the front door.

"You said my husband was shot," Kim pined as she opened the front door.

Lt. McCauley nodded.

"Point blank range," she verified, clearing her throat.

Both of them stepped out into the night air. Although it was mild for December, Kim didn't notice.

The officer nodded again.

"He was shot three times with what we believe to be ..."

Kim stopped and wrapped her arms around her stomach. She let out such a gut-wrenching wail that Lt. McCauley found it difficult to suppress his own tears.

Kim wept uncontrollably in his arms and then suddenly pushed herself away.

"Let's go. We have to go. My baby is all I have left now."

She pulled a tissue out of one of her coat pockets to wipe her face and started down the front steps. She stopped briefly and pulled several more tissues out of her purse, realizing one wouldn't be enough.

"Mrs. Sanborn. You'd be more help to your son if you stayed here."

"No! I'm going."

"What if someone finds him and calls you. You won't be home to take the call."

His objectivity stopped Kim in her tracks. She turned to face him.

"Let us handle this search, Mrs. Sanborn. I promise you we'll find him." The Lieutenant paused and then diplomatically corrected himself. "If he's out there, we'll find him."

By the time he had finished his last comment, Kim was standing next to him at the base of the steps.

"You're asking me to trust you?"

Lt. McCauley nodded.

"You can trust thirty years of police work."

Kim bit her lip.

"And you can trust those officers out there, many of whom have children. They'll stay out there for as long as it takes. Christmas or no Christmas."

He offered to chauffeur Kim back up the steps.

"You have my word as an officer ... and as a father of two."

Kim allowed herself to be shepherded through the front door.

"I forgot to turn the lights off," she reminded herself as she stood just inside the door.

The lieutenant tested a hesitant smile.

"You have a right to be forgetful tonight," he empathized.

"How would they know who to call?" Kim asked softly, as she stood glued to the marble tile in the alcove.

"They?"

"You know, the people who find Graham. How would they know to call me?"

"Oh, they'd probably call the police station. Unless they know you. Do you know anyone in the Aztec Drive, Sun Circle area?"

Kim shook her head before she spoke. "No, I don't think so."

"If anyone found a child that age, unattended at night, they'd most likely call us," he repeated himself.

"I know what you're trying to say. That means my son could spend the night away from me until your people piece things together."

"No. No, Mrs. Sanborn, I hope we'll have your son back to you within the hour, maybe a couple of hours."

Kim shot him an irritated look.

"I promise you we'll do the best we can."

"What if you don't find him?"

"We will."

"But what if you don't?"

"If your son is not in the neighborhood ... " He hesitated, choosing his words carefully. " ... and if someone, a passerby or local resident, or one of my men doesn't find him soon ... " He paused again. " ... then he's probably ... well, you're likely to get a ransom note or phone call."

Kim's knees suddenly went weak, prompting her to reach for the lieutenant's arm.

Lt. McCauley seated Kim on the sofa and settled himself beside her.

"Mrs. Sanborn, I think you ought to stay here in case your son has been kidnapped. Our chances of finding him are reduced after the first six to eight hours he's reported missing. I think we've got a head start on this one. Besides, we don't know if kidnapping is an issue yet. Let's hope he's been found already. It really would be better if you stayed here."

Kim shook her head, feeling suddenly sick to her stomach.

"Mrs. Sanborn, is there anyone I can call to stay with you. Family? A friend?"

"Yes. My parents. I should have called them already. What am I thinking? Jerry and Pauline Spencer. They live right over there." Pointing toward the front of the house, Kim moved past the cocktail table and stepped quickly over to the living room window. A premeditated poke with her index finger through the mini-blinds showed her that her parent's house lights were lit. A frown broke across her worn face. "I've got to call them so they'll come over. I'm surprised they haven't seen your car by now."

She backed away from the window and routed herself toward her cell phone. It was perched on the kitchen counter where she had left it.

The lieutenant followed her through the archway and advanced as far as the kitchen table. He saw the abandoned spaghetti and garlic bread on top of the stove.

The crayoned pictures posted on the refrigerator door displayed her son's handiwork. Potted plants hung from the vaulted ceiling, forming a rich green canopy over the round glass-topped dinette table. Three table settings were poised dutifully around the table. The center of the table cradled a pink poinsettia. The light from the chandelier over the table ricocheted off the glass surface eulogizing an aborted meal.

This whole night stinks, he thought to himself. *Whoever killed her husband is probably celebrating now... and spending this family's money. What a crying shame. And this family ... this poor family's Christmas has been turned into the worst possible nightmare.*

Frustration showed on her grief-stricken face as she fumbled with her parents' number twice in a row. Glancing at Lt. McCauley, she shrugged as she punched the number once again.

"I only have to punch one number," she lamented, " and I can't seem to get that right."

He threw her an understanding smile as he turned the stove off and was about to offer his assistance when she suddenly breathed her success. "I've got them. It's my father," she announced. "Daddy," her voice trailed off. It was obvious from the frozen look on her face that she wasn't going to be able to continue. Lt. McCauley started toward her.

Kim started to cry and held the phone out to Lt. McCauley. He could hear her father's baritone voice clearly through the receiver.

"Kim, darling. Is everything all right?"

The lieutenant assisted Kim into the closest kitchen chair and then spoke into the phone.

"Hello, Mr. Spencer, this is Lt. McCauley with the Raleigh Police Department. I'm across the street at your daughter's house."

§   §   §   §   §   §

"Buster, I told you not to call me here!"

"What was I supposed to do? You didn't say nothin' about his boy bein' with him."

"He wasn't supposed to be. Mrs. Sanborn generally picks him up," his employer hissed.

Buster grimaced, but remained silent.

"Damn it to hell," his nefarious client continued huffily, pounding the phone booth with his hands. "Can't you do anything right?"

We be in hell already, Buster thought in answer to his employer's tirade. Buster started to speak but let his thoughts take over again: *This conversation ain't goin' nowhere. All this jerk wants to do is give me a hard time.* He looked through the car window at Graham and then canvassed the area around the car.

"What you want us to do with the boy?"

"I don't know," shouted the other malefactor nervously. "Just let me think for a second."

"Take all the time you want," teased Buster nonchalantly.

His employer sighed heavily through the phone..

"Where is he?"

"In my car."

"In your car?"

"We ain't nowhere where anyone can see us."

"Damn it, Buster, it wasn't supposed to go down like this."

"No kidding! You was the one who said this would be easy."

"I know, I know. Look, take him to your place."

"My place!" The police are swarming all over Raleigh lookin' for that boy."

"Your place, damn you. Just for a couple of days. Just until I figure this thing out."

Buster gave him a disgusted sigh. "My woman's takin' a chance, too. So it's gonna cost you more money. We didn't figure on no kid."

"All right. All right."

"That's a thousand dollars more."

"What? I don't have that kind of money. I've already paid you five grand."

"That was for dumping the old man. The kid's extra."

His accomplice sighed.

"Okay. But I don't have that kind of jack on me now."

"You better get it," Buster threatened. "I done my part."

"Yeah. Okay. Give me a few days."

"No. You've got 'til tomorrow. I ain't taking no heat on this one. The kid's your problem."

His nervous client let out a heavy sigh.

"I'll get you the money tomorrow. In the meantime..."

"The kid's taken care of. You just take care of your end," Buster interrupted.

"Everything else went okay then?"

Buster smiled, "Yeah," he grunted, nodding his head absentmindedly. "I done the job right. And now I'm trying to cover your sorry ass."

His accomplice's impatience came through the phone.

"Did you ditch the gun?"

"Of course. It's fish bait in the bottom of Jordan Lake."

"You dispose of anything else traceable?"

Buster thought a moment.

"Yeah," he replied nonchalantly. "I threw the car keys into the lake, too. And oh, yeah, I got these." Buster said, producing a handful of credit cards. "I still got the credit cards and his watch. You said to make it look like robbery. So I did."

"So long as you get rid of the evidence. I don't want any loose ends."

"You mean any more loose ends. We've got a four-year-old loose end. I'm keeping his money though. I figure it's a bonus."

"What money?"

"The bank money."

"What do you mean, the bank money?"

"We made a withdrawal."

"You idiot. You forced him to make a withdrawal?"

"We used the ATM. Chill out before you have a cow. No one saw us."

"How do you know? Any number of people could have seen you. And the ATMs have cameras mounted on them. You idiot!"

"Ease off! I told you nobody saw us. You got no cause to worry 'bout my end. I'm not the one who screwed up. Just make sure you don't screw up tomorrow," Buster threatened.

"I told you I'd have your money."

"That's right. And the kid. Don't forget the kid."

The angry employer sighed heavily into the phone.

"You know I got the kid with me. Don't you be trying nothing foolish now. Like turning me in."

After a slight hesitation, the accomplice spoke agitatedly.

"Don't you go paranoid on me. Why would I want to turn you in? I wouldn't do something stupid like that."

"No, you're right. You won't do something stupid like that. I'll see to that. You get my drift?"

"Just produce the deliverable when I call you tomorrow."

"The deliverable? Aw, you mean the kid. Like I said, you take care of your end. I'll take care of mine. Merry Christmas, Santa."

CHAPTER FOUR

There were days when Kim could hardly make it out of bed. Getting up, doing anything at all took more effort than she could produce. Everything took a conscious, deliberate act of will. And these days she had more won't power than willpower. Grief was her morphine, deadening her to a world she no longer wanted to be a part of.

It had been three torturous weeks since Jim's funeral and Graham's disappearance, and she was not plugged back into life yet. And she didn't care. She wouldn't allow anyone to infiltrate her emotional fortress. She remained socially impregnable, untouchable, isolated. She shut herself off from people, from help, from the outside world.

Her house became her safe house. And her own cocoon was betraying her. Home repairs and regular maintenance didn't care about her grief. Spent light bulbs didn't ask if it was okay to burn out. Spoiled food in the fridge needed to be composted. Overdue bills needed to be paid. The length of her fingernails demanded a manicure. Her soiled clothes were heaped onto an already overstuffed hamper.

Although her father had mowed the lawn several days before, he wasn't aware of the stopped-up sink in the upstairs bathroom. But Kim was very much aware of it as she stared into the backed-up mess. She felt a certain kinship with the sink and the fridge and the hamper. They were all under siege. Kim stared at the recalcitrant plumbing. Where was Jim?

Suddenly Kim stiffened, as the rage she had suppressed so long tore from her. A vengeful growl detonated in her throat and exploded into a scream as it left her mouth. She stood there, with arched back and chin lifted toward the ceiling, much like a wolf baying at the moon, screaming at the top of her lungs. Both hands were clenched in fists so tightly her fingernails dug into her palms, leaving crescent-shaped indentions in the soft tissue.

She had succumbed to her abysmal grief, screaming her anger unapologetically at Jim's photo nearby.

"Damn you. Why did you leave me? You know I don't know how to do this stuff. I don't want to do this stuff."

She slammed her clinched fist down hard on the ceramic sink.

"I miss you both so much. It's not fair."

She felt more tears come.

"You said we'd grow old together. I want my son! You said you'd never leave me. I want both of you here!"

She slumped her body slowly along side the sink cabinet until she sat on the floor.

"I wouldn't have to call a plumber if you were here. Or a painter. Or an electrician. You've left me with a life that needs too many repairs. Damn it. It's not right. Too many things are hitting me all at once. I don't want to take care of anything. I don't want to do anything. I don't want to live."

Kim elbowed the front of the cabinets in a fit of despair. When she realized she hadn't hurt herself or inflicted sufficient damage to the cabinets, she elbowed them again.

"I hate you for leaving me. I hate God for taking my son. And I hate this house."

She sprawled on the floor, kicking everything she could reach—the base of the toilet bowl, the bottom of the Jacuzzi, the cabinet doors, the tiled floor.

Screaming at the top of her lungs, Kim gave the Jacuzzi another vicious kick—and then another—and finally, another. Her anger turned into uncontrollable sobs as the tirade depleted her physical energy. She wept as she had never wept before.

In a short while, physically exhausted and emotionally spent, she fell asleep.

§   §   §   §   §   §

Kim's family and close friends were quite concerned about her and tried to dislodge her from her grief, but she refused to be pulled from her emotional straight jacket.

She was surrounded by her loved ones. Her parents lived across the street; her good friends, George and Constance Lee, lived on one side of her, and her best friend, Pamela, lived on the other side. Pamela's sister, Karen, lived in Asheville, but flew to Raleigh each week to visit Kim.

Kim measured progress in steps: first one, then another, and the next, as far as the bathroom, then the dining room, and the sun room. Her grief took her back to the murder and kidnapping experience dozens of times. Her angry visits to the police precinct and State Bureau of Investigation offices left her depleted and confused. There was no progress in finding Jim's murderer ... no ransom notes ... no indication that Graham was still alive. Kim felt lost, drained, helpless.

Phone calls, flowers, cards, and visits from dozens of her ballroom dance colleagues showed Kim people cared. Sympathies extended to her from the presidents of the International Dance Sport Federation, the United States Ballroom Dance Sport Association, and the Fred Astaire Dance Studios in America all remained sealed in the envelopes on the night stand.

Pamela had downloaded hundreds of e-mail messages and kept Kim's Caring Bridge correspondence up-to-date so Kim could stay current privately. A lingering glance at the neatly stacked pages of e-mail correspondence forced a slight smile to form on Kim's dry, swollen lips. She thought about the chic, fashionable world of ballroom dancing, its outlandish costumes and glamorous competitions, its quirkiness and its politics.

Virtually every developed country in the world had its ballroom devotees. Its influence sent couples and single people alike to college gymnasiums, suburban country clubs, church recreation centers, and dance studios to learn the art and science of dancing.

Her Cinderella world had come to an end. Jim was dead and that special princess side of her had died, too. Their stunning achievements as professional dancers would never be repeated. She knew she would never be the same, feel the same, dance the same way again. There was a growing awareness that her championship dancing career was over. The desire to compete was gone. It was buried with her husband.

Many of the well-wishers on the printed e-mail list would have been competitors in a few months. Although Kim knew she and Jim would have been favored to win the World Championship, a few couples on that list would have been serious contenders. All that had changed now. The Sanborn's wouldn't be going to Blackpool, England this May or any other May.

She had dreamed of the world championships as a child. She and Jim had danced together as school children, then as high school sweethearts, and finally as husband and wif. They had danced together for twenty-four years. Even her pregnancy four years ago had not slowed their championship hopes. And Graham. Dear little Graham, had danced before he walked. He was a natural. She kept him with her everyday at the dance studio. He had style. He had soul. He had panache for a four-year-old. He would follow in their footsteps. Everyone knew it. He was Blackpool bound, too. She had dreamed it. He would be tall and thin, yet masculine. As smooth as Fred Astaire and as playful as Gene Kelly. With his father's looks and his parents' championship genes, Graham would have been the flagship of the next generation of Sanborns.

Kim started toward the e-mail print-outs, but stopped at the foot of the bed. *Thanks for loving me, all of you,* she said to herself, *but I'm just not ready for you yet.*

"Kim, are you all right?" came a voice from the living room.

"Yes, I'm ... I'm sorry, Pamela. I'll be right there."

She turned abruptly from the bed and walked measuredly through the doorway and into the hallway leading to the living room.

It was Tuesday evening and the sun was just setting into a beautiful patchwork of magenta and violet. Pamela had just exited Kim's office downstairs and was standing beside her sofa, sipping a cup of Hazelnut Cinnamon coffee.

"Kim, are you all right?" Pamela repeated as she placed her coffee cup on the ceramic coaster.

Kim threw her a fragile smile.

"Some of me is all right, but all of me isn't."

"I know, it's going to take time," Pamela agreed, making room for Kim to join her.

Kim settled in beside her and took her own cup of coffee off the end table.

"Thank you for down-loading those e-mails, but I haven't gotten to them yet."

Pamela smiled and then symbolically patted the large white envelope she had placed on the cocktail table when Kim was in her bedroom.

"These can wait, too."

"More e-mails?"

Pamela nodded and smiled.

"Thanks anyway. I suppose I should read them. All of them."

"When you're ready. You'll read them when you're ready. Please don't feel I'm pressuring you to..."

"No. You're not," Kim interrupted. "I don't feel that way about it at all. I appreciate your thoughtfulness. It's just that ... it's so hard."

Pamela patted Kim's free hand.

"Let's talk about something else."

Kim formed her lips into a tight smile and her eyes brightened a little at Pamela's sensitivity.

"How about a warmer?" Pamela asked.

When Pamela rose to refill their coffee cups, she raised an eyebrow at Kim. "You're going to get through this, you know. You've got that 'show-must-go-on' moxie in you."

Kim acknowledged her compliment with a smile, but then lowered her gaze to her crossed hands on her lap when Pamela left for the kitchen. After Pamela had done a proper job on the coffee refills, she re-entered the room and handed Kim her cup of coffee.

"Thanks for taking such good care of me. You and Mother particularly have been wonderful."

"What are friends and family for? I've had my share of misfortune. Believe me, I can appreciate what you're going through. Kim, I think you're doing wonderfully well, all things considered."

Kim closed her eyes and tightened her lips slightly. She remembered how Pamela had dealt with her dear friend Geoffrey's death, and the unbelievable threats to her life.

"I mean it. I'm so proud of you," Pamela continued. "You've lost two wonderful people. And that precious little boy. I ... I don't know how you've managed to hold yourself together like you have."

"You call this holding myself together?" Kim attempted a fractured laugh as she looked slowly around the room. "My house is a mess. The Christmas tree would still be up if Dad hadn't taken it down. The only housecleaning that's been done is what Mother and you have done. Ben has taken care of the business this past three weeks. The bills are piling up. I haven't opened my mail. My nails need a serious manicure" she lamented as she glanced at Pamela's well-manicured nails. "My hair's a mess. Yeah, I'm holding it together, all right."

Pamela put down her coffee and took Kim's cup out of her hand.

"You're mending inside. You're grieving the only way you know how. Don't be so hard on yourself. You delegated the business stuff to Ben. He's your business partner. He can take care of it. I was here when you called for your next nail appointment. And your hair appointment. And the eye doctor. You wouldn't have made those calls if you weren't coming out of it. You're easing yourself back into life. You're going to make it, Kim. I don't doubt that, and I don't want you doubting yourself, either."

"Did you ever consider becoming a therapist?" Kim asked as she squeezed Pamela's hand.

Pamela chuckled.

"I just want to be a good friend."

"You are," Kim replied, squeezing her hand again. "You are a dear friend."

Pamela placed her hands over Kim's.

"Is there anything I can do for you before I go?"

Kim looked quickly around the room again.

"Yes. As a matter of fact, you can. You can put all of the cut flowers Ben sent me outside in the sunroom."

Pamela's gaze followed Kim's exaggerated arm gesture.

"My word, woman! How many vases has he sent you?"

"One for each day since the funeral."

"That's three-weeks worth."

I know!"

The women's eyes met in the middle of Kim's last statement.

"I guess he wants to brighten up my days."

"He's over-doing it a bit, isn't he?"

Kim nodded, "Ya think? He's sending flowers because I won't see him."

Pamela sent her a puzzled expression.

"I haven't seen much of anyone since the funeral, and well ... Ben can be a bit tiresome," Kim admitted.

Pamela sent her a corroborating head nod.

"To tell you the truth," Kim said, "he makes me a little uncomfortable. You know how he has always had a thing for me?"

Pamela nodded again. She remembered how Ben competed with Jim for Kim's interest before her marriage.

"Is that jerk coming on to you—at a time like this?" Pamela asked.

"Oh, no," Kim responded quickly. "It's just that he's called every day ... and he's smothering me with flowers. He hasn't done anything improper. No advances. Nothing like that. He's just too attentive. I wish he'd keep his mind focused on our business. I'd like to buy him out, but the students love him and he's the top-rated dance instructor in the region. And I have to admit, he really is a good business partner. I should be thrilled he's around; after all, he won the silver medal at Heritage last year. But honestly, Pamela, he just makes me feel creepy sometimes."

"Well, you need a loyal business partner right now, while you take some time to heal," said Pamela.

"You're right. It's just that I'm afraid his idea of taking care of business extends beyond the dance studio. But at least he's running the studio while I'm going through this. And you're right. I know I'm in the healing process. But it's so hard. I keep going up to Jim's office, and staring at his laptop computer. His latest manuscript is still on it. I've even made a few editorial corrections, like I always did for him. Isn't that crazy?"

"No, it's not crazy. Oh, Kim. I'm so sorry this had to happen to you."

"What am I going to do, Pamela? Yesterday I spent four hours just sitting in Graham's bedroom, cuddling his toys and stuffed animals. Remember that panda bear you gave him last Christmas?"

Before Pamela could answer, Kim wrapped her arms around her own shoulders and pantomimed hugging a stuffed animal.

Pamela reached for Kim and the women held their embrace for a short while. Kim finally released Pamela and cradled her guest's hands in her own. She sighed before she spoke.

"I'm going to do my best to hold it together."

"I know you will."

Using Kim's energy as reaffirmation, Pamela gently pulled her hands away and lightly smacked her own knees. Then she raised herself from the sofa.

"You want all of the bouquets in the sunroom, right?"

"If you don't mind. Here, let me help you," Kim volunteered, as she elevated herself to Pamela's level.

A half hour later, Kim was sitting in a dimly-lit living room reflecting on Pamela's visit. She resisted the urge to lie down on the sofa, fearing she might drift off to sleep. She stood, stretched her stiff muscles, and walked slowly around the sofa before she switched on the lights in the living room. *Let there be light,* she announced to herself. *Lord, how I need some light in my life.* Then she turned out the house lights and settled for the muted lights from the street which leaked through the front window blinds.

She took her grief with her as she wandered aimlessly into the kitchen, and then back into the living room on her way upstairs. She hesitated in front of the spare room door, a door that had remained closed since that fateful Christmas Eve. The Christmas presents were still there, those multicolored monuments to an aborted Christmas. Kim stared long and hard at the door before her trembling hand touched the knob. Then, as if the knob were on fire, she jerked her hand away and retreated to her bedroom.

Once safely locked in her room, she crawled mournfully out of her clothes, tossed them in the corner, and wrapped herself in one of Jim's flannel shirts. She climbed into his side of the king-sized bed and curled up under the afghan her mother knitted for them as a wedding present. Her fatigue was her sleeping pill, causing her to drift quickly into dreams of Jim and Graham, and happier times.

She awoke with a start after a particularly vivid dream, and realized it was morning. A glance at the lighted dial on the face of the digital clock on the night stand told her it was ten-forty.

"I'm right on schedule," she told herself out loud. "It's after ten and half of the morning's spent already."

She sighed heavily, pulling her knees up to her chin. A rush of air left her lips again, but she made no attempt to unwind herself from the covers, her sense of urgency long since deflated by weeks of bereavement.

"I want my family back, God. I don't want to live without them."

She leaned over and turned on the night stand lamp. Heavy sediments of golden lamp light jumped on her face, illuminating the corners of the master bedroom.

Pushing another pillow behind her back for support, Kim slowly surveyed the bedroom. Her lethargic gaze caught the menagerie of cosmetics and perfumes which covered her dresser top. The cluster of nail polish bottles beside her hair brush looked like a small band of pilgrims sporting black top hats. The black lace bra she'd discarded yesterday was draped over her favorite music box, giving it the appearance of a bear stretching itself out of hibernation. The packet of e-mails Pamela had compiled for her was still poised on the bureau. She attempted a smile, but settled for a counterfeit grin. She wasn't ready to forgive the world for destroying her family.

"It's not fair, God. It's not right to take someone's happiness away like that. It's cruel. What did we ever do to deserve this?" Then her disbelieving heart surrendered to a rational mind. "Sorry, God. It wasn't you who took them. It was the creep who took them. It was the society that produced the creep in the first place!"

The cool silence of the room enveloped her introspection and self-pity. Glancing back at the jumbled up bra, Kim thought: *Hibernation isn't so bad. Someone once said rest itself is a weapon.*

"Rest itself is a weapon," she repeated her thought aloud. "Well, then, I must really have myself some humongous weapon." She allowed a small laugh to escape her lips.

As she sat up in bed, the expression on the face of her twin in the bureau mirror caught her attention. It was pleading with her: *Kim, darling, you've just got to get rid of those unsightly half moons under your eyes. And those lips, those lips were made for lipstick and smiles. Those beautiful nails need a serious manicure. And that hair! You can't possibly go through another bad hair day.*

"I've got to pull myself together," she chastised herself aloud.

She steeled her gaze at the woman in the mirror.

"You've got to get it together, young lady," she said as she shook a finger at her double in the mirror. "This isn't like you. You're a doer. Everyone says you can do anything you set your mind to do. You've got to find your son, and you can't find him lying here, feeling sorry for yourself."

Kim squinted her eyes, intent on giving her double a thorough examination.

"You can't allow this thing to destroy you," she reminded herself.

And you've got Graham to think of. The thought struck her, causing her to shiver. Goose bumps colonized her arms, forcing her to rub them vigorously.

"Graham," she whispered disconsolately. "My dear little Graham. Mommy's going to find you. I haven't forgotten about you. I've pined for you day and night for three weeks. I love you, honey. I've prayed to God every day for your safety. I want you here. I want our nightmare to end."

Her watery eyes lowered her gaze to the picture of Graham on her dresser. It was a studio portrait. He was wearing red shorts and a white top. His blonde hair and blue eyes favored his father's, his mouth and chin favored hers. Her nostalgic examination found the prominent birthmark on Graham's right knee. It was in the shape of a star, about the size of a pea. It was on the inside of his knee and was dark brown in color.

Kim smiled as she remembered Graham's first reaction to it. He was just beginning to become aware of his own body, his hair and eye color, baby teeth, and any cuts or scratches he inherited from falls or tricycle accidents. When he was two years old, she introduced him to the game of naming parts of his body as she pointed to them. She would point to his nose and he would say "nose." She would point to her own eye and he would point to his and say "eye." His first attempt to say star sounded more like "tar." But, he was only two years old then. She teared up. He was so proud of his "tar."

It's his lucky star, Lord. Please help me find him. You know where he is. Give me the strength to find him. Forgive me if I've done anything to cause this. If only I had picked him up instead of Jim, they'd both be alive today. It's all my fault. I was so set on picking up that dance statue before Christmas. But it was for Jim. The gift was for him, Lord. You know how much we loved dancing.

She spied the book Pamela had given her next to Graham's picture on her dresser. Intuition prompted her to take a peek at it. It was written by two Unity ministers from Durham. Pamela said she should read it. "It will change your life for the better," Pamela had told her.

Kim walked over to it and ran her hand over the book cover.

"More Straight Talk About Spiritual Stuff," she said aloud, mouthing the book's title. She turned the book over without taking it off her dresser. A quick glance took her eyes to one of the quotes on the jacket: *Spiritual growth is not stunted by unanswered questions, but by unquestioned answers.*

"Yes. I've got a few of those!" she said, recognizing that's exactly where she was emotionally. Her eyes migrated to the next quote: *It's time to question traditional religious views that perpetuate the myth of an anthropomorphic God in the sky who favors some and punishes others.*

"Oh, my God," she exclaimed. "That's exactly how I feel!"

She reeled in her curiosity and picked up the book. With measured anticipation she opened the book to the heading 'Anthropomorphic God.' Her undisguised longing for answers prompted her to read the description:

As you continue to unfold your spiritual nature, you come to understand that there is no external, anthropomorphic force that acts upon you; that guides you if you're dutiful; that heals you but not someone else, or heals someone else but not you; that rewards believers, but punishes sinners; that sacrificed His Son to purge the world of sin, but then allows humankind to sin anyway. This is the established mainstream religious view. But in the principle of unity which physicists, neuroscientists, and metaphysicians have set forth, you are not simply the creation of God, molded and shaped and set on the path of life 'down here' in skin school. You are the Force or Presence of the Eternal Presence we call God expressing Itself as you.

Her mouth dropped as far as her eyebrows raised, but her immediate reaction was one of solemn agreement.

My God. What if they're right? She said to herself. "They are right!" she spoke out loud, as if to confirm her own growing conviction that a God in the sky who truly loves us would never allow the atrocities that we hear about in the news everyday.

Her thoughts settled around the implications of what the excerpt she had just read meant. The depth of their assertion resonated with her completely and carried her thoughts and her gaze to the large brown manila envelope sitting on the bureau. It contained Jim's personal effects the night he was shot. She remembered signing for it when she identified his body. She had forgotten about it. But there it was, staring her in the face, flaunting the reality of his death.

Kim closed her eyes tightly, and placed the book gently on the dresser. Then she retreated to her bed behind her and sat on the edge of the bed. Then she pulled her legs up and placed her arms around her knees so that she teetered on the edge of the bed.

Wrestling with the finality of Jim's death and Graham's disappearance, she laboriously lowered her bare legs off the edge of the bed and heaved herself up. Her joints cracked and ached in lactic protest at having to move. Lethargic legs carried her past the book and manila envelope on the dresser toward a photo of Jim on the bookcase.

She stopped respectfully in front of the photo, siphoning all the strength she could from the confident expression on Jim's face in the photo.

"Oh, Jim. You didn't deserve to die that way. Your last moments must have been horrifying. Why would God want to put such a decent, loving man through that. No, wait! A loving God wouldn't do that. Those Unity ministers are right," she admonished herself.

I'm beginning to believe there's no white-bearded, white robed man in the sky, she admitted to herself.

She touched the photo of Jim's face with her fingertips, running her fingers over his eyes and nose, and stopping over his mouth. Peeling her fingertips from his lips, Kim brought them to her own lips and kissed them, sending them back once again to rest on the photo.

"I love you," she sighed softly. "I'll always love you."

Her body stood statue-like, frozen to the carpet in front of the bookcase. *You are my soulmate,* she pined to herself.

"We did more in seven years than most married couples do in fifty, didn't we, babe?" She reminisced aloud.

She caressed his face again and tearfully focused on his stately features. His eyes, more hazel than blue, were set in sockets above well-formed cheeks, prominent and warrior-like. His perfect set of teeth magnificently showcased a smile so completely intoxicating that he could mesmerize — instantly — anyone, friend or foe, caught in its glow. *You had an uncanny ability to win friends and influence people,* she reminisced. Her silent eulogy produced another installment of tears.

"Why couldn't you influence the animal that killed you?" Kim shouted angrily.

The two vases of cut flowers that Pauline and Constance had placed on the ledge of the bookcase fell victim to her outburst as she wrathfully swept them cleanly off the shelf. She watched the contents of the vases spill onto the cream-colored carpet. The wall near the bookcase also felt the effects of her outburst. Its surface was christened with the water and fragments of the flowers from the spent vases.

"He was too good a man to have this happen to him," she wailed tearfully, beseeching a God she wasn't sure she believed in anymore. "It's not fair. How can you give someone extraordinary happiness and then take it away from them? I want Jim back! I want my baby back! I want my life back!"

Kim leaned against the bookcase for support. Her outburst had drained her.

"Why aren't criminals and low life taken away to make the world a better place? Jim never hurt anyone," she whispered, vacillating between the God she thought had abandoned her after Jim's death and Graham's disappearance and the God Presence she was beginning to consider as more Principle than the God she once believed in.

"And Graham." She started to sob again. "What did he ever do to deserve this? I want my baby back."

Her sobs carried her into a heap on the floor at the base of the bookcase. Hot tears spilled over their mascara-less rims and down her cheeks, moistening Jim's flannel shirt.

"It's not right," she murmured, "I thought you reaped what you sowed. What did we sow to reap this?"

She raised her red-rimmed eyes toward the ceiling.

"What did we sow to reap this?" she repeated indignantly. "If that's a fundamental Christian principle, it should be consistent with cause and effect. So what did we do to cause this? I want to know. What did Jim do? What did Graham do? What have I done to deserve this?"

Brushing the tears from her cheeks with the back of her hand, she fired another soul-searching barrage at the universe.

"We've been good to people," she paused, wiping the next installment of tears away. "So if we sowed good, why didn't we reap good? I refuse to believe we did anything to cause this. My husband died and my son was taken from me. We have reaped what society has sown? Is that how it works? If you're blaming a four-year-old little boy for the sins of a wayward generation, I don't want anything more to do with you! Graham didn't sow any of this, he's innocent, God. You know he's innocent."

She took a deep breath and let it out slowly. *I'm serious. Those two Unity ministers are making a great deal of sense,* she broadcast to herself.

"I'm going to need an answer to that question before I trust you again—no, believe in you again," she said out loud. "Do you hear me, God?" She paused for a moment. "I want your answers, God, not your silence!" She gritted her teeth. "You simply underwrite everything, don't you God," she exclaimed, stringing her thoughts together. "It's up to us to draw from your power to make the human experience work. That's it, isn't it?"

She seemed comforted with amping up her understanding. "O ... ka ... y," she sighed out the words. *If there's no geography in Spirit like the two authors said, then there's no separation between you and me,* she assured herself.

"Maybe I should be looking inside myself instead of outside of myself for you," she reasoned, feeling like she was beginning to piece things together.

She placed her arms on top of the knees which she had pulled up to her chest, to improve her sitting position. Then she lowered her head onto her crossed forearms and remained motionless for several moments. When she lifted her head, her gaze fell on the brown envelope again.

The sight of the manila envelope brought her to her feet. *Part of Jim is in there,* she said to herself. She wanted to hold a part of her deceased husband again. To touch his things. To say good-bye to personal items that were no longer valid without him.

She moved slowly on bare feet across the carpet and came to a halt beside the package. Glancing mournfully at her double in the mirror, she sent herself a frail smile.

Kim picked up the envelope and gently opened the seal. The front of the envelope bore Jim's incident report number along with several other bureaucratic scribbles that looked more like graffiti than documentation.

Before she lifted the flap exposing the contents of the envelope, she pressed the folder against her heaving breasts and summoned the courage to commence her examination.

She walked decidedly over to the foot of the bed and poured the contents onto the plush quilt. Then she took her place alongside the scattered personal effects.

Her taciturn gaze spied the Mont Blanc pen she'd bought Jim when he landed his first bestseller. *I'm surprised that's still here,* she marveled, as she plucked it off the bedspread and laid it aside. She nervously picked up his wallet and cradled it in her hands before she opened it. Everything but the wallet-sized pictures, library card, and insurance cards was gone. The secret packet where Jim stashed his mad money was empty, too.

Kim wasn't surprised. The killer had taken everything from her.

The watch Jim bought in Germany was there, along with eighty cents in loose change, three quarters and a nickel. The car keys were missing, and so was Jim's college ring.

So that's why the police asked for my car keys and advised me to have the locks changed. She remembered having to give her car keys to her father so he could drive Jim's car home after it was released from the precinct impound.

The mini-recorder and the tape of Jim's interview with Rick Chrystler was there. She picked up the recorder, smiling as she recalled how Jim had hung on to this recorder, in spite of her pressuring him to try the newer technology. He claimed it was like an old friend to him, and he insisted on keeping it. Jim had written the date and subject of the interview on the label.

She studied Jim's handwriting briefly. A weak smile slipped across her face as she admired his penmanship. Even on such ordinary surfaces like cassette tape labels, his handwriting was superb. She added the tape recorder to the pile of keepers, then realized she had kept everything.

"This is hard," she consoled herself aloud. "These personal items know what happened. They know who killed my husband. They know what happened to Graham." She took a deep, shuddering breath. "If these things could only talk."

Kim gathered up the items from the bed and placed them in her top dresser drawer.

Another thoughtful glance in the mirror at the reflection of the semi-composed woman told her that she had just stepped past an emotional hurdle. A small smile of self-congratulation etched itself across her flush face, bringing her tightly-sculpted lips into a slight upward curve.

"One small step for widow-kind, one giant step for grieving wife."

She slowly unbuttoned Jim's flannel shirt and pulled herself out of it, exposing the body of a young woman who took care of herself. Her striking angular elegance was accented by well-proportioned, although not large breasts set above an isthmus of a waist. Her long, thin thighs and legs were unblemished. They were the legs of a dancer and her flat tummy was the product of years of conditioning.

Her coal black hair hung in languorous folds like swatches of velvet, cupping her oval face, framing it perfectly. She gave her hair a couple of perfunctory tosses and started toward the bathroom, but stopped just inside the door. Then she wheeled around and snatched the remote from its perch atop the CD player.

"I could use some soft music while I shower," she said, deciding on the spur of the moment. Then just as quickly she changed her mind and tossed the remote on the bed.

"I don't think so," she broadcast aloud, as she turned once again toward the bathroom.

Standing with her face tilted toward the overhead spigot, she allowed the hot spewing water to cascade over her face and hair and breasts and thighs. She remained motionless, eyes closed, hands at her sides, feeling enlivened by the chlorinated waterfall.

Her sighs were sighs of catharsis as wave after wave of hot water cleansed her weathered soul. She stood there until she had washed off three torturous weeks of bereavement.

Suddenly she remembered the erotic showers the two of them enjoyed when Graham stayed overnight with her parents. She reached impulsively behind her head to grasp the imaginary back of Jim's neck, to pull his lips closer to hers. Instead she found the prickling pressure of falling water as it bombarded her outstretched palm.

Undeterred, she lifted her other hand, palm up, and let the spigot send its hot water over both her palms. Then she stretched her hands as high as she could and arched her back, pretending she was reacting to his embrace. A short while later she came to her senses.

"Don't do this to yourself," she chastised herself aloud. "Jim's dead. He's not here. He's not coming back."

She reached over mechanically and turned off the spigot.

No, she reminded herself, *Jim's still here. A part of him will always be with me. He's my soulmate. Our souls are united forever.*

"There's no geography in Spirit," she chimed emotionally, remembering what the two ministers had written.

Comforted with that assertion, Kim stepped carefully out of the shower, toweled herself dry, and used the blow dryer on her hair. Then she ran her fingers through her silken hair and shook her head from side to side as if to complete the aeration her fingers began.

She let her bathrobe fall to the floor as she glided into the bedroom toward the chair her favorite jeans occupied. Although they had small holes in each of the knees, the jeans gave her a sense of freedom and comfort. And that was something she needed now. So without hesitation, she confidently sheathed herself into frayed jeans that were an air-conditioned old friend.

Next she rifled quickly through the second shelf in her walk-in closet and lifted one of her favorite cashmere sweaters, a black one, from its cubby hole. Electing not to encumber her breasts with a bra, she pulled the sweater over her head and let it cascade down over her tanned torso.

"Jim always liked me bra-less," she gave herself an approving grin.

The last thought about Jim prompted her to retrieve the cassette from her dresser drawer, while she used her free hand to snatch her hair brush.

"It's an interview tape, but it'll have his voice on it," she spoke softly and deliberately.

Needing to hear the sound of his voice, she loaded the tape into the combination CD/cassette player and rewound it. She settled back on the bed and began to brush her hair while she waited for the tape to begin.

She squinted her eyes when she heard what sounded like a car motor and some kind of rhythmic beating. She leaned closer.

"Heart beats," she whispered. "It sounds like heart beats. That's strange."

She didn't have time to edit her thoughts. The next series of dialogues sent chills up her spine.

"You know my name, but I don't know yours. Do you mind telling me who's carjacking us?"

"That's Jim's voice," she said in a raised voice. "Oh, my God!"

A look of puzzlement crossed her face when she heard another more caustic voice.

"Do you mind shuttin' your face up?"

Kim's eyes widened and her mouth flew open.

"Jus' keep drivin' and shut the hell up."

The beginning of real panic set in when she realized the context of the dialogue on the cassette tape.

"It's not the interview tape," she screamed. "Oh, my God! Oh, my God!"

She was distraught at hearing Jim's panicked voice, but when she heard Graham crying in the background, her gut-wrenching wail reached every corner of the house.

Her calm of a few moments ago had vaporized. She was listening to her husband negotiate for his life and the life of their son.

A smothering feeling enveloped her, causing her to turn off the cassette player.

The room was silent again except for the sound of her own labored breathing.

"Oh, my God," she repeated softly, cupping her hand over her mouth. She was completely undone by this turn of events.

She eased herself onto the foot of the bed and punched the start button on the cassette player. But her emotions got the best of her, forcing her to shut off the recorder again before it continued its horrible message.

Not a single lead in three weeks. Not one iota of evidence. No ransom calls or notes. Not one clue as to what happened. Her thoughts worked as rapidly as her heart sank. And all along, first-hand evidence was buried in the brown manila envelope.

A pitiful smile formed on her lips as she threw her hands up in mock surrender and lowered them immediately.

"Jim knew he was going to die," she said softly. She coughed, then cleared her throat. "He wanted to make damn sure the murderer didn't get away with it."

She cleared her throat again.

"Oh Jim, I love you, honey. You brave, brave man."

She lifted herself from the foot of the bed and tearfully pushed the start button. A sheer act of will kept her glued to the electronic account of her husband's slaying.

Her labored breathing competed with the recorded message as the mechanical humming of the car's motor pierced her ears again. The sound of her husband's anxious heart beats accelerated her own as she placed her hand over her own pounding chest.

A nauseous feeling washed over her. She thought she might vomit when she heard her husband's pleas for mercy.

CHAPTER FIVE

K im focused her attention out the window some fifteen feet away from Captain Deveraux's office as Lt. McCauley and several other officers listened intently to the kidnapping account on the tape. She had exited through the open door, and was standing outside the captain's office to put more real estate between herself and the gruesome account. After listening to the grisly narration in her bedroom the night before, she could not bear to hear it again.

She looked out the outer office window. The weather was as cold and bleak outside as she felt inside. Raleigh had its first taste of winter overnight. An ice storm, moving through the pine state, blanketed the capital city with a thin coat of ice.

Her weary eyes followed the crystalline calligraphy of ice-laden tree limbs and bent-over shrubbery as the morning sun danced off the thin crust of ice, brightening every branch and bough. She noticed a beautiful cluster of gnarled rhododendrons, long time residents of downtown Raleigh. Their wintry foliage was laminated with ice. Each plant stubbornly bore the icy insult, spreading its branches in all directions to distribute the weight.

Today's weather is in unbelievable contrast to yesterday's summertime temperatures, she thought sadly. What a difference a day makes. One day the temperature is in the 50's, the next day it's hovering in the teens. One day I had a family. The next day, I'm a widow ... and a single mom.

Sharp blasts from the section of the tape she dreaded hearing the most broke her reverie.

"Bang! Bang, bang!"

She jerked uncontrollably each time a round went off and the sound of her husband's last desperate gasps sent shivers through her. Three sharp barks of the pistol had ended his life and destroyed hers.

She closed her eyes and braced herself against the window sill, anticipating her son's recorded scream followed by his pitiful pleas to stay with his father.

When the sound of her son's scream came, she shivered. She bowed her head and wondered why she hadn't distanced herself further away from the morbid recording.

She leaned her head against the cold window pane when she heard the sounds of the recorded scuffle as the murderer yanked her son from the back seat. She clinched her teeth at the murderer's profanity and scowled at his cold-blooded arrogance. When she heard the solid thud of the car door as it slammed shut, she shivered again.

But it was her son's last pleas that caused her to collapse against one of the precinct desks nearby.

"Daddy! Daddy! Daddy... Daddieeeeeeee...!"

The tape continued, but it was the recording of Jim's interview which had been taped over.

From the corner of his eye, Lt. McCauley saw Kim falter and rushed out of Captain Deveraux's office to her side.

"Mrs. Sanborn. Are you all right?"

Kim nodded, then shook her head.

"No," she admitted, choking out her reply. "No, I'm not all right."

Lt. McCauley looked at her sympathetically as he supported her with his hand under her elbow.

"I don't know about you, but I could use a hug after hearing that tape," he said reaching out to her.

A faint smile creased her lips as she accepted his surprise hug. They stood in mournful solidarity, sharing in silence what mere words were too impotent to grasp.

Finally Kim leaned back slightly and trained her eyes on his weathered face. There was a toughness in the determined lift of his head. And his face was etched with the tensions of a lifetime of police work he would never reveal.

He wasn't wearing expensive cologne and his surprisingly well-fitted sport coat covered a white dress shirt that was frayed in several of the button holes. But his eyes revealed a wealth of feelings, empathy, caring.

"Thank you," she spoke softly. "Thank you, Lt. McCauley."

He grinned in an engaging way.

"It's just part of the job," he replied soberly.

"No, it's not," Kim retorted quickly. "I could tell from the first time I met you that you care about people."

His smile was followed by an embarrassed glance away from her.

"You feel up to speaking with Captain Deveraux? The evidence you've produced is just the break we've needed."

Kim tightened her lips and nodded, allowing the lieutenant to escort her into the captain's office.

"Mrs. Sanborn, we're doing our best to find your son and your husband's killer," Captain Deveraux said, looking directly at her. "The tape will help. We've got a complete description of the killer now, and his name, thanks to your extraordinary husband."

"Then I hope you can do something about it! I've just spent three weeks in hell wondering what happened to my son. I think it's about time I got help from your office. You said you were doing your best to find Graham, well, I don't believe you have done your best. The only thing I've gotten this past three weeks from this office is excuses and apologies."

"Mrs. Sanborn, we haven't the manpower. We..."

"You haven't had the interest...or the heart. If he were your child, you'd spare no resources. You'd leave no rock unturned. You'd find the manpower. Am I right, Captain?"

Lt. McCauley glanced at her and then at Captain Deveraux, but remained quiet.

"Mrs. Sanborn ... the lieutenant and I ..."

"I'm right, aren't I? You haven't made my son or my predicament a priority, have you?"

"I beg your pardon ..."

"No, beg my forgiveness," came her caustic reply.

Lt. McCauley sighed heavily as he squeezed her arm gently. He could tell she had just pushed one of the captain's hot buttons.

"Mrs. Sanborn, we're going to act on the evidence you've provided. And you're right about one thing—our best hasn't been good enough. So I am going to ask for your forgiveness. And I understand your anger. So give us another chance to show you what we can do."

Kim studied him for a moment, then nodded showing the slits in her eyes.

"I want you to find my son, and I want my husband's killer prosecuted."

"We'll do all we can to accomplish both those goals. You have my word on that."

Kim pulled her coat collar tighter around her neck and narrowed her eyes at the captain.

"I'm going to hold you to that promise."

She excused herself, eyeing both officers cautiously on her way toward the open office door. As she walked toward the elevators, she heard Graham's frantic little voice erupt again in her troubled mind:

Daddy! Daddy! Daddy ... Daddieeeeeeee ...!

§ § § § § §

74

"Is he ready?" the bearded man asked.

"Yeah," Buster tilted his head toward Graham, who stood wide-eyed behind him. He was dressed in a different set of clothes and was washed and groomed to perfection.

"Whatcha doin' with the beard?" Buster asked his employer.

"Think, Buster. Use your head. Why do you think I'm wearing it?"

Buster shrugged his shoulders and threw his disguised confederate a devilish smile. "Because, it's hunting season. Child-hunting season. Right?"

Summoning the courage to speak, Graham took a tentative half-step forward.

"I want my daddy and my mommy."

The bearded visitor looked past Buster at Graham.

"Hi, son. You doing all right?"

Graham was motionless except for a nervous tug at his trousers.

"My woman told him he was goin' home today." Buster explained quickly. "I didn't tell him no different."

"Yeah, yeah. That's okay," his accomplice replied, groaning his impatience.

Buster's girlfriend, a beautiful, shapely woman in her late twenties, stood behind Graham. One of her hands was resting on top of his blonde head. The other was holding a small backpack which contained clothing and a few toys she'd bought during his month-long stay.

"Is he taking me to my mommy?" Graham asked pitifully as he looked at the woman.

She knelt beside the youngster and cupped her hands around his tiny face. Then she kissed him on the forehead.

"Trixie wants you to be a brave little man today," she encouraged, straightening his coat collar.

She quickly placed the white knit cap on his head. A few of his golden locks escaped from under the hastily

placed hat, prompting her to tuck them back under with her
jeweled fingers.

"You be a good little boy now. It's a long way to
Atlanta," she added, glancing at Buster's accomplice.

"He's gonna take you for a ride," Buster said, pointing
to the bearded man.

Graham divided his look between confusion and relief,
but remained silent. Although he was comfortable around
Trixie, he felt traumatized by Buster, who made it clear from
the start he didn't like having him around.

"Here's the rest of your money," said the sandy-haired
malefactor as he handed Buster a brown paper bag. "Don't
spend it all in one place."

Both Buster and Trixie smiled, but Buster showed his
distrust by peeking in the bag.

"It's all there. One thousand dollars," verified his
employer.

"It's a pleasure doin' business with you."

The other man huffed and retreated a few steps toward
the front door of the apartment.

"I've got a long drive. It's best I get going." He looked
at Graham. "Come on, son! I'm going to take you home."

Trixie felt Graham stiffen slightly so she kissed him,
leaving a lipstick stain on his forehead.

"Everything's gonna be all right, darlin'." She spoke
softly, looking him directly in the eyes. Then she saw the red
lipstick impression she'd left on his forehead. "I'm sorry,
baby," she laughed, "you can't go to Atlanta lookin' like
that, can you?" She grabbed a tissue and erased the red
smear.

Graham threw her a fractured look and then forced a
smile. Before she stood he threw his arms around her neck
and squeezed her tightly.

"Aw, honey, everything's gonna be all right," she whispered, reciprocating his hug. "Didn't Trixie tell you everything's gonna be jus' fine?"

She stood again, this time holding Graham in her arms.

Buster leaned over, snatched the backpack off the floor and placed his hand behind Trixie's back, forcing her to move closer toward the front door. He handed his employer Graham's belongings while Trixie pried herself away from Graham.

The man who stood impatiently at the front door leaned toward Trixie and pulled Graham to him.

Graham felt the bearded man's strong grip and threw Trixie the most forlorn look. Although his lips began to quiver, he remained quiet.

As the self-appointed chauffeur vanished through the doorway, carrying his human cargo, Trixie closed her eyes. When she opened them again she saw Buster's indignant gaze coming back at her.

"I told you you couldn't keep him. I warned you not to get attached to tha kid, didn't I?"

Trixie nodded.

"So forget about him. Look." He held up the bag of money. "We got plenty of money. And there's plenty more where this come from."

He moved quickly past Trixie and put his brown leather jacket on. "Let's celebrate," he said, raising his voice jubilantly.

Trixie stood with her back to him, facing the door. A solitary tear drifted off the rim of one of her heavily mascaraed eyes.

"I'm gonna miss you, little man," she pined. "You're such a sweet little muffin'."

"Trixie! You ready?"

"Lord," she whispered, looking toward the ceiling. "Take care of that precious little boy. You left your mark on him—that perfect little star on his knee. So, stay with him, you hear? Find him a good home."

"Quit starin' at the damn ceiling and git your coat on."

I don't know how you're gonna do it, Lord, she thought sadly, *but you need to get him back with his natural mamma. It ain't right, what we just did. It ain't right at all.*

"Hey, what's wrong with you? Let's go!" Buster yelled.

Trixie wiped another tear from her eye with the side of her index finger.

"Yeah, sweetie. Just gimme a minute."

§   §   §   §   §   §

Kim sat on the back of the couch with one of her arms across her lap. The other arm supported her on top of the couch. Her eyes were closed as she listened to the last part of the tape.

Her parents were sitting trance-like on the couch in front of her. Jim's parents, Marie and Gary Sanborn, were standing next to her. No one spoke and all of them were wiping tears away.

Kim had called them when she returned from the precinct to announce her discovery of the tape. Her parents and Pamela had arrived at her house within minutes of her call. It took their collective discipline to postpone hearing the recording until Jim's parents could join them from Wilson, North Carolina.

Kim thought she was all cried out, but when the other women wept, she couldn't hold back the steady flow of her own tears. The men's eyes weren't dry either, but all of them managed to maintain their unsteady composure.

Marie collapsed against her husband, forcing him back against the curio, which creaked its resistance. Several of the collectibles inside the cabinet fell onto the glass shelves and made a sound like breaking glass, bringing everyone's attention to the couple's dilemma.

"Sorry," apologized Gary, standing unsteadily beside his distraught wife. He steadied her and looked apologetically at the others.

"There's nothing to apologize for," consoled Jerry. "The tape's quite graphic."

"This is a shock for all of us," Pamela added quickly, squeezing Marie's arm as she helped Gary escort his wife to the couch.

Pauline grasped the hand Marie held limply on her lap, patting it a few times. Then she handed Marie a couple of tissues.

"I'm so sorry," Pauline whispered.

An unsteady silence engulfed the room. All of them were shocked by the recorded account of the carjacking.

Kim leaned over the back of the couch, burying her head in Marie's silver gray hair.

"I'm so sorry everyone," she whispered. "I...I guess it was a bad idea to play the tape. But I thought we all needed to know what happened."

"It's okay. We wanted to hear what happened to Jim," the others replied softly, almost in unison.

"You did the right thing. We're family. We all needed to hear it," Jerry spoke for all of them.

"He didn't have a chance," Gary commented, as he stared at the floor.

"It looks like he did the best he could, the best anybody could under the circumstances," Jerry added.

"I don't know how he stayed so calm," Pamela added.

"Our son was in the car," Kim stated softly, but emphatically. She struggled to stop the next installment of tears, but then surrendered to them.

Marie swallowed hard and waved for another tissue to clear her nose. Pamela rescued her and extracted one for herself as well, then she moved next to Kim.

Gary paced angrily across the living room. For the first time in his dignified life, he felt like smashing something. His son's murderer was the sole candidate of his mounting rage. The idea that anyone could be so inhuman, so unfeeling, so callous, enraged him to the point of vigilantism.

"I want to spend five minutes alone with him when they catch him," he seethed.

"Gary!" his wife admonished.

"I'm with Gary," Jerry chorused. "I'd like some quality time with him too!"

"That's all I want," Gary bellowed. "Give me five minutes with that son-of-a ...!"

"Gary! I'll not have you using profanity. I know you're angry, but ..."

"Angry. Angry! Hell! I'm livid! I'd kill that filthy piece of garbage if I could get my hands on him."

Marie closed her eyes and bowed her head, too embarrassed to look at the others.

Jerry threw Gary a sympathetic nod. He couldn't get his thoughts working fast enough to offer a suitable reply, but he felt he had to say something to stop the cascading awkwardness.

"That's not going to bring Jim back," he reasoned, looking Gary directly in the eyes.

"I know that. But it would help me revenge the murder of my son. And it would give me a chance to beat Graham's whereabouts out of him."

Kim interrupted her father-in-law's tirade. "Jim's dead. And we can't bring him back."

Gary stared blankly at the glass-topped coffee table to avoid the stares of the others.

"Can we talk about a live grandson? Lt. McCauley says he thinks Graham might still be alive," Kim continued.

Her father-in-law looked at her, mimicking the others' surprised looks.

"Oh, honey, I hope so," chimed Marie.

"Do you really believe it?" echoed Pauline.

All eyes were trained on Kim as she continued. "It's been three weeks since..." She swallowed hard. "Since the funeral. "

"But no phone calls or ransom notes, right?" her disheveled mother politely interrupted.

Kim nodded her head.

"You all already know that. That's not something I'd keep from you."

"But we've got hard evidence now," shouted Gary, referring to the tape.

"Thanks to Jim's quick thinking," Pauline chorused. Then she lowered her head and closed her eyes, embarrassed at repeating the obvious.

"Let's give Kim a chance to finish, good people," Jerry protested. "She's trying to explain what might have happened to our grandson."

Marie nodded and buried her nose in the tissue again.

"Yes, of course," Gary said, realizing how much his tough rhetoric upset the ladies. "I'm sorry, honey," he apologized to Kim. "You don't need a gray-haired old man's macho commentary."

"That's okay," she replied charitably. "Apologies aren't necessary. We're all upset and angry. We've lost two people we love." Kim spoke more softly than usual and clung to her tissue. "Lt. McCauley thinks it may be more than a kidnapping," she continued, forcing the words past her pounding heart.

A series of gasps filled the room. Before anyone could interrupt, Kim continued. "Since we've gotten no ransom

notes or phone calls ... and no reports of his being found ..."
Kim stopped to clear her throat. "He ... he thinks there is a
good possibility Graham may have been sold."

"Sold!" Pauline shouted, unable to contain herself.

"Sold?" Gary echoed.

"You mean illegally adopted on the black market?"
Pamela voiced her horrified appraisal.

Kim nodded.

"Oh, my God," shrieked Pauline, who was coming
completely unglued. "Our dear little Graham. Kidnapped ...
and sold."

"Then, if that's true, we may never see him again,"
cried Marie, as she sank further into the soft folds of the
couch.

"Now hold on, all of you," Pamela cautioned. "We
don't know that for sure. It's only one of the possibilities."

Jerry knew of at least one other possibility. He
suspected their grandson had been murdered. Four-year-old
or no four-year-old, Graham had witnessed his father's
execution and would be considered a liability.

"People," Gary spoke firmly, but guardedly, as if
reading Jerry's mind. "We must also consider the possibility
that our grandson might have been ... killed ... too."

"What a horrible thing to say," Marie chastised him.
"Surely you don't believe that. Gary, honey, how can you
say such a thing?"

"I'm not going to accept that," refused Kim. "Graham's
still alive! I know it! And I'm going to find him no matter
how long it takes."

"He has to be alive," Pauline cried, "our baby must be
alive."

"The Lord wouldn't let anything happen to him," Marie
said, trying to reassure everyone.

"The God you're referring to let Jim die," Kim accused,
"and that God let His own Son die a horrible death two

thousand years ago." Kim was asserting her newfound perspective on the relevance of an anthropomorphic God in the sky. "What makes you think He'd spare my son?"

"Oh, Kim, honey, you don't mean that," Pauline sobbed.

"Yes ... Yes, I ... think I do, Mother! I'm beginning to question my religious beliefs. All I know is I've lost my family. Jim's gone and I may never see my baby again."

"We mustn't give up hope, dear," consoled Marie. "And we mustn't give up on God. We've got to hold on to hope."

"That's right. Hope's all we've got ... and prayers," Pamela offered, wiping her own tears away.

"Faith is all we've got," Kim replied quickly, "the faith that we can work all things together for good. I'm sorry, Pamela, but hope is wishcraft. And I'm not supporting wishcraft when it comes to getting my son back."

Oh, Graham honey, be strong wherever you are, Kim cried to herself. *Mommy's going to find you and bring you back home, I promise. I swear by all that is good and decent and right...*

She looked at the people who surrounded her in her spacious living room. The family wasn't a whole family anymore. It would never be complete without Jim and Graham. With a maternal instinct that was a surer guide than reason itself, she knew she would never rest until she found her son. Kim Sanborn, mother, dancer and widow knew she must supplant hope with faith, fear with courage, grief with determination.

"I'm going to find my son," she announced confidently to the group. "However long it takes. I'm going to find Jim's killer and I'm going to find out what happened to my son!"

CHAPTER SIX

Jerry, get over here!" Pauline screamed into the telephone as she shot another worried look at her daughter. Kim had collapsed like a discarded mannequin against the back of one of the living room chairs. Her face was ashen and contorted. She was holding her stomach, writhing in extreme pain.

"What's wrong, dear?" Jerry shouted.

"There's something wrong with Kim," she screeched. "I don't have time to explain. I think we'd better take her to the hospital. Please hurry."

"I'm hanging up now," Jerry fired his response. "I'll be there in less than a minute."

Pauline hung up the phone and rushed back to her daughter. When she heard a knock at the front door she started to leave Kim to answer it, then remembered it was unlocked. "It's unlocked. Hurry!" she called.

"He must have run down the street," she said, announcing Jerry's arrival to Kim, who was doubled-up in pain next to the high-backed chair. "He's here, sweetie. Everything's going to be all right."

Her fifty-seven year old husband bolted into the room. "Where is she? What's wrong?" he yelled.

"She's over here," Pauline shouted. "On the floor by the chair."

Jerry stepped around the glass-topped coffee table and planted himself in front of his daughter. He lifted Kim with his wife's help and escorted her slowly to the front door. Each step registered the excruciating pain on Kim's face.

"Did you eat anything or drink anything," he asked breathily, "that might have..."

Kim's vigorous head shake negated the rest of his inquiry.

"I've already asked her that," added Pauline.

Kim tried to say something, but was silenced by another sharp jab of pain which multiplied exponentially with every step.

"Did she fall or..."

"No!" his wife interrupted.

Jerry was as confused as he was concerned.

"Then what?"

"All I know," Pauline countered as she released Kim long enough to grab both women's purses and drape Kim's coat over her daughter's shoulders, " ... is that Lt. McCauley called to announce a few leads based on the evidence from the tape Kim gave him. We were leaving for the police station when Kim collapsed."

By this time, the trio had reached the front door. Pauline looked outside and asked, "Jerry, where's the car?"

"The car!" Jerry shouted. "It's still over at the house. Your call scared me. I ran over ... "

"Oh, Jerry," lamented his wife. Her fear translated into frustration.

"I'll get it," Jerry exclaimed, making sure Pauline held Kim tightly before he dashed out the front door.

By the time he backed the car up Kim's curved driveway, the women were waiting, arm-in-arm, at the sidewalk. In her haste to get Kim to the car, Pauline hadn't noticed it was raining.

"There's not an umbrella anywhere in the car," Jerry apologized. "And I didn't want to take time to look for one."

"Doesn't matter. No time for that," bellowed Pauline. "Help me get Kim into the back seat."

Jerry ran to the rear of the car to meet the women and flung the car door open. "Be careful, honey. Take it easy. There you go."

After the anxious parents deposited Kim in the back seat, Pauline wordlessly took her position beside her daughter, while Jerry slid quickly behind the steering wheel and hit the gas.

Suddenly Pauline screamed, causing Jerry to swerve the car before he brought it to a complete stop.

"What in God's name happened?" Jerry asked, turning toward them.

"She's bleeding!" Pauline shouted.

Both of their gazes locked onto Kim.

"I've missed ... I've ..." Kim spoke softly, breathing in short bursts. "I've ..." she gasped.

Her confused parents exchanged horrified looks.

"Oh, dear God in heaven," shouted Jerry.

Pauline looked at Kim's blood-soaked coat and then at her daughter. "Honey, are you having ... did you and Jim ... Oh, God, you're having a miscarriage."

Jerry reacted the only way he knew he could. He floored the accelerator.

§   §   §   §   §   §

Joyce and Julian Fergusen stood just inside the doorway to the bedroom they had quickly redecorated, and admired the four-year-old boy sleeping in his new bed.

"He looks so peaceful, doesn't he?" Joyce said in a hushed voice.

Her husband nodded his head and smiled as he squeezed her arm.

"I'm so thankful we finally have a son," she said, breathing a joyful sigh. "And I don't care if we got him illegally. They were going to put him in a foster home as a ward of the state."

"I know, dearest. I know."

"That wouldn't have been right."

"I know, honey. You don't have to convince me. I'm on your side, remember?"

"He couldn't help it if both his parents were killed in that automobile accident."

"Joyce, we've been over that a hundred times already," he protested mildly.

She grabbed his arm and leaned against him contentedly.

"Thank you for agreeing to adopt him so quickly." She raised her hand and cupped it to his bearded cheek.

"Well, honey, it wasn't like we hadn't talked about it."

"I know."

"We've been trying to adopt for a long time."

He kissed the palm of her hand.

"The man from the adoption agency, Mr. ..." she cut into her own inquiry, "what was his name?"

"Mr. Unser," her husband rescued.

"Yes, of course, Mr. Unser," she repeated, and tapped herself on her forehead with her palm. "Mr. Unser said the State of North Carolina would have bounced that poor little boy around from one home to another for the next couple of years. That's a horrible way to treat a child." She glanced up at her husband for confirmation.

"Doesn't seem right, does it?" he agreed.

"No, there's something awfully wrong with the system when children are treated that way. It forces people like us to break the law to save a child from being shuttled from one bureaucratic hole to another. America's supposed to be the richest country on earth, but we mistreat our children. Our country's going to pay for that some day."

"I'm just glad we had the money. Twenty-five thousand dollars doesn't grow on trees, you know."

"I know. But look at him. Isn't he beautiful?"

"You're sure you don't mind keeping his given first name?" she whispered, catching her husband's signal for her to lower her voice.

He hugged her as he leaned down to whisper into her ear.

"I think Graham is perfect." He smiled as he squeezed her shoulder. "It's his name and he's used to it. There's no point in putting him through an identity crisis along with everything else."

Joyce nodded sympathetically.

He kissed the side of her head, lingering there as she focused her attention on the small crop of blond hair barely visible above the brightly decorated bedspread. The small teddy bear they'd bought lay next to him like a toy sentry.

"Graham Allen Fergusen," she cooed, adding her father's name as Graham's middle name. "It sounds really nice, doesn't it?"

Her husband showed his approval by hugging her tightly with one arm.

Joyce pulled a picture from her husband's shirt pocket. It was one of dozens of pictures they took of Graham when he arrived.

"Julian," she exclaimed, holding the picture so both of them could admire it. "We are the proud parents of a beautiful son."

He formed a tight smile. *Yes, we have a son,* he thought. *I'll feel a lot more comfortable in a year or so when I know for sure we've gotten away with it.*

Oblivious to her husband's concern, Joyce focused her admiring gaze on the picture of Graham. She rubbed her fingertips across the photograph and stroked the birthmark on his knee.

That's so cute, she thought contentedly. *It's amazing how perfect a star it is.*

Until two days ago, all of their efforts to adopt a child were perfunctory stumblings through the approval process. Today the couple was standing in their son's room—a room filled with new furniture and toys—a room filled with hope.

Tomorrow, we'll go shopping again, she promised Graham in her thoughts. She thought about the birthmark on his knee. *But we'll have to cover you up for a while,* she addressed the birthmark. *Julian says we shouldn't take any chances. You are beautiful, birthmark, but you're a dead give-away. It's a shame we have to be so careful. But it's a small price to pay for a son.*

Suddenly she felt her husband tug on her arm. Julian motioned for her to follow him. She wordlessly obeyed him, but stole another quick glance at Graham before she left the room.

Once they were outside the room Julian put his arm around Joyce's shoulder and said, "Let's take our son to the game."

"What game?"

"You know," he coaxed, "the Super Bowl. They're showing it on the big screen down at the club. Graham can see his first professional football game." He hesitated thoughtfully. "I guess it'll be his first game. I don't know if he's ever seen one. What do you think?" He looked at Joyce, then quickly answered his own question. "At age four, it'll probably be his first game."

"You're not taking him to the club, Julian."

He threw Joyce a sour look.

"Of course I am."

"Oh, Julian."

"It'll be great! They have a sixty-one inch TV."

"And plenty of cigarettes and alcohol, too." she accused. "It's no place for my four-year-old son."

"He's my son, too, Joyce," Julian raised his voice.

Joyce signaled for him to lower his voice by putting her finger over her mouth. Julian moved further down the narrow hallway toward the dining room.

"I'm taking him with me," he scowled. "And that's final."

"How could you spoil it?" she lamented.

"Spoil what?"

"Our evening. The first full evening with our son."

Julian continued his retreat, detouring around the dining room table on his way to the living room.

"I'm going to see what's on ESPN," he murmured. "You need to chill out."

Joyce stood in the hallway, clutching the photo of Graham. A solitary tear began its salty trip down her cheek.

§   §   §   §   §   §

"Hi, Kim, this is Pamela. Just wanted you to know I was thinking about you."

Pamela hesitated, waiting for Kim to pick up the phone.

"Are you there?" she asked, hesitating again. "Guess not. Okay, then. I'll be brief. Karen called from Asheville last night and I told her about Jim's tape and about it being the only lead the police have. She has a friend who is a psychic. According to Karen, her friend has helped police locate missing persons."

Pamela took a deep breath.

"I know this sounds really funky, but I feel like we need all the help we can get. It's been six weeks now and we still don't know what's happened to Graham."

The painful memory of her own accident three years before pushed its way into her consciousness.

"I really believe I would have used a psychic to locate the man who stalked me two years ago," Pamela continued. "It might have saved me from getting into a very bad situation. Anyway, I've got her name and phone number if you want them. Let's talk about it if you're interested. Okay? Better go before I'm cut off. Call me. Love you. Oh, I'll be home most of the afternoon until around five. Then I'm going out. Should be home again about nine. See ya."

She put the phone down, then reversed her decision and dialed another number.

When the connection went through, the recorded greeting indicated she would have to leave another message: *After the beep, please leave your name, phone number and a brief message.*

Pamela waited for the mechanical robot to end its recorded instruction.

"Karen, this is me. Looks like I'm zero for two. I just called Kim and got her answer service, too. I told her about your psychic friend and asked her to call me if she's interested. I'll call you and arrange for the four of us to meet. You know more about this than I do. Kim may not be receptive to getting a psychic involved, but then again, she might. I'll call you as soon as I know something."

An after-thought sent a slight smile across Pamela's face. The image of Karen's faithful German Shepherd jumped into her consciousness.

"Give Hans a hug for me. I'll call you as soon as I know something. Oh," she added, "I've already said I'll call you. I always ramble when I talk on these things! Anyway, bye, sis. Love ya."

Pamela glanced at the oil painting of an angel Karen bought her for Christmas. The angel attentively stood behind two young children, a blonde-haired boy who was kneeling and a little golden-haired girl who was standing. Both children were affectionately absorbed in petting a collie who seemed to take great pleasure in receiving the attention.

Karen believes in angels, Pamela reminded herself. *She believes they're all around us. She calls them Spirit sponsors.*

She lifted the painting from its miniature brass easel on top of the dresser. Her eyes focused on the children and dog.

They look so happy. So innocent. So protected. Her gaze settled on the little boy's smile and his rosy cheeks, and finally on his golden hair.

It's the same color as Graham's hair, she realized.

Her impromptu assessment forced her eyes up to the wispy outlines of the angel. The artist had done an excellent job depicting the heavenly figure. It's angelic wings rose majestically above and extended past the soft shoulders of the holy figure. Her shimmering gown was a diaphanous blend of muted pastels, lavender, white, gold, and pink, as it caught the effervescent rays of the sun slanting through the trees in the glen. The edges of the gown were transparent, bathing the nearby trees and flowering shrubs with a heavenly veil of divination.

"I hope you've sent one of your best guardian angels to protect my friend, Kim," she addressed the angel on the canvas. Then she tilted her head toward the ceiling to petition a higher Being.

"If you've got a couple of angels to spare, particularly if they're good at protecting children, I think Kim's little boy, Graham, could use them right about now."

Pamela lifted the painting over her head so that it was between her face and the ceiling.

"And while I'm affirming angelic connection," she raised her voice slightly, "you can send a couple over to the Raleigh Police Department. They need all the help they can get."

When Pamela lowered the painting, she sighed mournfully.

God, Eternal Presence, Infinite Isness, you've got to help us. We can't do this alone.

When the phone rang, Pamela quickly placed the painting face up on the bed and looked quickly around the room for the phone. She spied it on the night stand and plucked it up, not bothering to look at the caller ID.

"Hello, Pamela," came Pauline's excited voice.

Her shrillness forced Pamela to jerk the phone back a few inches from her ear.

"Pauline! You sound upset," Pamela answered, squinting as she waited intently for Pauline to continue.

"We're at the hospital."

"The hospital?"

"The emergency room at Rex."

"Rex?" Pamela echoed.

"It's Kim, dear. She's asked for you."

"K ... Kim," stuttered Pamela.

"She's had a miscarriage," Pauline said, choking it out. "She's all right now, but she wants to see you. Can you come?"

"A miscarriage? I didn't even know she was ... Of course, I'll come. I should be there in ten or fifteen minutes."

"You don't need to hurry, dear. She's stable now. We're in room 6050."

"Room 6050. Okay, I'm leaving now. Bye."

"Thank you. Bye."

Pamela glanced at the angel as she tossed the phone next to the painting on the bed.

"Did you hear that? We need Kim's Spirit sponsors NOW! She's just had a miscarriage."

As she snatched her purse and car keys off the pillows on her bed, she threw a sour look toward the ceiling.

"Come on, God! The poor woman's been through enough, hasn't she?"

CHAPTER SEVEN

An interesting trio gathered in Kim's kitchen. Joining Kim around the oval glass-topped table, enjoying freshly-brewed Macadamia-Nut coffee, were Pamela, her sister, Karen, and Karen's psychic friend, Linda Amos. After the customary pleasantries were exchanged, Kim gestured for Karen to begin the meeting.

"Pamela didn't tell us about your miscarriage until we got here last night, Kim," Karen said. "Are you sure you're all right?"

"We can certainly come another time," chimed Linda.

"No," said Kim, her voice strong and clear. "I'm fine. I specifically told Pamela not to tell you till you got here. I was afraid you wouldn't come. I can't stand another moment thinking there's nothing I can do. When she told me about you, Linda, it gave me the lift I needed. I'm definitely ready for this meeting."

"Good," said Linda. "Shall we get started?"

Kim nodded her head and sat up straighter in her chair.

Linda looked at her and said, "I understand that you have been seeing a strange white dog here on your property."

Kim sent Linda a puzzled look. "Well, yes, I had mentioned that to Pamela. But what does that have to do with anything?"

"I believe it could be very important. Unusual occurrences like the appearance of strange animals,

94

reoccurring dreams, unexpected visits from people you haven't seen in a while, generally represent attempts by the Universe to help people in need. They are messages from God. I call them Divine Prompts. Unusual appearances like these can be significant. When is the first time you saw him?"

"Him? Oh, the dog. I saw him the night Jim died," Kim answered, rotating her coffee cup between her hands, "I stayed up all night while they searched for Graham." She looked intently at Karen. "Does she know about Jim's tape recording?"

"Yes, I've told Linda everything," Karen confirmed. "You did say I could tell her anything I thought would be relevant, didn't you?"

Kim nodded and then re-established eye contact with Linda.

"My parents stayed up with me. In fact, we stayed up all night. We were in the kitchen drinking coffee. That's when I first saw him, the white dog. He was in my back yard."

Linda scribbled something in her notebook and motioned for Kim to continue.

Kim repositioned herself on the chair and clasped her hands in front of her, resting her elbows on the pillow she held on her lap. Karen remained dutifully silent in the chair next to Kim, sipping her coffee.

"I didn't pay much attention to it at the time," Kim sighed deeply. "But then a week after that I saw the same dog, and then two weeks ago I saw the dog again."

Kim looked steadily into Linda's eyes.

"And then, a few days ago, when I came home from the hospital ... after the miscarriage ... ," her voice quivered, forcing her to take a sip of coffee.

The other women waited in respectful silence.

"I think the dog might be an illusion—you know, with losing Graham ... and well, you know with everything that's happened," Kim continued.

She paused to look at Pamela, who was having difficulty keeping her coffee cup on its saucer. After she took a deep breath, Kim smiled at Linda.

"I'm willing to try anything to get my son back. And Karen says you're good. So, I'm very comfortable exploring how you might help."

Linda smiled and adopted a pose similar to Kim's as she placed her elbows on the table and leaned toward her hostess.

Karen used Linda's hesitation to describe how she had met her psychic friend, while Pamela politely excused herself so she could brew more coffee.

She explained how she'd met Linda at a conference on extra-sensory abilities a couple of years before, and how they had immediately become friends. She proudly announced that Linda Amos, astrologer, therapist, and psychic, was one of the most documented, laboratory-researched psychics in the Western Hemisphere. As a former director of the CIA's radio physics lab and Special Projects Chair, Linda had won international acclaim as a bona fide psychic with extraordinary extra sensory abilities.

Her decision to leave the agency was announced with extreme regret by the government paraphysics community in 1992. Karen explained how Linda co-founded the Phoenix Institute a year later—an organization which uses credentialled psychics to locate missing children and victims of various crimes.

Linda sent Kim an embarrassed smile.

"Thanks, Karen," Kim replied, looking thoughtfully at Karen and then at Linda. "I'm glad you started with Linda's experience. I had no idea that people with Linda's skills and abilities existed. But I need your help, Linda, and I feel like you're here by divine appointment."

Linda smiled and started to speak, but hesitated to allow for Pamela's entrance.

Pamela joined them at the table and refilled all four cups, ending with her own. Then she set the empty pot on the tray next to the dish of apple Danishes and sat in the chair she'd vacated a few moments before.

"Tell me more about the white dog," Linda suggested before she took a sip of coffee.

"As I said before, I saw him again when I got home from the hospital, after I had my miscarriage." Kim kept her voice steady. "He was sitting just off the patio on the grass. As I eased myself closer to the kitchen window, he stood on all fours and watched me. I know he saw me." Kim paused. "I saw him the next day, too. It was then I noticed it."

"Noticed what?" Karen interrupted.

Linda glanced at her and frowned her disapproval at the interruption.

"Okay. Okay. Sorry!" Karen responded as she pantomimed her embarrassment by pretending to zip her mouth closed with her fingers.

Satisfied with Karen's comedic apology, Linda returned her attention to Kim.

"What was it you noticed?"

"I thought it was a wound or some kind of blemish at first. Or a stain or something. I couldn't get close enough to see at first."

"A blemish? Or a stain?" Linda repeated.

"It was neither; the spot turned out to be a patch of black fur on his right hind leg." Kim pointed to her arm, outlining the size of the spot as she described it.

"Interesting," Linda commented briefly, but seemed satisfied to let Kim continue.

"How large an animal is he?"

"Around fifty pounds. And I would guess he's about one or two years old. He let me pet him for the first time yesterday," Kim announced. "I've been feeding him and he has stayed. I don't know whose dog he is. I've never seen him around here before."

Linda's raised eyebrows were accompanied by a smile. "What kind of dog is he?"

"He looks like a shepherd mix, or a husky, or maybe even a Great Pyrenees."

"When you petted him, did you check to see if he had an identification tag?"

"Yes, as a matter of fact, I did." Kim seemed pleased with herself. "He had no identification other than the patch of hair on his leg."

"Like your son's birthmark?" interjected Linda as she straightened herself in her chair.

Both Kim's and Karen's eyebrows disappeared into their bangs. Kim felt goose-bumps travel up both her arms while Pamela's surprise matched Karen's mouth open.

"Come to think of it," Kim stated, "you're right! It is in the same place as Graham's birthmark!"

Karen rubbed the goose-bumps on her arms.

"What does that mean?" Karen asked. This time she was too absorbed in her question to worry about protocol.

"I'll tell you in a moment." Linda looked into Kim's engaging stare. "But first I want to know if you've seen anything else out of the ordinary."

Before Kim could speak, there was a knock at the front door, which caused her to flinch.

"I'll get it," chimed Karen as she bolted toward the door carrying a half-empty coffee cup balanced in her hand.

Both Kim and Linda remained seated and exchanged smiles.

"How long can you spend with me?" Kim asked Linda.

"As long as you need," the psychic replied sympathetically.

Kim's smile broadened.

"Thank you. Are you sure?"

"I'm quite certain."

They both followed Karen's enthusiastic voice as she greeted the unexpected visitor.

"Hi, Lt. McCauley. How nice to see you," greeted Karen. "Please come in."

He advanced into the kitchen behind Karen and saw the women seated at the table.

"Oh, I'm sorry. I didn't know you had company," he apologized, halting his advance diplomatically. "Perhaps there's a better time ..."

"Nonsense," exclaimed Kim, as she rose and extended her hand. "You know you're welcome here anytime."

Kim grasped Lt. McCauley's hand firmly, then pulled him closer to her and presented him to Linda.

"Linda, this is Lt. John McCauley of the Raleigh Police Department. He's helped us so much. He's become a friend." She turned to the officer. "Lt. McCauley, this is Miss Linda Amos."

"Pleased to meet you." He smiled as he took her hand in his.

Linda politely returned his firm handshake.

The lieutenant broke off his eye contact with the other two women and addressed Kim.

"Mrs. Sanborn, may I have a few minutes?"

Kim nodded her consent.

"Please excuse us," she addressed the other women, who were standing next to each other like a police line-up.

Kim led the lieutenant into the dining room and then turned to face him when she reached the stately cherry wood curio.

He looked her squarely in the eyes.

"We've found the mint green Camaro."

Kim stiffened. Her right hand shot up to her throat.

"It was abandoned in the woods near a farm in Zebulon."

A half-censored question fell from her trembling lips.

"Was Graham ... did you ...?

Lt. McCauley shook his head.

"No, there was no sign of your son. We canvassed the farm and searched the woods. And several of the farms nearby. We didn't find any trace of Graham." He paused and gently took hold of Kim's arm. "But that's good news."

She threw him the most mortified look.

"Really. Trust me, it is good news. That whole area is fairly isolated. It would have been the perfect place to ..." he purposely hesitated. "It would have been the perfect location to bury your son's body."

Kim let out a groan which pulled the other women to them.

"It's okay. Everything's fine," Kim whispered. "They've ..." she explained, clearing her throat, "found the get-away car."

At her request, Lt. McCauley quickly repeated what he had told Kim. Then he picked up where he left off.

"Mrs. Sanborn, I believe your son's alive."

All of the women released a collective gasp, with Kim's being the most pronounced. After a moment Kim steeled her gaze on the lieutenant, who looked as if he had more to say.

"If he intended to kill your son and bury him, that stretch of woods was isolated enough to have given him the time and real estate he needed to do it. There were two more sets of tire tracks in the area. We figure they are the ones from the car he switched into when he ditched the Camaro."

"So ... so what are you saying officer?" Karen forced the words from her mouth.

Kim's lips remained silent, but her eyes spoke volumes. She was reluctant to have her own suspicions confirmed.

The lieutenant preambled his next statement with a lengthy sigh.

"I believe your son is alive," he repeated, "and because ransom money was never mentioned, I believe we have a case of first-degree murder and kidnapping. The robbery was premeditated, too. And we think your husband was murdered because the killer wanted to tie up loose ends. You son's kidnapping may be linked to a series of kidnappings in a three state area."

Kim started to sob and was immediately embraced collectively by the other women.

"So you think my baby's alive?" she sniffled.

"We don't know that for sure, but I believe he is," assured Lt. McCauley. "At least, that's the way it appears." He took a half step closer to the women. "We're investigating several adoption agencies that have questionable ties to the black market."

The tears streamed down her cheeks again and Kim's knees buckled, causing the other three women to tighten their support. They escorted her over to one of the dining room chairs, lowered her into it, then stood protectively beside her.

Lt. McCauley followed their migration and knelt in front of Kim, who patted the tears from her eyes with a tissue.

"We are doing everything we can to locate your son. Your husband's description led us to the Camaro. I know it has been extremely agonizing for you. It hasn't been one of my better months either. I've taken it personally. I've let myself get too emotionally involved in this case."

Kim clasped his hand in both of hers.

"The hardest thing is not knowing where my baby is. Or what has happened to him." She squeezed his hand for emphasis. "Every time the phone rings or the doorbell sounds, my heart stops."

"I know," he sympathized. "I know."

"I don't know how she's done it, officer," announced Pamela. "She hasn't had a good night's sleep in weeks. She's been to the murder scene a hundred times. Do you know the people of Raleigh have created a monument of flowers at the scene in memory of Jim?"

Lt. McCauley smiled his understanding.

"I know. Since this made the news, people from all over the city have memorialized the spot. I've never seen such an outpouring of love and affection."

Kim blinked back the ever-present tears, as she maintained her white-knuckled grip on his hand.

"Well, I've got to be going now," he apologized. "Looks like you're in good hands." He winked at Karen, Pamela, and Linda respectively.

As he stood, he placed his hand on Kim's shoulder and gently forced her to remain seated.

"I'll call when I know something. We'll find out if any of those agencies are involved. And we're doing this thing by the book. I promise you that."

He returned Kim's smile.

"Ms. Justice," he addressed Karen. "And Ms. Justice," he addressed Pamela, "It's nice seeing you again. And Ms. Amos, it was a pleasure meeting you."

"Oh, Lt. McCauley," Pamela said, commenting on Linda's behalf, "If we need to see the car, the Camaro ... may we?"

He threw her a surprised look.

"I mean, have you towed it yet? May we see it? May we go where you found it?"

The other women knew exactly where Pamela was going.

"It's been impounded for evidence," the lieutenant responded. "Why do you want to see it? We've already checked it out."

"We understand," Kim said quickly, "but if we wanted to see it, could we?"

"Until the investigation is over, we ..."

"We'll go with you," Karen interrupted. "That way you can make sure we don't touch anything. You know, disturb evidence."

Kim was tempted to tell Lt. McCauley about Linda's psychic abilities, but decided against it. Despite Linda's national recognition, she was certain the Raleigh Police Department wasn't ready for psychic intervention.

All four women waited for the detective to speak.

"I'll have to think about it," the lieutenant dismissed them. But Kim's disappointment forced him to reconsider. "I'll check with the captain and see if we can work something out."

"Wonderful!" Karen replied.

"Thank you," Kim echoed, squeezing the lieutenant's arm.

"Mrs. Sanborn, ladies," he said softly, nodding his respect again as he left.

When he vanished through the front door, Pamela made a startling announcement. "Kim, I don't know if you know this or not, but Lt. McCauley has postponed his retirement until he catches Jim's killer and brings Graham back home."

Surprise flung Kim's mouth open.

"Officer Wells told me. I thought you should know."

"I had no idea. He never mentioned a word of it to me. It's just like him to do something like that, bless his heart."

"I knew there was something about that man I liked," chorused Linda.

The laugh which escaped Karen's lips produced a smile on Pamela's and Kim's.

"Let's hope he'll be able to retire soon," Pamela interjected.

"I'll toast to that," Linda agreed as she picked up her half-empty coffee cup and lifted it jubilantly in front of her.

Both Kim and Karen followed suit, with Pamela completing the caffeinated toast.

"Lukewarm," Karen and Linda said in unison, as they sipped the coffee.

"Time for another coffee run," Pamela shouted. "Who wants some hot coffee?"

The others made it unanimous by giving Pamela thumbs-up signs.

Linda checked her watch. "Eleven-thirty-five," she said softly.

"Oh, we've almost used up the morning, " Kim said. "I'm afraid we haven't made the best use of your time."

"My goodness, don't worry about that. I have all afternoon. I would like to call my office though. Is that all right?"

"Of course," Kim replied, granting her request immediately. "Use the land line over there." She pointed toward the phone stand in the hallway.

Linda lifted the phone from its cradle and held the phone up to her ear.

"That's funny." She raised one eyebrow as she looked at Kim. "There's no dial tone."

"Hello, is this Kim?" came the voice from the other end of the phone line.

"Hello," repeated Linda, as her eyes widened in surprise. She looked at Kim, "There's someone on the line for you."

"Who is this?" questioned the caller.

"You've reached the Sanborn residence," volunteered Linda, quickly regaining her composure.

"Is Mrs. Sanborn ... is Kim there? This is Ben Dare."

"Certainly. Just a moment, please ... " Linda extended the receiver toward Kim and whispered, "It's a Been There. Is he kidding? Been there? Did I hear him correctly?"

Kim smiled as she accepted the receiver, then covered it with one hand as she quickly explained, "Ben Dare, and yes. That's his real name. Ben's my business partner at the dance studio. He's taking care of things for me right now while ..." Her voice trailed off as she broke eye contact with Linda and held the phone to her ear.

"Hi, Ben. What's up?"

"Just wanted you to know the showcase practices are going very well and the competition enrollments have reached an all-time high. Thought you'd like good news for a change. I didn't want you to worry about the studio."

"Thanks, Ben. What a guy! You sure you don't mind this extra work?"

"Are you kidding? I'd do anything for you. You know that."

Kim rolled her eyes and made a face at Pamela. Both of them were very aware of his interest in Kim.

"I know, Ben. It means a lot to me not to have to worry about the business. I've sort of dumped on you, haven't I?"

"Don't give it another thought. The studio is operating just fine. Kyle and Dawn have picked up your students and Nikki doesn't mind coming in on Saturdays. Everything's under control," he advised.

"Things going that well without me, are they?" Kim pouted, letting a mischievous laugh break through. It was a luxury she had not enjoyed very often since that fateful night.

"It's good to hear you laugh. Things never go as well in your absence. You know that. Irene and I are a little behind in our prep for Blackpool, but our frustration pales in comparison to yours. What are you going to do about a dance partner, Kim? Forget I said that. I know it's terribly difficult for you now, so I'm going to change the subject. Oh, I've got something for you from your students. A gift. How 'bout I bring it over?"

Kim placed her palm over her forehead, rolled her eyes again, and retreated quickly into an excuse.

"No. Actually now is not a good time. Thanks anyway, Ben. I have company."

"Company? Oh, was that who answered?"

"Yes. She's a friend of Karen's." Kim glanced over at Linda and winked. "And as of this morning, a friend of mine, as well."

Linda placed her hands in a prayer position on her chest and smiled, using her lips to form the words thank you.

"That's terrific," Ben said. "No problem. Suppose I drop it by later?"

"Okay," Kim said, hesitating slightly as she fidgeted with an earring. "That will be fine. But I don't want to put you to any trouble."

"No trouble at all. I'll see you later today, then."

"Bye," Kim sighed, wishing she hadn't consented to his visit.

"Bye."

Unaware that she was making another face, Kim looked at her vigilant observers.

"He makes you uneasy, doesn't he?" Linda guessed.

Kim confirmed Linda's observation by raising her eyebrows. "Yes. Pretty obvious wasn't it. Ben does make me just a little uneasy." Then she corrected herself. "But, Linda, he's really a nice guy. And he's really helping with the studio. He used to be infatuated with me. But when I married Jim, that became ancient history. I don't know why I'm so uncomfortable around him now."

"Because he's a pest," accused Pamela as she plucked her coffee cup off the tray. "He's always had a thing for you and for the last month or so he's been trying to push himself on you, Kim. You know as well as I do, that's the truth. Everyone knows it."

"I know," Kim admitted half-heartedly, "but he's never been anything less than a gentleman around me."

"Maybe so." Pamela's tone was somewhat patronizing. "But you're a widow now." The words jumped out of her mouth before she could pull them back. She gave Kim a hug and whispered into her ear. "And a beautiful one, at that. Young widows usually become fair game to people who pretend they want to help. You'll be surprised at who will hit on you."

The shrewd glint in Pamela's eyes told the other two she meant it.

"Okay, okay. I know you're right. You've made your point," Kim said. "I'll be careful. But I can tell you, Ben Dare is harmless."

"No man is completely harmless."

"Well, this almost completely harmless man is saving my business," Kim countered, pointing an accusing finger at Pamela.

"That's true. We've got to give that to him." Pamela pretended agreement. "If his interests aren't amorous, I can tell you what they are. I don't know why I didn't see it before. Now that Jim's dead, Ben and Irene have to be favored to win the world championship at Blackpool."

Kim sighed heavily.

"Pamela!" Karen said crisply. "What an awful thing to say!"

"No, she's right," Kim added quickly. "The thought occurred to me, too."

"Hey, you two," interrupted Linda. "Why don't we change the subject?"

Kim's face brightened as she extended her hand and took hold of both Pamela and Karen's hands.

"Lt. McCauley thinks your son is alive," Linda tactfully reminded them.

"I've felt that way from the start, but I was too afraid to admit it," Pamela confessed.

"Kim," Linda spoke with uncontested authority. "I believe your son might be alive, too. And I believe there is a way we can find out for sure."

Kim eased herself onto a nearby chair.

"How? I don't understand. How can you be so sure?"

Linda motioned for the other women to sit.

"If you feel up to it, I'd like to hear more about the white dog," Linda said calmly. The expression on her face was serious and her manner was direct. "I'll probably want to see the Camaro, too, if Lt. McCauley can run interference for us. But for now, let's focus on your white canine visitor."

"If it'll help find my son, I'd tell you about the white dog, the woodpecker that's been hammering on my rain spout, the flowers Ben sent me, and any other strange thing that's happened to me lately."

Linda chuckled "If the dog's appearance means what I think it does," she said reflectively, "your son is not only alive, but is being protected by divinely appointed messengers."

Kim's face was a commercial of excitement as she scooted herself to the edge of her chair cushion.

"Linda, excuse my indelicacy, but you'd better not get my hopes up without some degree of absolute certainty. What you're telling me is that you know something that the best law enforcement minds don't know."

Linda nodded her acknowledgment and showed absolutely no sign of hypocrisy.

"I've seen Linda's work before," Karen interjected. "If she thinks there's a relationship between the white dog and Graham's whereabouts, there must be one. I'm positively confident in her ability. You needn't doubt her for one minute."

Kim drew in a deep breath and a flicker of expectancy flashed across her face. She studied her talented guest psychic for a moment.

"Okay, I'm going to trust you. But be careful of the claims you make," Kim cautioned.

"Kim!" Karen said quickly.

"No. I mean it," Kim continued. She glanced soberly at Karen, but then steadied her gaze on Linda, who remained calm and non-defensive. "I want to believe you. But I don't want to believe in false hope. Earlier tonight you asked me if I was ready to meet you. Well, I hope you're ready for me, because I cannot ... I will not subject myself to well-intentioned incompetence. I'm sorry if I've offended you, but that's how I feel."

The others remained silent, waiting for Linda to respond.

"My dear Mrs. Sanborn," Linda began, looking compassionately at her hostess. "I am not a prophetess of false hopes. If your son is anywhere, dead or alive, within a thousand miles of this place, I'll find him. You have my word on that. I do not take my psychic abilities lightly. I do not flaunt them for personal gain. I am not here to benefit monetarily from your tragedy. I am here because I am Karen's friend, and because I truly believe I can help you. I have no other motives. I have no other agenda.

"I understand your caution and your grief. As the One Source is my witness, I would never take advantage of you or anyone else. You may doubt my integrity now, but I am depending on your integrity and your courage later.

"I cannot save your son. He's in the Universe's capable hands. But I can find him for you. If you're willing to give me a shot at finding him, I'm more than willing to accept your doubts until you get to know me."

"Once upon a time," Kim began slowly, "there was a large white dog who had a small patch of black fur on his right hind leg ..."

CHAPTER EIGHT

To the best of my recollection, I've seen the white dog a half-dozen times. He was wary of me at first. He kept his distance at first and would retreat a few steps if I got too close." Kim paused to take a sip of coffee. She smiled and lowered her head. "Yes. I know you're not supposed to feed stray animals, but I felt there was something special about this dog. I left food and water in dishes on the patio every evening, and in the morning the dishes were always empty."

"You said he's allowed you to pet him?"

"Yes, I've been able to pet him almost every time. Isn't that strange? And his visits are getting longer. It's almost as if ... you're going to think I'm crazy ... but I think he wants to tell me something."

"You're not crazy at all, Kim, and I'll tell you why I believe you're having very special encounters with this dog a little later. Anything else you can tell me about him?"

"He seems to know me better than I know him. I don't know why I feel that way, but ... well, I think it's his eyes. It's like he looks through me. Understands me. Grieves with me. Has anyone ever described an animal like that to you?" Kim searched Linda's eyes for reassurance.

"Many times," she replied immediately, smiling as she straightened herself in her chair. "You are experiencing a primordial connectedness with the animal kingdom. Scientists who research animals in the wild report the same feelings, so you're in good company. What you're experiencing is real. I must defer any further explanation for now, but I promise I'll tell you what I think your encounters mean later. Okay?"

"Okay."

"Have you had any other unique encounters with animals, birds, or insects over the past month?"

"Animals, birds, insects?" Kim questioned, throwing Linda a confused look. "What do they have to do with anything? What do insects have to do with helping me find my son?"

"More than you realize," Linda responded calmly as she watched Kim's face melt into contours of bewilderment. "I believe any unique encounters you've had with certain creatures these past few weeks might be significant. Or at least instructive," she corrected herself.

Kim locked her eyes onto Linda's, then pulled them away reflectively. She decided to give the psychic some latitude.

"I've only mentioned this to my parents and Pamela. Karen, I don't know if Pamela mentioned it to you or not, but last week my house was invaded by hundreds of lady bugs."

Linda's eyes lightened, and her hands flew to her pen and paper.

"They were everywhere. They literally covered the tops of every window sill in the house. They were on the ceiling, in the curtains, on the window ledges, crawling up the glass in the sun room. Mother helped get them out of the house. She wanted to vacuum them up, but I couldn't do that. So we used three-by-five index cards and scraped them into canning jars and Tupperware containers with lids."

"You know they won't hurt you, don't you?"

"Oh, yes. I know. It's just that there were so many of them. Hundreds—thousands. I'm still finding them occasionally. And when I do, I capture them in a glass or jar and liberate them outdoors. It's been a very interesting experience!"

Suddenly Kim snapped her fingers and jumped to her feet. "The groundhog! Linda, I just remembered. I've seen a groundhog. I took some plastic bottles and cans out to the recycling bin early last Wednesday morning, and there he was. He was sitting on his hind legs at the end of my lot, watching every move I made. I've never seen a groundhog inside the city limits before. And that seemed very strange to me because I thought they hibernated in the winter."

"That's right, and since you saw him in January, his visitation is extremely significant. Groundhogs don't usually come out of hibernation until winter's over. You've had an interesting January, my dear."

"Pamela saw him, too. And so did the Lees. As a matter of fact, George video-taped his visit. He was only here a little while—he was gone by lunch. The groundhog, that is, not George."

Both Karen and Linda smiled, realizing Kim's clarification was unnecessary.

Kim led the women through several more of her encounters with the animal world, sending Karen to the kitchen during an especially vivid description of her afternoon with an aggressive black snake which had gotten in the house.

Linda listened intently to Kim's accounts and took copious notes, stopping occasionally to clarify one of Kim's descriptions or to ask a question.

Karen prepared a late lunch for them during Kim's account of her unusual sightings. By the time Kim finished her story, the women had finished eating lunch, as well.

Linda jotted down a few more insights while the other women tidied up the kitchen.

"Let's take a few minutes to stretch and relax, and then I'll interpret what I've heard," Linda instructed, as she closed her note pad with a snap. Then, not wanting to be seen as trying to get out of clean-up work, she asked, "Can I help you in there?"

"You stay where you are," Karen ordered. "We're almost finished here. I need a pit stop, and then we'll be ready to hear what you have to say. I, for one, can't wait."

Kim had half a cup of coffee left and decided to warm it in the microwave while they waited for Karen. "I've drunk way too much of this stuff," she said as she held her cup up and stared at it. Then she shifted her gaze toward Linda.

"I'm afraid I didn't give you much to go on, did I?"

"On the contrary," Linda disagreed. "You've confirmed Lt. McCauley's suspicions." She grinned. "Actually, your animals have."

Kim threw her a confused look.

"When Karen joins us, I'll explain."

"Explain what?" Karen repeated, catching the end of their conversation.

"Sit," invited Linda. "I'll begin by telling you that I believe Graham is definitely alive." She trained her eyes directly at Kim.

Kim forced a brittle smile and clasped her hands in a prayer position as she raised them to the bottom of her chin. Her emerald gaze studied Linda.

"How do you know he is alive? You know how much I need for him to be alive. But how can you be so sure?"

"Kim," Linda began, softening her voice and lightly touching Kim's hands. "You have been searching for your son a little over six weeks now. Except for a few clues and an officer's intuition, there have been no concrete developments in the case as far as the Raleigh Police Department is concerned."

Kim nodded her agreement.

Pamela eased her chair closer to Kim so Linda wouldn't have to turn her head back and forth to address the three of them.

"Your own maternal instincts and your strong faith tell you that Graham must be alive. Am I right?" Linda asked.

Kim confirmed the psychic's assessment by closing her eyes and nodding her head.

"You must trust your instincts and remain faithful, my dear. You must not give up or give in. I believe your son is alive and well for several reasons."

Kim's eyes widened in response to the psychic's pronouncement. *She said he is alive and well,* Kim repeated to herself. *Alive and well.*

"Whenever I closed my eyes and thought of your son this afternoon, I saw him surrounded by a golden orb, a shimmering cocoon of golden light."

Kim swallowed nervously.

"If he were ill or injured, I would have seen him encased in an ashen or murky light, a dull light. If he were dead, he would have been surrounded with a black sphere or I wouldn't have sensed his energy at all. I feel he's alive. I sense his energy in the ethers."

Kim repositioned herself in her chair to straighten herself. She accepted the tissues Karen offered and tried her best to compose herself.

"Now, you have enough on your mind these days without my complicating your life by explaining the structure and dynamics of psychic intuition. Everyone has psychic ability. It's just undeveloped in most people. Perhaps at a later time, you will want to know more about how to develop your own psychic abilities." Linda smiled and leaned slightly toward the trio of women who sat attentively across from her. She grasped Kim's hand before she continued.

"As for now, just know that the subconscious mind warehouses the richness of human transpersonal experience. Taken for granted, our divinity, or as the psychologists call it, our transpersonal experience, is generally unexamined, unappreciated, and unused. It keeps its secrets hidden in our subconsciousness or comes to us in dreams, waiting for its human host to wake-up. To varying degrees, people all over the world are waking up. We only have to trust our connection with the Eternal Beingness which underwrites all that is in this dimension and in all dimensions. That's part of the problem with the human race—we think we're smarter than the Presence that is the Ground of All Being."

"Then I could locate my son, if I were trained to go inside, into my subconsciousness?" exclaimed Kim.

"Well, it's more like your super-consciousness, my dear, which is a much higher octave than your subconscious. Your psychic abilities are lying dormant, for the most part, within you. And like any ability, they must be uncovered, developed, and honored. You will only feel his presence first, until you have sufficiently developed your psychic abilities. You may even see images, or sense circumstances that communicate his presence. It is not uncommon to pick up thoughts, or partial thoughts of loved ones. But these thoughts usually come to us as intuitions, urges to do or say something, or déjà vu experiences."

"Linda says most people don't slow down long enough to find their psychic abilities," Karen inserted exuberantly. "The universe is wired in our behalf. All we've got to do is listen to it, feel it, see beyond appearances, trust it."

"Thank you, Karen. Kim, she is exactly right. But there is much more to share with you this afternoon. I want to remove all doubt with regard to your son's state of being. I can feel a live connection with your son. I feel his energy. Faintly, but nevertheless it's here. I feel distance, as if his spirit is bound by forces—forces that seem selfish, but not evil. I sense an uninterrupted stream of consciousness in regard to your son's energy. If he were on the other side, there would be different signs."

"What kind of signs?" Kim asked quietly.

Linda leaned back into the curve of the high-backed chair and crossed her legs. She wanted her body language to communicate the confidence she felt.

"There are natural ways, extra-sensory ways to feel the interconnectedness between human emotions and heavenly spirit. All living things are connective divine tissue. We all come from the same Source. Some of us can simply feel that connection more than others. When you mentioned the sudden appearance of a white dog, I knew immediately that your son was alive. And the interspecies occurrences within weeks of your son's disappearance confirmed his survival for me."

Kim let out an extended sigh of guarded relief. Her eyes were riveted on Linda's.

"The ground hog and lady bugs," Kim spoke softly. "That's why you asked me if I saw or heard anything unusual?"

Linda nodded, but maintained eye contact with Kim.

Karen smiled. She knew what was coming.

"All forms of life are here to remind us that we are part of the Divine Matrix. I call it the Field of Infinite Potential."

Pamela winked at Kim who immediately got her drift. She knew Pamela was referring to the book by the two Unity ministers who had mentioned 'the Field' in their writings.

Linda noticed their side 'chatter,' but continued her description of the interconnectedness of sentient beings.

"The most common belief the ancients share is that our spiritual guides employ animals to send us messages of hope and healing and protection."

"Amazing," whispered Kim.

"Animals represent the basic, more instinctive, emotional and attitudinal side of life," Linda continued. "They are here to remind us of the evolutionary primordial drives and instincts we must overcome, control, or modify in some way. The ancients knew that visible things like animals, plants, insects, buildings, structures of any kind are symbols of invisible forces within each of us. The Bible, and other sacred writings from the world's major faith traditions, remind us that we have dominion over animals, that is, our primordial instincts, It also teaches us to learn from them, too!"

Kim's interest crept onto her face.

"For example," Linda continued, "birds symbolize lofty ideas, aspirations, and inspiration. Fish symbolize intuition and creative insights from the depths of the subconscious, because water stands for human emotions. Insects teach us about industriousness, fertility, resurrection, leaps forward, and so on."

"I'm learning things here this afternoon I never thought of before. I had no idea," Kim confessed.

"You're not alone, my dear." Linda spoke evenly. "Most people have no idea about their inter-connectedness with the living things around them. I call it the kinship of all life. Every living thing is connected to the whole. How can we truly be self-conscious if we forget or deny our proper place in the natural world?"

"I never thought of it that way," Karen commented. "Looks like we humans aren't as smart as we think we are."

All of them laughed. Pamela was especially pleased to see Kim loosen up.

"Actually, my dears," Linda jumped in, "we are as smart as we think we are. We just don't think far enough. For example, I believe one of the worst things that ever happened to the human race was the invention of the wheel."

Both Kim and Pamela's mouths dropped open at the same time.

Karen had heard Linda's explanation before and enjoyed watching Kim's and Pamela's reactions.

"I'm serious," Linda pitched her assertion. "What if, instead of inventing a physical thing, a round mechanical object to get us from point A to point B, the ancients used mental transference? Suppose they had gone internally, into the subconscious mind, and developed mental constructs to project us from point A to point B? Like levitation, bilocation, or molecular transference!"

The amazed looks on the two women's faces encouraged Linda to elaborate.

"Just think where we'd be today. We could mentally project ourselves from New York to Los Angeles. From North Carolina to Bermuda. From the Earth to Mars in a matter of seconds.

"From Raleigh to wherever my son is," added Kim, sadly.

A sudden hush fell over the room as the other women realized the gravity of Kim's statement.

"Yes, my dear," Linda spoke softly, choosing the words carefully, "I believe that would be possible, too."

In an attempt to introduce some levity, Linda decided to share a quick story before she explained the significance of the white dog. Then she reversed her thinking, believing Kim needed an immediate interpretation of the symbolic significance of the white dog and the other messengers from the animal kingdom.

"Kim, dear, I believe the white dog was sent by your Guardian Angel to you to tell you Graham is alive. Our universal inter-connectivity works in mysterious ways. And I believe the dog's soul is connected with your son's soul. The dog's markings are the Universe's way of showing you Graham's nonlocal connection with the white dog. If Graham were dead, you would be feeling a sense of heaviness, of displacement or disconnection. Your melancholy would be tripled. Your sense of loss would be deeper than you could imagine. You would not have received help from the natural world. Instead, you would have received psychic signals from Graham's disembodied soul—like the smell of his hair or clothes, or an apparition of him in this house. He would have communicated with you personally somehow."

Kim brightened a little, although she remained silent.

"The dog is marked in a specific way to get your attention. That's a sign of hope, not resignation. The dog's presence itself means good tidings. You said the dog looked like a white Great Pyrenees or Husky?"

Kim nodded.

"He is probably a combination of a herding dog and a hunting or retrieving dog. Therefore he symbolizes guardianship and protection. The color white stands for innocence, purity, cleanliness, union. Black generally means absorption, the unknown, darkness, the negation of self. The black patch of fur on his hind leg corresponds to Graham's birthmark. It means Graham's energy is still vibrant and healthy. He may have been torn from you, Kim, but he is held firmly by the universe. As I said, the color white is a unifying principle. Remember the old saying: 'the whiter the paper, the darker the blot.' Well, we may not know where he is now, but I believe a probable connection is immanent. Whenever a child is taken like this, the whole universe is aware. Whoever took your son cannot hide him for long. I believe that with all my heart. It is a message to you that the dog is linked with your son's energies—and with your energies—or he wouldn't have shown up. His marking is no coincidence. It is a powerful totem."

Kim smiled weakly, wanting to believe in Linda's extraordinary explanation.

"I believe the white dog is proof that Graham has spiritual protection. The dog came into your life as a spiritual totem. So you must ask yourself questions like: How can I express more faith? Do I believe Linda or do I want to believe her? Am I remaining faithful to my belief that he is alive? How can I seal the connection? How can I protect myself from doubts and depression? To what extent will I trust the connection? How can I use the dog to connect me with my son's energy?"

You're right, Kim reasoned before her thoughts erupted into speech. "You're right. I can protect him through my prayers and positive thoughts. I can visualize him being well. I can act on hunches and help the police somehow. I can learn what the white dog has to teach me. I can believe the inter-connectivity you mention is real. I can ..."

"Take care of yourself," Pamela interrupted, referring to Kim's reluctance over the past month to get the rest she needed and to eat properly.

"You're right, Pamela." Kim agreed. "I've got to protect myself from getting sick or I won't have the energy or the health to find Graham."

"You have the support of some other powerful totems, too." Linda reminded her. "The ground hog you saw represents the mystery of death or loss without dying. The lady bugs stand for resurrection, too."

"I'm afraid I don't understand," commented Kim.

"The groundhog is known for its burrowing or tunneling ability. It goes into hibernation and spends four to six months in that subterranean condition. Hibernation symbolizes death without dying. It suggests a time of sleep or soul-searching before a reawakening."

Kim's puzzlement prompted Linda to elaborate.

"I believe the groundhog you saw symbolizes Graham's disappearance from your physical presence. He has gone from light into darkness, but he is alive in captivity. He will remain under cover, out of sight, so to speak, until you magnetize him to you. You must accept his disappearance but believe in his return."

"How long?" Kim asked, coughing nervously. She took a sip of her cold coffee to moisten the dry spot in her throat. "Do you have any idea how long it will take to get my son back?"

Linda exchanged sympathetic glances with Karen and Pamela. Both women knew the degree of ethical accountability associated with predictions of this sort.

"I wish I knew. There are too many factors that can come into play. There's an old saying," Linda paused, "It goes something like this: if you don't want to know…"

"Don't ask," Kim completed her statement and then sighed heavily. "I want to know even if it upsets me. Okay?"

Linda clasped both of Kim's hands in her own as she studied the young mother.

"Remember I said that groundhogs usually spend from four to six months in hibernation?"

Kim's only movement was a slight tick in her left eye which belied her composure.

"It could be four to six weeks, four to six months, or… four to six years before you see your son again."

Kim collapsed against the back of her chair, forcing a break in her grip with Linda's outstretched hands.

"Oh, no," Karen whispered aloud while Pamela closed her eyes and shook her head slowly.

Kim couldn't get any words to fall from her lips.

"That's only an observation … a guess," voiced Linda. "I'm not claiming it as fact and I certainly hope I'm wrong. But I think the numbers four and six are significant. That dear little boy could also just as easily come home in the next four to six hours." She paused, "But I don't think that's reasonable. Do you?"

All three women stared blankly at Linda and no one spoke for a while.

Linda was the first to break the silence.

"Kim, dear, I think it means that you may have to prepare for reuniting with your son later than sooner. I'm not ruling out sooner, but I believe you will have to employ patience, trust, and faith as your chief allies. I'm sorry, dear."

"There's nothing to be sorry for," Kim dismissed her apology. "You've given me hope. I believe now more than ever that my son's alive. I'm not sure I totally understand the animal symbolism, but what you have said makes sense. My heart tells me you've spoken the truth. But my head tells me to hold out for the hard, cold facts."

"That's okay," Linda agreed. "Just remember, facts are only facts so long. So far, the facts haven't helped you find your son, or more importantly, confirmed whether or not he is even alive. If you believe my ... shall we call them psychic facts ... you know he is alive now. So all I can say is pay attention to the animal totems that surround you, particularly the white dog.

"Believe in your own instincts. Trust your intuitions. Force negative thoughts out of your mind. Universal love and your soul connection with Graham are in charge. Let the Universe help you."

"Okay. Thanks, I'll try. I mean, I will do it! " Kim promised. "I hope the Universe sends me more signs. More confirmations. I need to open my psychic eyes, don't I?"

"Open your heart first," Linda emphasized. "Don't look for signs per se because signs are based on hope. And hope means you aren't sure something will happen. Switch hope to faith. Faith is belief in your connection. Most people believe things when they see them. Life generally works the other way. People see things when they believe them. Love opens doors. Love turns darkness into light and love will bring your son back to you."

"I've seen Linda help too many people find their loved ones to doubt her," Karen ratified.

"I hope you're right. I want to believe you're right."

Linda smiled thoughtfully.

"I'd like your permission to hold a few of Graham's things," Linda said. "I'd like to see if I can get a read on his whereabouts."

Kim couldn't keep the look of surprise off her face. A quick glance in Karen's direction satisfied her that Linda was serious.

"What kind of things?" Kim asked innocently.

"A photo, clothing, artwork, toys. Anything that he came into contact with often. And especially anything he last touched when he was emotionally upset."

Kim stood quickly and left the room.

"She's taking this pretty well," Linda commented to Karen, who had stood up and stretched when Kim left the room.

"Surprisingly well," affirmed Karen. "Kim's a lot like Pamela. They're both intelligent business women. Resourceful. Independent. Pragmatic. Left brained. So something like this, employing a psychic as a resource and talking about the inter-connectedness between animals, insects, and humans is a bit far out for her. I know she thinks angels are real. And she's interested in topics like Zen, metaphysics, and spiritual places throughout the world. But the spirituality of animals—that's a growing-edge for her."

"Me, too," exclaimed Pamela. "And thanks for the compliments. Resourceful business woman. Pragmatic. Independent."

Linda raised her eyebrows and tilted her head to one side.

Karen laughed. "I mean it. You two are alike in many ways. You know more metaphysics than Kim, but I'm pleased that she's handled Linda's animal totem philosophy so well!"

"Then perhaps I'll share an insight with Kim that will open her spiritual eyes a little further," Linda proposed. "Do you think she can handle a bit of cosmic counseling?"

Karen rolled her eyes and made a noise like a punctured tire.

"Hmmm. Yep, I believe she can. You certainly captivated her. She's a strong woman. And she's lost faith in a legal system that seems both impotent and disinterested in helping her find her son. Like the rest of us, she knows the answers are always there if we just know where to look. It's knowing where to look that's the problem. I'm glad she agreed to ask for your help."

Pamela nodded her agreement, and was about to say something when they heard Kim coming back.

Kim reappeared carrying one of Graham's baseball caps, a framed photo, and a pair of pants and shirt. In her left hand was his stuffed teddy bear the police found in the car. She was also wearing tears which found their way down her face.

"Will these do?"

"Perfect," assured Linda. "But would you take his photo out of the frame? Although the glare-free glass is transparent, glass serves as a barrier."

"How about another picture. A snapshot?"

"As long as it's a recent photo of Graham," cautioned Linda. "Residues of his energy will have faded too much on older photographs."

"I've got a wallet-sized one of the one in the frame. The police found it and this teddy bear in the back seat of Jim's ca...car," Kim replied softly. "Give me just a minute."

"That's perfect. The bear may still have trace amounts of the emotional environment your son experienced that night."

"I've ... I've also got that taped account of his voice. Graham's screams were recorded on Jim's cassette tape that night," Kim added, trying to keep her fragile composure.

"Yes, bring that, too," Linda directed. "I may be able to intuit something from the tape itself. Good. It's good that you have the tape."

"It's a copy of the tape. The police have the original," Kim reported softly.

"That's okay. Bring it. I'll do my best to sense its psychic value."

Kim turned to take her leave.

"Kim," Linda said in a tone that retailed her concern.

"Yes?" Kim replied as she turned to face the others.

"You don't have to bring the tape if you don't want to." Kim's tight lips softened in a frail smile.

"There's a chance it may help, so I want you to hear it."

"Are you sure, dear?"

"Yes. Definitely," Kim responded soberly. "I'll be back shortly. I want to find my son,"

"You'll have plenty of help. You're being helped now, in ways you aren't even aware," Linda affirmed.

"Help me to recognize how I'm being helped."

"That, my dear, will be my greatest pleasure, next to witnessing your reunion with your son."

"I want that more than anything."

"Good," cheered Linda. When Kim retrieved the copy of the tape, Linda gently gathered the snapshot, the bear, and cassette and placed them on her lap. Then she picked up the bear and held it in front of her. She closed her eyes and let out an extended sigh.

"She's making the morphogenic connection so she can determine his general whereabouts," whispered Karen. "She'll be able to tell how close he is. She picks up on his vibrations, on his proximity to the articles she's holding."

Kim's anticipation took her breath away.

A few moments later Linda placed the bear on the table. Then she picked up Graham's clothing and repeated her breathing routine. She did the same thing with his cap. Next she repositioned herself in her chair and picked up the photo with one hand and the cassette with the other.

In a few minutes Linda began to sway slightly. The geography of her face changed continuously from frowns and lip tightness to eye twitches and head shakes.

"Is she all right?" Pamela whispered, inching closer to her sister.

Karen glanced quickly at Kim and Pamela, who were both sitting on the edge of their seats.

"Yes, she's fine. Let's sit quietly so we don't disturb her."

Almost immediately, Linda winced and then jerked violently three times in succession. Tears found their way down her cheeks as she began to breathe heavily.

"Are you sure she's okay?" Kim whispered.

Karen nodded and placed her finger over her lips to silence Kim, who was becoming increasingly unnerved.

Pamela came to her rescue and hugged Kim to stabilize her.

Linda lowered her head and then raised it as if she were watching something. Her eyes remained closed, but the rapid eye movements telegraphed her excitement as the pupils raced back and forth under her eyelids. She began to quiver from head-to-foot and her head bobbed up and down several times before she assumed a relaxed position. Her breathing returned to normal as she composed herself. Then she slowly lifted her head and opened her eyes.

"I was able to see glimpses of your husband's heroic struggle with the carjacker," Linda began. "Your son was in the back seat with the felon."

All three women widened their eyes.

"At one point in your clairvoyance, you jerked three times. What happened? What did you see?" Kim asked.

"I heard three gun shots," Linda replied immediately. "I saw him kill your husband."

Kim closed her eyes, but held her head steady.

"When he pulled your son out of the car, I was able to see the initials H.A.T.E. tattooed on his knuckles."

"That's right. That's what Jim recorded on the tape," Pamela verified enthusiastically.

"And you've picked up on it just by holding the cassette in your hand?" Kim addressed the fatigued psychic.

"I also got a glimpse of the killer."

The other three women froze.

"You saw him?" Kim raised her voice.

Linda nodded.

"He was wearing a green skull cap and brown jacket. Leather, I think. He had blue eyes and some hair was missing on his left eyebrow. It looked like a cut had left a scar across a portion of the eyebrow.

"That's more than the police have been able to find," Pamela exclaimed.

"You've gotten more information holding the tape than the police did listening to it," Kim said as she stood on excited feet. "The killer had blue eyes and a scar over one eye. And you saw that. That's incredible."

"He took your son with him. He put him in the green Camaro Lt. McCauley told us about tonight," Linda continued. "I saw him drive the car away. There was another person in the car. A woman. A woman with long black hair. Mid twenties, I think."

"I'm calling the police," Pamela said excitedly. "They need to know this."

Kim tossed an appreciative smile at Linda and then addressed Pamela.

"Lt. McCauley's phone number is on the freezer side of the fridge under the panda magnet."

"There's more," Linda said, in a voice loud enough for all to hear.

Pamela stopped in front of the refrigerator and held the phone at her side.

"There's something else the police should know."

Kim's puzzled look was duplicated by the others.

"He's not here," she whispered emphatically.

"What?" Kim raised her voice in desperation.

"He's nowhere in Raleigh. Or Cary. Or Durham. He's nowhere within fifty or sixty or a hundred miles of this place."

Kim's gut-wrenching cry produced sympathetic tears in the other women's eyes.

"Where is he then?" she cried dispiritedly. "What have they done with my baby?"

Linda sat beside Kim and cradled her hands in hers.

"My sympathetic sphere is limited, my dear. Most of my location work is done at the scene of the crime or in private residences like yours where I can see, feel, and touch mementos of the deceased or missing. If the victim is moved beyond a certain radius, I can't pick up on the energies. I'm sorry, dear. I'm sorry to disappoint you."

"Isn't there anything you can do?" quizzed Karen.

Linda looked at the two of them, contemplating her next comment.

"Yes. As a matter-of-fact there is. Have either of you ever heard of remote viewing?"

The astonished look on each of their faces told her she needed to explain.

"Remote viewing is the ability to correctly perceive and describe detailed information about a remote place, person, or thing, regardless of the normal boundaries of space and time."

"Could you repeat that?" Karen asked for all of them.

Linda obliged, repeating it slowly.

"Incredible," Pamela confessed.

"Good remote viewers can find any 'target' anywhere in the world," Linda reported. "The remote viewer is able to see a mental picture of the person or object and describe its location accurately."

"What do you mean by target?" Kim asked worriedly.

"A target is an object, a place, or a person that the remote viewer is asked to locate. It's not a target in the sense of something to be destroyed, like a military target. The purpose of remote viewing is to find something mentally. A person, place, or thing."

"Are you telling us you're a remote viewer?" chanced Kim.

"No, my dear. Oh, heavens no. I believe I could be with some training. But it's an extra-sensory talent that I have not developed to any great extent."

Kim frowned her disappointment. "Then you must have had a reason for mentioning it." Frustration was etched across her face.

Linda's face beamed as she stood. She reached for Graham's ball cap and the wallet-sized photo.

"I know someone who is an extraordinarily talented remote viewer," she exclaimed proudly.

A glimmer of hope returned to Kim's eyes.

"I'm not sure what all of this means. I've never heard of remote viewing. But if you think it can help ... you know I'll try anything to get my baby back."

Linda's sympathetic gaze settled on Kim as she squeezed both her arms lightly.

"How legitimate is this remote viewing? I don't think I can handle it if it's not going to work," Kim announced cautiously.

"My dear, I cannot absolutely, positively promise you that he can find your son. I wish I could. We are only now beginning to understand some of the rules associated with altered states of consciousness like remote viewing. But I can promise you this. I believe with all my heart that he can help us find that dear little boy. He's an extraordinary psychic. If anyone can find Graham, he can."

She placed her fingertips under Kim's chin, gently lifting her face.

"We live in a loving universe and there is an overall plan of which we are not fully aware. There is a conciseness out there," Linda made a sweeping motion with her hands to indicate expansiveness. "A cosmic precision," she continued. "And when bad things happen to good people, we don't know enough to see the precision. We blame God. We blame ourselves. We lose hope. We forget who we are. The best thing we can do is to become part of the solution and not perpetuate the problem. We can only do our best. We must seek our truth and follow our hearts. There is no other way, my dear."

"But what if you're unsure of your heart?"

"It's not your heart you're unsure of, it's your ego telling you not to take a risk. The ego wants to protect the status quo. It doesn't want to take chances. It certainly doesn't want to accept our interconnectedness, or the existence of angels, or psychic ability or astral travel, or using one's psychic ability to locate a missing child. Egos wear blinders, but spirit believes in possibilities. Taking blinders off our fragile ego means it would have to give up control to something greater than itself. And it refuses to accept a subordinate position. I remember someone saying once that the word ego is actually an acronym. It stands for Easing God Out."

"This is all a little beyond me. Are you saying that I have to let go and let God? I always thought that was such a cliché."

"It may be a cliché, but think about it. There is divinity in all things, and in order to consciously experience that divinity, you must work with the cosmic material at hand. You must trust that it is available to you at precisely the right time. That's what letting go means. It means believing in the inter-connectivity that is a fundamental function of wholeness," Linda explained, then continued.

"Forgive me for a long answer to your short question. Remote viewing is not a respected science yet in the United

States. Except for a few organizations like the CIA and the paraphysics community, especially in the Soviet Union, few people know about its scientific worth."

"Do you trust it?" Karen asked, trying not to sound pessimistic.

"Trust remote viewing as a bona fide extra-sensory skill?" Linda clarified.

Karen nodded, hoping her question would lighten Kim's emotional load and her own curiosity.

"Let's put it this way. I have absolute trust in my own experience. And my experience says that remote viewing is one of the many extra-sensory gifts we are endowed with. The real question is do I trust Joseph Wood's ability as a remote viewer?"

She smiled compassionately at the mesmerized trio who stood apprehensively in front of her as if they had walked into an episode of Twilight Zone.

"And your answer would be ... " Pamela found herself leaning toward Linda anticipating her response.

"I trust Joseph completely. I'd trust him with my life. I'd even walk blindfolded behind him through hell if I had to. He's real. He's meticulous. He's compassionate. And most of all, he owes me big time."

After joining them in a pinch of laughter, Kim looked directly at Linda.

"Would you call him for me?"

"It would bring me great joy if he could help you."

Tears fell from Kim's watery eyes again.

"In the meantime, my dear, clichéd or not, you must let go and let your I-Am-ness which is God expressing as your Higher Self do Its work."

"Is that an order?" Kim retorted, allowing a tiny smile to form at the corners of her mouth to signify her growing awareness that Linda's, Pamela's, and Karen's God was beginning to make sense.

"No, my dear, it's a reminder of Divine Order. And things like unusual animal sightings, spontaneous healings, heavenly signs, and even life traumas that teach us important spiritual lessons are the vocabularies of answered prayer. Be vigilant, my dear, and trust in Divine timing."

Kim looked at her appreciatively.

"And the white dog?"

"Open your mind and heart to what he has to say. He is one of the vocabularies of prayer I just referred to. Learn his language. Become fluent in it and he'll lead you to the path marked reunion with your son."

Kim walked over to the kitchen window and peered through the mini blinds at the empty dog food bowl.

"I know some of his vocabulary already," she said softly. "It's called tithing with food and water."

A quick scan of the back yard convinced her the white dog wasn't there so she turned toward Linda.

"I feel more at peace now than I have felt in a long time, thanks to you, Linda. And you, too, Pamela, Karen. You have my eternal gratitude. Oh, Pamela, you can make that call now. When Lt. McCauley asks how we got the information, tell him my husband told us."

The other women smiled and watched in respectful silence as Pamela punched Lt. McCauley's phone number.

CHAPTER NINE

Although it had been three hours since her guests left, the subject of their lively conversation still danced in Kim's thoughts.

The silence of the house wrapped itself around her as she surveyed her room furnishings, pausing occasionally to focus her attention on one of the many collectibles which stood sentinel-like on the shelves.

The walls were a riot of color, hosting a variety of oil paintings and water colors, mostly of European harbors—pictures they had bought overseas—and commissioned dance scenes of her and Jim. The cathedral ceiling in the living room and the openness throughout the house gave the interior a feeling of spaciousness and freedom.

The carpet downstairs was fairly new, replaced at Jim's insistence a week before Thanksgiving two years before. She'd been quite comfortable with the original carpeting, but he'd wanted to spend some of his huge book advance, so she welcomed his generosity.

Her visual inspection settled on the snapshot of Graham lying on the coffee table. Her vision blurred for an instant, but then cleared. Sighing heavily as she picked up the picture, she raised it to her bosom and hugged it.

"Baby, I'm coming out of hibernation," she promised aloud. "I'm going to learn some vocabularies of prayer. I'm going to find you, honey. Mommy's going to try her best to find you." *No more hibernation. I'm coming to get you,* she affirmed silently, as if summoned by his thoughts. "I'm coming to get you, baby," she re-addressed the snapshot. "And I'm sending you dog energy and groundhog energy and ladybug energy." She looked around quickly to see if she could spy any lady bugs. Then she lifted Graham's picture to her lips and gave it a quick kiss.

She held the photo out at arm's length and said, "Linda says I must trust in the extra-sensory connection between animals and humans, nonlocality and morphogenic fields. Somehow the white dog is linked to you. If she is right, I've got to find out what that linkage is so I can use dog energy to find you."

As she made that statement her eye caught a piece of note paper next to Graham's cap, in the chair Linda had vacated hours earlier.

Kim pulled the typed note and the small cap onto her lap. The note was on Phoenix Institute letterhead and identified the text as Observation Sheet #304. A yellow post-it-note was attached which read: Read this. It was signed: your favorite psychic, Linda. The one page text was entitled: *Tippy.*

Tippy, a year-old mixed breed dog, acquired the daily habit of depositing his stools on a small rug in the kitchen. He also adopted the repulsive habit of eating or scattering the cat droppings he found in the litter box.

Kim grimaced her confusion and remembered why she and Jim had postponed adopting a pet until Graham was older. She collected herself and began reading again.

His owner tried everything she knew to correct his bad habit. She yelled at him. Shook her finger at him and rubbed his nose in his poop. Nothing worked.

"You shouldn't have rubbed his nose in it," Kim chastised the pet owner aloud. She found her place in the text again and continued.

His manufacture and transportation of smelly goods, as we jokingly referred to it, started several weeks after his owner rescued a stray cat. Because the woman decided to keep the cat indoors, she introduced a litter box.

"Good choice," Kim smiled. "It's a lot less messy that way."

Tippy observed his master scooping out the cat poop and thought it was a neat game. He stood intently by as his owner "played" with the poop.

Kim produced another sour look.

Tippy liked the smell of the cat's leavings and thought that copying his roommate's behavior would please his owner. Since his owner made such a fuss over the cat's daily deposits, Tippy decided to leave a few deposits of his own.

What's more he wanted his owner to know who left the gift. So Tippy chose the rug in the kitchen as his dump site.

When the owner yelled at him for his "mistakes" on the rug, Tippy grew even more upset and changed the dump site to an area near the cat litter box. The competing smells and territorial violation upset the cat, who changed the location of his droppings.

"Oh, no!" Kim said, smiling broadly as she glanced unconsciously at her own carpet.

I was able to help the owner get inside the heads of her two confused "siblings." Once the owner realized Tippy's good intentions, she was relieved.

Kim laughed. "Poor choice of words, Linda."

She was able to see how the difference in elimination protocols led to the confusion of both pets.

We spoke to the animals just like they were people and I explained what the owner's new expectations were for each of them in terms of their "general deposits" The owner also lavished praise on Tippy whenever he left his deposits outside. In a few weeks both animals resumed their normal routines and the mistakes on the rug disappeared.

Explanation: Animals understand many of the words their owners use because they're familiar with human language. They "get" your instructions, emotions, or thoughts and even images behind the words, even if they don't fully understand the words. Since animals are not socialized to believe that words or symbols are the only way to communicate, they do not lose their innate telepathic ability and sensitivity as most humans do. (See The Journal of Interspecies Telepathic Communication.)

Linda Amos, Director, PI

Appreciating Linda's cleverness, Kim thought about the appearance of the white dog.

"So you're here to give me gifts, are you?" she asked rhetorically as she walked to the kitchen window. To her surprise, he was there—standing just off the patio, looking at her through the window.

She started toward the kitchen door, but re-routed herself when she heard the phone ring. Another quick glance out the curtained window produced a frown when she realized her canine friend had vanished.

She caught the phone on the third ring.

"Hello."

"Hi, Kim, this is Ben. Does the invitation still hold?"

Kim sighed as she remembered the now-regretted invitation. His call triggered another thought before she could speak.

Oh no, the vocabulary of Ben Dare.

"Kim, you still there?"

"Yes. I'm sorry, Ben. Something was on my mind."

"Well, it certainly wasn't me," he laughed good naturedly.

"I'm sorry," she repeated, wishing she hadn't been so rude.

"Forget about it. Your company left yet?"

"Yes, several hours ago. Oh, that's right. You wanted to hand deliver some sort of gift, didn't you?" She smiled and almost giggled as she thought about Tippy's pungent gifts described in Linda's memo.

"Yep. And you know what they say. Beware of good-looking dance instructors bearing gifts."

His patronizing voice reminded her of her disdain for pushy salesmen and spineless politicians. Her first reaction was to cancel the visit, but her promise to Graham leaked into her thoughts: *Get out of hibernation. Listen to the vocabulary of prayer.*

"I'm going to propose a change of plans," she countered, as her voice picked up strength.

"It's okay to change your mind as long as you stay in the line of dance," he bantered diplomatically, using dance terminology as a pun.

"Ugh, Ben! That was so bad. You punsters are all alike."

"I'm just trying to stay on the dance floor."

Kim smiled weakly.

"You don't have to try so hard. I'm not calling off your visit."

"Good. So we're still on then?"

"Yes. Same time, but different place."

"I didn't realize we set a time."

"You're right. So let's set one," she recovered. Although she kept up with the surface play of their conversation, she disliked this sort of small talk. She tapped her nails on the table top as she waited for his response.

"Your call," he conceded, sensing her impatience.

"Okay, how 'bout the studio? I'll meet you there in say, thirty or forty minutes? It'll be good to get back, if only for a visit. I've missed being there."

"Great! Why don't you make it an hour from now? And then let's grab something to eat—I'm buying! What do you say?"

Kim hesitated. She wasn't sure she wanted to be pulled out of hibernation by Ben. *You promised Graham*, she criticized herself. *Ben's trying to be nice. So cut him some slack.*

"Sounds like a plan to me. See you around five-thirty."

"By the time you get here, I'll know where I want to take you," he prophesied jubilantly.

"You can take me anywhere," she bantered, "as long as it's an up-scale restaurant and as long as it's the Stonewood Grill."

"Stonewood it is," he agreed.

As she hung up the phone, Kim reflected thoughtfully on their relationship. She first met Ben at the Birmingham Ballroom Dance Competition in 1989. Each of them eclipsed their respective partner's talents and were surfing dance competitions for another partner. They were both rising star champions in the Fred Astaire circuit. When they

decided to team up, they won two national championships—
one in American smooth dance and the other American
Rhythm. Then Kim and Jim began a partnership of marriage
and dance.

In addition to his tremendous athletic ability, Kim
attributed Ben's success at competitions to his extremely
good looks and political savvy. Presidential in appearance,
he had the Astaire look: thin, but muscular frame, an air of
confidence and fitness, and an impeccable dance posture.
He had the perfect look for his craft.

His mother was the widow of Chester Dare, the
billionaire and co-founder of Teletek, a monumentally
effective account security firm that developed a fool-proof
account management system for large data users. Money
was no object for Mrs. Dare or her only son. When he got
bored with his management position at his father's firm, Ben
decided to open a dance studio, and begged Kim to partner
with him.

Ben's ability to manage the day-to-day operations of the
studio allowed Kim to market the sport to baby boomers and
retired executives who had both the time and the money to
indulge themselves.

Over the years, he promised her that if she ever grew
tired of Jim, he would spend his millions on her. Only once
had he ever made a serious play for her. When she objected
strongly to his overture, he apologized and begged her to
continue their partnership. Kim agreed, with the proviso that
their relationship remain strictly business.

When Jim wrote his first bestseller, Ben hosted a
celebration gala at Myrtle Beach that lasted three days. He
had even used his media contacts to arrange for Jim to
appear on *Oprah, Good Morning America, the Today Show*
and *QVC* to hype his book. Internet sales alone rocketed
Jim's book to the top of the international bestsellers list.

Her only real objection to Ben was his obnoxious charm. Kim chuckled as she thought about Ben's subtle advances and peripheral passes that could be construed as playfulness if it weren't for the hint of impropriety that danced in his eyes.

"He's one of those guys who grows on you in spite of himself. He's like kudzu!" Kim laughed out loud as she pushed her thoughts free of roasting Ben. Realizing what time it was, she walked into the bedroom to change clothes and prepared to visit her dance studio.

§ § § § § §

The deep-pitched ring of the phone jolted her out of the only good night's sleep she'd had since she had dinner with Ben three days before.

Thinking it was the alarm clock, Kim reached over spastically and tapped the alarm button off on the digital clock. She stared at the clock and tapped it again when the phone rang a second time.

"What the .. oh, it's the phone." She raised her voice. "What a way to start a day."

She grabbed the receiver before it had a chance to snipe at her a third time. Before she spoke she glanced at the red letters on the clock face. *Seven-ten,* she confirmed to herself.

"Yes," Kim whispered as she wiped the sleep out of her eyes.

"Kim?" came the overly officious voice on the other end of the line.

Kim straightened, still trying to blink off the night's sleep. She knew she had heard that voice before, but couldn't place it.

"Yes, this is she," Kim sputtered. "Who is this?"

"Oh, I'm sorry, Kim, this is Linda, Linda Amos. I hope I haven't called you too early."

"No, no. I…" Kim stumbled through her reply. "I'm usually up before this, but I…" She yawned her reply. "You caught me grabbing a few more Z's this morning," she laughed. "I think I'm awake now."

"Forgive me. I feel so badly," apologized Linda. "Suppose I call back."

"No … no … no," Kim objected, as she stretched her mouth into a wide yawn. "I'm fine. I'm awake."

"I know this is short notice," Linda began, "But Joseph can see you tonight."

"Joseph?" Kim spoke lamely.

"Joseph Woods, the remote viewer I told you about," Linda replied quickly.

"Oh yes, of course."

"He's in the middle of a lecture series and he's at Duke University today. His administrative assistant, Sandi Weiss, told me where to find him."

"Oh, okay."

"He speaks this afternoon at three-thirty, at Duke. Karen, Pamela, and I are going and would like for you to join us."

"That would be great." Kim was fully awake now. She climbed out of bed as she spoke, and shook out her hair. "I'd like to hear him. Is he speaking on remote viewing?"

"Yes. His program is called Extra-Sensory Treks. He's using some new slides as part of his presentation. He's a really good speaker, too."

"Sounds interesting. I think I'd like that." Kim stretched her legs, first to the left and then to the right.

"Terrific. You'll be glad you went. I can't wait for you to meet Joseph. I've told him all about you. See ya later."

"Okay, thanks. Oh, wait a minute. Linda?"

"Yes, I'm here."

"Can he … will he be able to see me tonight?"

"Oh, brother! How could I forget the most important part? Joseph has agreed to see you this evening after his presentation. He's agreed to locate Graham. Are you up to it?"

"Of course, Linda, that's great. Thank you. I promised you I'd listen to all vocabularies of prayer. And Joseph might be capital letters."

"I'm thrilled you can join us. Is it all right if we grab a light dinner on the way back from Duke, and then come to your place for the remote viewing?"

"That'll be perfect."

"Good. Consider it set, then. Now let me put Karen on. She's handling the logistics. See you later."

"Good morning Sis," Karen greeted her with a crisp caffeine-saturated voice. "Had your second cup of coffee yet?" she asked playfully.

"No, but I've had my third yawn."

"Oops," Karen winced. "We did call kind of early, didn't we? Sorry."

"It's okay. Really."

"You sure?'

"I'm sure. Linda tells me you're the logistics mavin."

"Well, actually Pamela is, but she's jogging. So we decided to call you before you left this morning."

"Was I going somewhere?"

Karen cleared her throat.

"We wanted to catch you just in case you were going somewhere today ... this morning."

Kim sent her a hearty laugh.

"Sounds like you're penitent enough. When were you planning to pick me up for this Duke adventure?"

"Around two-fifteen. That all right?"

"Two-fifteen is fine. I'll be ready."

"Good. It should be fun." Karen's tone was jubilant. "Casual dress is fine. I'm wearing a sweater and jeans."

"Great! Casual works for me, too."

"Okay. We'll see you at two-fifteen."

"Oh, wait Karen ..."

Karen hesitated before she pulled the phone away from her ear.

"Would you put Linda back on for a minute?"

"Sure, hold on."

"Hi again," Linda said. Her voice sounded pleasant, but diplomatic.

"Hi, Linda. I wanted to ask you a couple of questions — to be ready for this presentation. Do you mind?"

"Of course not," she agreed. "What kind of questions?"

"About remote viewing and extra-sensory ..." Kim paused as she searched for the appropriate technical terminology. "... stuff."

She felt embarrassed for using such a wimpy word, but it was the only one she could think of at the moment.

"Sure. But you must realize, my dear, that I'm not an expert on the subject. And Joseph's presentation this afternoon should be very enlightening."

"I'm sure it will," Kim agreed, "and I'm looking forward to it. I'd just like to get a little background information so I don't feel so stupid."

"You're not stupid, young lady," Linda chastised good-naturedly. "We must work on the things you say about yourself. But that's another matter. What would you like to know about remote viewing?"

"Would you tell me exactly what it is again and how it can help me find Graham?"

"Let's take first things first. What is remote viewing?" She paraphrased Kim's question. "Remote viewing is the ability to perceive and describe in detail information about objects, people, or things that are considerable distances away from the viewer. The viewer sees, or as Joseph says, feels things in the targeted area, even if it's hundreds or even thousands of miles away."

"I still find that hard to believe," Kim responded, shaking her head slightly.

"You'll hear Joseph describe it in more detail today," Linda assured Kim. "The experience is like a feather brushing across his mind and moving about softly and lightly before it settles into the lower regions of his subconscious."

Kim nodded her understanding into the phone, but remained silent.

"Joseph says when he tries to grab an image, to hold onto it mentally, it's like attempting to catch the down from a pillow as it drifts lightly through the air. It escapes his grasp if he grabs for it. If he waits for it to settle, he can see it clearly for an instant before it evaporates."

Kim reached up to grasp an imaginary feather in response to Linda's description, and mentally saw it flutter evasively away from her outstretched fingers.

"I see," Kim volunteered her understanding. "Then the images are very ephemeral. They dissipate quickly."

"Yes, that's right. Generally, they last for only a few seconds. The viewer catches them mentally, then records them on tape or sketches the images on paper to capture them."

"You mean he actually jots the address down on paper?"

"Not the address. The location. He can see the physical surroundings. He describes what he sees and commits the images to paper so he doesn't forget what he's seen."

"Oh."

"According to Joseph, this is done for several reasons. Drawing, art work in general, is a right-brained activity and therefore a non-logical function of memory. Since images come from the right hemisphere, drawing them seems to produce less mental static and keeps the visual channels clear."

Kim lifted her eyebrows unconsciously. *I do know something about hemispheric differences. After all, I'm a professional dancer,* she thought.

Linda's voice brought her attention back to the conversation.

"Also, researchers know that some viewers do better by combining their artistic skills with verbal. Others simply describe what they see. Either way works, but in every case, viewers are able to commit their mental trek to paper."

"That makes sense," Kim interjected.

"Joseph does both," Linda continued. "You'll see that today when he shows his slides and this evening when he tries to locate Graham."

"Do you really think he can find Graham?" she asked guardedly, trying her best not to let the dry spot in her throat cause her to cough.

With the phone still glued to her ear, Kim headed toward the bathroom as she waited for Linda's reply. Once she got to the sink, she pulled one of the small cups out of the dispenser and filled it with water. Then she sipped the cool liquid as she listened to Linda.

"I believe he will do his best," Linda asserted confidently. "He's one of the top remote viewers in the world, and one of the most scientifically-tested, as I told you last night. Describing his credentials that way sounds horrible, doesn't it? He's not a laboratory animal. Although I'm sure there are times he feels like one. The government still hires him for his remote viewing ability for highly-classified targets.

"His session with you tonight will go something like this: He will want a quiet place. One free of electronics, phones, and outside distractions."

Jim's study will be perfect, Kim thought. *Although I'll have to remember to unplug the phone and turn the laptop off.*

"He will want some drawing paper, a stack of pencils, a tape recorder, and a glass of sparkling water of some kind, Evian or Pellagrino, whatever."

"I can handle that."

"Oh, and be thinking of a specific time you want him to concentrate on the target. Sorry ... I mean Graham. That's very important. The date, of course, will be today's date, but the time's important, too."

"I'm not sure I understand," Kim lowered her voice almost to a whisper, trying her best to sound intelligent.

"The reason he has to have an exact time and date is because objects have histories. They have a past and a present. He also has to consider the difference between existence and reality. Existence is subjective, reality is objective. You'll learn more about that this afternoon."

Kim frowned her confusion. "I understand that people, places, and things have a past and a present."

"And a future," Linda interjected strongly. "When Joseph targets an object or a person, he is not limited to current reality with regard to collecting extra-sensory information. Since remote viewers work outside the space-time continuum, they have to be able to place their targets in the context of the current need."

Kim stared at her reflection in the mirror. Her look of puzzlement began to melt into one of astonishment.

"You mean remote viewers like Joseph have to be able to differentiate things from the perspective of the present, past, or the future?"

"You got it. Unless they are instructed to concentrate on a target in a particular time frame, viewers pick up information or fragments of information from any era associated with that particular person or location."

"That's incredible. That's simply incredible."

"Joseph believes there are alternate realities. He believes in what quantum physicists call parallel universes.

And somehow our past, present, and future are intertwined in those universes. There are electromagnetic universes, microscopic universes, ultraviolet universes, subatomic universes. Even our subconscious is a universe. All of these have both empirical and non-empirical forms. And then there's the multiverse, but that's another subject."

"I've never thought about it that way. So, we're surrounded by universes."

"My dear, we're interconnected with and within those universes. People like Joseph Woods and myself, who have allowed ourselves to step out of ordinary consciousness into the world of extra-sensory phenomena, know there's more to the visible Universe than meets the eye. What we generally call reality is only a very small part of what is real. People's perceptions may or may not be the same thing as reality."

"But it does seem real to that person, doesn't it? I've found that if you can change a person's perception, you can help him or her change their reality, too."

"I believe that, too, Kim. As a psychic I know everyone and everything is connected to everyone and everything else. We are brothers and sisters, parents and children to each other. Some people have special visual ability. Others have a special sense of smell or hearing or touch or taste. And because we're connected in some way with everything that is, I believe people like Joseph can see long distance across the space-time continuum while others can only dial locally."

"You're referring to his ability to find my son."

"Kim, darling," Linda spoke slowly, calculatedly, "he will find your son. My only concern is if we will be able to interpret enough out of what he sees to locate your son."

"Oh, Linda," Kim struggled to speak with a tight throat. She took another sip of water. "I'm scared. I want so badly for this to work. I don't want to get my hopes up, but I don't want to not get them up, either. Does that make sense?"

"It makes perfect sense. I understand completely, my dear. Each of us is nothing less than the universe in dialogue with itself. We'll find your son if we're aware enough to pick up the signals, if we're able to move past the arrogance of our intellects and into the wisdom of our feelings."

"You make it sound so cosmic ... so supernatural," Kim confessed.

"Not at all, dear. It's really pretty simple. We just make it hard by trying to find scientific proof for everything. We need to approach life as children, with wonder and awe and faith."

Kim reached for a tissue, blotted her tears, and took another small sip of water to ease the shakiness of her voice.

"Thanks, Linda."

"You are more than welcome. And now, before we hang up, any more questions?"

"Well ... yes. Actually, I have one. I know I've kept you on the phone way too long, but it's a quick one. I promise."

"No problem. Ask away."

"I'm not sure how to ask this. It hasn't come up, but how much is Joseph's fee? I'm not sure I can afford to do this."

"Aw, honey, there is no fee. Joseph doesn't charge relatives."

"But Linda, I'm not related to Joseph."

"Oh, yes, you are. Joseph found his son five years ago. He and another youngster were washed downstream during a hurricane and drowned. He remotely located where they were miles downstream. You have more in common than you think. Joseph is not doing this for money. He's doing it because he wants to do it. It's his nature."

"So he must be one of those million-dollar words," Kim remarked.

"Million-dollar words?"

"Yes. In the vocabulary of answered prayer," Kim clarified.

"He's priceless, my dear. Priceless!"

CHAPTER TEN

He was not at all what Kim expected. His intense brown eyes seemed to penetrate her, catalog her, accept her. His high forehead rose above a slightly receding hairline and most of the gray settled on the area above his temples and down his well-groomed mustache and beard, giving him a distinction that belied his age.

Kim thought he was striking in appearance and his six-foot frame was well-built and angular for a man his age.

He looked conservatively professional except for the hint of ruggedness that caught her attention. Although his light gray herring-bone jacket was tailored, he was dressed in belt-less jeans and sandals. He appeared comfortable. And confident. Ready to practice his craft.

Linda managed to isolate him from the press of admirers who stood patiently in line behind the four of them.

"Mrs. Sanborn ..." Linda stopped herself in mid sentence when she caught Kim's look of disapproval. "Kim," she corrected herself, "this is Dr. Joseph Woods."

"Joseph will do quite nicely," he reprimanded her mildly and then followed his playful reproof with a wink.

"I'm sorry," Linda defended, trying her best to retreat gracefully.

"No apology needed," he assured her as he gave her one of his patented hugs. Joseph turned his attention to Kim, stretching his hand out to her as he smiled his greeting.

"It's a pleasure to meet you, Joseph," said Kim, returning his firm handshake.

"Same here. I'm looking forward to this evening, when I can give you my undivided attention. Linda has briefed me on your situation. I hope I will be able to help."

Kim closed her lightly mascaraed eyes momentarily and then reestablished eye contact.

"I hope so, too. Thank you."

"And you must be the operations manager Linda told me about," Joseph said, taking Karen's hand. "Linda's description of you doesn't do you justice. You are much more beautiful and taller than I might have guessed."

"It's a pleasure meeting you. Linda certainly has sung your praises. And her description does do me justice!" she responded playfully. "I'm Karen Justice. Justice is my last name. And I'd like to introduce you to my sister, Pamela, Pamela Justice."

"Pamela, you're just gorgeous. You must be a model. No, modeling wouldn't do you justice! " Joseph pitched his appraisal, attempting to extend Karen's just desserts.

"I'm not a model. But thanks for adjusting your greeting," she smiled as she gave her sister a quick wink.

"I kinda did, didn't I? I just like to ... make people comfortable. But I meant it when I said how breathtakingly beautiful you are."

Pamela gave him an embarrassed smile.

"Let's just end the 'justs' guys. Don't you think," Karen rescued the three of them.

Linda smiled at Joseph and gave the women corroborative winks.

"I am honored to have such a distinguished group in my audience today" he addressed the quartet. "and ... I have reserved seats for you right up front."

"Terrific," chimed Linda. She glanced at the people lined up behind them. "Guess we'd best occupy those seats so you can greet the other guests."

Joseph stole a glance at his watch. "You're right. My program starts in fifteen minutes. See you after the presentation."

The women found their seats and entertained themselves with small talk as the auditorium filled. Linda leaned over to address the other three women when they were all seated.

"Joseph likes plays on words," she announced. "He does that all of the time. It's his way of breaking the ice when he meets new people."

"I think he's cool," cooed Pamela.

"And Linda," continued Kim, "Your description of Joseph didn't do him justice."

The quartet brought out into respectful giggles, recognizing they were down front where everyone could see —and hear—them. They settled down and awaited the platformer's introduction of the speaker.

The audience's applause carried Joseph to the podium.

The women were as spell-bound as the other audience members when Joseph began his slide-enhanced presentation. His flare for oratory and his ability to engage the audience made his program thoroughly entertaining.

Kim was not alone in her new-found appreciation for remote viewing. When Joseph closed his program, he received a lengthy standing ovation.

The women watched Joseph patiently sign autographs for those admirers who bought his merchandise. He answered questions, listened to rambling stories, and finally posed for quite a few photographs. When he took his leave from the last guest, he walked confidently toward the four women.

"I think that's a wrap! I'm starved. Let's grab something quick and then we can get down to the real business at hand."

"Joseph, that was a phenomenal presentation. You really made it all seem so understandable—and believable!"

"Well, thank you ma'am. I consider that high praise." Joseph mimicked a vaudevillian bow.

As they accompanied him out of the auditorium, their barrage of compliments chaperoned Joseph merrily toward the car.

§ § § § § §

The trip to Raleigh was filled with laughter as Joseph recounted his initial attempts to learn remote viewing. By the time Pamela pulled the car into Kim's driveway, the women were prepared for another, more serious investiture of Joseph's time.

As soon as everyone was comfortably seated in the living room, Kim started toward the kitchen.

"How about a glass of wine before we get started?" Kim asked over her shoulder.

"Not for me, thanks," came Joseph's immediate reply. "I'm working."

Both Linda and Karen's smiles were met by Pamela's raised eyebrows. Kim's repentant look added to their enjoyment.

"Oops! I'm sorry, Joseph. I didn't even think about that," apologized Kim.

"No problem," empathized Joseph. "I'd love a glass of sparkling water though." He winked at Kim diplomatically and addressed the other three women. "I certainly don't mind if you have a glass of wine. I won't be offended in the least."

"Well, okay then," Karen politely acquiesced to Kim's offer.

"I could use a glass, too" Pamela announced unapologetically.

"Me, too," added Linda.

"Okay, three glasses of wine coming up," Kim announced gracefully, waving at Pamela to stay seated. "And one for me, too."

"I thought Ben was joining us," stated Pamela, as she accepted her glass of wine.

"He is," answered Kim. "He'll be here around six-twenty. He had to give a dance lesson to one of our silver-level students."

Karen looked at Joseph. "Ben is Kim's business partner. He's been managing the dance studio this past month."

"He's a real character. It'll be interesting to see what he thinks of remote viewing," added Pamela. "I'm not sure how much depth Ben's capable of."

"Pamela! I'm surprised at you. He's a good friend, even if he is a little eccentric," Kim countered, throwing Joseph an uneasy glance.

"I'm just surprised he wants to come tonight. He doesn't seem to be the type of person who'd be interested in remote viewing."

"He's interested in Kim, that's why he's coming here tonight," Karen said, smiling at Joseph.

"He's quite an opportunist," Pamela interrupted. She glanced at Kim and raised, then lowered her eyebrows several times in succession.

"Cut it out, guys! No more wine for you, Pamela!" Kim laughed in spite of herself. Then she turned to Joseph.

"Ben's a friend who can sometimes be a little overbearing. He means well, but his timing as far as relationships go, is generally way off. He wanted to hear your presentation this afternoon, but he had to be at the studio. To be honest, his interest in coming this evening surprised me. I hope it's all right with you. I didn't know how to say no. He's done so much to help me . . ."

Joseph sensed Kim's uneasiness and decided to short-circuit her anxiety. With a flourish that was knight-like in its calculated smoothness, he stepped between Kim and Pamela and offered them his arms in a gentlemanly fashion.

"No problem. As long as he doesn't interfere with the viewing, he's more than welcome. Now, shall we get set up? I'd like to have the room ready by the time your eccentric guest arrives. He should fit right in, don't you think?"

The three of them, arms interlocked, walked in mock formality in a circle, orchestrated by Joseph, who was unsure where to take them. Kim realized his predicament and took the lead, guiding the pretzeled group toward the staircase. As they got to the landing Kim gently disengaged her arm and led the trio upstairs, speaking over her shoulder. "I thought Jim's study would be a good place to do this."

The abandoned office was cleared of computers, phones and electronics. The smaller of the two desks was cleared off, except for a half-dozen sharpened pencils, a tape recorder, drawing paper, and a glass sitting next to a bottle of Pelegrino.

The phone was wrapped loosely with its cord and wedged between the two computers. A small hide-away couch was tucked into the corner adjacent to the window, which had its mini-blinds drawn shut.

The shelves and walls were speckled with plaques, photos, and other awards—monuments to her husband's prodigious literary achievements. The covers of his three bestsellers were displayed nicely in gold-leafed frames on the wall immediately above the larger of the two desks. An entire wall, floor-to-ceiling, was covered with bookcases crammed with books and reference materials. Tucked away on one of the shelves was a family photo album, a nostalgic reminder of happier times.

"I hope this office will be okay." Kim said, realizing it's limitations.

"This will do fine," said Joseph. Then he turned to Linda. "Okay if we move that office chair over next to this one?" He pointed to the padded chair pushed under the larger desk.

"Whatever you need is fine," said Kim.

Linda rolled the chair over to the smaller desk and waited for Joseph's next request.

"Kim, would you be so kind as to bring some blankets or bed sheets in so we can cover the bookcases?"

Kim threw him a puzzled look.

He smiled and then mimicked her puzzled look.

"The more nondescript the viewing environment, the less mental clutter there will be. Short-term memory soaks up what you see and stores the images in the immediate environment. When that happens, the subconscious will include information about some of those objects with information from the target. If that occurs, I may experience mental overlay, static or jamming."

"Oh, of course. I'll get some blankets and sheets right away."

"And Kim, it would be better if the sheets do not have designs on them or multi-colors."

Kim thought for a moment.

"Do they have to be the same color?" she quizzed.

"No. They can be white, pastel. Even dark. Just solids—not prints."

Kim nodded and moved quickly toward the door leading to the hallway.

"I'll help," volunteered Linda, who caught up to Kim as she retreated through the doorway. The ring of the doorbell interrupted their mission.

"I'll get it," chorused Pamela as she headed toward the front door.

"I didn't realize there was so much involved in a remote viewing," confessed Kim.

"There are a few more things he will need, I'm sure," Linda said, smiling gratuitously, "but I promise you, you won't have to call an interior decorator."

The two women exchanged smiles.

"Did somebody call in the Marines?" came a voice from downstairs. It was Ben. He had just negotiated the first landing and was carrying a Styrofoam cup of coffee he'd snagged before he left the dance studio. Pamela led him toward the study, rolling her eyes as she heard his comment.

"Hi, Ben," Kim greeted. "Looks like at least one Marine is here."

Ben halted his advance and saluted Kim.

"Sergeant Ben Dare reporting for duty, Sir ... Ma'am ... Boss."

"Have you ever hung sheets?" Linda countered, trying to keep their mission on track.

"Oh, Ben," Kim raised her voice, feeling somewhat embarrassed at having neglected a proper introduction. "This is Linda Amos. Linda, this is Ben Dare, my business partner."

Linda nodded.

Ben was a bit more abrupt.

"No, but I've been under a few." Ben replied, hoping to produce a laugh.

"What?" flushed Linda as surprise flung her mouth open.

"Sheets."

"Ben, " Kim chastised, "You'll need to clean up your act immediately or leave."

Reeling from Kim's unexpected sharpness, Ben lifted his hands and extended them, palms up toward the two women who glared at him from the top of the stairs.

"What did I say?" he pretended his innocence.

"Forget it." Kim replied firmly. She glanced quickly at Linda, and then looked askance at her prodigal guest, who was frozen on the third step.

"Ben, you know what this evening means to me. I need you to be on your best behavior tonight. That means you'll have to employ a little reverence and respect. Can you do that?"

He recovered quickly, placing his hands in a conciliatory prayer position.

"Sorry for the misfire," he said apologetically. "I promise to be on my best behavior. Ms. Amos, Kim, Pamela, Karen. You have my sincere apology. May I start over again?"

Before they could speak, Ben retreated down the steps and leaped past Karen, who followed him with her mouth open. He placed his half empty coffee cup on one of the end tables and retraced his steps to the front door. With his characteristic flair, he opened the front door, stepped out momentarily and then re-entered smiling broadly.

"Good evening, everyone. Am I in time for dessert?"

His antics were met with cold stares as the women focused their attention on the self-appointed clown at the front door.

"I see our last guest has arrived," Joseph said evenly, as he and Pamela met the women at the top of the stairs. He'd overheard the ruckus and wanted to salvage the evening for Kim's benefit.

"Yes," agreed Kim as she buttoned up her dissatisfaction with Ben's antics. "Joseph, this is Ben Dare. Ben, this is Joseph Woods, the famous remote viewer I told you about."

"Pleased to meet you," Ben acknowledged. "Is there anything I can do to help?"

Kim and Linda exchanged glances.

"Yes, there is," Pamela answered dismissively. "You can help us paint the office with sheets."

Kim's eyebrow flash forced Ben into immediate compliance as he walked gingerly across his previous retreat route and began his ascent to the second floor.

"Any chance for a warmer," he ventured, glancing back at the coffee cup still sitting on the end table.

"Actually, folks, I'd rather no one carry food or drinks up here," announced Joseph. "I'd like to limit any possibility of distractions during the viewing session."

"I hadn't thought of that," chorused Karen.

"Me either" followed Pamela.

The rest of them exchanged charitable head nods.

Ben followed Joseph and the two women into the office while Linda helped Kim retrieve the bed sheets they had intended to collect before Ben arrived.

When they returned with the sheets, Joseph instructed Ben to place the sheets over the bookshelves and secure them to prevent the sheets from falling. Linda helped Karen cover the three-shelf high bookcases with the teal-colored and mauve bedspreads while Pamela helped Kim cover the framed photos and awards on the walls.

Kim hesitated for a moment just before covering Jim's bestseller covers on the wall behind his desk, but was able to do it with Linda's sympathetic support.

Joseph lit the desk lamps and then doused the overhead lights to produce a more dimly lit room. He rearranged the record-keeping paraphernalia on the smaller desk to suit his needs and positioned the tape recorder.

After instructing the others to find their seats, he settled back in the one reserved for him. Adopting his most serious voice, he announced his intentions to the group.

"All of you heard my presentation this afternoon, except Ben." Joseph established eye contact with the reformed clown.

"I spoke with Karen this morning," Ben defended. "So I know a little about remote viewing and what Kim hopes to accomplish here."

"Good. That's good," complimented Joseph. "That makes my job easier."

Although his voice was well-modulated, Joseph spoke more softly and with less urgency and intensity than he did earlier in the day. He glanced at the digital clock on the desk.

"It's six fifty-eight," he announced as he moved his attention to Kim, who was situated to his left. "You asked me to begin my search for your son at exactly seven-fifteen Eastern Standard Time today. Is that still the desired time for launch?"

Kim nodded her head several times.

"Good. Then I have seventeen minutes," he asserted as he glanced at the clock again. "I have seventeen, now sixteen minutes to prepare you and myself for the launch."

Almost in unison the other members of the group repositioned themselves in their respective chairs. Ben's actions were slightly behind the others, but he settled in and remained obedient.

"If any of you needs to cough, sneeze, clear your throat or make a pit stop, now would be a good time. Otherwise I'd like you to wait until the session is over."

He waited for their collective enrollment. Satisfied that each of them was comfortable and committed, he tossed them a collusive smile.

"I can't tell you how important it is to maintain the strictest silence once we begin. I generally do not have so many people in the viewing room with me. Usually there is only one other person besides myself. However, Kim asked me to make an exception because she feels she needs your support. This isn't a laboratory test tonight, so I have consented to your presence. But I do have a few rules. Once the viewing begins, I prefer that you remain in this room.

However, if you absolutely must leave for some reason, please leave quietly. And if you leave, please do not come back in until we're finished. Is that understood?"

The group's reaction was staccatoed head nods, sequentially beginning with Pamela and ending with Kim who sat across the desk from Joseph.

"I'll begin with a meditation to center myself," Joseph continued. "You may wish to manufacture your own visualization, meditation, or prayer." He looked at Kim. "I think I'll add a prayer or two of my own tonight."

Kim threw him a grateful smile. "Thank you," she whispered.

Linda gave Kim an encouraging nod. *Me, too,* she pantomimed as she raised her hands in a prayer position.

Joseph patted Linda lightly on the shoulder.

"Linda has agreed to serve as my navigator. Linda, when the clock indicates seven-fourteen, I want you to say 'It's time.' That will be my signal to begin my mental trek." Linda nodded, repositioning herself comfortably into her chair.

Joseph looked around the room slowly, making eye contact with each person individually. As he visually circled the room, he said, "Linda is the only person who will speak besides me. She knows what to ask and how to ask it so it won't interfere with my viewing. As navigator, she will ask questions to guide my process. No one else is to speak. Understood?"

He waited for a confirming nod from each participant in the room before he continued. Then he turned to look at Kim.

"Kim, I shall do my best to locate your son. I fully believe I can locate him. I have the photo of Graham you supplied me and will meditate on it to connect with his spiritual energy field."

Kim began to wring her hands nervously.

"Now Kim, I want you to relax. I want all of you to relax. This will take some forty to fifty minutes. Perhaps longer. It will be positively exhausting for me, I can assure you. I've done enough of these sessions to know how taxing they can be. So, I repeat, if you feel you cannot sit in one position for the next hour, please leave now. You may rejoin us for the debriefing."

Kim bit her lower lip. *I'm already exhausted, Joseph,* she announced to herself. *My son's been missing over a month. If another forty or fifty minutes means I'll find him, I can sit very still.*

When no one left the room, Joseph added somewhat mechanically, "Just as an aside, researchers generally agree and my own experience confirms that there are four sufficient conditions which contribute to a successful remote viewing session. They are time, date, location and the target's energy."

Linda unconsciously nodded her agreement.

"Successful remote viewing occurs when at least three of the four are known by someone. Generally speaking, what happens is that two or three of the known elements act as a mental address for the fourth element."

He focused his attention solely on Kim.

"Kim, we know two of those elements. One, we know the time."

He looked at the red numbers on the digital clock.

"In seven-and-a-half minutes, it will be seven-fifteen. Seven-fifteen is factor number one. Factor number two brought us to your home tonight, that's today's date. Factor number four is your son. You are supposing that your four-year-old son is alive and will most probably be sleeping at seven-fifteen tonight, wherever he is residing. So that leaves factor number three, his location, as the unknown quantity."

Kim's breathing quickened.

"I know what your son looks like, and with three of the four factors known, I believe we have a good chance of locating his spirit's bio-physical address."

Kim tried valiantly to still the shaking sensation that seized her, but she heard the blood thundering in her ears. Conscious of her own escalating tenseness, she motioned for Pamela to move closer to her.

Ben helped Pamela move her chair nearer to Kim's. Then moved his chair to her left.

Too nervous to object to Ben's unsolicited support, Kim settled back into her chair, nervously anticipating the whereabouts of her son.

"I will concentrate on the star on his knee," Joseph reported, "on his Vital Body and mental field, and on his angelic face." He looked around the room. "Everyone, take a few deep breaths and focus your attention and thoughts on Graham Sanborn."

He squinted slightly, studying Kim.

"Kim, let's locate your son."

"I'm ready," Kim commented softly. She reached over and grabbed both Pamela and Ben's hands and squeezed them.

Joseph turned toward Linda.

"Remember the signal?"

"Yes, when it's seven-fourteen, I'll simply say: 'It's time'."

His smile thinned to a straight line as he turned his face from her and closed his eyes. His slow inhalations filled the room as he began his sequence of relaxation exercises. Finally, he sat still. The only evidence of his breathing was the occasional rise and fall of his chest.

The others watched in silence as Linda leaned toward the digital clock.

"It's time," she whispered aloud, sending Joseph on his mental rescue mission.

Seven minutes passed. Joseph remained trance like, frozen to his chair.

The numbers seven-thirty flashed on the clock face.

Joseph tilted his head to the left, tightening his already shut eyes. Linda placed her finger directly over the record button on the tape recorder.

Another minute and a half melted away.

"I'm beginning to see an image," Joseph reported.

Linda pushed the record button.

"I'm getting an impression ... of something that looks like ... it's very high ... it's ... no, wait a minute ... there are two of them ... ahhh ... towers of some sort."

He improved his posture in his chair.

"I seem to be positioned above and to the right of them ... feels like I'm getting hit in the face with cool air ... wind ... considerable turbulence ... towers are darkened ... look like huge black obelisks against a darkening background ... sky, I suppose ... yes ... I seem to be coming from a position above lights ... multi-colored lights. I get the feeling that some of the lights are moving ... traffic perhaps ... red ... white ... yellow."

He leaned forward, placing both elbows on the edge of the desk top.

"I get the sense that it's evening ... lights ... specks of light everywhere ..."

There was a pause of several seconds.

"Go to the black obelisks again," Linda interjected softly, "what can you tell us about them?"

"I seem to be hovering above them ... equal distance from both ... lights are set on the top of each. I don't get that they are lighthouses. Lights on top are too small ... ahh ... huh ... each has some sort of design on top ... like a sculpted piece of metal. I can't make out ... no, wait ... one has a series of half circles ... arches ... yes, arches ... the arches seem to encircle a small dome ... ahh ... moving closer to the other obelisk ... light at the top seems to be attached to something ... a steeple ... a huge rod or spike. Yes, that's it ... a steeple."

He sighed heavily.

"Shouldn't have to work this hard ... sides of obelisks seem to reflect light ... darkened glass panels. Viewing them from ground level now ... must be twenty-thirty stories ... huge buildings."

"Describe the area immediately around them," Linda instructed.

"Sidewalks ... rows of trees ... wide streets. I see ... let's see ... there seems to be a shopping plaza ... a mall perhaps. Garage ... parking garage ... yes, it's a mall. I sense I should move past the mall. I feel like I'm in the middle of ... I'm on the outskirts of a business park ... an industrial park ... offices ... street lights ... intersecting highways. No, just streets ... intersections."

Joseph lifted his closed eyes toward the ceiling.

"I'm in the middle of a large complex of houses ... I get the impression that everything is similar ... the resistance that I feel is that my surroundings are fairly nondescript. I get the sense that ... oh, wait ... no, I lost it. There ... no ... why can't I ... I can't seem to zero in ..."

"Would it help if you pulled back? Suppose you take a panoramic view," Linda inserted.

"Perhaps. Let's see ... Oh, ah ... there we go again ... the obelisks ... darkened sky again ... I'm at an oblique angle now ... considerably above the twin towers ... I'm going in again ..."

He lowered his head slowly, inching it closer to the surface of the desk top. When he stopped, the tip of his nose was less than an inch from touching the note pad on the desk.

"I feel a barrier of some sort—a resistance. Oh, it's a house, front porch ... medium-sized rooms. Wallpaper. Grandfather Clock. Wooden floors covered with scatter rugs. I'm getting an impression of metal ... some sort of rounded ... wide-mouthed instrument. No, I feel it's like ...

not a musical instrument ... more like ... ahh ... older. It's polished ... I can't ... it resembles an old musket. Yes, that's it ... now I've lost it ... I've got a flash of a ... no ... The words Sesame Street come to mind."

Kim cupped her hands over her mouth to muffle her gasp. She started to shiver, but was steadied by Ben.

"I see a moving star ... yes. That's it. It's ... yes, it's a small black star."

Kim struggled to compose herself. She dug her nails into Ben's arm as she rose from her chair.

Joseph squinted his eyes again and moved his head from side-to-side.

"Some sort of train ... monorail ... I'm sensing a public transportation line. A metro system ... If I could get ... still can't quite ... No, I have a strong sense ... It looks like, yes ..."

"Graham!" Kim cried, reacting to Joseph's description.

Joseph's eyes snapped open, and he turned to face Kim, whose outburst had been reduced to sobs.

"Oh, Joseph, I'm so sorry." Kim apologized. "Have I ruined it?"

Joseph patted her hand.

"I'll try again. Sometimes I can reconnect after an interruption. Other times I can't."

"This is ridiculous," said Ben. "Kim, I don't like it one bit. This guy's getting your hopes up. How do we know he isn't a fake?"

"For heaven's sake, Ben, sit down," said Kim, wiping her eyes roughly with one hand and pushing Ben back toward his chair with the other. "I'm sorry, Joseph. We've ruined your viewing, haven't we?"

Joseph sighed and directed his irritation at Ben, who had risen to his feet.

"I propose we stop for tonight." Joseph countered softly.

Linda pulled her chair back from the desk, as Joseph came from behind the desk to get closer to Kim. He took her hands in his and said gently, "The connection is broken. But I've gotten quite a bit of information. I saw something that resembled a monorail system near a business park."

He glanced at the others. "I need for you to remain where you are a few minutes longer. Mrs. Sanborn, can you give me a few more minutes? I have a few images I want to capture on paper so I won't forget them. It is absolutely necessary that I save everything. My scribbling may prove to be invaluable later. I don't know for sure, but oftentimes my dootling unlocks secrets which would otherwise be lost."

Kim was noticeably shaken, but managed to stay fairly composed. She clung to Pamela's hand as she slowly nodded her head. "Of course. I want you to take all the time you need. I want my baby back." Her voice turned to a choked sob as she squeezed Pamela's and Ben's hands tightly.

"I believe the monorail system I saw is in Atlanta, near Perimeter Park," Joseph confirmed confidently. "I did not sense he was in danger. The wide-mouthed metal object appeared to be encased in some sort of display. I feel your son was in a home or apartment. I'm not sure which. The only thing that came to me in regards to a physical address was the letter 'P'. I sensed an up-scale neighborhood."

He turned his chair toward Kim and steeled his gaze onto hers.

"He's definitely in a metropolitan area. The images I got tonight were cluttered with interference. By interference, I mean that there were too many similar objects nearby. Except for the twin towers which left indelible impressions, many of the other details were difficult to decipher. I wish I was able to extract more, but I think the few strong images in the viewing have sufficient psychic weight to warrant a search in the Perimeter Park area. I'm sure he's there, Mrs. Sanborn. I'd stake my reputation on it."

"Thank you," Kim whispered as she pulled him into a bear hug.

CHAPTER ELEVEN

No! Absolutely not!" Captain Deveraux raised his voice. "I'm not sending anyone to Atlanta on the word of a psychic, no matter how famous he is."

"He's more than a psychic, he's a remote viewer," yelled Kim. Her defiance was inextinguishable.

"I don't care if he's General Robert E. Lee come back to life. I'm not sending any of my men to Atlanta and that includes you, lieutenant." Captain Deveraux looked contemptuously at Lt. McCauley. "For Christ's sake, John, have you gone off your rocker, too?" fumed the captain.

"That's precisely why I'm going with Mrs. Sanborn."

"What? Because you're off your rocker?" hissed the captain, veering from disbelief to flippancy. "I always suspected you needed help, old boy. And now you've removed all doubt."

"You said it, sir!" Lt McCauley spoke evenly and with considerable poise. "That's exactly why I must go —for Christ's sake. Didn't Jesus say 'suffer the little children to come unto me'? And I'm not just going for Christ's sake— I'm going for Graham's sake—and for Mrs. Sanborn's. I promised her I'd find her son!'"

Captain Deveraux frowned at the two crusaders.

"You're both crazy. You've gone completely mad."

His mouth tightened in aggravation as he fondled nervously with his pager.

"No. You're wrong about that," Kim countered. "What is crazy is that this past two months I've lost my family. I've tried everything I know to find my baby. I've trusted you to find the killer. I haven't slept. I hardly eat. I'm tired. I'm angry. I've distributed posters. I've called everyone and anyone who could help me. Graham's picture has been circulated on milk cartons. I've made personal pleas on national television," she paused briefly, allowing her insubordination to boil. "What is absolutely absurd is that I've had to depend on my dead husband and two psychics to provide the only clues in this case."

Her tears started to flow, infuriating her all the more.

"And when I try to help myself ..." She severed her own remark, moving quickly to her left to block Captain Deveraux's attempt to close his office door. "You want it closed?" she blasted. "I'll close it!"

Kim grabbed the door and slammed it vigorously, rattling the glass partition dangerously close to shattering it.

Captain Deveraux stood in muted exasperation. His first inclination was to save face. A quick glance through his office windows confirmed that the entire precinct's attention was diverted to his office. He looked at the iron-willed woman again.

"And when I try to help myself," she repeated, "all you can offer me are sanctimonious bromides and bureaucratic excuses. I refuse to accept any more of your excuses. You've already admitted you don't know where to go from here. Well, I've just produced another lead for you, and I expect you to take me seriously. It may not be the kind of lead you expected, but it's more than you've ever produced."

Kim grabbed her coat and purse.

"Well, I know where I'm going. I'm following up on the only lead we have. I'm going to Atlanta."

She wheeled around abruptly and walked toward the office door.

"Mrs. Sanborn," Captain Deveraux spoke to the back of her head. "I'm really sorry. I don't have the manpower to spare. The Mayor would have my head on a platter if he knew I took your psychic seriously. Please don't lower yourself by grasping at straws. In heaven's name, let us do our job."

Kim reversed herself and faced the captain again.

"I've heard enough of your pious froth and lame excuses. That's all you've offered me. Well, Mr. Bureaucrat, I want you to do your job. But it looks like your definition of your job and my definition are worlds apart. So stay out of my way. And if I upset the Mayor ... or upset your delicate political apple cart ... by grasping at the extra-sensory abilities of psychics ... that's just ... well, that's just too damned bad!"

She wiped back the tears that inched their way down her cheeks.

"You're supposed to keep the streets safe. And if they become unsafe, you're supposed to make them safe again and keep them safe," she blasted. She started to say something else but sniffled defiantly instead. She sniffled again, but this time accepted a tissue from Lt. McCauley, who moved beside her.

"Do you have any children, Captain Deveraux?" she asked, speaking more softly now.

"Two. A twelve-year-old son. My daughter is eight."

"Do you love them?"

He threw her a mechanical smile.

"Of course I love them."

"If something happened to them, God forbid, would you do anything for them? Would you go to any lengths to make sure they're safe and healthy?"

Captain Deveraux could see where this was going and decided not to go there.

"Mrs. Sanborn, I don't think ... "

"Answer my questions," she pressed, stepping boldly toward him.

"Yes, I'd do everything I could. Everything within reason. Everything within my power."

"You'd even to go Atlanta, wouldn't you? Or Kosovo! Or Ramallah, or Afghanistan. Or the moon!"

"Mrs. Sanborn ... "

"You'd go there on a psychic's advice," she raised her voice as her eyes formed into slits of fury. "You'd go on the advice of a remote viewer. And if you had to, if you were desperate enough, if your heart ached enough, you'd go there on the rantings of a madman if it meant getting your son back."

She took another half step toward him, her voice getting louder with each word.

"So I'm grasping at an unorthodox straw, Mr. Public Servant. And I'm holding on for all I'm worth." She choked back the tears. "Because I want my son back." She lowered her voice, sobbing as she turned slowly toward the door, "I want my baby back."

The captain stood silently behind his desk, sympathetic but unrepentant.

By the time Kim managed to collect herself enough to open the office door, Lt. McCauley intercepted her.

"Wait just a minute, Mrs. Sanborn," he said, coughing nervously as he gently touched her arm. Then he turned to Captain Deveraux, "Captain, I wish you would reconsider."

Kim focused her attention on Lt. McCauley, who remained at her side.

The captain shook his head.

"Lieutenant, you know I can't do that. You know I couldn't get the approval."

Lt. McCauley sighed and lowered his gaze so that he could see the tips of his black dress shoes.

"Well, I don't need to get the approvals," he announced. He looked at Kim, catching her confused expression. "Unless I need your approval, Mrs. Sanborn."

Kim's eyes narrowed into slits again, but she didn't speak.

"May I accompany you to Atlanta?" he asked, smiling broadly. "Luck favors momentum, you know."

Kim's weariness dissipated once she realized what he was saying.

"Oh, Lieutenant ... please ... I ... you don't ... " she stumbled through the syllables.

"Just say yes," he teased. The light which danced in his eyes made his sixty-two year old face seem younger.

"Oh, Lieutenant, do you mean what I think you mean?" she surrendered. Her heart pounded with joy. "Yes! Yes," she squealed as she threw her arms around his neck.

"What's going on here?" Captain Deveraux pleaded. "You're not thinking of doing what I think you are?" he picked up on the gist of Kim's statement.

The Lieutenant raised his eyebrows.

"I can't spare you now. You're not going to Atlanta," the captain objected.

"My sister lives in Alpharetta," the Lieutenant volunteered calmly as he winked at Kim. "We could stay with her."

"Lieutenant, what the hell are you talking about?"

"I'm referring to this," he replied confidently as he handed his badge to his superior.

"Oh no, I'm not going to let you do that," protested Kim as she attempted to wrestle his shield back onto his jacket pocket.

"I promised you I'd help you find your boy," he reminded her. "And I intend to keep my promise."

He cupped her face between his huge palms. Then he kissed her on the forehead just below her hairline.

"You can add an old lunatic to your list of psychics and madmen."

Kim wept tears of joy as she clung admiringly to him.

"John. Please. Don't do this," the captain pleaded mechanically.

"It's already done," he declared, smiling as he placed his shield and revolver on the desk. "Consider this early notice for a late retirement," he bantered. "A long overdue retirement."

"John. Are you sure you want to do this?"

"When I get back from Atlanta, I'll officially sign the retirement papers. And give me something other than a gold watch. I don't wear one, remember?"

The Lieutenant turned toward Kim.

"Are you ready, partner? We've got a trip to plan."

He helped Kim slip into her coat and escorted her through the maze of precinct desks and on-lookers.

As they approached the elevator, Officer Wells rushed up to the Lieutenant and shook his hand heartily. "Did you do what I think you did?"

"Past due, wasn't it? Looks like you'll have to find another partner."

"I'm going to miss you, you old flat foot."

The two officers embraced.

"Take care of yourself," Lt. McCauley advised his young partner.

Officer Wells smiled. "You, too."

"Thank you," Kim said, taking a deep breath. "I can't believe you're doing this."

The officer returned her smile and nodded his bald head reverently before he reestablished eye contact.

"I've been considering retirement for some time now. I mentioned it to your friend, Ms. Justice, the other day. "But, don't thank me yet. You can thank me when we find your son."

The elevator bell announced the presence of the steel cage and the automatic doors opened, inviting the pair to enter. The officers embraced again before the Lieutenant chauffeured Kim into the hydraulic box and pushed the button which predicted their descent to the lobby.

§ § § § § §

When the elevator doors opened, Kim slipped out ahead of the lieutenant, who was still limping from the fall he suffered the first day they arrived in Atlanta. That was three weeks ago and their search was limping along at about the same pace as the lieutenant.

They had gotten nowhere and both of them were beginning to doubt the findings of the remote viewer. They'd canvassed the north end of the Atlanta metro area from Marietta to Alpharetta, including Perimeter Park, to Roswell, Norcross and Smyrna. Every street with the letter "P" on the city map had been marked and checked out.

The flyer campaign failed and neither the Atlanta police nor the Raleigh police were able to provide them with any more leads. The Internet produced swarms of responses, but zero leads.

It was as if Graham had dropped off the face of the earth.

"Kim, we need to grab some lunch. It's almost three o'clock," the retired lieutenant pleaded.

"I know. I know," Kim verified. "I'm just ... it's hard to stop, you know? Oh, John, what are we going to do?"

The past three weeks had dissolved their previous formality and they were now on a first name basis.

"Devise a better plan," he suggested, breathing heavily, "because this one isn't working." John sighed as he hobbled over to one of the park benches bordering the terrace.

Kim sat down beside him.

"You poor man. That hip's really bothering you, isn't it?"
John rubbed his thigh and repositioned himself.

"What's bothering me is our lack of progress. It's
February twentieth and we still have no idea where he is."

"Here," Kim said as she outstretched her arms.

"Yeah, here. Somewhere in this city of millions ... " he
countered, abbreviating his own comment. "Kim, honey,
I'm beginning to believe ... "

"Don't you dare say it," she cut him off.

"I think our Mr. Woods has led us on a wild goose
chase."

Kim frowned, realizing she was beginning to feel the
same way.

"I want to believe he's right. I felt sure he was. And a
part of me still does," she confessed.

"I know, honey. I thought we might get a break, too."

"I dreamed about Graham again last night. It was so
real, I couldn't get back to sleep after that."

"Kim, honey. You've got to stop doing that to yourself."

"But I can see him, John. He's dressed in blue striped
pajamas and he's calling out to me."

"Kim, honey ... "

"I know he's here! He has to be here! We've got to trust
in Joseph's skill, and in our own intuition. We've got to keep
the faith."

"Okay. Let's grab some lunch at the mall. Then we'll
pass more flyers around there. Maybe we'll get lucky.
Maybe somebody's seen him. Maybe we'll see him."

"I'll drive your sister's car. You need to rest that leg."

§ § § § § §

"Hello, Mrs. Fergusen?"

"Yes, this is she."

"This is Mr. Unser. From the adoption agency."

"Oh, yes. How are you?"

"I'm fine. I'm just checking to see how Graham is getting along. It's just a routine call."

"Oh, Mr. Unser. We're so happy. Graham is such a sweet little boy."

"That's fine. Ah ... you haven't had any problem with him in pre-school or socially, have you?"

"My goodness no. He's a perfect little angel. Of course, we have taken the precaution of ensuring that he wears trousers whenever he's outside. You know, to hide the birthmark, as you suggested. And we've trimmed his hair. He looks so cute."

"Ah ... that's good. Say, Mrs. Ferguson, I have some rather unpleasant news for you. I hate to be the bearer of bad tidings, but ... well ... you know, I wouldn't be doing my job if I didn't help you and your husband take good care of Graham."

"What is it, Mr. Unser?"

"Some of Graham's unsavory relatives are rustling a few legal feathers up here over Graham's custody."

"Oh, no!"

"It's more of an inconvenience than a problem. My office should be able to handle their concerns. But in the meantime, I want you to be very careful who you talk to about Graham. As a matter of fact, I'd prefer you to be extra careful. You see, although you saved him from becoming a ward of the state—with the state's blessing, of course—the boy's relatives are questioning the proceedings. Basically that's all they're doing. We didn't know the youngster had any living relatives until a few weeks ago."

"I see. What do you suggest we do?"

"Just sit tight. Ah ... on second thought, ah ... Mrs. Ferguson, didn't you tell me your family lives in Virginia?"

"No. Julian's family does. Mine lives right here in Atlanta. Why?"

"Well, I've got an idea. Until this thing cools down a little, could you ... do you suppose you could take your son to visit his grandparents in Virginia? Just as a precaution. Several of his unscrupulous relatives are in Atlanta on a business trip. They don't know Graham is living with you in Atlanta, of course. But we'd hate for them to run into you. You know what I mean? Atlanta's a big city, but I've seen the strangest coincidences happen in cases like this. Could you spend a couple of weeks in Virginia?"

"I don't think that would be a problem at all."

"Good."

"Julian probably couldn't get off work, it's too short a notice. But I certainly could take Graham to see Julian's parents."

"That's fine, Mrs. Ferguson. Sorry I didn't call you sooner. I'm embarrassed to say it, but I misplaced your file and couldn't find your phone number. Otherwise I would have called you three weeks ago."

"Three weeks ago! My goodness. Have they been here that long?"

"Well, ah, I didn't want to upset you before we knew more about their intentions. They want to get their hands on the boy's inheritance, but as I told you, there is none — never has been. For some reason his relatives think Graham has inherited a fortune. His parents were poor and didn't even own a home. I don't know what their real intentions are. As I said before, we didn't even know he had living relatives until a few weeks ago. Besides they are not the kind of people who should be allowed to raise children, if you know what I mean."

"Yes. Yes, we do, Mr. Unser. We appreciate your willingness to help us."

"Oh. My pleasure. That's what I'm here for."

"If you think of anything else we should do from here, let us know."

"You just let us handle it from this end, Mrs. Ferguson and have a pleasant trip to Virginia."

"Thank you. We'll leave as soon as possible."

"Wonderful. I just want to make sure that dear little boy stays in a nice home."

"Thank you. We do, too!"

§   §   §   §   §   §

"Good-bye, Sis," John said with a cheerfulness he did not feel.

"Good-bye," Kim said sadly, as she hugged Louise for a second time. "Thanks for letting us stay here—and use your car. I feel so badly that we tied it up for so long."

"Don't give it another thought. What's five weeks among friends?"

"A long time if you're related," joked John.

Both Kim and Louise laughed.

"Yes. I guess that's true," Louise agreed.

"Oh, you two stop it. I think we all got along together just fine."

"I think so, too," confirmed Louise, as she helped Kim take her luggage out of the trunk.

"It sure would have been nice to be taking one more home with us."

The two women grew silent.

"Tomorrow's Graham's birthday," pined Kim. "I hoped he'd be home on his birthday."

"Maybe his birthday is the day, " Louise replied hopefully. "Maybe we'll witness a miracle. You believe in miracles, don't you?"

John bowed his head to conceal his disappointment.

"I thought we had one," lamented Kim. "I thought this trip was our miracle." She looked directly at Louise. "I'm not going back empty-handed though. I would never have met you if it weren't for this trip. You're so incredibly kind."

"She got that from our mother's side of the family. Our father's side was too steeped in law enforcement to be nice."

"John, that's not true. Papa's side had good hearts."

"Well, if you say so," he teased, winking at Kim. "I s'pect we'd better get to our gate. The plane's due to leave at eight-fifteen."

The women embraced again.

"Thanks for driving us to the airport," Kim said as she grasped both of Louise's hands. "I wish we could have met under happier circumstances."

"There will be happy times again. We'll be able to celebrate Graham's homecoming someday."

"Sis, I'll be back down in a couple of weeks. They're going to throw a good riddance party for me later this week. Then I'm going to put my house up for sale. As soon as I get things squared away, I'll call you."

"Okay. Are you sure about that now?" Louise quizzed her older brother.

"Yep. Besides," he added, winking at Kim, "I've got to keep my eye open for that youngster."

"I feel so grateful to you two. You're pretty wonderful, you know."

"I'm going to handcuff you if you don't start toward that gate, young lady," he chastised Kim affectionately.

"Bye," Louise whispered to them both as they disappeared through the sliding glass doorway.

Kim chanced one more look at the short, gray-haired woman who opened her house and heart to a desperate widow from North Carolina. She watched tearfully as Louise got into her car.

Graham, honey, Kim whispered to herself as she stepped quickly alongside John. *Mommy's not giving up. I want you home. I'm going to find you if it takes the rest of my life.*

§   §   §   §   §   §

"Graham, honey, we're almost home." Joyce encouraged, as she walked him toward the escalator that led downstairs to baggage claim.

Graham's lips formed a smile as he held onto the crayon book his foster grandparents bought him, then peeled his eyes from her quickly.

"Wait, Mamma. I dropped my crayon."

As he bent over to retrieve his blue crayon from the tiled floor, he failed to notice the couple who walked quickly past him, blending in with the hundreds of other travelers in the crowded terminal. The man was an older gentleman who limped slightly. The young woman at his side had just taken a tissue out of her purse and wiped the latest installment of tears away.

CHAPTER TWELVE

She cried all day. It was Monday, March twelfth—Graham's birthday. Kim wanted so much to celebrate it with him. She'd visualized a homecoming celebration complete with banners, cake, and balloons.

Her pragmatism had prevented her from decorating the house for the anticipated homecoming. But her faith produced the small poster placed behind the metronome on the piano. In blue lettering were the words: WELCOME HOME, GRAHAM.

Pamela had printed it out on her laser printer and presented it to Kim before she went to Atlanta. They'd had such high hopes.

Kim's red-rimmed eyes were scratchy, salty from fatigue, and the puffy half moons under her eyes gave her the appearance of a woman who had just experienced ten miles of bad road.

"It's your fifth birthday," she sobbed aloud. "You're five years old and I can't even kiss you. Or hold you. Or see you open your presents."

Presents. A sudden realization erupted from her despair. His presents.

"His Christmas presents," she raised her voice dejectedly. "They're still in the spare room."

She grabbed a glass of water from the kitchen and headed upstairs.

Depression has centrifugal force, she remembered. *It moves things away from you. It pushes everything to the periphery.*

She opened the spare room door and moved her eyes solemnly around the room.

It's a good thing my parents and Pamela cleaned up around here, she observed silently. *I haven't done any legitimate cleaning in two months.*

She formed a brittle smile as her swollen eyes found the floor mirror to her left. Her twin in the mirror was mascara-less and disheveled.

"I've lost all interest in cleaning and eating and the studio," she addressed her double. "But, of course, you know that."

Kim sighed, but her sigh turned into a frown.

"I don't care if I pay the bills. I don't even want to go out. I've lost my taste for chocolate. I don't exercise anymore. And I think I've given up trying to find my son."

She eased herself onto the carpet in a sitting position.

"I don't care about this house. I don't care about make-up. I don't care about wearing my bra. I don't care about you either," she ranted, pointing savagely at her reflection in the mirror.

She spied her shoes lying on the floor next to the bureau and noticed their reflection in the mirror. She leaned over, raised herself on her hands and knees, and crawled over to one of the shoes. Engulfed in self-pity, she grabbed the shoe and hurled it toward the mirror.

"I hate you," she screamed as the shoe struck the angry twin in the mirror, cracking the glass and sending the top of the mirror crashing against the wall.

When the mirror rocked forward again, it sent her a contorted, jagged image of herself.

She laughed as she viewed herself on all fours.

"That's quite an improvement," she said, giggling at herself. "But you look a little rough around the edges."

Her giggles escalated into a hearty laugh as she glanced at her reflection.

"Do you get the point?" She collapsed into a fit of laughter. A few moments later she rolled over to the bed and sat up, viewing herself from a different angle. Kim closed her tear-filled eyes. The laughter of a few moments ago evaporated into sadness.

"The point is, young lady," she addressed herself mournfully, "the point is, if you had picked Graham up when you were supposed to ... " she blunted her own sentence. She swallowed hard. "If you had only done your shopping earlier."

She began to sob.

"Both of them would be alive today," she condemned herself.

She smothered a small gasp, but was unable to stop the flow of tears that sent her sprawling back onto the floor. Unfathomable grief forced her to bury her face in her hands. Her gut-wrenching wailing filled the empty house, cleansing it with the tears of a woman who was close to giving up hope.

"Wait a minute," she blunted her own deflatement. "What am I doing to myself? I didn't cause this! I'm living in a world filled with other people who make decisions and take actions that affect other people. If I was in the car, I could have been the one killed!"

She scooted herself up so that her back was against the bed. She remembered something she had read on the blog the two ministers had posted on their website. She found herself becoming attached to their writing and webinars.

They shared a different perspective on the concept of fasting. *Fast from the belief that life has to be filled with suffering and struggle, and tragedy and calamity, and unemployment, and an empty wallet,* she quoted the authors to herself.

"It's not what happens to you, they said," she mouthed out loud, "It's how you respond to what happens to you. It's the value you attach to the 'fluff' of outer appearances."

She pulled her leaden body back to its previous sitting position. As her sobs hiccuped their way into each of her short breaths, another glance into the shattered mirror arched her eyebrows. There in the ruptured mirror, refracted in the cracked shards of glass, was the reflection of the white dog.

Her gasp brought her head around as she turned toward the doorway.

Not ten feet away, just inside the doorway, stood the white dog. His majestic head was tilted slightly and his dark eyes were riveted on her.

As she wheeled around on her knees to face him, he began wagging his tail.

"How did you get in here?" Kim asked softly.

He cocked his snow-white head first to one side, and then the other.

"I must have left the door open downstairs," she explained, more to herself than to the large pup that stood before her.

"Heard me crying, did you?" she asked rhetorically.

The dog barked, startling her.

"Oh, well, thank you for checking on me. I'd like to ... would you let me pet you?"

Kim reached over slowly to pet him. Instead of backing up, the dog closed the distance between them and allowed her to stroke his ears and head.

Kim settled next to him and continued to shower him with affection.

"Oh, so you're not wearing a collar," she commented as she inspected his neck.

"I wonder where you've come from. No one from around here seems to have a white dog. I've checked."

The dog's busy tail showed her he enjoyed being the beneficiary of her lavish attention.

Kim's eyes brightened.

"How would you like to stay here with me tonight?"

She moved her caresses from his neck to the top of his head.

"Would you like that?"

When he barked his consent, Kim remembered her conversation with Linda about the extra-sensory bond between animals and humans.

"I'll consider that a yes, young fella. Suppose I name you. Let's see ... how about ... White Knight? No. Chance seems appropriate. What are the chances I'll find my son? Oh, wait. How about ... Hope! I certainly need hope. What do you say about Hope for your name?"

The dog stutter-stepped in place and answered her with a muffled bark.

"Good," she said triumphantly. "Hope it is."

She found her legs and led Hope to the bedroom door.

"Come on, boy. Let's get something to eat."

Hope followed her obediently down the hallway. When she got to the landing, she stopped. Hope was tailgating her, but managed to avoid a collision.

"Tomorrow," she promised herself aloud. "I'm going to straighten and clean the spare room. And I'm going to start with the Christmas packages. I'll leave Graham's where they are and the dance statue needs to come out of hiding, too. But I'll recirculate the rest. It's about time, isn't it, Hope?" she shot a quick glance at her newly adopted companion. "Better late than never. Right?"

As she began her descent downstairs, she mentally reprimanded herself: *I wish I had taken my parents up on their offer for lunch today. And Pamela's offer to stay with me on Graham's birthday. I probably could have saved myself a river of tears and a wasted day.*

When she reached the living room, Kim stopped and leaned over to pet Hope.

"But I've got hope now, don't I, Hope?" she greeted him, pleased with her semi-private pun.

"Now, let's see how you got in here, young fella."

One look through the kitchen doorway confirmed what she suspected. She'd failed to close the outside kitchen door.

Must have left it open during my pity party this morning, she guessed. *It must have been open all day. I'm lucky Hope is the only one who took advantage of my hospitality!*

"Nothing like trying to heat the outside, huh, boy," she addressed Hope, as she closed the door with her foot.

"There, you've given me more energy already," she praised Hope. "I'm beginning to feel like I might make it through this yet."

She escorted Hope over to the refrigerator.

"Let's see if I can find something in here for you to eat. Temporarily that is ... until I can buy you some decent dog food."

Her search was interrupted by the telephone.

"Excuse me, fella," she apologized, "I'll be right back."

She felt lighter somehow and more enlivened as she reached for the phone.

"Hello."

"Hi, Kim. This is Ben."

"Oh, hi, Ben."

"How 'bout a quick bite to eat?"

"Well, I don't know. It's pretty late," she countered, offering a half-hearted excuse.

"Look, your folks told me they invited you to lunch and you turned them down."

I turned Pamela down, too, she added to herself.

"I know you're feeling bad about your trip to Atlanta."
Kim's whole body tightened at that reminder.

"And I know today is Graham's birthday. I don't want
you to be alone today of all days. If you don't want to grab
something to eat with me, at least call your folks. Or do
something fun with Pamela. Please. Don't do it for me. Do
it for yourself."

As she listened to his petitions, she knew he was right.
She had promised herself to stay out of hibernation. The
Atlanta fiasco crippled her emotionally. She knew she must
start climbing back out.

"Okay," she whispered softly.

"Suppose I just drop something by then? Chinese?
Pizza?"

"No. That's okay," she repeated. "I'll go."

"Subs? Chicken?"

"Ben," she raised her voice. "Didn't you hear me? I said
I'd go."

"Oh, great! You mean go out to eat?"

"Yes."

"Terrific. How 'bout the Stonewood Grill again?"

"Okay."

"I know we ate there last time I took you out, but ... "

"Ben!"

"What?"

"You're doing it again."

"Oh, I'm sorry."

"I'll be ready in an hour."

"Great! I'll pick you up at five-thirty."

"Would you bring me a bag of dog food when you
come?"

"Dog food!"

"Yes. Good dog food. Nutritious dog food."

"Okay. Are you keeping someone's pet, or did you get
a dog?"

"Let's just say—I've got Hope."

§   §   §   §   §   §

She was alone at home again, except for Hope and a cup of cappuccino. Despite an evening chill, she decided to plant herself in one of the cushioned patio chairs in the gazebo and absorbed herself in giving Hope's back some attention. She needed to settle because her stomach was full. Although the vegetable lasagna lessened the effects of the wine, she was still floating with the buzz from the carafe of red Beaujolais Nouveau she so willingly consumed. The extra wedge of cheese cake added an extra nudge of discomfort.

It was a good meal. And Ben made sure that the platoon of waiters, waitresses, and scurrying busboys limited their intrusions. Ben had reserved her favorite booth. Situated at the far end of the dining area, it was surrounded by plants and protected by a beautiful stained glass partition. Its location shielded them from the normal high pitch of conversations and the monotonous clink of silverware on the pewter plates, common to the restaurant.

She had refrained from telling Ben it was her and Jim's preferred booth. Some things should remain secret. *Besides,* she justified to herself, *the memories associated with this booth are priceless. There's no room for anyone else.*

As she sipped another taste of liquid mud, she smelled the richness of the spiked cappuccino. The sugary taste of Amaretto caught her taste buds.

"You are being mighty generous with the liquor tonight, aren't you?" she reprimanded herself.

Another light sip lifted her eyes toward the heavens. The almost full moon assumed command of the darkened sky, turning nearby trees and shrubs into ghostly shapes which swayed effortlessly along the perimeter of her property.

The yapping of small dogs from several streets over filled the night air, but Hope didn't seem to mind their canine chatter. The occasional chorus of birds that penetrated the darkness had a soothing effect on Kim.

Another sip of nostalgia pulled her gaze up again toward the star-studded canopy overhead. She continued to stroke Hope, who was quite comfortable in his new home.

"Which one of you is shining over my little boy?" she addressed the stars. "Please help me. The police haven't been able to find him. Missing children organizations haven't been able to help me. Two psychics haven't been able to penetrate the cloud that separates us. A mother's love ... hasn't ... helped either."

Her eyes moistened.

"I've done the best I can. You know I have, my darling Graham," she added for emphasis. "The flyers with your picture that we've distributed all over southeastern United States haven't gotten us anywhere."

She brushed a tear off her cheek with her fingertips as she gazed at the flickering firmament.

"I'm sending my love out to you to keep you safe. Please come back home to me. I affirm – no, I declare in this now moment, that my prayers will be answered."

She steadied her eyes on Hope, who was lying on his belly enjoying the back rub. Kim ran her fingers through his thick fur admiring his rich white coat.

"You're so beautiful. Pure white, except for the wonderful black spot of hair on your hind leg."

His powerful muzzle was closed. And his eyes were dark reservoirs of dynamic energy. His majestic head was resting on his front feet.

"You precious thing," Kim spoke softly. "You're here to comfort me, aren't you? To reassure me. God, the Eternal Presence," she added, "underwrites all being and nonbeingness. So, Graham's rescue is entirely possible. And I'm willing his rescue in this now moment!"

She fixed her gaze on Hope, who looked up at her. "Well, young fella, ask your Employer to hurry. I want my son back."

She caressed his neck and ears again. His fur was soft and cool. As she stroked the back of his head and moved her fingers along his shoulders and back, Kim felt his strength.

"You are special," Kim spoke, almost in a whisper. "You're my Spirit Sponsor."

She eased her hands along his ears again and then embraced his face, running her fingers under his jaw and down the side of his powerful neck. Her caress forced Hope to his feet and prompted him to place his muzzle in her lap. Kim smiled when he glanced at her as she stroked his head and ears. She felt the pressure of his lower jaw and throat on her lap as he swallowed his enjoyment.

"I'm not alone, am I boy?" Kim asked rhetorically, appreciating the dog's significance. "I think you've been assigned to me by Graham's loving energy. I think you're here to keep me company because of Graham's magnetizing energy. I know I've told you that before, but it helps me to say it."

She leaned back in her chair and gazed solemnly at the moon. Her tearful gaze found the glittering specks of light in the blackened sky. *There seems to be more of you now,* she thought reverently.

Just then a soft breeze caressed her face and hair and she thought she heard a faint rustling nearby, like the brush of angel wings.

§   §   §   §   §   §

"Absolutely not, Julian. You're not keeping those guns around here," Joyce barked.

"What's gotten into you, Joyce? I've always kept my private arsenal around the house. You know that."

"And I've never liked the things, either," she screamed. "And you know that! I don't mind your hunting rifles, shotguns, and handguns, but the AK-47s and that awful Vepr rifle. Why do you need those?"

His eyes were filled with defiance.

"So why this sudden outburst? I ... "

"Because we have a son now, you idiot." She sliced into his heated retort. "And I don't want him hurt."

"Damn it, Joyce, what do you take me for?" he said, trying his best to marshal his composure. But his wife was good at pushing too many buttons. "I've been around firearms all my life. I know how to use them. And you would too, if you'd get down off your high horse long enough to handle one."

"I'm afraid of those things," she yelled. "How many times do I have to tell you that?"

He brandished an angry smile. "Until you hear how stupid you sound."

When her tears started, they gushed, and the failure to stop them doubled her anger.

"So I'm stupid, am I?" she lashed at him. Her irascibility escalated. "You're the one who's stupid, you insensitive, loud-mouthed jerk. Suppose Graham shoots himself with one of the guns? You keep them loaded, you know."

"I either keep them locked or the magazines clear," he rebuffed, unable to conceal his contempt.

"Not your .9 mm. Or the .45 caliber behind the night stand," she sputtered, launching her counterattack.

"They're both in our bedroom. He doesn't go in there."

"How do you know? You're at work all day."

"You're at home," he exploded. "You keep him out."

"That's the point, Julian. That's exactly the point. I don't want to have to worry about Graham hurting himself. And I don't want him to think he's a prisoner in his own home. Can't you see that?"

He shot her a contemptuous look.

"And I don't want to be a prisoner either," she repeated, agitatedly. Apprehension tightened her throat so that she coughed.

Julian sighed heavily and although he understood her point, he gave her a disapproving stare.

"I suppose you're right," he conceded. "I'll empty the two hand guns and hide the clips. Are you satisfied?"

Joyce threw him a sorrowful look. She opened her mouth to speak, but only a sigh leaked out.

Oh, Julian, she lamented at his unrepentance. *What's happening to us?*

"You make it sound like it's my fault," she surrendered.

"You're the one who hates guns. You started this whole damned discussion tonight. A discussion we've had a gazillion times," he blasted.

She felt crushed by his fierceness and by his complete disregard for her concern about Graham's safety.

"I know. And I'm sorry if I've upset you," she apologized. "But, Julian, can't you see my concern about providing a safe environment for our son?"

"I just told you I'll empty the two handguns. Damn it, I'll do it right now so I can have some peace tonight," he snapped as he began his grudging retreat toward the master bedroom. "Of course, now I won't feel like any of us live in a safe environment. How can I protect my family without a loaded gun around?"

Joyce ignored his comment. She was more concerned about his unwilling compliance over an issue they hadn't been able to resolve. Nothing had been settled. It would be another spiteful stalemate.

She tucked away a hollow smile and made an about-face as she pushed her way past the living room sofa. She sighed deeply as she wandered through the sliding glass doors and came to a halt next to one of the lawn chairs that sat in silent vigil on the uppermost landing of the custom deck.

Depression lifted her red-rimmed eyes upward to the thousands of tiny specks of light that dotted the night sky.

"Star light, star bright, first star I've seen tonight. I wish I may, I wish I might, have the wish I wish upon a very special star tonight," Joyce recited and then cried aloud.

I wish for happiness, she prayed silently. Just then she felt a tug on her arm. It was Graham.

He clasped her hand in his and leaned the side of his face against the top of her hand on her lap.

"Oh, honey, what are you doing up? It's way past your bedtime. Are you okay?"

"I heard you fighting."

"Oh, honey, we weren't ... we only had a loud disagreement. I'm sorry. Did we wake you?"

"I don't like it when you fight," he said sleepily.

She cupped his angelic face in her trembling hands.

"We won't argue anymore. How's that?"

Graham nodded as best he could with his little head pinned.

She pulled him to her and pressed his head against her breasts.

A soft breeze mingled her airborne hair with his golden strands as they huddled beside the chair. She gently released her embrace and kissed him on the forehead.

They exchanged smiles as their eyes met.

"Time to go to bed," she whispered. "Suppose I say a prayer with you after I tuck you in."

Graham nodded as he pulled slightly away from her.

"Can we pray for my new daddy?"

"Oh, honey, that would be very nice."

CHAPTER THIRTEEN

Kim ran her fingers through Hope's thick coat of hair and the dog responded as he always did, by tilting his head toward her and blinking his affection with his onyx-colored eyes. He studied her for a while, then settled back to enjoy her nonchalant massage.

Kim was relaxing on the deck after taking a break from packing up the house. She had decided it was time to move on with her life. The house held more bad memories than good ones now. Despite her resolve, the packing was taking an emotional toll on her.

"Tomorrow's our third anniversary," Kim announced solemnly, as she playfully tugged at his ears and ran her fingers along the underside of his muzzle.

Three years, she reminded herself. *Three years since I've seen my little boy. Three years of fruitless searches. Three years of running up to youngsters in the mall who resembled Graham in appearance, only to come face-to-face with my denial.*

"Well, boy," she spoke aloud to Hope, whose ears perked up at her voice. "We're off on a new adventure ... a new home." She felt a tear slide slowly down her cheek and let it meander to her chin before she took care of it.

She'd visited Atlanta twice since her ill-fated inaugural trip, but her last trip had been a year ago. While her searches were unsuccessful, her friendship and love for both Louise and John had deepened. John kept his promise to her and divided his time between his retirement pursuits and well-orchestrated searches for her son.

Kim had retired from championship ballroom dancing, refusing lucrative offers from the international performing arts community. Although her announcement had surprised many people, her retirement devastated Ben, both emotionally and professionally. His efforts to dance with Kim ended with her retirement and his partnership with Nisaba dissolved because of his efforts to dance with Kim. Ben's gamble cost him a chance at the World Championship in Blackpool, but Irene had fared better. She and her new partner won the International Standard Championship.

Kim had become a novelist. Louise was a novelist and had gotten Kim interested in fiction. They attended several writing conferences together and kept in constant touch. She introduced Kim to her agent, and although her agent was most charitable, Kim knew that until she produced marketable bodies of work, Louise's agent would only pretend interest. But Kim knew she was hooked. Soon, she had convinced herself, she would write the great American novel.

Ben had made himself indispensable. He tripled the number of dance studios, adding one in Durham and another in Chapel Hill. In spite of her objections, he raised her salary enough so she could stay at home and write. Although she depended on him and considered him one of her closest friends, she resented his romantic overtures.

Hope voiced his objections to Ben by growling everytime Ben visited Kim. Kim tolerated Ben because she felt indebted to him. He had helped shepherd her through the worst three years of her life.

She blinked her eyes several times to pull herself out of her self-induced hypnosis. Her gaze settled on the stepped planters that displayed daisies, impatiens, hyacinths, azaleas and holly. The crescent-shaped yard formed a kind of amphitheater.

"I'm going to miss you," she addressed her yard. She breathed deeply as she lifted her face toward the rich canopies of tree tops. The sky was a flawless wide curve of blue. *Clearing morning skies mean a premature sun,* she reminded herself as she took another deep inhalation. The mingled scents were a symphony of olfactory delight. She loved the smell of her back yard..

"Ummm," she groaned her appreciation as she listened contentedly to the teeming polyphony of bird songs which filled the morning air.

The yard would be a quiet place if only the best birds sang, she reflected silently. Leaving her eyes closed she inched her reconnoitering fingers closer to her coffee cup until they found it. Then she opened her eyes and lifted the cappuccino to her lips.

She sipped another taste of the caffeinated brew and reached down to pet Hope, who rolled onto his side. She accommodated his well-rehearsed antics by rubbing his stomach vigorously.

Hope showed his delight by lying motionless, except for one of his hind legs, which began to move in syncopation with Kim's affectionate raking.

She smiled the kind of smile pet owners give their contented pets.

"You've certainly been a loyal pup," she praised as she patted his stomach and chest.

She raised herself to a standing position, to Hope's disappointment.

"Well, young fella, I've got to do more packing. The movers will be here tomorrow and I promised the moving company I'd be ready for them."

She peeped into the empty coffee cup.

I need another jolt to get stay invigorated, she convinced herself, and glided through the patio doors into the dining room.

The only thing in the kitchen left unpacked was the cappuccino machine. Everything else was in boxes.

Anyone walking in here would know my priorities, she thought, laughing at herself.

She filled her cup and pivoted toward the cluttered dining room. Cardboard boxes were indiscriminately stacked everywhere. She had placed the lighter ones on top. Boxes filled with books lined the walls. Others, filled with knickknacks, covered the dining room table.

When her gaze settled on the cluster of boxes in the corner near the front door, her eyes moistened. Some of Jim's clothes and accessories were in those boxes. His writing awards and dance awards were there. His favorite books and jigsaw puzzles were packed too.

She had kept some of Graham's clothes and toys, including his Christmas presents, all his photos, and his favorite coloring books. She decided to sacrifice the large stuffed giraffe, who was wedged between some of the boxes to be given away.

"You're lucky you lasted this long, you old Grinch. You stole my Christmas, remember?"

As she inventoried her discards, she reminded herself that, except for the few nostalgic pieces of Jim's things stored in boxes upstairs, these boxes held the remnants of her life with him before her widowhood.

"Jim, I'm sorry honey. I just can't live here anymore. I know you would want me to go on, make a new life for myself. If I stay here, I'm going to limit my world to your office and our son's bedroom. I know you understand. Some of these things are emotional weights that I need to let go of."

Kim spied an open box containing the two patchwork quilts Karen had made her. One was sewn out of Jim's flannel shirts and the other was stitched out of Graham's shirts and trousers, which was more of a bedspread than a quilt due to its lighter fabrics. Both were treasured possessions. She closed the box by juxtaposing the flaps and then sealed it with tape.

This is one box I'm going to keep in the car with me, she thought to herself. *I'm not going to take any chance of the movers losing these.*

When she backed up to improve her view of the cardboard mountain of boxes in front of her, she brushed one of the coffee tables with her leg, sending her coffee cup sliding toward the edge.

"Oh, no you don't," she said, as she grabbed the half full cup of coffee off the table. She took another sip of the addictive cappuccino as she renewed her inspection.

Looking at these empty boxes isn't going to get them packed, she reprimanded herself.

Just as she settled down to wrap one of the brass and glass table lamps, the phone rang.

She quickly set the lamp down and reached over a small box to retrieve the phone from off the kitchen counter.

"Hello, Mrs. Sanborn?"

"Yes."

"This is Sergeant Wells. Remember me?"

"Sergeant Wells? Sergeant ... oh, yes. Sergeant Wells from the Raleigh Police Department," she rescued herself. "How are you?"

"I'm fine."

"It's been a long time," she stated the obvious. A momentary panic gripped her. "What are you doing calling me this morning?"

"I'm glad it was you. I wasn't sure you had the same number. I pulled your file and ..."

Kim's breathy gasp on the other end of the line caused him to hesitate.

"Are you calling about my son? Have you found him?" she shrieked, fearing what he might say, yet driven to know.

"No, but we've got someone who knows something about the disappearance of your son."

"Oh my God. Oh my God!" she screamed. She began to hyperventilate before she could stop herself. "Is he alive? Do you know where he is?"

She almost dropped the phone. Her lips were numb and the ringing in her ears made it difficult to hear Sergeant Wells.

"Mrs. Sanborn, can you meet me at the emergency room entrance at Raleigh Community Hospital?"

She gasped again.

"The hospital?"

"Yes. Raleigh Community. We have an accident victim who fits the description of the carjacker."

Kim grew silent.

"He's ... He's at the hospital?" questioned Kim.

"Yes."

"I've got to sit. Let me sit for a minute," she whispered as she scrambled for an empty kitchen chair. As she sank into its wicker seat, Hope moved to her side.

"Mrs. Sanborn?"

"I'm okay. I'm sitting. I'm okay."

"I know this comes as quite a shock to you, but it's imperative that you come to the hospital as soon as you can."

"What? Why?"

"The man we believe killed your husband is dead. But the other person that was in the car is in serious condition and will only talk to you."

The urgent tone of Sergeant Wells' voice snapped Kim out of her emotional merry-go-round.

"I think you'd better hurry if you want to find out where your son is. She's in pretty bad shape."

Kim rallied as if she'd been shot out of a cannon.

"I'll be there in five minutes."

Kim carelessly slipped her cell phone in her hip pocket and started toward the front door, but reversed her direction when she heard the phone drop to the floor. She quickly reinstalled the phone, this time in her front pocket, and wheeled around, tripping over Hope.

"Sorry boy. You okay?"

Hope followed her toward the front door.

"Stay here, boy. I'll be back soon. I'm sorry fella. I know you don't understand all of this."

She snatched her purse from the kitchen counter and then scoffed at herself for not thinking more clearly. She made an about face and tripped over Hope again as she pickpocketed the phone from her jeans.

"Dad, this is Kim. I need another fast ride to the hospital."

"What's wrong, honey?" Jerry exclaimed, totally caught off guard.

"I'll explain on the way. Hurry."

"I'll be right there, darling, as soon as I slip some shoes on."

"I'll meet you at your house. I'm on my way over."

This time Kim slipped the phone into her preferred back pocket and apologized to Hope again as she sprinted out the front door.

§   §   §   §   §   §

Kim and her parents walked nervously behind Sergeant Wells as he led them through a maze of hospital corridors. The dimly lit aisles were lined with medical equipment and blocked in several places by carts loaded with supplies or hampers stuffed with soiled linens and hospital gowns.

The familiar smells of antiseptic and gauze filled her senses and the sterility of the surroundings accelerated her steps. One of the partitioned cubicles was open as she passed by, giving her quite a jolt when she saw the condition of a young girl lying on the hospital bed.

As Sergeant Wells led them further down the emergency room hallway, Kim could see a uniformed policeman standing in front of a curtained partition at the end of the corridor. The officer nodded to Sergeant Wells as the four of them approached.

"You'd better make it fast," he addressed his sergeant. "The doctor says she doesn't have long."

The sergeant glanced at Kim as he opened the nylon drapery for her to enter.

"Go on in. We don't have much time. I'd better warn you, she's not a pretty sight."

Sergeant Wells motioned for Kim's parents to wait in the hallway. Jerry nodded concurrence and escorted Pauline over to where the uniformed officer stood.

Kim slanted her way past Sergeant Wells and stepped hurriedly into the cubicle. She took a few tentative steps over to the woman lying on the hospital bed.

The woman's bloody forehead was wrapped in gauze and one of her legs was heavily bandaged. Dried blood etched her nose and mouth and her breathing was labored. Each fractured breath sounded raspy as she fought for air.

Her arms were sheathed in tubes which ran alongside the bed and up to the plastic bags filled with plasma. A screen to the left of the bed blinked her vitals.

"Her name is Trixie Maddox. She's Buster's girl friend. She's got a rap sheet as long as his," Sergeant Wells informed Kim.

Kim moved closer so the dying woman could see her.

"Trixie. My name is Kim Sanborn. I'm Graham's mother."

Trixie's eyes eased open and rotated in their sockets as she struggled to keep herself from slipping into oblivion. She blinked several times as she focused on the outline of Kim's face.

"I'm ... I'm sorry, honey," Trixie whispered in a voice that was almost inaudible.

Kim leaned closer to her.

"I've ... I've ... " she drifted, "I've done a very ... bad thing."

She breathed laboriously.

"Trixie, I want to know where my son is," Kim asserted, raising her voice.

Sergeant Wells motioned for Kim to calm down.

Kim tightened her lips and gave him a perfunctory head nod. She intended to find out what happened to Graham.

"Trixie," Kim raised her voice only slightly this time. Although she was afraid that she might lose Trixie at any moment, she wanted to shake Graham's whereabouts out of her.

"Trixie, where is my son?"

The semi-conscious woman raised her hand slightly as her blood-shot eyes refocused on Kim.

Kim gently clasped Trixie's hand in hers.

"He's ... I loved that little boy ... I ... " she confessed, coughing up blood.

Panic gripped Kim. She thought she might vomit.

"He's somewhere ... " she said softly, rasping heavily, "in ... " she whispered, swallowing hard. "Atlanta, Georgia."

Kim shivered convulsively, muffling the scream she felt lift from her throat.

"Somewhere ... " Trixie continued, "somewhere near the king and queen."

Kim knew exactly what she was referring to. The king and queen were two office buildings north of downtown Atlanta in Perimeter Park. Their tops were constructed in the design of chess pieces. She'd seen them many times during her trips to Atlanta to find Graham. And Joseph Woods had drawn them during the remote viewing session over three torturous years ago.

"Where, Trixie? Where?" pressed Kim, as she squeezed Trixie's almost limp hand.

Trixie's eyes were closed but she reopened them. She coughed up more blood before she could speak again.

"I ... I tried to ... find ... out, but," she said wearily. Her voice was a whisper now.

Kim leaned over so that her ear was next to Trixie's mouth.

"But he ... would never ... tell me."

Kim closed her eyes. *This whole session is emotional piracy,* she wailed silently. *I'm never going to find Graham.*

"I'm so sorry ... you ... never ... " she wheezed, "deserved this."

Kim's eyes widened.

Trixie murmured something unintelligible.

Kim lifted her ear from its position directly over Trixie's mouth and leaned down to speak into her ear.

"Trixie, you said he. You said he wouldn't tell you ... Who is he?"

Trixie blinked her eyes.

"He never ... told me ... Don't ... " her breathing was extremely labored. "Don't think ... he ever ... would ... " She slowly inhaled a lengthy fractured breath.

Kim winced. She could feel Trixie slipping away and knew she couldn't do anything about it. She tuned her emotional antennae to catch the slightest whisper, the faintest murmur which fell from the dying woman's mouth.

"He who, Trixie? You said he. Do you mean Buster?."

"No. No. Not... You ... know him. Be ... Ben ... Ben Dare ... He knows ... where your ... boy is."

Kim snapped herself backward as if she were slapped.

"What did you say?"

Trixie used all of her strength to squeeze Kim's hand to pull her closer.

"Ben ... Be ... Ben Dare. He.."

"Ben Dare?" Kim exhaled his name. "Ben? No! No way! Not Ben!"

Trixie groaned, reverting Kim's attention back to her.

"For ... give me ... I ... in over ... my ... head ... Ask Ben ... Your little boy ... I...loved..." she exhaled fully as she expired.

Kim released Trixie's limp hand and reverently placed it on the dead woman's stomach.

I forgive you, she gave Trixie a silent benediction. "I forgive you," she repeated aloud. "But Ben Dare is going to have hell to pay!"

When Kim turned to face Sergeant Wells, she had fire in her eyes.

"He's going to have hell to pay!"

CHAPTER FOURTEEN

Where's my son?" Kim demanded fiercely, as she moved quickly toward Ben. Her tone was harsh and the steel in her eyes spoke volumes.

Ben's eyes widened in response to her savage greeting. Before he could speak, she launched another salvo.

"Where is he?" she said huffily as she marched up to his desk and placed her hands, palms down, on its lacquered surface. Then her volatility carried her around his desk for a frontal assault.

Ben had the most incredulous look on his face.

"What are you talking about?" he asked. His eyes danced in their sockets as he moved them quickly from Kim to Sergeant Wells, who had come in behind her.

Kim shortened the distance between her and Ben and grabbed his shirt. "You know damn well what I'm talking about. Graham! Where is he? Where's my son?" She clipped his chin as she swung at him. Her fury unnerved him.

Ben glanced uneasily at Sergeant Wells, who had just grabbed Kim's shoulders. Then he raised his arm as Kim accelerated her vicious attack.

By this time Sergeant Wells had restrained Kim, who wasn't at all pleased with his intervention.

"Graham?" Ben questioned nervously. "I ... I don't understand." He threw her a pleading look.

Kim started angrily at him, not buying his confusion for a minute.

"Mrs. Sanborn, please let me handle this," Sergeant Wells cautioned, as he respectfully restrained her.

Ben glared at Kim, unsure what his next move should be.

Kim grudgingly allowed Sergeant Wells to pull her to the front of Ben's desk. Then he gave her befuddled business partner a calculated stare.

"Do you know a Buster Matthews?" the sergeant asked.

Ben blinked his eyes, then widened them quickly.

"Buster Matthews," he repeated, taking his eyes off Kim and then back up to Sergeant Wells. "No. Can't say that I do."

Kim tightened and huffed an indignant sigh.

"Liar," she screamed, and then took a breath through gritted teeth.

"How about a Trixie Maddox? Do you know her?"

Ben shook his head.

Kim lunged over the desk at Ben, and made it difficult for Sergeant Wells to restrain her again.

Ben inched back a few more steps. "What's wrong with you, Kim?"

She swung at him with her right fist, which she had been able to free from Sergeant Wells' relaxed restraint, missing Ben's face by inches as he dodged her punch.

"Mrs. Sanborn, Mrs. Sanborn," Sergeant Wells petitioned, "let me handle this!"

"You're going to tell me where my son is if I have to claw it out of you," Kim addressed Ben as if she didn't even hear Sergeant Wells' admonition.

"Officer, what is she talking about?" Ben pleaded, using the desk to stay out of her reach.

"Then you don't know either of them, Buster Matthews or Trixie Maddox?"

"No. No, I don't. Why do you keep asking me these questions?"

"Because she knows you!" blasted Kim, "and she told us you know where Graham is."

"Mrs. Sanborn," rebuffed Sergeant Wells.

"I'm telling you I've never heard of them, and I don't know what Trixie what's-her-name is talking about."

Ben eased himself behind his office chair and looked at Kim pleadingly.

"Kim, darling, I don't know where Graham is. My God, woman, I've tried to help you find him. I've stood by you all these years. Kim, I love you. I'd never do anything to hurt you."

"Then how did she know you? Why would she tell me you know where my son is? She had nothing to gain by it. It was her death bed confession."

"What?" he asked as he coughed nervously.

"Ms. Maddox died in the hospital less than a hour ago," reported Sergeant Wells, wishing Kim hadn't divulged the woman's death. "She was a passenger in Buster Matthews' car. They were involved in a high speed chase and lost control of the car on South Saunders Street," Sergeant Wells clarified. "Mr. Matthews fits the description of the murderer who carjacked the Sanborn's car three years ago."

Ben slumped in his chair, then rose to his feet, staying safely behind the desk.

"You said he fits the description of the killer," Ben cautiously verified. "Does that mean he's ... Is he ... ?"

"He's the killer, all right," Kim confirmed. "He was dead before I got there, or I'd have killed him myself!"

"Now Kim," Sergeant Wells winced at her admission. "We were able to speak to him before he died, Mr. Dare. I have a few more questions to ask you."

"Then we've found ... you've found the man who killed Jim," Ben said nervously, as he addressed the sergeant.

Sergeant Wells nodded.

"We believe so."

Ben nodded his head a few times.

"Good," Ben whispered. "Did he say anything ... was he able to tell you anything before he ... before he died?"

He moved his eyes quickly from Kim's defiant stare and focused on the sergeant's face.

"Suppose I ask the questions, Mr. Dare."

"Oh, yes, of course. I'm sorry. It's just that in spite of what Kim thinks, I want to ... Kim, darling, if he said anything before he died that can help us find Graham ... "

"He was dead on arrival," blasted Kim. "I'm sure you're real broken up about that."

"Oh," Ben responded, hesitating slightly before he continued. "That's too bad."

"Mrs. Sanborn, please! We agreed I'd do the talking, remember?"

"How did she know you, Ben?" quizzed Kim, ignoring Sergeant Wells.

"I have absolutely no idea," he replied. Ben looked at her pleadingly. "I don't know the woman. How many times do I have to tell you?"

"Until I believe you!" Kim screamed.

Anticipating her heightening volatility, Ben volunteered his own explanation.

"Maybe she was a student here. I don't remember anyone here by that name, but I can check to make sure. Maybe she saw me at one of the local bars or nightclubs," he alibied. "Maybe she knew one of my old girlfriends."

He looked pathetically at Kim.

"Maybe she saw us at a restaurant or showcase or dancing exhibition. I don't know how she knows me ... knew me. I swear, Kim, I have no idea why she used my name. It's absurd to think I had anything to do with Graham's disappearance. This ... this whole thing is crazy. It's a set-up, can't you see that?"

He walked slowly from behind his desk, calculating each step. When he reached out to Kim, her lurch forward tightened Sergeant Wells' grip.

"I'm not going to leave it at this," he declared solemnly. "I love you too much to let anything come between us. Surely you must know I'd never do anything to hurt you. Kim, how could you even suspect me?"

His attempt to reach for her again was deflected by her flammable stare.

"I want to believe you, Ben," she admitted sourly, trying her best to extinguish Sergeant Wells' hold on her. "But if I find you had anything to do with ... "

"I can't take it anymore," he burst out. "You're looking at me as if I'm on trial here. Kim, I didn't do anything wrong. You've got to believe me," he pleaded. "Please believe me."

"I'm trying to believe you," she repeated breathily, "so give me something to believe."

"Mr. Dare, until we can sort this out, I'd appreciate it if you would stay in town, in case we need to reach you," Sergeant Wells interjected, sounding as agitated as he appeared official.

"Yes. Of course. I'm not going anywhere. I've got a business to run and a very special woman to convince of my innocence."

Kim met his pleading gaze with the unsparing scrutiny of her own.

"Ben, I'm going to find out the truth," she declared. The suspicious curve of her perfectly-formed eyebrows flattened as her face softened.

"If you'd give yourself a chance to let me into your life, you'd know I'm telling you the truth," Ben predicted soberly.

Kim forced a tight smile and glared at him as she prepared to exit the office.

"I'll be in touch, Mr. Dare," Sergeant Wells announced as he filed out behind Kim, who he corralled with his right hand firmly on her back.

They walked a few steps down the narrow aisle toward the ballroom before either of them spoke.

"You're not going to arrest him?" Kim asked.

"We're not done with him yet. We need corroborating evidence. He's either a very good liar or he's telling the truth. Just when I thought he was rudderless, he seemed to find sure footing. Looks like he handled the surprise visit pretty well."

He held the front door open for Kim and waited for her to exit before he spoke again.

"We're searching their apartment. Maybe we'll find something there," he continued. "We found a letter in the decedent's purse from her mother in Portland. That's how we found their apartment. Neither carried a driver's license and the car they drove was stolen. We're going through their apartment as we speak. I'll call you as soon as I know anything."

"Oh, no you don't. If you think for one minute I'm going to sit at home while you follow-up on the only lead we've had in three years, you've got to be crazy. There's no way I'm letting this go."

Kim's parents stood beside their car and waited for their daughter and Sergeant Wells as they approached.

"What happened? Was Ben there? His car's out front," Jerry spoke rapidly as Pauline rushed up to Kim.

"He says he didn't have anything to do with Graham's abduction and that he's never heard of Trixie Maddox or Buster Matthews," Kim reported mechanically. "We're on our way to Buster and Trixie's apartment."

"Kim's agreed to stand just inside the front door, so she can identify any of your grandson's belongings. If we find any," Sergeant Wells reported. "We hope we'll find evidence leading us to your grandson," he repeated himself. "I'm allowing Mrs. Sanborn to accompany me. However, I'd like you two to wait for your daughter at home. Their house is part of the crime scene, so we don't want it compromised, if you know what I mean."

"I'll call as soon as we know anything," Kim promised her parents. She gave her mother a parting kiss. "I'll come right over as soon as I get back. I promise."

Each pair got into their respective vehicles and Sergeant Wells motioned for the Spencers to leave first. He didn't want them sticking around the studio to conduct their own investigation.

"Mrs. Sanborn, I'm allowing you to go with me on one condition. You can stand just inside the front door of the apartment," he reminded her. "And under no circumstances are you to make any attempt to interfere with this police investigation. Is that understood?"

Kim sighed as she rolled her eyes and then nodded obediently.

"Good. Good," Sergeant Wells addressed her as he started the car. "I'm going to say this as diplomatically as I can, Mrs. Sanborn. I'm willing to keep you involved as much as possible. However, you must let me do my job. I understand your frustration. I'd be as anxious to find my child as you. Especially after three years. So, if you'll abide by the rules, you can participate in the investigation."

"I understand," she patronized. "I'll stand as quiet as a mouse at the door unless you summon me."

Sergeant Wells smiled at her, knowing there would be a tigress, not a mouse, standing at the front door.

"It's a South Raleigh address. We should be there in eight to ten minutes."

After they drove several blocks, Kim turned to face her chauffeur as he checked in with the precinct. She waited patiently for him to complete his routine call.

"Depending on what we find there and how long it takes, I have a request," she stated.

The sergeant glanced at her quickly, then diverted his attention back to the street ahead.

"A request, huh?"

"Yes. I'd like to stop by the hospital on my way back home. I want to see the body of the man who destroyed my family."

The sergeant was immediately sympathetic to her request.

"Of course," he spoke softly. "Of course."

§   §   §   §   §   §

A thorough search of Buster's apartment came up empty. That was two weeks ago, and Kim was sitting in her parents' living room staring blankly at the settlement check she held in her hand. She'd sold her house, but decided not to rent the townhouse she originally planned to occupy, opting instead to stay with her parents until she knew what she wanted to do.

Her parents were wise enough to allow her to bring Hope with her. Her depression had returned, and along with it, hopelessness and despair. She had caught a cold, which settled in her chest. The antibiotics seemed to be working, but the hacking cough kept her weak and unsteady. Hope did not leave her side.

John McCauley's phone call two weeks earlier had lifted her spirits, when he informed her he was renewing his search for Graham based on Trixie's death bed confession. But a call from Linda Amos the next day left her dismal again. Kim learned that Joseph Woods was out of the country touring spiritual places. He was somewhere in Europe and couldn't be reached. Kim wanted him to try to locate Graham again, since they were now fairly certain he was in Atlanta.

An unbearable ache settled in on her. Her breathing was laborious and she felt as if someone were standing on her chest. The effect was suffocating.

She filled her despondency with sleep mostly, waking occasionally in obedience to her bodily functions or to the coaxing of her parents as they forced food and fluids down her.

Her refusal to see Ben made him more eager to see her and her parents' distrust of him compounded his plight, heightening his obsession for her.

Kim placed the unsigned check on top of the hard cover book on the end table beside her. It was Louise's most recent novel and she'd autographed it for Kim's parents. Kim suspected her mother had left it out, hoping she would want to read it. Kim had picked it up a few times, but had not opened it. Getting serious about a novel meant sitting in one position, and what Kim really wanted to do was wrestle the truth out of Ben.

Her parents were at the Wednesday night church service, so Kim was alone except for her loyal canine companion who was sprawled on the floor against her chair.

Suddenly the doorbell rang, bringing Hope to his feet. His protective eyes focused on the door. When it rang a second time, Hope answered it with a bark.

"Hope. It's okay, boy. Let it ring," Kim ordered softly.

Its third ring was accompanied by Ben's slurred voice.

"Kim. I know you're in there. Please let me talk to you."

The doorbell trilled again.

"Kim. Please! Don't be this way. I don't want to lose you."

Ben knocked on the door, giving the doorbell a rest.

"It's not right. You're not giving me a chance."

Hope was at the front door sniffing at the bottom of the riser and growling at the commotion. The dog's aggressiveness forced Kim out of the chair.

"So you want to see who it is, do you? It's Ben. You remember Ben don't you, old fella?"

Hope barked his agreement.

The doorbell sounded again, accompanied by heavy knocking.

"Kim, I'm not leaving until you see me. You've got to let me explain myself. I ... "

"Okay. Okay. I'm coming. Stop your hammering before you break the glass."

"Kim, please. I'm getting wet out here. Let me in."

She opened the interior door.

Ben straightened himself once he saw her through the storm door.

"Kim, I've got to talk to you. You've got to listen to me."

Her frown melted into a grimace when she saw that he was drunk. His usually meticulous appearance was disheveled. His shirt sleeves were rolled back to his elbows and his hair was tussled. There was grass and mud stain on one knee of his expensive trousers and he was soaking wet.

He smiled childishly as he tried to hold himself vertical.

"Can I come in?"

"You've been drinking." Kim gave him a sour look.

"Just a little. Please don't hold that against me. I've never been this unhappy before," he whined.

Kim shook her head and sighed.

"You've been drinking," she repeated.

He wiped his wet hair back from his face and caught himself before he stumbled against the door facing.

"Please."

"You do look pathetic," Kim chastised, grinning as she unlocked the outer door. "You may come in, but you'll have to wait at the door until I can get some towels."

"Yes, ma'am," Ben agreed, trying unsuccessfully to shield his slur.

Kim closed the front door behind him and motioned for him to remain still.

"Hope, if he moves from that spot, eat him."

A look of surprise flickered across Ben's intoxicated face.

When the dog took several steps toward him, Ben decided his immediate compliance was both prudent and healthy.

"Your wish is my command," he told Kim, as she left to retrieve the towels she promised.

Hope changed his stance to a sitting position, but his eyes never left the unsteady guest.

"Hope, you know me boy. Don't you remember me? I've been here before. I'm not going to hurt your master."

Kim returned shortly, carrying a blanket, towels and newspaper.

"He doesn't like me, does he?"

"Here. Take your wet jacket off and dry your hair with these," she ordered, as she handed him several towels. "Put your shoes on the paper."

She assisted him as he lowered himself to the floor to rid himself of the wet shoes. When he made a play for one of her breasts, Kim pushed him away, causing his head to crash against the front door. Hope moved nervously beside Kim, unsure what to do.

"Try that again and you'll be Hope's dinner tonight," she warned. "I'm serious, Ben. You said you wanted to talk."

Ben nodded without saying a word and fumbled his way out of his shoes. When he finished his partial disrobement, he allowed Kim to help him to his feet. This time he made no attempt to fondle her.

Kim led him to one of the mahogany chairs in the foyer and spread newspapers and then a blanket over the chair seat.

She motioned for Ben to seat himself.

"I could use a pot of coffee," he confessed.

"Coffee will not help you get sober," Kim snapped. "If you're plastered, you're going to have to wait several hours for the alcohol to leave your system on its own. Drinking coffee won't make your body metabolize alcohol faster."

"You're kidding," he winced.

"No, I'm not kidding," she confirmed as she continued to make sure the water-logged drunk didn't spread his wetness onto the hardwood floor.

"I've always loved you," Ben slurred as he pushed a strand of damp hair off his forehead.

Kim put newspaper under his shoes by the door, then eased herself onto the chair next to Ben.

He reached out to clasp her hand, but she pulled back.

"You see," he pointed out, sighing heavily. "That's the kind of thing that's taken its toll on me. Your lack of affection. Your pulling back like that." His despondency roughened his whining voice.

"Ben, you said you wanted to tell me something," Kim sliced into his blubbering.

"I know. I know," he slid into her abruptness, and then looked at her pitifully.

"Ben, you've got to know I still don't trust you. I'm allowing you in here tonight because I thought you've decided to come clean. You'd ... "

"I know you're still grieving for Jim and Graham," he began, measuring his disclosure. Then he fidgeted a bit when Kim's irritation became evident. He brushed several strands of wet hair off his forehead again and sent his bloodshot eyes apologetically toward hers.

"I know what it looks like, but I honestly didn't have anything to do with Jim's death and Graham's disappearance."

"Ben, the past three years have been a nightmare for me. If I hadn't considered you my friend, you wouldn't have gotten in here tonight."

He gave her a sheepish look, but didn't say anything.

"If it wasn't for you and my family ... and some very dear friends ... I don't know what I would have done. But as I said, I don't trust you now. I've lost faith in you."

Ben's hands were automatically solicitous as he reached for her hand. But Kim leaned back in her chair to avoid even touching him.

"You need to tell me what you've come here to tell me, or I'm going to ask you to leave."

Ben whined his disappointment, but a quick look at Hope reminded him to keep his hands to himself.

Kim forced a smile when she realized Ben's discomfort with Hope's presence.

"It seems I'm not the only one who's getting negative vibes from you," came Kim's icy observation. "I thought you were a good friend all these years." She pruned what she was really thinking, and then she purposely hesitated, knowing her next comment would meet with considerable resistance.

"Ben, you say love me, but I'm not so sure about that. I'll never forget the look you gave me when Sergeant Wells and I burst into your office at our dance studio. I used to consider you a dear friend, but you haven't been the Ben I used to know since the carjacking. You're ... different. There's ..." She abbreviated her own review when he started to speak, and waved him off. "There's a dark side to you now, Ben. I can feel it. It was probably there all along, but my grief must have blinded my discernment."

"I love you. What do you mean I have a dark side?" He started to stand.

Kim tightened her lips and made sure he remained seated by pushing firmly on his damp shoulders.

"This past two weeks ... especially due to what's happened this past two weeks ... " she corrected herself, swallowing agitatedly. "There's obviously been a major ... a significant strain on our relationship. The police are still investigating you. I'm still investigating you! I don't know what to believe about you anymore."

Ben looked at her sorrowfully.

"I don't trust you, Ben," Kim repeated. "You've got to earn my trust again!"

He dropped his gaze momentarily and then lifted it, diverting it again to the safe harbor of his fidgeting feet.

"What can I do to win your trust back?" he pleaded, shifting nervously in his chair. "I can't stand being away from you. I've accepted your not dancing anymore. I really have, but we should be together. We're meant to be together. You've got to let Jim go."

"Now wait just a minute, Ben. You don't want to go there. No one can ever replace Jim. I'm not interested in you or anyone else. I've made that quite clear many times. The issue here is you. Friends don't lie to friends. And they don't hurt friends. Or their families."

Kim studied his flushed expression. The twitching in his left eye, accompanied by his nervous coughs fueled her suspicions.

"You can help me understand why Trixie said you know where Graham is."

"We've been through this a thousand times." he raised his voice. "I don't know how she knew me. I've told you,

I've told the police. I've volunteered to help you find him. You've got to believe me."

"Help me to believe you, then. Give me some logical explanation. Tell me why your name was on a dying woman's lips."

Kim was yelling by the time she finished her inquisition. She leaned menacingly toward him.

"I don't know," Ben lashed back. "Do you believe a black woman's lies over my loyalty? 'Cause if you do, there's no hope for me. Please, darling, you've got to trust me. You've got to believe me. I'd never hurt you."

Ben slid off his chair and landed in a heap on the floor in front of her. He eased himself up, buried his head in her lap, and started crying.

Kim's disgust prompted her to rise to her feet, sending him crashing to the floor.

Hope jumped to his feet about the same time Ben found his knees.

"What's wrong? What have I done?" he pleaded, reaching for her. However, a tentative glance at Hope kept him on his knees.

"You confessed! You've just confessed! I can't believe it. You ... you just confessed."

"Confessed? What are you talking about?"

"How did you know she was a person of color?" Kim's voice was calm and her manner was composed, but her tone was laced with venom.

"What?"

"You said she was a black woman. How did you know that?"

"I don't remember saying ... did I say she was black?" he stumbled through his explanation. "It was in the papers. Her identity was in the papers. Come on, Kim, what's wrong with you?"

He lifted one knee off the floor in an attempt to stand.

"Nothing in the papers said she was a person of color, Ben. Only her address and a description of the fatal accident were listed."

"You must have said it the day you and that arrogant police sergeant interrogated me at the studio," he alibied. "Do you know how embarrassing that was? That was a nasty thing to do to a friend."

His slippery smile infuriated her.

"You know her race because you knew her, you slimeball," she blasted. "And if you knew her, you had something to do with my son's kidnapping ... and Jim's death, you piece of garbage!"

Hope barked, picking up on Kim's highly emotional outburst.

Ben jerked back slightly, but held his ground. He began to shuffle across the tile floor toward her.

"Where is he, Ben? So help me I'll sic Hope on you. I'm not kidding!"

The hair bristled on the dog's neck and back as he inched forward between his master and the drunk on the floor.

"Come here, boy," Kim called to Hope as she motioned him to her side.

"I came here tonight to make things right between us."

"You're not my friend anymore, Ben. I don't think you ever have been. I don't know how you're involved or how that woman knew you, but you're going to tell me tonight."

"Kim, this isn't like you. Look at me. I'm on my knees. I'm begging you to accept me, and to believe me. Oh, wait a minute. I remember where I ... how I knew she was a black woman. Officer Wells told me. He told me the last time he questioned me at the studio. Yes, that's when it was. You've got to believe me."

"You're a liar!" Kim fumed.

"No. No, darling. It's true. I swear to you on my mother's grave."

"Make it your grave."

"What?"

"You heard me. Stay right there. Don't come any closer. I'm going to call Sergeant Wells right now. If he confirms your claim, we have more to discuss. If he doesn't, I'm turning you in."

Then she caught herself.

"That is, if I don't let Hope have you first," she raised her voice. "So help me God, I've half a notion to let to let Hope tear you apart!"

Ben knelt, frozen to the floor while Kim dialed Sergeant Wells' number.

"You move one inch and I'll sic Hope on you!"

"Hello, Sergeant Wells. This is Kim Sanborn. Do you have a minute? I've got ... "

"Okay, okay. Hang up. Please hang up," Ben said quickly.

"Just a minute," Kim instructed the officer. She lowered the phone, but kept the connection open and pushed the speaker icon.

"Graham wasn't even supposed to be in the car."

His confession came at her like a sledgehammer. She took a step back to brace herself on the staircase bannister.

"Sergeant Wells," Kim spoke guardedly and authoritatively, "Did you hear that?"

"Yes, I did! I'm on my way. "

"Kim, I never meant for Graham to be involved," Ben confessed. When he reached out to touch her, she recoiled immediately, sending Hope closer to Ben's position.

"Where's my son? What have you done with my son?" she screamed. "Where is he? Tell me or so help me I'll ... "

"What—Kill me?" Ben finished her savage threat as he rose to his feet. He grabbed both of her arms sending the phone crashing to the floor.

Hope barked his disapproval, sensing the game the humans were playing was getting out of hand.

"I'm already a dead man. You've killed me emotionally. You've never let me get close to you," he said through clenched teeth, squeezing her arms. "What was I supposed to do, ice woman?"

"Ben, you're hurting me."

"You've never shown me one ounce of affection. If I can't have you, no one will."

"Ben, please stop! You're hurting me! Hope, sic him, boy!"

Hope jumped on Ben, tearing at the clothing on the arm nearest him.

Ben kept his arms around Kim, forcibly kissing her on the lips, ignoring both her protestations and the vicious tug of Hope on his shirt sleeve. Wincing as he ravaged her mouth and neck, he seemed oblivious to Hope's escalating attack as he tried to turn his lust up a few notches.

His hasty kisses became rougher, more frenzied as he struggled against the two of them. He moved his free hand to Kim's throat. Finally he screamed in agony as Hope sank his teeth into Ben's left elbow. The dog drew blood.

"Kim. Kim. Are you all right?" came Sergeant Wells' voice over the phone on the floor. But the magnified commotion blanketed his involvement. "I'm a couple of minutes away."

Ben screamed again as he began an encumbered retreat toward the living room.

Hope tried his best to bring the two hundred pound man to the floor.

Ben's punches to the dog's head and neck only served to tighten Hope's vice-like grip. Hope's persistent growls grew into more pronounced statements of determination.

" Call him off. Call him off ... Okay ... Okay. Damn it ... Okay. Yes, I had him killed. I figured with him out of the way, you'd turn to me—love me— let me ... take ... Come on, Kim. He's killing me."

"I heard him, Kim," declared Sergeant Wells, holding the steering wheel with one hand and his cell phone with the other. "I'm almost there!"

"My God!" An invisible scream filled the inside of her throat. "You had Jim killed!" She yelled, needing to hear herself say it. "You murdered my husband, you no-good piece of ... damn you, Ben! You ... you're going to pay for this." Her face turned to stone. "I hope he kills you!" she threatened as she watched Hope shake his arm. "Sic him, boy. Tear his arm off!"

"Call him off," Ben shouted. "He's shredding what's left of my arm off!"

"Where's my son?"

"Kim, ple ... lease call ... him ... off."

"Where's Graham?"

Hope rocked his head from side to side tearing at Ben's arm. Unable to weather the searing attack, Ben kicked at Hope, who kept circling Ben to avoid his frenzied kicks. Writhing in pain, he punched the dog, who growled his commitment to neutralize Kim's attacker.

"Call him off. I'm bleeding—a lot! He's going to kill me!"

"Where's Graham?"

"Please ... get him to stop. He's tearing my arm off!"

"I'm going to let him kill you if you don't tell me where Graham is."

"Okay, okay, get him off me ... I'll tell you. Just ... Just get him off."

Kim's seething anger caused her to hesitate a moment before she called off her dog.

"Hope," she shouted. "Come here, boy. Stop! Hope, come here!"

The dog released his victim's arm and moved to Kim's side, still growling his protectiveness at the man who assaulted his master. His muzzle was bloody from the encounter and his snow white hair was matted with a considerable amount of Ben's blood.

"Look at my arm!" Ben whispered, having lost the energy to voice his anger. "He bit through an artery. Oh, my God! You've got to get me to a hospital. I'm going to bleed to death if you don't help me. Please! Look at my arm! Help me. Please!" Ben struggled onto his right side, using his good hand as a tourniquet. "That damn dog of yours severed an artery!"

"I'm going to sic him on you again unless you start talking."

"But I'm bleeding to death!"

"That's what it looks like, so you'd better tell me where my son is," Kim snapped, throwing him one of the wet towels from his chair by the front door to control the bleeding.

Kim leaned over to pet Hope, who waited for her permission to renew his assault.

"I can't believe you're this heartless."

"You murdered my husband, you creep, and stole my son, and now you're bleeding all over my parent's hardwood floor. If I were heartless, I'd let Hope tear your heart out. Now, where's my son?"

"Hand me another towel so I can stop this bleeding and I'll tell you."

Kim hesitated before she threw a soiled hand towel at him.

Ben quickly placed the hand towel over the one already pressed on the wound and applied pressure to control the bleeding.

"Where's my son?"

"I'm feeling a little faint," Ben announced as he leaned back against the chairs.

"You're stalling. I'm about five seconds away from turning Hope loose on you again."

"This alcohol's made my blood thinner. I can't get it stopped."

"I'll call an ambulance after you tell me where Graham is. Officer Wells should be here any second. If you expect to be alive when either arrives, you'd better tell me where my son is. NOW Ben," she shouted.

She threw him another hand towel from the pile of towels on the floor as she flaunted the cell phone in front of him.

"Oh, wait," she blunted her perfunctory assistance, "I'll need to call on my parent's land line. My cell phone's still connected to Sergeant Wells," she smiled.

"They'll be on their way as soon as you ... I'll quit stalling when you quit stalling," she said in a measured voice, tossing him a third towel to add to the bundle of blood-soaked towels covering his arm. "Now, where's Graham?"

"I'm not going to prison over this. It's your word against mine."

"You're wrong about that," Kim smiled. "Sergeant Wells and I have kept the connection open on our cell phones. He's heard everything that's happened tonight!"

Ben threw her a horrified look. "You've... He's..."

"You'd better tell me where my son is before you lose consciousness."

Ben looked at her through unrepentant eyes.

"We were the couple who should have gone to Blackpool."

"What?"

"It should have been us," he lamented. "I've always been the better dancer."

"You killed Jim because you wanted me to be your dance partner?

"I had Jim killed because he was in the way. I..."

Kim screamed to control her rage.

"Your stalling's going to get you killed! Why did you take Graham away from me? Tell me, or so help me I'll sic Hope on you again."

"I told you, I didn't know he was in the car. I only wanted to get rid of Jim. Do you know how much I loathed him? Do you? You belong to me. You've always belonged to me."

Kim stepped toward the pathetic heap of humanity sprawled on the floor.

"You really are crazy. You're sick!"

"And bleeding," he said. "I feel light-headed. I think I'm going to faint."

"For the last time, what did you do with Graham?" she shouted, holding on to Hope's collar.

He responded with a blank stare.

"Oh, no you don't. You're not checking out of here before you tell me what you've done with my son."

She released Hope and flew to the kitchen sink to get a pan of water.

"I'm going to pour this over your sorry head. If that doesn't work, I'm going to drown you."

Hope's barking caused her to turn toward Ben, who was crawling toward the front door.

"Ben!" she shouted. "Oh, no you don't!"

By the time she dropped the pan in the sink and sprinted out of the kitchen, Ben had cleared the front door.

Kim followed Hope out the front door. The dog growled his pursuit as he chased the injured man.

Before the dog reached him, Ben stepped into the street and stumbled in front of Sergeant Wells' car.

Ben didn't see the flashing lights until it was too late. The police cruiser hit him, driving Ben into the side of one of the parked cars.

"Ben," Kim screamed. "Oh my God, no!"

By the time she rushed up to him, Sergeant Wells had exited his cruiser.

She flung herself next to Ben.

"Ben, please, in heaven's name, tell me where my son is."

His eyes locked onto hers.

"Ben!" she screamed as she shook him. "Damn you!"

She resisted the pull of Sergeant Wells as he tried unsuccessfully to pry her away from Ben.

"It wasn't ... supposed ... to end ... this way," Ben said softly, gasping for air.

Kim fell on her knees next to him as Officer Wells relaxed his grip.

"He's with the Fergusens ... "

"Fergusen? Did you say Fergusen?" Kim whispered as she moved closer to him.

"Julian and ... "

"Go on, Ben ... Julian and who?" Kim lowered her ear closer to his blood-stained lips,

"Julian and Joyce Fergusen ... Alpharetta ... Georgia ... 140 ... 1401 Pres ... Prestige ... Circle ... Graham's there ... never meant ... to hurt you ... always ... loved you ... "

He reached for her hand and gave her a weak smile.

"I'm sorry ... I'm ... sorry."

He smiled again and then he was gone.

CHAPTER FIFTEEN

J ohn, hi!" Kim joyfully threw her arms around him, oblivious to the crowded airport terminal. "You didn't have to meet us here."

"A year's a long time," he declared, kissing her on the cheek. "We're both here. Louise's in the car."

"Wonderful. I can't wait to see her again. You remember my parents, don't you?" Kim asked as she grabbed her father's arm and pulled him closer to her. "Jim's folks couldn't make it. They're in Paris. We'll call them after we find out what happens here."

"Nice to see you again, Mr. and Mrs. Spencer ... Jerry," he greeted, extending his hand for a handshake. "Pauline," he added, greeting her with a hug. "Sorry Jim's folks couldn't make the trip. How was your flight?"

"Fine," Jerry answered for the three of them. "It was a smooth on-time trip."

"Yes, in fact you're even a few minutes early."

"We're lucky to be here at all, with Delta on strike. The other carriers are booked solid," Pauline corroborated.

"Did you check any bags?" John asked rhetorically. He noticed the women were only carrying their purses.

"Yes. Four," Kim stated emphatically.

"Four? Four suitcases?" questioned John. "Are you planning to stay for a month?"

"One for mom and dad, one for me. And two empty ones for Graham's things," Kim commented hopefully.

"You folks are prepared, aren't you?"

All three of them threw him determined grins.

"How far is Prestige Circle from here?" Kim asked.

"Oh, we're not going there," John censored, stopping beside the escalator which took them to Baggage Claim.

"What?" Kim asked, throwing him a most horrified look.

"He's not there. The Fergusens moved back with her parents six months ago."

Kim's confused look was mirrored by the ones on her parents' faces.

"After you called, I checked the residence out. I pretended to be a life insurance salesman," he smiled. "The couple living there knew the Fergusens. They lived in a smaller garage apartment, and moved into the Fergusen's home when they left. I told them a deceased relative left Graham some money. I didn't have to twist their arms for the Fergusen's new address. They're staying with the McDonalds. They're her parents."

"You cagey old fox, you," Kim squealed. "I see you haven't lost your touch."

"We're glad you're on our side, old boy," rallied Jerry.

"Sometimes mouthy neighbors are a help instead of a hindrance," John teased.

When they got to the baggage claim area, John elected to help Jerry retrieve the luggage while the women huddled nearby. Then he led them toward Ground Transportation where he knew Louise was waiting.

"It was very late by the time I got over to the new address last night," John confessed. "Atlanta's not an easy place to get around when you're in a hurry. It's a nice house. A fairly large one in a subdivision named after Joseph E. Wheeler. Wheeler was a Civil War general who fought for the Confederacy. And now, you know more about the subdivision than you care to know. Right?"

"Did you see him?" quizzed Kim nervously. "Graham, I mean."

"No. I snooped around for a while but the house was dark. Two cars were in the garage and the trash was on the curb. It appears somebody's still there."

He looked up suddenly.

"Oh, there's Louise."

She stood beside the car and waved at them. Her long hair looked like a silver shawl from a distance and the joyful expression on her face was a symphony of warmth.

"Louise," Kim shouted, running to her. They embraced like sisters and exchanged kisses before the others caught up.

After a quick round of pleasantries, the women found their seats while the men piled the luggage in the back of the SUV.

John drove them out of the terminal and headed toward Louise's house.

"I'm taking you to Louise's house first. She has your rooms ready," he assured them. Then, before anyone could speak, he continued. "I've arranged for Detective Brian Anderson of the Atlanta PD to meet us at the Fergusen's at ten-fifteen this morning. He'll have a court order with him. I've pulled a few strings and cashed in a couple of I-O-U's. I wanted to take care of the loose ends before you got here."

"You've been a busy man," Jerry praised.

"I figure we've waited long enough. I want to make this visit by the book. We should be able to take care of this thing in short order. We've got the law behind us and the element of surprise. Detective Anderson assured me he'd watch the place. I talked to him shortly before your plane landed. If the Fergusens are church-going people, they haven't left for worship service yet."

Kim looked at her watch.

Eight-fifty-five, she confirmed to herself. An hour and twenty minutes to go. She sighed nervously and squeezed her mother's hand in anticipation of Graham's homecoming.

"I still can't believe Ben Dare was in on this," John commented as he turned down the street heading to his sister's house. "He sure had me fooled."

"Me, too," Kim agreed.

"He fooled all of us," accused Jerry. "It's amazing how someone so close to you can be so evil without your being aware of it."

"And so good at it," added Pauline. "I never quite trusted him around my daughter," she admitted, squeezing Kim's hand for emphasis, "but I never thought he was capable of doing anything like this. He was a monster. A man without a conscience."

"Well, he had enough conscience to tell me where Graham is before he died," corrected Kim.

"Hope really did a job on him, didn't he?" John commented soberly.

"He nearly tore his arm off," Jerry confirmed, trying his best not to seem too pleased. "The police have impounded Hope, but only for observation. They aren't going to destroy him or anything like that, since he was protecting Kim. Pamela is going to pick him up for us and keep him until we get home tomorrow."

"Can we talk about something else?" Kim suggested. "I don't want to worry about Hope while I'm trying to get Graham back."

"I'm sorry, honey. We didn't mean to upset you."

Kim smiled her forgiveness as she gave her dad a few pats on the leg.

"Here we are," Louise announced, as they pulled into her driveway.

"You have just enough time to put your things in your rooms and freshen up before we have to leave again," John advised.

"Kim, you're in your old room," Louise clarified. "Jerry, Pauline, I'll show you to your room."

§　§　§　§　§　§

Kim nervously fumbled with her purse as they pulled up behind the unmarked police car parked across the street from the McDonald's house.

The contents of her purse included several pictures of Graham, his birth certificate and a recent picture of Ben Dare—at John's insistence. He hoped the McDonalds would be able to identify him as the fraudulent adoption agent. John theorized that Ben master-minded the kidnapping. When the car came to a complete stop, John motioned for his passengers to stay put.

"I'll be right back," he assured them, as he opened the car door. He walked toward Detective Anderson, who had already exited his car.

"John," the detective said, extending his hand.

"Brian," greeted John as the two shook hands firmly.

John introduced his carload as they peeled out of the SUV. Louise had elected to stay home so she could prepare a celebration lunch.

Detective Anderson led the rescue party up the porch steps and rang the door bell.

Kim stood silently beside him while the others planted themselves at the top of the front steps.

In a few moments, the front door opened and a well-dressed, gray-haired man stepped out to meet them.

His tanned face was a mixture of crevices and wrinkles, evidence of many years spent out-of-doors. He wore a yellow sweater over a white knit shirt. His gray trousers were pleated and cuffed, and his brown loafers were blemish-free and polished.

He looked at the posse on his front porch.

"Yes, may I help you?" he spoke calmly.

"Good morning, are you Mr. McDonald?" Detective Anderson asked as he brandished his badge. "I'm Detective Anderson, Atlanta PD. May we come in?"

Mr. McDonald surveyed the group quickly as he retreated half a step.

"What is it, officer?"

"May we come in? We have something we'd like to discuss with you inside."

It was all Kim could do to control herself from leaping past the old gentleman to find Graham. She was about to bolt inside when Mr. McDonald spoke.

"Yes, of course, officer. Please come in."

He backed out of the way as the group filed past him. Kim led the way, her eyes darting first one way, then another, as she visually toured the interior.

Detective Anderson grabbed her arm and turned Kim to face their elderly host. Before Detective Anderson could speak, someone else spoke from the hallway.

"Dad. Who is it?"

The young blond-haired woman entered the living room. Her uneasiness registered on her face as she stood beside her father.

"This is Detective Anderson," he announced politely, indicating who the officer was. "The others are ... well ... " he paused, waiting for the detective to enlighten them both.

"This is Mrs. Sanborn," he pointed to Kim. "Mr. and Mrs. Spencer are her parents," he continued, motioning toward them. "And this is their private investigator, Mr. McCauley." He thought that title would simplify John's presence.

John shot him a quick eyebrow flash to show his unpremeditated collusion.

"Private investigator?" repeated the man's daughter.

The officer nodded.

"Are you Mrs. Joyce Fergusen?" Detective Anderson asked, gently restraining Kim.

The woman hesitated for a moment, uncertain whether she should comply without knowing the reason for their visit. She managed to steady herself as she raised one of her hands to cover the V-neck in the white silk blouse she was wearing.

"Yes, I am she."

Kim appeared outwardly calm, but her insides were scrambled nerves. She wanted to shout for Graham, but bit her lip to keep her mouth from opening.

"Do you have a son, a seven year-old son named Graham?"

Joyce and her father exchanged nervous glances. The look of recognition on each of their faces betrayed them.

"Where's my son?" Kim exploded, before either the adoptive mother or her father could speak. "I want to see my son. Where is he?"

The rapidly-changing expressions on their faces went from confusion to surprise to nervousness as Joyce and her father reacted to Kim's outburst.

"He's not ... is he all right?" Joyce tripped through her reply.

"What do you mean, 'is he all right?' "screamed Kim. "Isn't he here?"

The commotion brought Mrs. McDonald to the aid of her family in the living room. Her face was a canvas of confusion as she entered.

Joyce shook her head.

"No," she said sorrowfully, and grabbed hold of her mother's arm. "He's been gone for almost a year,"

There was a collective gasp from the other two women.

Pauline's knees buckled, causing her to fall back against Jerry, who managed to steady her.

Kim's wobbly legs took her toward Detective Anderson who steadied her.

"Gone?" questioned John. "What do you mean gone?"

"My husband left me eleven months ago and took Graham with him."

Kim and Pauline wailed in concert as they reacted to the news.

"No ... No ... No!" Kim sobbed.

Pauline buried her nose in tissues and collapsed into one of the high-backed living room chairs.

"Detective Anderson, who are these people and what do they have to do with my grandson?" Mr. McDonald inquired sternly. "I think we are entitled to an explanation."

Detective Anderson deferred to John McCauley who, with help from Kim and her parents told the adoptive family the whole sad story.

John told them about the car-jacking and how Kim's husband was killed. He related the family's horror when they realized Graham was kidnapped.

Kim's parents tearfully described her life the past three years, her bouts with depression, her desperation, her illnesses, the disappointments. They spoke of her abiding love for Graham and of their daughter's determined efforts to find him.

Kim showed them Graham's photos. She pointed out the tiny star on his right knee to the chagrin of Joyce and her parents, who realized instantly they were, indeed, talking about the same little boy. Kim introduced his birth certificate and the hospital records indicating his blood type.

When she showed them Ben's picture, the three of them identified him immediately as the bogus adoption agent. Kim mentioned her trips to Atlanta and showed them Joseph's drawings of the king, queen and strange wide-barreled gun, which Mr. McDonald identified as Julian's blunderbuss.

He described it as a wide-mouth shot gun used in the seventeenth and eighteenth centuries. It was one of the many collectibles Joyce's husband, Julian, owned.

Kim described how Joseph telepathically located them from Raleigh, but was unable to obtain an exact fix. When Kim described Graham's blue striped pajamas, Joyce listened intently, then rose silently from her chair and left the room. She returned a few moments later, pajamas in hand and presented them to a tearful mother.

When their guests finished their heart-rendering accounts, Joyce and her parents told their own pensive story.

"I had no idea your son was stolen from you," sympathized Joyce.

"He told us, Mr. Unser—uh, I mean Ben Dare—that Graham's parents died in an auto accident," Mr. McDonald interjected.

"My husband and I tried for years to have a child. But I couldn't," Joyce expressed sadly. "We were in our fourth year of waiting for an adoption to come through. We were beginning to believe we were never going to have a child."

"My daughter's a good person," Mrs. McDonald declared proudly. "She would never intentionally do anything to hurt anyone."

"How did you meet Ben Dare, alias Mr. Unser?" John asked plaintively.

Joyce raised her eyebrows and took a deep breath.

"One of our friends told us about a man who ran an interstate adoption agency. We were so naive ... and desperate, we didn't ask the questions we should have, I guess. I'll take responsibility for that. Anyway ..." she stopped herself in mid-sentence to blow her nose, "we called him ... "

"Do you still have the number?" Detective Anderson asked.

"I think so, somewhere. I generally keep things like that."

"Before we leave, do you mind seeing if you can locate it?"

Joyce nodded her head.

"Sure, it will be in one of two places. I'm sure I can come up with it."

"Our daughter is not in trouble, is she?" her father inquired.

Detective Anderson shook his head. "Under the circumstances, I don't believe so," he assured them.

Joyce tightened her lips. "We called him and he said he was an adoption agent in North Carolina. We were so happy, we didn't ask questions."

"It turned out to be your Mr. Dare," Mrs. McDonald chimed in. "He used a fictitious name, according to what we know now," she defended.

"Betsie," Mr. McDonald waved her off. "It's okay, I think they believe us."

Hoping for confirmation, he glanced at Detective Anderson, who nodded his agreement.

"He said you were dead," Joyce tearfully addressed Kim. "He didn't tell us your names. He said it was against their policy to divulge specific family histories." She looked soulfully at Kim and her parents. "We were so desperate for a child that we ... and it was a boy ... Julian wanted a son to carry on the family name ... We took a second mortgage on our house to pay the adoption fee. Mr. Unser, ah, Ben Dare said Graham's surviving relatives weren't the kind of people who should have children."

Joyce closed her eyes.

"I'm sorry, I know how hurt and angry you must feel," she glanced at Kim's parents.

"He even concocted a story about the boy's relatives fighting over a non-existent inheritance," Mr. McDonald added excitedly. "He had us believing they might try to take Graham away from us."

"We were frightened ... and stupid," his wife confessed.

"Long story short, our desperation and emptiness caused us to buy his story hook, line and sinker," Mr. McDonald summarized.

"Then last June, June twelfth ... " Joyce said, struggling to compose herself, "I got home from a shopping trip ... There was a note from Julian ... on the refrigerator. He said he was taking Graham to North Carolina to teach him to be a man."

Kim closed her eyes. She felt leaden. Her nightmare was beginning all over again.

"He told us not to follow him," intoned Mr. McDonald. "Said we'd be sorry if we did."

"He ... he changed when he got involved with a local militia group here," Joyce explained.

"Week-end Rambos, I called them," criticized Mr. McDonald. "Idiots with guns."

"He took Graham with him to those stupid military outings despite my objections. Julian always had a fascination for guns," Joyce confessed. "Well, things got worse."

Both of Joyce's parents stiffened.

"We argued one Sunday morning because he forbid me to take Graham to church. It wasn't the first time we argued about that. But that morning was the worst we ever fought. He said no son of his was going to be called a sissy," she said tearfully. "He accused me of teaching him to be a sissy by going to church."

"We're church-going people," Mrs. McDonald declared. "As long as Graham was with our daughter, he went to church. Every Sunday. The only times he missed were the last couple of weeks before Julian left."

"We'd be in church today if Betsie and Joyce were feeling better," Mr. McDonald confirmed.

All Kim could do was to tighten her lips. She didn't know what to say.

"He was some piece of work, wasn't he?" John spoke for them all, as he frowned his disgust.

Heads bobbed around the room.

"Well, one thing led to another that morning," Joyce continued, "and he ended up slapping me hard to the floor."

"Turns out he broke her jaw," accused Mr. McDonald.

"And Graham saw everything," Joyce added fretfully. "He heard Julian curse me and saw him strike me."

"He would have been jailed if I'd had my way," her father added sourly.

"Dad," Joyce censored him.

"I know. I know, honey. We agreed to drop it. I'm sorry."

"Like an idiot, I forgave him," Joyce confessed. "And things got better for a while. Mainly because I did all of the giving. I gave in to expediency. I allowed him to turn my son against me. I got pretty good at avoiding Julian's fists."

Her father growled, unable to control his anger.

"Then two months later, June twelfth of last year, he left and took my son ... took Graham with him," she corrected herself.

The group sat silently and stared at one another. Suddenly, Mrs. McDonald rose from her chair and flung her arms out in front of her.

"Oh, how inhospitable of me. I haven't offered you anything to eat or drink. Please forgive me."

Her guests reacted almost in unison, politely declining her offer.

"We won't hear of it," dismissed Joyce. "You must have something. Besides, I want to show you some photo albums of Graham before you leave."

She looked at Kim, who was still clutching Graham's pajamas.

"Would you like to see his room?"

§   §   §   §   §   §

Pauline busied herself in the kitchen while Kim walked Pamela through the photo albums Joyce had given her when they were in Atlanta.

The extra suitcases they took with them to Atlanta were sitting on the floor, wedged between Kim's foot and Hope, who was sprawled contentedly next to her.

Joyce had insisted that Kim take any of Graham's belongings she could pack in the suitcase. Although Joyce kept a few items, due to Kim's persistent lobbying, she confessed how guilty she felt keeping any of Graham's things since his real mother was alive. Despite Kim's vigorous objections, Joyce had boxed Graham's toys and mailed them to Raleigh.

"We must have wept in each other's arms for at least an hour," Kim told Pamela. "I was so emotionally drained when we got home, I went to bed at eight and slept most of the next day."

"You still look a little zonked," Pamela informed her.

"And she'd better plan on resting the whole day today," interrupted Pauline, as she placed the coffee tray on the cocktail table.

"Drink," she ordered, narrowing her eyes playfully at Kim. Then she helped herself to one of the cappuccinos and found an uncluttered seat across from the two young women.

"They're really nice people," Kim footnoted. "I hate that they got pulled into this. They've lost a son and grandson, too."

The women sat silently for a moment, each fondling a piece of Graham's clothing.

"What are you going to do now?" Pamela asked as she placed one of her hands over the closed album on her lap.

"I'm going to find him," Kim asserted immediately. Her voice had a determined lift to it. "I'm not going to let him stay with that heathen," she hissed, referring to Joyce's estranged husband.

Pauline smiled. She knew that what her daughter lacked in investigative experience, she compensated for with traits of equal, if not superior value—determination, audacity, and common sense. She also knew Kim benefited from her father's resourcefulness and courage.

"John is flying up next week," Kim reported, "and we're going to devise a plan to bring Graham back."

"They're using our house as a base of operations," Jerry said proudly, taking advantage of his eavesdropping. He gently plucked the cup of cappuccino from his wife's hands and took a few sips.

"Get some of your own, you thief," scolded Pauline good-naturedly.

"Yes, ma'am," teased Jerry as he took another sip and handed her the cup.

"I've e-mailed Joseph Woods. Maybe he'll want to help us again."

Just then the phone rang. Jerry was the first to reach it. "Hello."

"Hello, Mr. Spencer. This is Joyce Fergusen. May I speak with Kim?"

"Yes, of course. Is everything all right?"

"Everything is fine. All things considered," she modified.

"Okay, just a minute and I'll get her."

He handed the phone to Kim, who stood behind him.

"Hi, Joyce," Kim greeted her warmly. "Didn't expect to hear from you so soon."

"I've just thought of something. I don't even know if I can do it. I'm not even sure you will allow it."

"Allow what? What are you trying to say?"

Joyce's sigh came through the phone

"I know you're going to look for Graham."

Kim's eyebrows lowered and she held the phone tighter to her ear.

"And I know my husband better than anyone else ... Well ... I ... I know his habits and his weaknesses ... and what he looks like. He may have changed his appearance when he left and doesn't look like the pictures I gave you."

"Joyce, is this going where I think it's going?"

The caller nodded her head and then realized she wasn't communicating to anyone but herself.

"I want to help you find your son. I have given it a great deal of thought and I think I know where to start."

CHAPTER SIXTEEN

The two women celebrated Graham's ninth birthday by lighting the candles on top of the large white-frosted cupcake they'd bought at a roadside grocery store in Bryson City. Almost two years had passed since Joyce joined Kim in her search to locate Graham.

They timed their breaths so they extinguished the candles simultaneously. Neither of them said a word as Kim pulled the candles, one-by-one off the cupcake. Joyce assumed the honor of peeling back the paper wrap from the cupcake and then halved it, giving the slightly larger piece to Kim.

The women washed the last morsels down with water and then sat silently, hugging each other. Their covenant was strong. They had become sisters through the crucible of shared motherhood. Their grief was the same. Each had lost a husband; each had lost two children.

When Joyce learned of Kim's miscarriage, she told Kim about her own. She became pregnant one year after adopting Graham and lost her unborn child when she was the unwilling recipient of one of Julian's beatings.

Kim collected the candles and cleaned them. Then she placed them in the pocket in her knapsack. She would use them to celebrate Graham's homecoming when they found him. Both women were frugal these days. Their combined financial resources were about to run out.

Joyce headed toward the bathroom. "Got to make a pit stop."

Kim raised an amused eyebrow as Joyce carefully climbed over Hope.

"I'm going to read for a while. Is that okay?"

"Of course, you read every night."

Kim extricated the penlight and book from her duffel bag and settled back under the covers to devour a couple of chapters of Louise's latest novel. It was a suspense thriller and it was number two on the New York Times bestsellers list.

One day I'm going to write one of these, Kim thought to herself, *and it's probably going to be about a mother trying to find her lost son.*

Joyce returned shortly and glanced out the window before she got into her bed. Although there was six inches of snow on the ground, the RV was well-insulated and kept the harsh winds out.

"I think I'll sleep on top of this thing tonight," she announced to her roommate, who was too absorbed in her reading to hear Joyce's comment.

Joyce stretched herself out over the bed covers. Like Kim, she had lost weight and was more muscular. Her beauty was dimmed by the scar above her right eye. Julian had put it there during his last assault on her. She had tied her blonde hair into a short ponytail earlier, but took the band off so her hair could lie naturally over her shoulders.

She was an attractive woman and she wondered what the last twenty-four months of weathering the elements would do to her overall complexion as she aged.

"Kim, can I interrupt your reading for a moment?"

"I think you already have," Kim smiled.

Joyce pretended innocence, but decided to honor her intrusion.

"Do you think he'll recognize me?"

"He, who?"

"Julian."

"Oh."

"I'm serious. I've cut my hair, lost weight. I'm even leaner than I was before we got married. He'll see me in clothes he's never seen me wear before. I mean, look at me ... "

She waited for Kim's undivided attention.

Kim peered at her from over her reading glasses.

"Look at the clothes I'm wearing."

"Sweat pants and a white polar bear T-shirt. Yep, I can see where he might not recognize you."

"He's never seen me in sweat clothes. I was never like that."

"So you think the new 'Rambo-style you' will appeal to him more than the punching bag wife?"

Joyce glared at Kim.

"I can't believe I'm even having these thoughts. I hate him for what he's done. Am I an absolute idiot?"

Kim stared at her thoughtfully.

"No. No, you're not an ... absolute idiot," she bantered. "You haven't seen your husband in almost three years. It's perfectly natural to want to look good, maybe even a little sexy to show him what he's missed."

"Isn't that crazy?"

"No. Well, yes! But it's also caring enough about yourself to show even the most obnoxious jerk that you've improved, that you're a better person, that you've survived his abuse. It's proof you don't need him in order to be a successful woman. To be happy and fulfilled and content and healthy, thank you very much."

The change of tone caused Hope to lift his head. Assured that all was well, he lowered his head again and was intent on going back to sleep.

"That's exactly what I'm thinking. I don't need him to feel successful or fulfilled. When we were married, I felt dependent on him. He made all the important decisions."

Kim gave her a suspicious look.

"You're not thinking of reconciliation, are you?"

Joyce bowed her head.

"Joyce!" Kim raised her voice.

Her roommate winced.

"The thought did cross my mind."

"Oh, for heaven's sake, Joyce. He beat you! He stole Graham. He took a coward's way out."

"I've changed these past three years. Maybe he's changed, too."

"Well, in that case, I can answer your question," Kim asserted, deciding to censor their protracted debate.

"What question?"

"The one about will he recognize you."

"Oh?"

"He'll recognize the scar over your right eye."

Joyce sat there, more numbed than stung by Kim's heavy remark.

Kim discarded her book and sat up to face Joyce, who was fighting back the tears.

"Sometimes you can be a real stinker," Joyce lashed out at Kim through her tears.

"Aw, honey, I'm so sorry I hurt you, but I don't want you to make that kind of mistake," Kim countered, cupping her hands around Joyce's face. "You deserve better and I'm afraid he's probably changed for the worse. Besides, if he doesn't give me my son back, I'm going to kill him and I wouldn't want you to take offense."

Kim smiled as she touched her forehead to Joyce's, then she pulled back enough to stare at her friend.

"I know you're right," Joyce admitted.

"It's not a question of being right," Kim countered. "It's called getting in touch with reality. And the reality is, abusive husbands cannot rehabilitate themselves without help. And I doubt very seriously he's getting any help where he is."

She brushed back Joyce's tears, using her fingertips to wipe the salty deposits off her cheeks.

"I only had Graham the first four years of his life. You had him for another three. So help me God, if that man has turned my son into a heathen ... I am going to kill him," Kim threatened. "And I positively, absolutely am not going to let him hurt you either. I don't want either of us to be under any illusions here. He's not coming back to you. And he's not going to give me back my son without a fight. He's on the run and he's managed to keep himself well-hidden. So he knows what he's doing and I believe he thinks he's gotten away with it."

Kim released Joyce and both women repositioned themselves in their respective beds.

"But I know a couple of things. Because he's human, he'll make mistakes, and since he thinks he's gotten away with it, he won't be as careful. He's living in a world of false security. Someday, he'll slip up and when he does—I'll be there."

"We'll be there," Joyce said quietly, reaching out to squeeze Kim's foot. Then she got up and grabbed a sheet of paper from the breakfast table.

"John's got these photos posted everywhere across North and South Carolina, Tennessee, and Virginia."

She was referring to the photo of Julian and Graham that Joyce had supplied them two years before. John converted the photo into a poster and the three of them had pooled their resources to reproduce thousands of copies. The posters were everywhere: grocery stores, convenience stores, malls and shopping centers, parks and recreational facilities, day cares, schools, and even a few post offices.

"Sooner or later someone's going to see them. They've got to eat and sleep. And they've got to have health care of some sort. And Graham has got to be in some kind of school."

"You're right, Kim. We've got to find them. And let me tell you something else we've got to do. When the two of us get to Karen's tomorrow, we've got to eat a home-cooked meal for a change and take a bubble bath that won't quit."

Their laughter filled every corner of the RV. Hope raised his head and looked at the two women who had disturbed his sleep. He extended his gaze this time to show his disdain before he plopped his head back down on the bedding.

"Oh, look Kim, we're interfering with Hope's beauty rest."

"That's what you get for sleeping with two women, old boy," Kim countered, laughing at her restless pet. Then she addressed Joyce again. "You were saying?"

"I'm going to buy a bottle of bubble bath and pour all of it in the tub with me. I'll probably soak for a hour."

"And after my hour-long bath, I'm going to curl up on the couch and read every book Karen has in the house," cooed Kim.

"Sounds wonderful," cheered Joyce. "You got me hooked on those two New Thought ministers from Durham," she confessed, "and Karen has bookcases of metaphysical literature."

Kim looked up reflectively.

"Yes. She has a goldmine of really good New Thought books."

Then Kim looked around their current quarters.

"Sleeping in different rooms to get some sleep," Kim teased, voicing her own requirements for creature comforts. "Particularly since you snore."

"I don't snore!"

"Joyce, you do so."

"Well, maybe a little ... "

"Ho! Ho! More than a little. You keep me up a lot of nights with your snoring."

"Well, how 'bout you?"

"Me?"

"You stink up the tent with your nail polish."

Kim looked at her fingernails and then flicked them at her.

"I aerate the RV every time I do my nails. And I always do them early in the evening."

"But it still smells up the RV."

"I can't believe we're talking about this. We've got to get some sleep. We need to get an early start tomorrow."

"I know, I was only relieving some tension," Joyce confessed.

"I'll call Karen on our cell phone before we leave tomorrow," Kim informed her. "That way, she'll know when to have the bath water ready."

Joyce threw her a devilish smile just before she purposefully let out a counterfeit snore.

"Joyce!"

"Just kidding ... "

§   §   §   §   §   §

Kim gorged herself on mashed potatoes and meat loaf, but decided to tackle the apple pie later. She watched from her vantage point on the sofa as Karen showed Joyce her latest sculpture, a clay model of Hans, her German Shepherd.

Getting the kudos she expected from Joyce, Karen enthusiastically produced several of her oil paintings. They were exquisite renderings of the Asheville area and included a beautiful summertime rendition of the world-famous Biltmore Estate.

All of her oils, water colors, and sculptures sold well. So well, in fact, that Karen enjoyed the luxury of a sustained two-year waiting list for her work. Although she used to teach piano and voice to aspiring students, her music was less of an escape for her now.

Kim admired Karen. To the uninitiated, Karen seemed vulnerable, possessing only an ordinary means of livelihood by producing oil paintings and water colors for the general public or an occasional commissioned bronze sculpture to ease her financial woes. But those who knew her knew how solid her spiritual—and financial—footing was. *Karen has simple tastes,* Kim thought to herself, *and is very philanthropic.*

Karen's spirituality continued to ground Kim, who was struggling spiritually ever since she lost her family. She used to believe in a male God in the sky, but now she was plagued by questions like: *What did I do to deserve this? Why did this happen to me? I thought prayers protected me, so how could God allow this to happen to me? If what happened to me was part of God's plan for me, what kind of God is that?*

She smiled admiringly as Karen threw her a thumbs-up sign in response to Joyce's appraisal of one of her paintings. Joyce was genuinely interested in Karen's artistry and the fun the two women were having had a soothing effect on Kim.

Kim's thoughts settled on Karen again. Her five foot four inches in height had a firm foundation ... slightly overweight, but far from being obese. Her small round face, covered with a light dusting of girlish freckles, kept her womanliness concealed, taking off the years instead of adding them. There was something slightly pioneer-like about her, almost colonial, most probably due to the lingering influence of growing up in Asheville.

Joyce's jubilant tone jolted Kim out of her reverie. The two women were headed toward her and Karen was carrying a framed canvas. Its canvas back was toward Kim, but she could tell it was a completed work.

"I've talked her into giving it to you now," boasted Joyce. She was referring to Karen's promise to unveil a special painting for Kim later that evening, celebrating Graham's birthday.

"I realize it's not the kind of gift you give someone who's on the road," Karen apologized. "I mean, it's not like you have plenty of wall space to hang it on right now."

"It's the perfect gift," Joyce squealed, fidgeting as she stood next to Karen.

Kim straightened herself and eased both her legs over the edge of the sofa cushions so her feet touched the floor.

"Are you sure?" Karen faltered.

"Karen!" Joyce coaxed, rolling her eyes. "Show it to her."

Karen turned the painting around so Kim could see it.

Joyce bit her lip and started to snivel immediately, reacting to Kim's sudden outburst of tears.

Karen added her own as the three mixed tears of joy with tears of sorrow.

"Oh, Karen, it's beautiful!" Kim praised, dividing her sobs with bits of nervous laughter to regain her composure.

Kim gently took the painting from Karen and held it approvingly on her lap.

"Do you really like it?" Karen asked rhetorically.

Kim huffed elatedly. "It's one of the most beautiful things that's happened to me in five years. I love it!"

Kim ran her fingers over its lacquered surface, stopping first on Grahams face and then meandering softly over to Hope's head and ears.

"You've got them standing in front of a lighted Christmas tree outdoors," Kim exclaimed. "The snow is beautiful and the sky is so blue."

She lowered her trembling fingers to touch Graham's face again. Then her eyes found the black spot of hair on Hope's right hind leg.

"Oh, Karen, it's absolutely ... it's so ... I will cherish it forever."

"I'm glad you like it."

Joyce handed Kim a tissue.

"You're dripping on the painting," Joyce warned good-naturedly. "You might melt the snow."

Kim's laugh was echoed by the smiles of the other two women.

"Looks like that's the excitement for this evening," chimed Joyce as she smacked her hands together.

The mild pop alerted both the dogs who arched their necks nonchalantly over their shoulders to investigate the sharp sound.

"I'm sorry, fellas," Joyce apologized, laughing at the pets' identical reactions. "Didn't mean to interrupt your siestas."

Her comment brought a second look from Hope who settled again. The dogs were lying on their sides back-to-back on the wide stone hearth. There was a reciprocity, a somethingness between them that sealed their kinship. Karen referred to it as their Kim-ship. No doubt the dogs felt that connectedness.

"They are certainly expressions of nowness, aren't they?" Karen observed.

"They've definitely chilled-out" Joyce agreed.

When the two women turned to face Kim, they realized she was still totally immersed in the painting.

"Think we can pull her away from it?" mused Joyce.

"Let's not even try."

"How 'bout a slice of your apple pie?"

"Sounds good to me."

"Think we should leave her any?" Joyce teased, as she tilted her head slightly toward Kim.

"She'll have to take her chances."

Although they brushed unnoticed past Kim on the impromptu dessert run, their movement toward the kitchen was not undetected by the pair of dozing canines.

Sensing an opportunity for an unscheduled snack, the pooches ambushed the two women and stood beggar-like at their respective dishes waiting for handouts they suspected would come.

"They've got this down to a science," declared Karen.

Joyce followed her nod with a snicker.

"Professionals. No doubt about it."

Hope barked his impatience while Hans growled his support.

"Can't put anything past these two."

"We can give them Kim's piece," joked Joyce.

"Oh, no you don't," warned Kim, hearing her name mentioned. She entered the kitchen and pointed an accusing finger at the co-conspirators. "Sic 'em, boys," she signaled to the dogs. "They're trying to steal my dessert."

Both dogs wagged their tails, almost on cue, enjoying the excitement.

"Karen," Kim said as she walked up to her hostess. "Thank you. I shall treasure the painting the rest of my life." She hugged Karen tightly, extending her embrace for several moments.

While the three women fussed over facial tissues, the dogs publicized their growing appetites.

CHAPTER SEVENTEEN

Good morning, John Boy. What are you doing up so early? It's only seven-twenty," Karen said, yawning. "I haven't even had my second cup of coffee yet."

"Well, then, you'd better get with it. The day's a-wastin'," he teased as he pulled the phone closer to his ear.

"John McCauley, you sound mighty chipper this morning."

"I've found a couple more spots," he asserted, referring to the drawings Joseph Woods provided two years earlier of structures built into the side of a rock crevice or cliff. When Linda Amos had located him in England, he used his remote viewing ability from across the Atlantic, mentally locating Graham again.

"I thought you'd about covered them all."

"You'd think so, wouldn't you?" He checked his ledger. "Let's see, in five years seven months and six days, we've investigated three hundred seventeen sites across a four-state area. We've traveled through the most rugged, unforgiving mountainous terrain I've ever had the displeasure of trekking through in my sixty-six years of living on this planet. I've seen more bad weather, ticks, and snow than a lost grizzly. And it looks like I'm about out of another transmission on my truck."

"Oh, no, John. You poor thing."

"It's these cotton-pickin' mountains. They're hard on cars and tires and old fools."

Karen laughed as she steadied the coffee cup she held in her hand.

"Are the others up yet?"

"Kim is. Joyce's still asleep."

"Put Kim on the phone, please. I want to divvy up the new locations so we can get crackin' again."

"She's in the sun room polishing her nails. I'll take the cell phone to her. If you hear static over the phone, it's because I'm carrying it with me."

"I thought she cut those fingernails a year ago so she wouldn't have to mess with them."

"She did. They're normal length now," Karen reported, looking at her own. "Well, they're longer than my stubs, but she's keeping them glossy with clear polish."

"Hum ... m. Crusades like this sure change your living habits, don't they?"

"And your perspective on life. You sure find out what's important. Okay, John, here she is."

"Good morning, general. Any luck in Bristol?"

"A little bit of this, a little bit of that. I met an old retired Boy Scout master at Golden Corral last night. One thing led to another and by the time we got to dessert, I knew everything about him. And he knew everything about me. I told him about our search for Graham."

Kim put the phone on speaker, as she lip-synced a thank you to Karen, who handed her a fresh cup of coffee.

"Kim, honey, if I live to be a hundred, I'll always be amazed at how God works. It's like, if you try hard and your heart's in the right place, God will suddenly clear a log jam or give you insight or send someone to help you."

"And the God of my understanding says it's the Eternal Presence expressing as us that guarantees the timeless connection." Kim clarified. "You were talking about your discussion with an old Scout Master," Kim said dismissively, not wanting to give his Higher Power credit for taking so long for something that an omnipresent God should have taken care of years ago. She missed Graham, and her emptiness was still too constant of a companion to feel close to an absent God she believed had abandoned her.

"Yes. Well, the Scout Master invited me to stay at his house last night. I met his wife. She's a petite little thing. Reminded me of you. Ah ... yes ... what was I going to say ... Oh! I showed him our ledger of locations and explained what they all had in common. You know, the house or cabin built into the side of a hill."

Kim sipped her coffee, waiting patiently for him to get to the point.

"Well, as it turns out he helped the Boy Scouts of America catalogue trails and campsites throughout the Southeast. He's also mapped areas for the U. S. Geological Survey and the Forestry Service. Long story short, I've got four more locations for us to check out."

Kim sighed heavily, lifting her eyebrows in resignation.

"I suppose that's good news. I don't know whether to be elated or disappointed. We've been to over three hundred locations so far ... "

"Three hundred seventeen, to be exact," John inserted with a snicker, "but then, who's counting?"

"Okay, three hundred and seventeen, with how many more on the ledger?"

"Let's see, including the four new ones ... eleven. Eleven more. Of course, that's as of today."

"Sometimes I wonder if we're not fooling ourselves."

"What do you mean?"

"Maybe we've misinterpreted Joseph's drawings."

"Now, honey, don't go doubting your own instincts or his remote sensing ... ah ... remote viewing ability. Remember the accuracy of his Atlanta drawings."

Kim nodded her head wearily.

"Remember?"

"Yes."

"We've got to keep the faith," John encouraged. "Replace hope with faith ... And no, I don't mean your dog, Hope. I mean the kind of hope that wants something to happen. Hope is based on wishcraft and uncertainty. It's hoping something happens. "

"I know."

"Faith is knowing that what you want or need will happen at some point, when the timing is right. It's not a question of if, but when."

"I know," she repeated herself. "It's just that I hoped I would find him sooner than later and it's already later— much later than I imagined."

"Aw, honey. All I can say is hope is based on impatience and faith has patience as its ally. The first will get you ulcers. The latter keeps you centered and in control. That's what Louise told me when she tried to get her first novel agented, and then to get a publisher interested. Someone once said that the moment of absolute certainty never arrives. So ... we've just got to keep the faith. And that's my sermon for the day!"

Despite her slight irritation at the soundness of his wisdom, Kim smiled her appreciation.

"Now I know why you called this morning. You knew I needed a 'faith-lift.'"

John laughed appreciatively, but kept his collateral thoughts to himself. He knew Graham's birthday had been the day before and she was unable to celebrate yet another birthday with her son.

"Maybe we'll all get a lift when we find Graham at one of the remaining spots."

"That would be wonderful," cheered Kim as she saw Joyce sleepwalk into the sunroom. Kim lip-synched John's name for Joyce, who smiled in recognition.

"Oh, John, Joyce says hi."

"Give her a kiss and hug for me."

"I will," Kim promised, then remembering the phone was on speaker, continued, "She can actually hear you! Speaker phone is on! You know ... my nails..."

Joyce toasted John in absentia with her steaming cup of coffee. "Greetings!" she exclaimed, as she stepped safely over Hope, who was sprawled near the outside screen.

"Hi, Joyce! Either of you got a pad and pencil handy?" inquired John. "I'd like to give you these new locations."

"Sure. Just a minute."

Kim found the writing instruments on the wicker stand nearby. She checked to acknowledge her fingernails were dry, then placed the pad on her lap. She flipped the first two sheets over, which contained sketches of Karen's next art project.

"Okay, I'm ready."

"Location number one is one I'll check. It's Mountain City, Tennessee. I've got to drive right by it on my way back from Bristol. It's near Iron Mountain and Watauga Lake."

"Too bad you can't stop to fish."

John chuckled as he tugged at the bill on his favorite fishing cap.

"There will be plenty of time for that. I'll show that boy of yours where all of the best fishing holes are in North Carolina, Virginia, and Tennessee."

"Wouldn't that be wonderful? I hope you'll be able ... I know you two will get a chance to do just that."

"That's my girl. Now there's a location not far from where you are in Asheville. It's near Blowing Rock, tucked in the mountains near Hounds Ears and the Appalachian Ski Resorts. Grandfather Mountain is just a few miles away. I'll fax you a sectional map before you leave Karen's.

"I'll go with you to the next two locations before we split up again. One's near Piney Creek off of Route 93 near the state line and the fourth's called Low Gap. It's near Cumberland Knob just outside of Mount Airy. You got all of that?"

"Yep."

"I'll meet you at the entrance to the New River State Park on Wednesday morning. We'll have breakfast at Chick's Diner a couple of miles from the park's entrance, say around eight o'clock? Of course that's contingent on what we find before then."

"Eight o'clock is fine."

"We'll stay in cell phone contact, as always. Isn't modern technology wonderful? Cordless communication has certainly made our search easier."

Kim nodded. "Hurrah for wireless. You take care of yourself."

"You, too. Oh, remember ... when you find them, call the local sheriff and wait for me. Remember?"

"I remember. The same goes for you."

"I'm a team player," he teased. "Now remember, honey and I'm saying this for my benefit as well as yours and Joyce's. We all must stick to the rules we've made. It's been a long haul and we're all tired of bed bugs and mosquitoes, but we've got to stick to the rules of engagement, so to speak. People tend to make fatigue mistakes when they're tired. We don't know what we're going to run into when we find them. You've seen the horrible conditions of some of the places we've found up until now."

"Yeah, well, the RV has a lot to be desired, too."

John laughed heartily.

"My camper's not much better. Well, I've got to go. I'll check out the one here before I leave Bristol. I'll fax you the map of Blowing Rock in about a half hour or so. Oh, ah ... put Karen back on the phone, would you?"

"Sure. Take care."

"I always do."

Kim motioned to Karen who stepped into the sun room. She was carrying a plate of buttered toast.

"Hi again," Karen renewed her greeting.

"Would you do an old mountain man a favor?"

"John McCauley, do you need to spend a few nights back in civilization?"

"That's not what I meant," he protested, laughing good-naturedly.

"Oh, well, anyway ... you know you're welcome to stay here any time. So, what's the favor?"

"I could sure use some of your world famous, award-winning, zero-calorie, chocolate chip fudge brownies. Is that possible?"

"Still haven't found better brownies anywhere, huh?"

"Haven't even tried. Your brownies are peerless ... and so are you."

"Okay, okay. Flattery will get you everywhere!"

"Good. Then you'll satisfy an old man's sweet tooth?"

"Can't promise you zero-calories."

"Just promise me a dozen brownies."

"A baker's dozen, all right? I'll send them with Kim and Joyce."

"I'll save that extra piece for Graham."

§   §   §   §   §   §

Their breakfast at Chick's Diner was filled with laughter. John and Joyce got tickled at something he said and couldn't keep a straight face. It was the comedic relief they all needed to ease their combined disappointment at having to write-off two more locations.

The trio finished breakfast in less than an hour and Joyce decided to relieve Kim of her driving duties for the short trip up the mountain.

As they followed John's camper up Route 93 toward Piney Creek, Kim was glad it was Joyce's turn to drive. The steep forested road had a few guard rails and she was better at keeping the RV away from the graveled sides of the road.

Far ahead on the blacktop, the sun made reflective pools of tar into mirages which glistened and vanished, then glistened and vanished again as the car approached. The sun's warmth cast a golden glow on the houses tucked along the tree-lined highway. The shadows of the larger trees denied the sun's rays and lay like long black feathers across the pot-holed macadam.

The sky, no longer a dull gray, leaked a brilliant pastel blue, much like the sky of the oil painting Karen gave her.

The sprawling summits poked their rich tree lines high into the sky. Fissures, twisted spires, and serrated overhangs of miles of quartzite and granite cliffs stood as powerful testimonies to the geologic experience of the ancient mountain terrain.

The ridge lines are as corrugated as washboards, she reveled to herself. "Why, you can scrub your soul clean with the very sight of them," she whispered.

"What?" Joyce asked, unable to hear Kim clearly, "Did you say scrub something clean?"

"It was nothing," Kim dismissed. "I was only talking to myself."

"Oh, well, you know what they say. People who talk to themselves know a good conversationalist when they find one."

"Look at that!" Kim exclaimed, ignoring her companion's comment.

Joyce glanced quickly out the passenger's side window. Her eyes found the lake Kim was admiring. The trees lining the edge of the lake bank looked like irregular eyelashes, and the lake water was so still it looked like a gigantic flat sheet of metal.

"Beautiful," Joyce commented, mostly to appease Kim, who was totally absorbed in the metallic oasis.

Joyce jolted Kim out of her reverie when she pulled over to the side of the road.

"John's stopping," Joyce explained, realizing Kim was playing catch-up.

They watched as he waited for a car to pass before opening his pick-up truck door. He checked the moderately-busy road again before he walked back to the two women.

"I think the dirt road we want is back there a piece. If it's the one I think it is, it's about a quarter of a mile back. Sorry, I drove right past it."

"That's okay," Joyce consoled, throwing him an empathetic smile. "We do that a lot."

John smiled.

"It's not hard to do on these mountain roads. Be careful turning around. I'll see if I can find it this time."

"Oh, look," Kim raised her voice and pointed across the road behind John. "Two deer."

John wheeled around, stepping out of the women's line of sight. They watched a pair of white-tailed deer, a doe and a fawn, expertly navigate the road and disappear into the woods not fifty feet from their parked vehicles.

"A mother and her fawn stand for gentleness and innocence," exclaimed Kim, remembering her sessions with Linda when they discussed the spiritual significance of animals. "They're reminding us to establish a strong healthy connection with children before we send them out into the harsh world."

"Or re-establish a connection," added Joyce. "Maybe it's a sign. Maybe ... "

"Now don't you two start that. Maybe we'll find him today. Maybe we won't. Let's not get off-track."

The women knew he was right.

John slapped his hand gently on the top of the car, signaling his departure.

"Let me turn around first. Make sure the coast is clear before you follow."

Before he got to the rear of his pick-up, he stopped. Then he walked up to the left rear tire of his camper and kicked it.

The women could see him mumble something, but couldn't decipher it. His actions spoke louder than words when he kicked the tire a second time.

He pivoted toward them, throwing them a sour look.

"The tire's losing air," he yelled. "What do those deer have to say about their connection with trucks?"

Both Kim and Joyce exited the car and serendipitously used the extended stop to let Hope frolic in the woodlands.

By the time John finished his own road service, the liquid blue sky was punctured with spots of thick ashen clouds.

"Rain clouds coming in," John guessed. "A couple of hours, maybe three before we get wet."

"Let's hope it holds off a while," Joyce added. "The paper called for thunderstorms tonight."

"Good thing we repaired that hole in our roof," Kim reminded her.

Joyce winced her agreement.

John wiped his hands on a soiled rag he kept for those purposes and signaled his readiness to resume the trip.

By the time both vehicles headed in the same direction, it started to sprinkle.

"So much for a couple of hours," Joyce observed. "It's already started raining."

Kim raised her eyebrows, confirming Joyce's observations as she diverted her attention to the side of the road. She spied a beautiful cluster of gnarled rhododendrons cradled among the trees that lined the road. As long-time residents of the western part of the state, their flamboyant dignity was extraordinarily at peace in the cool drizzle.

When Joyce turned to follow John up the dirt road, she closed both of the windows in time to keep the dust from infiltrating the car.

Kim peered straight ahead. Each turn was a magnet for her attention as she anticipated a hopeful rendezvous with her son.

I don't know how many more of these dead ends I can take, she thought sadly to herself.

"Joyce, I should be excited. I know it's possible he could be here. This could be the one. But we've been on too many of these for me to get my hopes up, you know?"

"I know. I feel the same way. I'm sorry that my husband went off the deep end. If we'd had a normal divorce under normal circumstances, you'd already have your son back."

"It's not your fault. You can't take responsibility for your husband's insanity."

The women grew quiet as the rain pelted the windshield.

The surprise shower stopped almost as soon as it began, and the sunlight pushed weakly through the cloud cover, bathing everything in muted brightness. It had drizzled enough to soften the road dust so the women could see John's dust-speckled pickup.

They slowed their advance, staying two car lengths behind as he turned jerkily down a stretch of narrow road. Then John pulled off to the side of the road, allowing the women enough room to pull in slightly behind and to the left of his truck when he stopped.

They watched him consult his map and tilt his head first toward the map, then toward the empty road ahead. The women smiled when he tossed the map aside and pulled slowly ahead, taking care not to spin stones at them.

"How many times have we done that?" Joyce asked, amused at his confusion over which way to go.

"More times that I'd like to say. At least it's nice to know we're in good company."

John pulled back out onto the road, drove a short distance, then turned down another, more narrow road and headed slowly toward its graveled summit.

The women followed him more closely this time as the two-car convoy inched past the summit. They could see traces of a white log cabin through the thicket of trees leading to the clearing.

Kim's heart raced, as was its custom, every time they got this close to Graham's possible whereabouts. She swallowed nervously as more of the clearing revealed itself.

It was a small cabin siamesed against a rock face. Wooden steps led to the porch, which stretched the length of the front of the home. The cabin was cradled in a cul-de-sac of rhododendrons and pine. Its off-centered symmetry was a hodgepodge of make-shift lines, producing a disproportionate sense of homespun beauty and grace.

Whiffs of smoke danced out of the stone chimney and disappeared into the ashen clouds, which looked low enough and mean enough to dump liquid bullets any moment.

The fissures and crevices which scarred the rock face gave it the appearance of graffiti-etched walls.

A tangerine-colored pick-up truck was parked out front. The old truck looked weathered, but capable, and was burdened with a fishing boat tied with bungee cords to the truck bed. A large dog stood in the middle of the boat, barking at them.

A young boy about Graham's age ran around the side of the house. When she saw him, Kim almost leaped out of the moving car. He was dressed in blue jeans and a flannel shirt. His long blonde hair was partially covered by a red ball cap.

"Joyce, it's him! I know it's him! Oh, my God. It's got to be him," Kim screamed.

Kim glanced warily at Joyce, whose eyes narrowed as she studied the youngster.

John pulled his pick-up beside the tangerine heap and the women followed suit. Before Joyce brought the RV to a complete stop, she leaned her head out the window.

"Graham," she shouted. "It's me—mom."

Kim's heart leaped to her throat. She tried to talk but could only gag out something resembling a garbled facsimile of his name. Kim flew out of the RV and headed toward the stunned youngster.

"Graham, baby. Do you remember me? It's mommy."

Joyce tethered Hope to the steering wheel and leapt out of the RV.

"Graham, honey, we're coming to take you home," Joyce shouted again.

"Mother!" Graham shouted, recognizing Joyce immediately. Then his eyes shifted to the other woman, who wept as she shouted his name. He reestablished eye contact with Joyce, who trailed Kim by several yards.

Just as Kim got along side of his truck, John grabbed her, preventing her from taking another step toward Graham.

Suddenly a shotgun blast filled the morning air.

Whoom!

John had seen it coming. Out of the corner of his eye, he'd noticed a man dressed in a soiled T-shirt, patched blue jeans and suspenders, step out onto the front porch. When he saw the shotgun in the man's hands, he decided immediately to abbreviate Kim's trespass.

Joyce stopped in her own tracks, wide-eyed and horror-stricken, when the gun belched its shot.

Graham flinched but remained where he stood, dumbfounded at the violent reception.

The dogs were trading nervous yelps and seemed content to watch the humans make the next move.

"Graham, come up here, boy," the man ordered gruffly as he moved to the top of the porch steps.

"Julian, what are you doing?" screamed Joyce. "Don't you know who I am?"

He glared at her but didn't say a word.

"Dad. It's mom," clarified Graham.

"I know who it is, boy," growled Julian. "Rex, shut the hell up," he spewed, sending his irritation to the dog in the bed of the pick-up truck.

Kim stood with her hands over her mouth, staring at Graham, who divided his confused look between his father and the unarmed visitors.

"What are you doing here?" Julian asked in a voice roughened with resentment.

Joyce looked at Kim and then at John, who gave her a go-ahead nod, hoping Julian wasn't planning on getting too ecumenical with his buckshot. His own handgun, a Browning 9mm, was locked in the glove compartment of his truck.

"Julian, a lot has happened since you left," Joyce said cautiously, as she took a few tentative steps toward the front porch.

"Stay where you are! Don't come any closer," he warned, brandishing the shotgun.

"Julian, what are you doing? Put that thing down."

"You take one more step and I'll blow your meddling head off. You hear me?"

Joyce stopped and glanced fearfully at John, who motioned for her to retreat a few steps.

Kim had not taken her eyes off Graham and was inching away from John.

"Kim, no" he whispered. "This thing could go crazy at any moment. Don't move."

"He's my son, John! It's him! I'm not going back without him."

Graham tossed a confused look at Julian, who was growing more agitated every minute.

"What's she talkin' about? Who is she?" Julian yelled, pointing the shotgun at Kim.

"These people are here to talk to you," Joyce began. Conscious of the growing alarm rising in her throat, she decided to take a deep breath. "You've got to listen to them. That woman over there is Graham's real mother."

"What?" snapped Julian.

A stupefied look leapt onto Graham's face, flinging his mouth open. Kim thought there was a slight hint of recognition in his eyes as he studied her. She almost broke away from John's grasp, but he was able to hold her.

"Graham, honey, it's me." Kim identified herself, forcing her voice to stay calm and firm. "Don't you remember me? I'm your mother."

"What are you trying to pull?" Julian bellowed at Joyce. "Get these people off my property."

"Julian, you've got to listen to them. Whatever you think of me doesn't matter. You've got to ... "

"Get outta here!" he shouted. "All of you. Get the hell off my property."

"He's my son," Kim raised her voice. "I'm going to take him back home with me. You stole him. I've got proof in the car, if you'll just ... "

"You're not taking him anywhere!" Julian threatened. "You three better get the hell off my property," he bellowed, repeating his order.

"Mr. Fergusen," John interceded, "My name is John McCauley and I'm a private investigator. I ... "

"I don't give a shit who you are. You're trespassing and that gives me the right to shoot you if I have to. So I advise you to get outta here while you can still walk."

"Julian," screamed Joyce, "have you gone ... "

Whoom!

He fired into the air. Then he reloaded the chambers and pointed the business end of the shotgun directly at Joyce.

"If you aren't outta here in thirty seconds, I'm going to shoot you for trespassing. Now, that's your final warning. Move your asses outta here."

John ushered Kim into his truck while Joyce ran back to the RV.

"Graham, I love you," Kim yelled, poking her head out of the pick-up truck's window. "I'll be back. So help me God, I'll be back."

Tears flowed as she collapsed against the door.

"I'll be back," she yelled defiantly.

Julian kept his promise.

Whoom!

CHAPTER EIGHTEEN

There he is now," John announced as the three of them watched the sheriff pull steadily toward them up the gravel road. A second cruiser, trailing in a cloud of dust, was barely visible except for its canopy of flashing lights.

Kim tightened her grip on Hope's leash as she glanced at the clouds, which looked threatening again. The sky was being capricious, dividing itself between sunshine and islands of clouds. Hope's attention was on the approaching police cruisers.

Just what we need. More rain. Mother Nature must be as angry as I am over this, Kim thought.

She dropped her gaze and focused on the sheriff, who waddled out of his cruiser toward them. He was a dumpling of a man, as horizontal as he was tall. The uniform, which covered the considerable amount of flesh that migrated to his waistline, looked like mud sliding downhill. Except for the close-cropped hair over his ears and around the back, his head was completely bald.

His two deputies were both young, thin, and of average height. They filed in behind him dutifully as the sheriff approached the trio of out-of-towners.

"Thanks for coming so quickly, sheriff," John greeted, extending his hand.

The sheriff threw him a hurried look and then trained his large eyes on the two women as he gave John a perfunctory hand shake.

"You the one who called?"

John nodded.

"I'm John McCauley and this is Mrs. Sanborn and Mrs. Fergusen. We're all glad you're here."

The sheriff chewed on his tobacco briefly before he spit the words out.

"Pleased to meet you. I'm Sheriff Coleman. This is Roy and that's Howard."

The deputies tipped their hats, but remained silent.

The sheriff turned his head to one side and spit out a stream of tobacco. Then he wiped the residue of dark brown spittle off his stained lips with the back of his hand.

Kim's wince did not go unnoticed. The sheriff saw her disapproval out of the corner of his eye before he made eye contact with John again.

"Suppose you tell me what happened here this morning," the sheriff insisted politely. He glanced over John's shoulder at the pick-up truck, which John had parked catty-cornered across the road some thirty yards ahead of them to block the road in case Julian decided to take flight.

"And you can start by telling me why that pick-up's parked like that."

With intermittent help from the women, John recounted the whole story. Kim showed him photos and relevant documents, including newspaper clippings, posters, and Graham's early pictures on milk cartons. Joyce spoke of her marital woes with Julian, the illegal adoption, and of his kidnapping Graham. John summarized the confrontation with Joyce's husband and reiterated his role as a friend to both of the women and as a retired police officer turned private investigator.

"You say he shot at you?" the sheriff reconfirmed.

The women nodded their heads.

"He fired in our direction," John clarified. "No one was hurt. I'm not certain, but I think he just fired into the air."

"He probably just wanted to scare you," Roy hypothesized.

"Well, he succeeded," Kim corroborated. "We got out of there as fast as we could."

"You did the right thing by calling us," Sheriff Coleman praised as he spat on the road. "No use anybody getting hurt over this."

"Should I get the FBI up here?" asked Howard, who seemed to be the more senior of the two deputies.

"No. Hold off on that for now," cautioned the sheriff. "I want to see what we can do before we call the suits."

The sheriff and John exchanged collusive winks.

"I like to keep things simple. And the more people that get involved in this thing, the more likely it is that we'll make a mountain out of a mole hill. We don't need 'em yet, so let's keep the government out of it."

Kim had studied the sheriff ever since his arrival. She was turned-off by his extremely rotund figure, his ghastly tobacco-chewing habit, and the uncultured gruffness of his voice. But his uncommon sense and decisiveness changed her initial low opinion of him.

"Mr. McCauley, would you be so kind as to move your vehicle? I'd like to mosey on up there and have a talk with Mr. Fergusen. Roy, I'd like you to go with me. The rest of you stay here. Maybe we can get this thing all settled peaceful-like."

"I'm not leaving here without my son," challenged Kim. She took a few assertive steps toward the sheriff. "I've spent the last five years of my life trying to find him and I'm not about to go home without him."

The sheriff lowered his head and thought for a moment. Then he steadied his gaze on her and tightened his beefy lips before he spoke.

"Mrs. Sanborn, I'm well aware of your predicament ... and your anger. I don't intend leaving here without the boy.

But I don't want anyone to get hurt either. Now, I'm going to do my level best to get your boy back. But I'm going to do it my way. You got that?"

He spat again to give himself time for her rebuttal. He used his forefinger to swipe the dark juice from his mouth.

Kim hesitated to show her defiance before she nodded.

"Now I don't know much about Mr. Fergusen. Only what you three have told me. Since there were shots fired, I'm going to assume he's got a chip on his shoulder. Much like you, Mrs. Sanborn. Now don't take offense. But that's why you're staying here. You're upset. You're argumentative. You're impatient. And you're ... "

"A woman," Kim interrupted. "Isn't that what you were going to say?"

The sheriff smiled through tobacco-stained teeth and looked directly at her.

"You're tired. I was gonna say you're tired, and tired people make mistakes."

He quickly looked at the other two and then back at Kim.

Kim stiffened when he reestablished eye contact with her.

"I believe your story, young lady. Hell, you've got enough documentation and tears to fill a courtroom. I've got a ten-year-old boy myself. These two deputies know how much I love him. So, yes ma'am. I know exactly how you feel. I wouldn't want to leave without my son either."

The sheriff stooped to rub Hope's ears and then squatted in front of the dog. Hope allowed the sheriff to pet him and seemed to enjoy the officer's gentle roughness.

"I've got one of these, too. She's a smorgasbord. You know, a little bit of this and a little bit of that. She's older than this pup though. How old is he, seven? Eight?"

"I think so. He was a year or so old when I adopted him," Kim explained.

He stood facing Kim again.

"I might be an overweight, tobacco-chewing, smelly old country sheriff from Piney Creek, Mrs. Sanborn. But I'm a God-fearin' man. And I put family at the top of my list of values. It's up there alongside of freedom and the Ten Commandments. So I know right from wrong. And it was wrong for anyone to take your boy. And you'd be wrong if you didn't let me handle this by the book."

He broke his eye contact with Kim and caught Roy's attention.

"Roy, get on the horn and call Melvin Dyson and Jake Roskind. They're probably over at Chick's Diner by now. See if they know anything about Mr. Julian Fergusen, assuming he's using his real name. Find out how long he's been here. Where his boy... where he has Mrs. Sanborn's son in school. If he works anywhere, where he banks. I'd like to know that, too. Ask Ansel what kind of supplies Mr. Fergusen purchased recently. We know he's got a shot gun. I'd be interested to know if he's carrying anything else up there."

He looked directly at Kim. This time he tongued his tobacco instead of spitting.

"I'm going to see if I can reason with him if he'll let me. I'm generally pretty good at such things. I fully expect to leave there with your boy. I think Mr. Fergusen's just a little surprised and upset. If he's as honest and God fearing as the rest of the folks I'm sworn to protect around here, I 'spect he'll see the error of his ways and let the boy go."

"I hope so," Kim whispered.

"I'm not so sure," Joyce inserted worriedly. "Sheriff Coleman, you be especially careful. The Julian I met this morning is not the same Julian who left me three years ago. There's a veneer of coldness and hatred around him. I could feel it. He's angry at me. And he's angry at the world. I think he took Graham so he can live his life over again through Graham."

"What do you mean?" Kim asked sharply.

"Before he left, he spouted anti-government hate talk. Things like: 'if I had it to do all over again, I'd defend the real Constitution.' Or, 'if I were younger and knew what I know now, I wouldn't pay any taxes.' He irritated me then, but he scares me now."

"So he's probably been indoctrinating Graham with that kind of anti-government propaganda all these years," Kim exclaimed.

"I'm so sorry," Joyce apologized, forcing herself to look at Kim.

"We can't do anything about it now. Besides, it's not your fault. I just hope it's not irreversible," Kim replied.

The sheriff started to say something, but thought better of it.

"I'll pull my truck out of the way," John volunteered, knowing his comment would get everyone moving again.

The sheriff nodded.

"Look," Kim shouted, pointing past John, who stopped in his own tracks.

All eyes were on the road ahead as the tangerine-colored pick-up came to a sliding stop fifty or so feet from John's truck.

By the time the dust cleared, Julian was backing his truck as fast as he could up the rocky incline. Graham was in the passenger's seat, and although he looked confused, did not appear to want to exit the truck.

"Calm down everybody," shouted the sheriff, "he can't get past us. Even he knows that."

He looked at John again.

"Back your truck down now so I can pull up. Roy, come with me."

John backed his pick-up down the road and parked it facing the two cruisers. The sheriff and his deputy started slowly up the gravel road toward the cabin. The flashing lights on the sheriff's car began their syncopated pattern as the cruiser rounded the bend toward the cabin.

§　§　§　§　§　§

They watched intently as the sheriff's car made its way slowly toward them. The sheriff had doused the flashing lights for the return trip, since there was no need for them. The car stopped near the place Julian had turned his truck around, and both officers got out of the car.

Roy started down the hill while the sheriff busied himself with the police phone.

No other figure emerged from the cruiser.

Kim started to sob as she ran to meet the approaching officer. Joyce was at her side and placed her arm around Kim's shoulders to support her. John and Howard walked briskly behind them.

"I'm sorry," apologized Roy as he confronted the women. "He ain't givin' up your boy."

The combined efforts of John and Howard prevented Kim's collapse. Joyce wiped away a tear trickling down her cheek. "I was afraid of that," she said and shook her head.

"Why? Why can't I have my son back?" Kim asked, as she held on to Howard's arm.

"Because, Mrs. Sanborn, he ain't releasing him to us. But the sheriff's calling for more help. We're trying our best to get him back to you."

"Deputy," Joyce sighed, "she's not asking *you* why. She's asking the underbelly of humankind itself why."

He swallowed his confusion and squinted at her, unsure what to say next.

John pulled Kim into his arms in an attempt to console her, but Kim pushed him away.

"I'm never going to get him back, am I?" she sobbed, stepping back from all of them.

"Now you just hold on there a minute," John challenged. "They're not going anywhere. We've barricaded the way out. He's got to come through us and we're not letting him leave here with Graham. Come on now. We've come too far to give up now, particularly when we're this close to bringing him home."

He reached for Kim again and this time she allowed him to hold her.

"Look at me," he raised his voice, lifting her chin toward him. "We're not leaving this mountain until we take Graham with us. And that's a promise."

"Promise?" Kim asked, throwing him a fractured smile.

"Scouts honor. Now let's see what the sheriff has to say."

John and Joyce bookended Kim as they walked her toward the sheriff, who was still on the phone.

"We ain't going nowhere. You just get up here as soon as you can ... Oh ... Henry, bring a crackerjack team with you. You know who I mean! We want to keep everything as peaceful as we can. Do you copy?"

The sheriff leaned into his cruiser to put the phone to rest before he addressed Kim.

"Mrs. Sanborn ... as you've probably guessed, Mr. Fergusen was a bit hard to get along with. Actually, that's puttin' it mildly. He was downright testy. He's not going to give your boy back. He made that very clear. Now that doesn't mean you're not going to get him back. It just means we'll have to work a little harder at it."

The sheriff excused himself while he spat.

"I've just talked to Henry Van Dukkum. He's an FBI man. He'll bring some boys up here shortly and we'll get this mess all straightened out. In the meantime, we'll stay right here. I'm going to leave my cruiser here in plain sight of the house. Mr. Fergusen's got some thinking to do. So I'll give him a little more time to consider his predicament before I mosey on up there for another talk."

Kim waited for the sheriff to dispense the liquid soot again.

"Roy." The sheriff raised his voice. "You got ahold of anybody yet?"

The deputy put his field glasses down quickly and strode toward his superior officer like a child obeys a disciplining parent.

"Yes, sir. Got ahold of Melvin. And Ansel, too. Jake's delivering Katherine's baby so I didn't leave a message. Figured I'd catch him later."

"What'd you find out from Ansel?"

"He said he thinks they've been here close to a year, maybe fourteen months. He didn't recollect seeing him much at the store. Bought mostly food items he couldn't grow, blankets, candles, cigarettes, matches, ammo. Course you already know 'bout the ammunition."

The sheriff waved him on.

"Ansel never saw the boy. He don't remember him ever coming in to the store. Says Fergusen's got an orange pick-up, which we already know about."

"What kind of ammo?" the sheriff asked gruffly.

"What kind of ammo?" the deputy repeated.

The sheriff showed his irritation by intentionally spitting close to the deputy's boot.

"Oh," Roy said, jumping back instinctively. "Twelve-gauge shells, thirty-eight caliber, a couple of hundred rounds of twenty-two longs, dynamite."

"Looks like the boy's got an arsenal. Anything else?"

"That's all he told me. Oh, there was a woman come in with him."

The sheriff raised his whiskered eyebrows.

"Fergusen did most of the buying. She just nodded her head when he'd hold up somethin' he weren't sure about."

"Describe this woman."

"I didn't ask what she looked like. I guess I should have, huh?"

The sheriff sighed heavily and launched another salvo of brown spittle at his boots.

"Yep, I guess I should have," Roy answered his own question. "I'll get right on it." The deputy dismissed himself and ran toward his cruiser.

John looked at the women. "I didn't see any woman up there, did you?"

Kim shook her head while Joyce raised her hands, palms up, indicating her surprise.

"Roy."

"Yes, sir?" Roy skidded to a stop and wheeled around nervously.

"What about Melvin?"

"Oh, Melvin ... Sorry ... He said the boy ain't been in school. To his way of thinking maybe the woman's been teaching him."

"He knew about the woman?" quizzed the sheriff.

"Yes, sir. Don't know how though."

Usually the sheriff was a connoisseur of cool, but his deputy was pushing the wrong buttons.

"You want me to find out, right?"

"That would be nice."

"I'll get right on that, too."

The sheriff dismissed Roy and spat again before he addressed the others.

"I didn't see a woman. You didn't either it looks like. But I do remember seeing clothes on the line. That's not somethin' a man usually does."

"You don't miss a thing, do you?" John admired.

"Not much, but I sure missed a year's worth of Mr. Fergusen. I didn't know anybody was in Peck's old place. It's been vacant for years."

"Only campers and people passing through occupy it mostly," added Howard. "Nobody gets up here much."

"Mrs. Fergusen, you said he was one of them anti-government fanatics before he left. Is that right?" the sheriff recollected.

"Yes. He was pretty fanatical, all right."

"Howard, wasn't Peck some kind of survivalist or anti-government nut or something?"

"Yes, sir, sheriff. I believe you're right. He sure 'nough was."

"Did your husband ever mention anyone by the name of Peck Jefferson?"

Joyce's eyebrows pulled together as she backpedaled through her thoughts. "No. He didn't mention anyone by that name that I can remember. At that time he was just into the literature on the Internet, and all of the abuse he could dump on me."

The sheriff noticed the scar above her eye. He knew how the scar got there. Thirty years in law enforcement enabled him to recognize marks like that.

"Howard, call Jenny. Ask her to check Peck's file for anything that might help us. Maybe their paths crossed. Maybe they didn't. But one thing's for sure. He's holed up in Peck's old cabin and not many people 'round here even knew it was here, let alone occupied—includin' myself."

The sheriff waddled over to Roy's cruiser, picked up the binoculars and started back toward his car. He motioned for Kim to follow him.

He handed the binoculars to Kim.

"You mind keeping an eye on the cabin?"

Kim rallied quickly and smiled her appreciation.

"Let me know about any suspicious movement," he advised. He had just won Kim over with his sensitivity. She realized he wanted to give a desperate mother an opportunity to catch glimpses of her son. He was guaranteeing her a few stolen moments through the binocular lens. Kim knew he knew that wasn't enough, but it was the best he could do.

He checked his watch. Two-forty-five.

"John," he summoned, "would you do me a favor?"

The preoccupied detective took his eyes off of Hope, who was relieving himself over one of the sheriff's spittle puddles on the road.

"Sure."

"These people are hungry. Run down to Chick's Diner and bring us back something to eat."

"Of course."

"Roy's got a menu in the car. He knows what I want. Tell Chick to put it on the Mayor's tab."

John handed Hope's leash to Joyce on his way to Roy's cruiser.

"Oh, Howard, while you've got Jenny. Ask her to call the Mayor. We'll need to let him know about this situation, especially since the suits are on their way."

Kim narrowed her eyes into slits when she saw Graham step out on the porch. He was eating something off his plate, but her attention was directed more on his face.

Oh, Graham, honey. I love you so much, she lamented to herself. *You're growing up so fast.*

She peeled the binoculars off her watery eyes just long enough to wipe the tears away. Then she resumed her sentinelship.

She saw him holding a pork chop bone about shoulder level so the dog had to leap for his meal.

Tears flowed again as she watched him laugh at the antics of the hungry dog. Her trembling hands almost dropped the field glasses when Graham suddenly looked in her direction.

His blue eyes, Jim's eyes, were the eyes of a nervous nine-year-old, not the eyes of a zealot. His mouth was Jim's, too, and his well-formed nose and strong chin looked just like his father's. But his smile was like hers.

His face was a firmament of freckles and his golden hair was pulled back into a ponytail. He was slim, too thin, she thought and wished she could sprint up to him and lead him back to a more civilized environment. He was taller than most nine-year-olds, she guessed. His clothes were soiled, but he looked well cared-for.

Her heart ached and she suppressed a spontaneous urge to scream. Watching him like this was pure agony, but not seeing him was worse.

"Baby, I want to hold you so much."

A long sigh that was his name came from her numbing lips. Her nose began to burn as her grief manufactured more tears.

She flinched when Joyce touched her shoulder.

"Here," Kim said through salty lips as she handed the binoculars to Joyce. "Look."

Kim held tightly onto her friend and fought to hold back a flood of tears when a sudden inrush of air signaled Joyce's own maternal longing.

CHAPTER NINETEEN

Henry, your men in place?" Sheriff Coleman asked, as he unstrapped his holster.

"They're ready all along the perimeter. I've even got two posted on the rock cliff above the cabin."

"Then let's get this show on the road. Since you're in charge, I 'spect I'll follow you." The sheriff threw the FBI agent a quick wink.

Agent Van Dukkum smiled. He knew how Sheriff Coleman felt about bureaucracy. He also knew he had Sheriff Coleman's full support.

The FBI agent turned to Kim, who was standing beside the Mayor.

"Mrs. Sanborn, Sheriff Coleman and I are preparing to negotiate with Mr. Fergusen."

He glanced at Mayor Pritchard.

"We've informed the Mayor of our plan.

Kim's sigh was echoed by Joyce's.

Cluttering the rural mountainside was an assortment of rescue vehicles and police vehicles parked beside the sheriff's cruisers. The glare of red and blue lights flashed across dusty hoods and trunks, creating small islands of glistening color that disappeared, only to reappear again as the obedient strobes recycled their chromatic alarm.

John checked his watch.

Five thirty and it's beginning to get dark, he informed himself. *We've been here over eight hours. I'm glad we decided not to call Kim's relatives. No use upsetting them when we don't know how this thing's going to pan out.*

He handed the women their coats. The air was heavy with moisture and it had drizzled off and on all afternoon. The cool evening air communicated the overriding tension they all felt.

Sheriff Coleman glanced at the women before he scooted his two hundred sixty-pound frame into Agent Van Dukkum's unmarked government vehicle. He tightened his lips and sent his wiry eyebrows into skeptical arches as he pulled the car door shut.

Kim crossed her arms over her chest as she peered through the car window at him. Her apprehension caused her to shiver violently and detonated a bothersome series of eye ticks, as she watched the cruiser pull toward the cabin.

"You all right?" Joyce asked softly.

Kim nodded her head in slight successive movements, then reversed herself and shook her head worriedly.

"No, I'm not all right," she confessed, trying her best to control her shivering. "What if he doesn't let Graham go? What am I going to do? He's just an innocent little boy. Joyce, what if something happens to him?"

Joyce put her arm around Kim's waist and spoke softly into her ear.

"He's going to be all right."

"How can you say that? People are always saying that and then something terrible happens."

"I don't think God would bring us this far to ... Well, I don't believe He'd let us see Graham unless ... Oh, Kim, now you're upsetting me."

"You both need to calm down," John cautioned. "Turn hope into faith—remember?"

Kim squinted as she looked around John's shoulder toward her car.

"Speaking of hope—Where is Hope?" she asked nervously.

"With all these people here, I decided to put him in my pick-up."

"Oh. Good. Thanks, John. I'm glad one of us was thinking."

"Want me to check on him?"

"Would you? Actually, would you bring him to me? I think he'll be all right as long as I keep him on his leash."

John nodded and eased himself around some media personnel. They had moved closer when the sheriff and Agent Van Dukkum left, positioning themselves for the story they knew would come.

John was just a couple of steps from his truck when he realized the driver's-side window was down. Momentary panic sent him rushing to the open window.

The dog was gone.

John closed his eyes in disbelief.

"I forgot to close the window," he chastised himself. "How could I have been so stupid?"

A frantic search in the area adjacent to his vehicle proved fruitless. Hope was nowhere in sight.

Before he walked back toward the two women, John launched a hurried search among the parked vehicles and nearby woods. Finally, he headed past the curious barricade of on-lookers to where the women stood.

"Where is he?" Kim asked, looking into John's disquieted gaze.

"He's not there," he confessed. "He's not in the truck."

"What?"

"I left the driver's side window down."

"Oh, John, you didn't," petitioned Joyce.

"Look, you don't have to make me feel worse than I already do," he defended, "I'm sure he's around here somewhere. There's too many people and too much activity for him not to find something to hold his interest."

Neither of the women were comforted.

"I've got enough on me right now, I don't know what I'll do if something happens to Hope, too" Kim lamented. "I'm going to look for him myself."

"Okay. Okay. I'll renew my search, too," John added guiltily.

"I'm going with you," volunteered Joyce.

"Thanks."

Kim watched John's despondent retreat and huffed at him agitatedly when he chanced an embarrassed glance back at her. She watched as he disappeared behind one of the media vans. She headed in the other direction as she zipped her coat.

"Hope," she summoned. "Come here, boy."

§   §   §   §   §   §

When the shooting started, it sounded like a war zone. Small firearms fire punctured the night air, sending everyone scurrying for cover.

Howard pulled the two women down beside the sheriff's car, while Roy shoved the Mayor and a newsman against the rear door panel. On-lookers nearby either ducked behind the particular vehicle they stood next to or dove for protection behind a nearby tree.

John charged up behind the women and knelt beside Howard, who opened the driver's side door of the sheriff's car. He was fishing for the car radio.

"What happened?" shouted John.

"I dunno. I'm going to see if I can get somebody on the squawk box. All hell's breaking loose up there."

Kim peered over the hood of the cruiser only to be jack-in-the-boxed by John to keep her from catching a stray bullet.

"John, I want to see," she shouted angrily, still reeling from the fruitless one-hour search for Hope.

"Stay down," he ordered, irritated at her insubordination. "Do you want to get your fool head blown off?"

"Of course not, but my son's up there in the middle of all of that and for all I know Hope might be, too."

"And you can't help either of them, now can you?" John blasted. "Only God can."

"Yeah, right ... God." Kim rolled her eyes and looked away from John.

"Unit one. Unit one," Howard yelled over the gunfire. "What's happening up there?"

"We've got a situation here," the sheriff replied gruffly. "Stay where you are and stay down. There were a couple of shots fired from the house and this hotshot damn team of agents fired off a couple of hundred rounds before we could stop them."

"Oh, my God," Joyce shrieked as she cupped her hand over her mouth.

Kim was close behind with her sudden gasp.

"You need anything?" Howard queried nervously.

"My head examined for thinking this was going to work. Hell, a troop of tenderfoot cub scouts could have handled this better than these lame-brained bureaucrats. I knew I'd regret calling them in. Dammit to hell. They've got jurisdiction over something like this, but we might as well have invited the Keystone Cops."

The deputy started to say something, but censored his own input.

"Are those women all right?"

Howard looked at Kim and Joyce huddled nervously against the front wheel.

"Yes, sir. They're fine."

"The Mayor's fine, too," Roy cut in, "he's kneeling here behind your cruiser."

"Howard, put Mrs. Sanborn on," the sheriff ordered calmly, ignoring Roy's comment the Mayor.

"Push this button here to talk," Howard instructed Kim, "and let up on it to listen."

"Sheriff Coleman, this is Kim."

"Mrs. Sanborn, I'm awful sorry about all this. I hope your boy's all right. We got a little carried away up here. Henry's assured me it won't happen again. And I'm holding him to it."

"Thank you."

"Try not to get too upset. I'm gonna see if I can't straighten this thing out. 'Course, I'll need more help than I'm getting."

"Okay."

"By the way, are any of those newspaper people hounding you?"

"No, John and Howard have done a good job of running interference."

"Good. Can Howard hear me?"

"Yes, he's right here. Do you want to ... "

"Howard, you and Roy keep them sharks off both those women, you hear me?"

"He says yes," Kim relayed Howard's promise.

"John McCauley. Are you there, boy?"

"He's here next to me," Kim clarified as she handed the car phone to John.

"John, I want you to try to get ahold of that old scout master—what's his name. Rimmer?"

"Yes, you've got a good memory. His name is Pete Rimmer."

"Ask him if he knows anything about the area surrounding the cabin. Its history. Any special features about its terrain. He sounded like someone who was quite knowledgeable about topography. Do you still have his phone number?"

"I think so."

"Good, call Jenny. Tell her what she needs to know and get back to me. Howard, patch John through to Jenny as soon as we get through here."

"Yes, sir. He says yes, sir," Kim reported, moving the phone back to her mouth.

"You're getting pretty good at this, Mrs. Sanborn. Wanna job?"

"No thanks. This is as close as I want to get to someone pointing a gun at me."

"Smart girl. Roy? Is Roy still there?"

"Yes, he's right here."

"Roy, did you hear my conversation with Mr. McCauley?"

"He says yes."

"Good. Roy, get a-hold of Ned Beachley. He's an old retired forest ranger. See what he knows. It's eight-fifty. He's probably at the fire hall. Get to it, boy."

"He's on his way," Kim reported, feeling like a dispatcher.

"Ask Mrs. Fergusen ... "

Pow! Pow!

Pow! Pow! Pow!

Shots erupted from the cabin again, sending everyone for cover except for Kim, who tossed the phone at Howard and scampered quickly past John before he could tackle her.

"Graham," Kim screamed, as she sprinted toward the gauntlet of trees which cradled the cabin some hundred yards away.

John winced in pain as he rounded the front of the sheriff's cruiser. He had thrown his hip out reaching for Kim.

"Graham!" Kim yelled, running as fast as she could.

Howard stepped around John and took off after her.

Pow! Pow! Pow!

Pow! Pow!

Pow! Pow! Pow!

"Get down everybody," Roy ordered, pulling Joyce down next to the Mayor, who was hugging the side of the car.

"Mrs. Sanborn," Howard shouted on the run, "get down! You're gonna get shot!"

Pow! Pow! Pow!

Pow! Pow! Pow! Pow!

Kim tripped over a rock and hit the gravel road, skinning her hands and tearing her jeans on the abrasive surface. Before she could rise completely to her feet, Howard tackled her, sending both of them off the road and into the nearby bushes.

"Mrs. Sanborn, are you all right?"

Pow! Pow! Pow!

"Yes, I think so," she replied, as she hurriedly inspected herself. "I'm ... I think I'm okay."

"Thank God. Are you crazy? Why did you go off and do a fool thing like that?"

"I was afraid Graham might get hurt," she asserted, as she focused her attention on the cabin.

"I think all the shots came from there." Howard guessed.

"Where?"

"The cabin."

Pow! Pow! Pow! Pow!

"See," the deputy pointed as specks of light danced from one of the windows in the cabin. "He's firing from there."

The interior of the cabin was dark except for the sporadic bursts of gunfire coming from the window.

"Nobody's shooting at your son," Howard assured her as he panned the area around the cabin.

They were startled by the sound of feet behind them on the gravel, but breathed a sigh of relief when they realized it was Roy.

"She all right?" Roy asked breathily.

Howard nodded. "Man, you scared the hell out of me running up on us like that."

"You two gave our hearts a flip or two when you took off up here, too." Roy defended.

"Listen, " Howard commanded.

"What?"

"He's stopped firing," Kim reported the obvious as she started to rise.

Howard pulled her back down beside him.

"Mrs. Sanborn, please stay down. You don't know when he's gonna shoot next."

"I want to go closer."

"No!"

"Roy, ease yourself up to the sheriff and see what's going on."

"I'm going, too," Kim announced impatiently, wrestling to free herself.

"Oh, no you're not! Mrs. Sanborn, please. It's too dangerous."

"Oh, man," she growled, realizing his grip was too strong for her.

"Mrs. Sanborn, we're going to back down toward the others now. Okay?"

"No. I'm not going. I'm staying right here 'til Roy gets back."

A thunderclap startled both of them as its geologic power shook the ground.

"Looks like Mother Nature is going to use some fire power of her own," Howard predicted.

Kim peered through the darkness at the besieged cabin. It looked so diminutive now, half hidden, partly visible under the cloak of darkness.

"Mrs. Sanborn," the deputy pleaded, "let's go back to the cars. Roy will come back there and tell us what he finds out."

"No."

"It's gonna rain any minute."

"No."

"No sense in your getting wet ... or shot. Please Mrs. Sanborn."

A fierce lighting clash drowned out her objection as it's electrical charge hit near the cabin.

"That's it, I'm taking you back."

Their brief struggle was interrupted when Roy slid in beside them.

"Sheriff says all the shots came from the cabin," Roy reported.

"See, I told you," boasted Howard proudly.

Kim frowned her relief but renewed her push toward the cabin.

"He and Agent Van Dukkum are on their way back to brief the Mayor."

Lightning flashed again, sending its pyrotechnic fingers of fire streaking into the hillside.

"Howard, he called us and we weren't there," Roy reported, looking a little weathered.

"Who?"

"Sheriff Coleman."

Howard gulped nervously and tossed an embarrassed look at Kim.

"That's right. When I took off after Mrs. Sanborn, I left the radio on the car seat."

"It's not your fault. I took off after you. I'm the one he should holler at."

The deputies' chatter took the edge off the tense situation just enough to help Kim forget her fear for the moment. She gave both of them a sympathetic grin, and pretended to chew some tobacco before she spat imaginary sputum on the road.

"I'll vouch for you boys. Now do what you're told and git me back ta safety. Do you hear me?"

Both deputies snorted their delight at her portrayal of the sheriff. Another flash of lightning prompted them to lower their heads.

"Mr. McCauley answered the car phone. He told the sheriff what we were up to," Roy explained as they escorted Kim back toward the others. "The sheriff said Mr. McCauley told him I handed him the squawk box before I chased after you. But that weren't so. I jus' forgot about the phone. I figured we were in enough trouble so I didn't say no different."

Kim stumbled as she chanced a backward glance at the cabin. Both deputies steadied her as they pulled her further away from her son.

When they advanced to within a couple of yards of the vehicular barricade, they were mobbed by Joyce, the Mayor and the media. John, still hobbling from the recurring injury to his hip, watched from behind the sheriff's car.

Before the crowd pressed the deputies for answers, Sheriff Coleman and Agent Van Dukkum arrived.

"Hold on now. Everybody just settle down," ordered the sheriff, as he waddled around the front fender of his car. He wedged himself between the women and the media.

"Get that camera out of my face, boy," the sheriff lashed out at a newsman who hovered too close. "You folks will get your story."

"Sheriff, what happened up there?" one of the media people asked.

"We heard shots," another chorused.

"That's an understatement," criticized the sheriff.

"Is it over?"

The sheriff shook his head.

"Except for the initial exchange of gunfire, the rest of the shots you heard came from the cabin," he said, blinking toward the blinding light in his eyes. "I told you to get that damned light out of my eyes."

When the obnoxious cameraman held his ground, the sheriff stepped toward him and pushed him back a half dozen steps.

"Now you stay right here, son. I'm asking you real peaceful like. Believe me, you don't want to get my dander up."

The newsman froze, sensing that the sheriff was a man used to being obeyed.

"Now that I got everybody's attention, Agent Van Dukkum's got a few words to say."

The FBI agent moved next to the mayor.

"The subject is still holed up in his cabin. We believe there are three of them. Mr. Fergusen, the boy and an unidentified woman. We consider the subject to be armed and dangerous."

Kim closed her eyes and lowered her head.

Joyce looked straight ahead, almost trance-like as she heard her husband described as a criminal.

"Who's the woman?" someone from the crowd shouted.

"We don't know."

"Are you going to attempt to rescue the boy?" a reporter yelled.

"I thought that's what we've been doing," inserted the sheriff agitatedly.

"I think he means when are you going to rush the cabin?" one of the town's officials asked.

"We have no immediate plans to do so. Our objective is to end this stand-off as peacefully as we can," stressed Agent Van Dukkum.

"How long do you plan on sitting here?" one of the news people challenged.

"As long as it takes," replied the agent. "We believe Mr. Fergusen will give himself up. He's got the safety of the woman and a child to consider."

"Can you tell us more about them?"

"I'm going to pass on that for now."

"Where's he from?"

"No comment."

"Sheriff Coleman, can you tell us anything?" shouted a newsman.

"Agent Van Dukkum's got jurisdiction in this case," the sheriff responded calmly.

"We understand that, but do you have a comment?"

"Yes, sir. Direct your questions to the agent in charge."

"Listen, everyone. We'll keep you as informed as we can. Right now we've got work to do," Agent Van Dukkum said, glancing at his watch. "It's nine-fifteen. I really don't think the subject will do anything else tonight. So I suggest you all go home. For those of you who feel a need to stay, I'm going to ask you to drive back down to Route 93. We're expanding our perimeter."

Indignant objections rose from the crowd as they pressed him to reconsider.

"Roy. Howard. Help these people clear the premises," Sheriff Coleman commanded as he gave the defiant cameraman another shove. Then he stepped around the cameraman and faced Kim.

"You're exempt from the evacuation order and so are your two companions, so long as you all stay where you are told. No more of this putting yourself and my men in danger," the sheriff admonished Kim.

Kim bit her lips.

"Thank you," she whispered as she gently touched his arm.

"Mr. McCauley. Are you doing all right, boy? I couldn't help but notice you've been limping around here for the last half hour."

John raised his eyebrows and sighed as he patted his thigh.

"I'm okay. I've just aggravated an old hip injury. I'll walk it off in no time."

"Just the same, Roy, get Oscar over here. I want him to take a look at Mr. McCauley's hip. Oscar's a veterinarian. But he's as good as old Doc Jake. He's even looked after me a couple of times," the sheriff said, allowing a faint smile to cross his face.

"Thanks, but you don't have to ... "

"No trouble at all. Any more word out of you and I'll have Oscar put you in the kennel overnight," the sheriff threatened, winking playfully at John.

"That won't be necessary," John said, laughing heartily. Then he was hit by a disquieting thought. *Where's Hope? We still haven't found Hope.*

Kim was standing beside John when he panicked.

"What's wrong?"

"We still haven't found Hope."

"Hope." Kim glanced around the immediate area, then wiped away the tears that sprang to her eyes. "I've lost Hope."

"The shooting interrupted our search," defended the old detective. "I haven't given him another thought."

"He's around here somewhere," Joyce assured them as she zipped her coat up a little more. "He wouldn't go anywhere without us."

"I hope you're right," Kim agreed tentatively. She thought about his running loose during the commotion and of the chaotic gun fire. She lifted her head skyward. Except for occasional bursts of heat lightning, the sky was kettle black. The thick cloud cover had doused the stars, adding to the coating of melancholy which enveloped her.

Kim was barely aware of the medical advice Oscar gave John as he poked and prodded John's hip and lower back through his clothing. She focused her full attention on the sheriff, who was huddled with the Mayor and Agent Van Dukkum.

When Agent Van Dukkum adjourned the meeting, Sheriff Coleman waddled slowly toward Oscar.

"Is he all right, Oscar?"

The veterinarian peered over this spectacles.

"Nothing's broken. His hip's sensitive to the touch. Spending time in one of them Jacuzzi's would do him good. Otherwise the pain killers he's on will have to do."

"I'll be fine," John assured them, feeling uncomfortable with all the attention.

"It's going to be a long night. You're welcome to stay at my place," the sheriff volunteered.

"No, really. It's okay. I can spread out in my camper," John insisted. "Oh, Sheriff, I called Pete Rimmer, the scout master I met in Bristol. I left your number on his answer phone."

"Good. Howard, you let me know when Mr. Rimmer calls."

The sheriff turned to face Kim, who was leaning against his cruiser watching the cabin. He motioned for Oscar to follow him as he approached her.

"Mrs. Sanborn," he interrupted her solemn reverie. "I want Oscar to take a look at your hands."

The geography of Kim's face changed from sadness to surprise.

"Show Oscar your palms."

"They're okay. There's no need to ... "

"Are you two related?" interrupted the sheriff.

"Related? ... Who?" she asked. Her bewilderment was complete.

"You and that old broken down private investigator over there," teased the sheriff.

"Sheriff Coleman asked me to take a look at his bum hip," clarified Oscar, "and he gave this old horse doctor the brush-off. Looks like you're doing the same thing."

"Oh-hhh, I see. Do these need re-shoeing?" she asked, holding out her hands, palms up.

Unable to conceal the smile that inched across his face, the sheriff waddled quickly away, hoping to preserve what remained of his tough cop image. Kim's smile was a hymn as she admiringly watched his hasty departure.

"He likes you," Oscar disclosed nonchalantly, as he examined her mildly lacerated palms.

Kim's eyebrows disappeared under her bangs.

"Oh, I don't mean no disrespect. He's quite happily married. It's just that he don't let many people get through his hard veneer. He's got a tough exterior but a soft heart, as you've already guessed."

Kim's smile preceded her nod.

"Now, don't get me wrong. It's not that he feels sorry for you. I mean, he does ... a little ... but I don't mean it that way," he apologized, tailgating his comments the more nervous he got.

"I think I understand," Kim assured him.

Oscar nodded. "He respects women of quality. People of character in general. He's about the most decent and honest, God-fearing person that was ever raised in these parts. He's got a few rough edges, but they're reserved for folks who get his dander up."

"I'm beginning to see what you mean."

"Well, there you go. I've cleaned them off as good as I can. If you'll rub this salve on your palms and knees, I believe you'll be as good as new in a couple of days."

"Thank you, Oscar."

"My pleasure, ma'am."

He looked at the cloud-covered sky.

"We never did get that rain. Got plenty of thunder and lightning, though."

Kim copied his heavenward gaze.

"Nope. It's absence sure kept things a lot less complicated."

"Sure enough did. Well, I'd best be taking my leave now. You ought to get some rest, too. You want me to see you to your RV?"

"No thanks," she declined politely. "I think I'll just stay here a while."

"Good night then."

"Good night, and thank you."

Her sadness took her on an emotional roller coaster as she sat on the hood of the sheriff's cruiser, pining for Graham and heightening her concern for Hope. Engulfed in a parade of emotions, she decided to focus on the serrated outline of the tree tops made almost invisible by the storm blackened sky.

The night sky was bankrupt of stars and the chill in the air settled over everything.

After a while, Joyce plopped herself beside Kim and both women sat quietly, contemplatively, longing for an end to Julian's private war.

"Here. As long as you two plan on staying up all night, you may as well use this."

John handed them a blanket and then made a polite departure, promising to keep one eye peeled for Hope.

Their vigil was heavy with the unspoken as they huddled under the blanket. Needing a few cubic feet of quiet, neither of the women deviated from the privacy of her thoughts. Like self-appointed sentinels, they maintained their silent vigil.

After a while, the sheriff approached them holding two cups of coffee.

"How 'bout a night cap?"

"Where'd you get those?" Joyce beamed.

"I had the Mayor make a coffee run," the sheriff bragged, chuckling his delight. "He hadn't done anything all day ... except pay for meals. Course he doesn't know that yet."

"Thanks."

"Me, too," Joyce followed Kim's lead.

"Cream? Sugar?"

Both women declined.

"It's decaffeinated. Hope you don't mind."

"It's hot and it's wet," Joyce announced.

"Mmm ... mmm," Kim showed her appreciation as she treated herself to the hot liquid.

"I'm going to join Van Dukkum in his car up ahead. Howard's staying with his hunk of metal. If you need anything just holler."

"We'll be fine."

"You two stay wrapped up. It's supposed to drop to around thirty-five by midnight."

He turned to his deputy, who was sitting dutifully in the belly of the cruiser.

"Howard, you let me know if we get any calls. I 'spect I'll be up there the rest of the night." The sheriff motioned toward the agent's unmarked car, barely visible now except for a few glimmers of chrome which managed to escape the darkness.

"Enjoy the coffee now, you hear?"

"We will, thank you," Joyce replied as she took another sip.

"Good night," Kim whispered softly, as she brought the Styrofoam cup to her lips.

As Kim watched the darkness erase the sheriff's tan uniform, her eye caught a flicker of light emanating from the cabin.

Joyce saw it too, and shouted at the sheriff, who halted his own advance.

Both women bounded off the car, spilling their coffee in the process, and headed toward the sheriff.

The four of them started up the gravel road toward Agent Van-Dukkum, who had jumped from his car.

"Fire!" shouted Kim. "It's a fire."

The flames spread quickly from one end of the cabin to the other until it was fully involved.

Kim's scream was followed by Joyce's, as both women darted ahead.

"Come back here, you two," shouted Agent Van Dukkum.

"Ladies, what are you doing?" yelled Sheriff Coleman. "You can't ... "

His warning was abruptly cut short by an explosion that knocked all of them off their feet. Billows of fire mushroomed out of the cabin, sending smoke and flames skyward. Smoke enveloped the entire area. What used to be an intact cabin was reduced to a mixture of fiery red and orange ballast.

The cabin was fully involved.

Silhouetted against the backdrop of burning wood were the two women. One standing. The other on her knees.

"Graham," screamed Kim, her heart ripped asunder by the explosion.

The officers rushed up to Joyce, who had just fainted. Kim let out the most wretched, gut-wrenching wail they ever heard come from a human being.

Her dismantlement was complete.

CHAPTER TWENTY

The women watched mournfully as fire and rescue crews from Winston-Salem helped local emergency teams search through the smoldering rubble for bodies. The cabin was completely destroyed, leaving only the charred remains of the last vestige of hope of finding her son alive.

The women had stayed up all night, dividing their time gazing at the incinerated cabin and searching for Hope.

Kim's sorrowful gaze caught Sheriff Coleman staring at her from several feet away. His mouth was drawn tight and his hands were resting on top of his holsters.

She sent him a faint smile and watched him lower his burly head as he sighed.

He became more animated when Agent Van Dukkum walked up to him. The agent pointed toward the smoldering rubble and both men walked around to one side of the charred ruins.

The sheriff's summons to one of the firemen was inaudible from where she stood, as Kim watched the volunteer move further into the sooted ruins.

"Did you hear what Sheriff Coleman said?" Kim asked Joyce, who was watching them, too.

"No, but it looks like they've found something."

The women watched as the fireman carefully pulled a charred cylindrical piece of metal from what was left of the flooring.

Although it took her a few moments, Joyce suddenly widened her eyes as her mouth flung open.

"It's Julian's blunderbuss. Or what's left of it."

"What?" Kim asked, surprised at Joyce's discovery.

"They've found Julian's antique gun. The butt is burned off, but it's his gun!"

Joyce's guarded enthusiasm pulled both of them toward the growing number of rescue personnel who surrounded the damaged antique.

"That's Julian's old blunderbuss," Joyce announced as they joined the throng. "He doesn't go anywhere without it."

As soon as the words fell from her trembling lips, Joyce's hands covered her mouth. She threw Kim the most horrible look.

Kim's sharp mind seized on Joyce's frightful dilemma immediately.

"Aw ... no. Don't jump to that conclusion. You don't know he's dead. They haven't found any bodies yet."

"But he'd never leave it."

"What are you saying, Mrs. Fergusen?" Agent Van Dukkum quizzed.

When Joyce couldn't find the syllables, Kim spoke in her behalf.

"The gun is her ex-husband's. She thinks he's probably somewhere in the rubble because he'd never leave without it. It's a priceless antique."

"And if he didn't leave," Joyce interrupted, "he would have forced the others to stay with him."

'No, ma'am. You can put yourself at ease on that," Sheriff Coleman consoled Joyce. "We haven't found any bodies."

Joyce looked tearfully at the sheriff, who paused to scratch his sooty forehead.

"He's not here, Mrs. Fergusen. As a matter of fact, none of them are. They've vanished into thin air."

The women mirrored each other's gasp.

"How is that possible?" Kim marveled, unconsciously moving her hand to cover her mouth.

"Beats me. I don't know how they did it," responded the sheriff.

"We've looked everywhere," explained Agent Van Dukkum. "We searched the crawl space under both the cabin and the porch. Or what used to be the crawl space. Obviously there was no back entrance. There's nothing but solid rock behind the cabin."

"They managed to escape somehow," Sheriff Coleman reasoned. "They're flesh and blood, same as us. So we'll just have to figure it out."

His penetrating stare found Agent Van Dukkum.

"Henry, you ready for another go-round before lunch? We're going to find Mr. Houdini's escape route."

The agent nodded in agreement and both men started toward the fire chief who was beckoning for them.

Suddenly John came limping up beside them, using the wooden cane Howard found for him. Both men looked as if they had just lost their best friends.

"Sheriff," Howard yelled respectfully at this superior officer, "we got some news. But I'm afraid it's not good news."

Both men reported their disappointment at the lack of information they got from their respective sources. Neither Pete Rimmer nor Ned Beachley could provide helpful collateral data.

The sheriff's sigh showed more fatigue than irritation.

"Well, let's get to it. We got a boy to find."

Kim and Joyce retreated toward the battered old tangerine pick-up. They stood beside its blanched surface and stood quietly shoulder-to-shoulder.

Something on the front dashboard caught Kim's eye. When she glanced at it, she let out a cry.

"What? What is it, Kim?"

Wordlessly Kim moved toward the front of the truck and produced a ball cap which was jammed between the dashboard and the windshield.

"It's Graham's ball cap," Kim whispered.

Both women recognized it as the soiled Chicago Bulls cap he'd worn the day before.

Kim tearfully clasped it to her breast and closed her eyes to seal the world out. Then she raised the cap to her face and buried her nose in it, siphoning all of him she could through its sooty fabric.

Joyce leaned her forehead onto Kim's temple as the women braced each other.

Kim sobbed unapologetically, allowing her tears to dampen the cap's tightly woven fabric.

Joyce's intuition brought her head around to catch John's sympathetic gaze. He shook his head sorrowfully and maintained his distance, allowing them their privacy.

Kim pulled the cap from her face to look at it, but was unable to separate herself from it. She brought it crashing to her flushed face, as her emotions took hold of her. Joyce stabilized her fall as Kim slid backwards down the side of the truck, forcing both women to sit on the ground.

Kim's chest heaved as she wept uncontrollably for her son. For her own agonizing journey of disappointments and tears. For the surrogate mother who sat lovingly at her side.

Finally, her tears abated enough for her to look at Joyce, but she buried her face once again into the stale-smelling cap. Then she lowered it to her lap.

"Oh, Joyce. It's so hard."

"I know, honey."

"I've only got pieces of him."

Joyce wiped her own tears away.

"I don't know if I can take any more."

"Yes, you can. I know you can."

"I've lost both of them," she began to sob again as she fingered the hat. "He's wasn't a baby any more, was he? He was a ... young man ... Oh, Joyce ... Graham's gone."

Joyce shook her head. "We don't know that. We've got to hang in there. We can handle this. We're going to have to handle it." Joyce watched Kim fondle Graham's hat.

Suddenly Kim gasped, and looked at Joyce, her eyes wide in amazement.

"There's something here" she exclaimed excitedly. Her fingers struggled with something captured under the brim— a piece of folded paper tucked inside the band of the cap.

Kim's unsteady fingers fumbled with it, but she was finally able to open it.

Both women gasped when they saw its contents. The note read simply:

> *Mom and Mom,*
> *I'm sorry for all this.*
> *Love to you both,*
> *Graham*

The women were inconsolable now as tears flowed unabated down their faces. Kim reached into her pocket and pulled out a bundle of tissues and shared them with Joyce.

"Whew," Joyce recovered. "Did I say we could handle this?"

Kim managed a brittle smile through another round of sniffles.

They paid homage to the note again before either of them spoke.

"Here. You take this," she told Joyce handing her the note.

"Aw ... no ... I can't ... it's yours."

"No, it isn't. He wrote it to both of us."

"Aw, honey ... it's not right. You're his mother."

"He didn't remember me. You saw him yesterday morning. He called to you. No. You take it. Please."

Joyce struggled to hold back the tears she knew were coming, but failed to stop them from flooding down her reddened face.

"Thank you."

When she sufficiently composed herself, Joyce clasped the cap in Kim's hands.

"You keep this then. I'll scan his note with my phone and then we'll both have a copy."

Kim looked at her through swollen eyes.

Thank you, she mimed, unable to get the words out.

Joyce decided they'd better get off the cold ground, and helped Kim to her feet. As they held their respective mementos, their attention was drawn to John, who yelled at them as he pointed toward the leveled cabin.

"Look," he cried. "It's Hope!"

"Hope!" Kim screamed. "It's Hope!"

Hope's soot-tainted white coat was hardly visible as the women watched him dig at something near the back of the rubble.

Storing their mementos in their coat pockets, the women sprinted toward Hope. John hobbled toward them to join the reunion.

Hope was digging furiously at the firewall of the damaged fireplace. He followed his sniffing with several pawing attempts to dislodge a thick metal partition at the rear of the fire wall.

By the time they trudged through the rubble, the trio was met by several fireman who began tearing at what was left of the fireplace.

"Hope," Kim yelled "Come here, boy. Come here."

Hope started toward her, but reversed his direction, pushing his way past the firemen to paw at the base of the fire wall.

"Hope, come here, you stinker," Kim coaxed.

The dog tore himself away from the fireplace and greeted Kim nervously.

"Where have you been? Look at you. You're black with soot."

The dog licked her repeatedly as she knelt in front of him, and then reversed his steps to the fireplace.

"Sheriff, look here," commented one of the firemen, as Sheriff Coleman inched his way toward them. "This fireback doesn't sit on metal feet. It slides."

"Well. What do you know 'bout that!"

"That's strange," Agent Van Dukkum commented as he caught up with the sheriff.

"Give that thing a push. Let's see how far it slides," ordered Sheriff Coleman.

One of the firemen sat on the hearth and used his foot to push the fireback sideways, revealing a small opening.

A collective look of surprise washed over their faces.

"Now don't that beat all," the sheriff said as he leaned forward to get a better look. Then he straightened himself and addressed Kim.

"This dog of yours just earned himself one of Chick's soup bones," the sheriff said. Then he praised Hope by giving him a couple of hearty pats on the back. "Henry, looks like I'm over-qualified for that tiny hole. I'd like to see where it goes though. You think you can help me with that?"

Agent Van Dukkum nodded.

"Martha. Bob." Agent Van Dukkum motioned two of his smallest agents to crawl through the opening.

As soon as the agents cleared the opening, they were able to stand. One of the firemen provided them with battery-operated lanterns.

After a few moments, one of the agents reappeared at the fireplace entrance.

"Henry. There's a body in here. It's the woman."

§ § § § § §

Further investigation uncovered a hidden exit leading through a narrow passageway to a small cavern on the other side of the stone cliff.

Ansel identified the dead woman as the same woman Julian brought into the general store. She was shot several times. The agents found her lying on her back on a blanket. Her arms were crossed over her abdomen and a rose was tucked between her hands.

An open Bible was lying next to her and the rose suggested a hurried funeral. Her eyes were pressed shut and the coroner found traces of tobacco stains on her forehead indicating she was kissed several times.

She was a young woman, presumed in her early thirties. The coroner determined the wounds were caused by government issue assault rifles. Evidently, she was killed by hostile fire coming from outside the cabin.

"Henry, you're gonna have to explain how your men panicked and killed that poor woman," Sheriff Coleman announced.

Agent Van Dukkum sighed heavily.

"And I'm gonna tell you something else. I ain't gonna lie for you. You ordered your men to stand down until you gave them the signal, and they disobeyed that order."

The FBI field officer gave the sheriff the most pitiful look.

"It will all be in my report."

"But will it register in your conscience?" pressed the sheriff.

The agent looked away.

"Henry, I know you feel bad about this. Hell, I've made mistakes from time to time. But this is a reflection on me, too. And I'd hate like hell to have people think I had anything to do with it. Am I making myself clear?"

"Yes, sir."

"Now that that's off my chest, have your people typed that blood yet?" the sheriff asked, referring to the blood samples they found all along the passageway. "I've got some people here who are sure 'nough interested in the results," he added, referring to Kim and Joyce.

"Not yet. I'll let you know the minute I'm made aware."

"Good. Oh ... ah ... Roy thinks they used horses to make their getaway."

"Horses!"

The sheriff motioned for Agent Van Dukkum to follow him to the cave entrance.

"Looky here," he said, pointing to the broken ground under the straw. "See those hoof-prints?"

"I'll be damned. They were hidden by the straw." Agent Van-Dukkum admitted as he surveyed the interior of the cave. "Except for the small armory of weapons he stockpiled here, it just looks like a storage room. There's no indication of feed bags or horse manure in here to suggest a stable."

"Uh ..., yes there is." The sheriff's eyes brightened. "You're standing in some right now."

Agent Van Dukkum lifted first one foot, then the other.

"Dammit. Why didn't you warn me?"

"It was too late. You was already baptized."

§   §   §   §   §   §

Federal agents and sheriff's deputies coordinated their search over the next few days. They found three horses tethered to trees in a clearing eight miles from the cave entrance. The dirt access road which lead from the clearing to Route 93 was wide enough for a vehicle.

Tire tracks perforated the slightly moist ruts on the trail, verifying that the subjects had a six to seven hour head start.

The sheriff informed Kim and the others that the blood samples did not match Graham's blood type. But they did match Julian's and medical care facilities within fifty miles, including private doctors offices, had been alerted.

Due to Sheriff Coleman's insistence, Kim and her posse stayed at his house during the course of the local investigation.

"Sheriff and Mrs. Coleman, you've been so wonderful this past week," Kim praised. "I don't know how I can thank you enough."

"You don't have to, dear. We enjoyed having you. All of you. I just wish it could have been under different circumstances," Mrs. Coleman replied as she stood next to her husband.

"Well, we owe you so much," Kim confessed. "May we pay you for this week?"

"Woman, you better put that billfold back in your purse before I lock you up," Sheriff Coleman protested playfully.

"He's just looking for an excuse to keep you here, dear," said Mrs. Coleman, as she smiled at Kim.

Joyce began the departure ritual by hugging Mrs. Coleman. Both John and Kim followed suit. The men exchanged firm handshakes and Joyce waved her good-bye to the sheriff.

Kim stood facing the thick-veneered law officer. When the sheriff extended his right hand for her in a handshake, Kim veered past his outstretched arm and hugged him.

"Why you old coot, you," Mrs. Coleman teased, "you're blushing."

The sheriff frowned his embarrassment and re-directed his attention to Kim.

"Get on outta here now and find that boy. And may God be with you."

Kim tissued a tear away as she turned to follow Joyce to their RV.

The Coleman's placed their arms around each other as Kim waved farewell. They watched with heavy hearts as the caravan of two vehicles disappeared.

"Mary, we need to keep them on our prayer list," he said to his wife. "Those young-uns need all the help they can get."

When the sheriff's ten-year-old son came running out of the house to show them the gift Kim gave him, he was squeezed tightly by an introspective father, who held his embrace longer than the lad was used to.

CHAPTER TWENTY-ONE

Kim settled back in her ornate wicker rocking chair, enjoying the sun room she had built onto the deck the year before. Although two other beautiful pieces of wicker furniture vied for attention, this rocker was still her favorite.

Hope slept in his usual spot near one of the sliding doors. He was around twelve years old, and was wearing out. The lumps on his chest and around his rib cage were typical for an older dog, but were not cancerous. He was old for a Great Pyrenees, but his overall health was good.

"I'll walk you in a little while," she whispered as her eye caught the nervous twitch of one of his front paws.

She lifted the cappuccino to her lips and took several swallows. She was still hooked on the sweet mud-colored broth and used it to give herself a jump-start every day.

Kim inspected the preponderance of plants that decorated the glass enclosure. Hanging from hooks were scores of reed and brass baskets bearing a profusion of exuberantly lush green plants. Philodendrons and Peace Lilies thrived in well-tended pots. Dwarfed ficus trees, sporting their variegated leaves, filled the corners. Spider plants, resplendent with runners, and ivies of all kinds hung from expertly-placed hooks.

She looked at the wicker chest that supported her bare feet. It was a convenient storage bin for the bird seed and corn she used to feed the animals.

"It's so good to be home," she sighed. "I really do think these road trips are worse than our mountain searches were."

She brought the cup of hot liquid to her lips again as she rifled through the basket of mail that accumulated in her absence. Kim had just gotten home from a twenty-city book tour. Her first novel turned out to be a mega-hit and had enjoyed the number one spot on the *New York Times* Bestseller's list for forty-three weeks.

As she mindlessly sorted through the mail, Kim reflected over the last few years. She had started the novel two year's after the cabin explosion in Piney Creek. Even now, Kim got shivers down her spine as she remembered that horrible experience. John's hip injury had side-lined him, forcing him back to Atlanta for surgery, but she and Joyce steadfastly continued their search for Graham.

For two long, exhausting years they had followed every possible lead, with no luck at all. Finally, the women decided to end the crusade. Both women had depleted their savings, as well as the money each of their parents had given them. Joyce returned dejectedly to her parent's home to live with her mother. Her father had died from a stroke the year before.

The only tangible outcome in their seven-year search was the consolation that Graham knew they were searching for him.

The youngster had managed to write a note to Joyce in care of the editor of the Piney Creek newspaper. It arrived several months after the daring escape from the cabin. Joyce had given Kim a copy of the letter, which she knew by heart:

Mom -

I don't know if you'll get this. It's the only way I can think of to try and write to you. Dad and me are on the run. I can't see you now. Dad says it's dangerous.

I love you. I was glad to see my other mother—I always thought she was dead. Tell her I love her, too. I love Dad, too, and he needs me now. I'm OK and learning more than if I was in school.

Love, Graham

The letter upset Kim, but she understood Graham's loyalty to his fanatical father.

Graham contacted them once more during the three years it took her to write her first novel. He used the Piney Creek newspaper again as his communications outlet. In that second note, sent last year, he informed them he was a teenager and apologized for not keeping in better touch. He and his father were members of a paramilitary group, and were always in hiding.

In that second letter, Graham shared some of his memories. He admitted he couldn't remember his old address, or his grandparent's name. He only remembered calling them Grandpa and Nanna. That's why he wrote to the newspaper. It was his only link to his mothers.

He confessed Julian's reluctance to provide him with Joyce's address and phone number, declaring Julian's hatred for Joyce and her parents.

Kim kept both notes in a box along with his ball cap and a copy of the hastily scribbled message Graham had left for them in the tangerine pickup. Joyce had scanned a copy for Kim to add to her collection of memorabilia of her son. She kept them in a special box next to several other memento-packed treasure chests in her walk-in closet.

She revisited them occasionally, carefully fondling each piece of clothing or toy or crayon-scribbled page. The boxes were her memorabilia urns, treasured reminders of the son ripped from her arms ten years ago.

She took another addictive sip of cappuccino and watched the squirrels in the feeder devour the peanuts she tossed out for them. Several blue jays and a pair of cardinals pecked their allotment of seeds as they tentatively shared the feeder with the bushy-tailed rodents.

Her contemplative eyes settled on several young squirrels and an aggressive duo of young jays as they scavenged for food near the feeder. The jays were especially bold as they crowded the squirrels.

Graham's fourteen, Kim reminded herself, *almost fourteen and a half. I wonder if his hair is still pony-tailed. Has the birthmark on his knee faded or is it still recognizable as a star? Why doesn't he run away and come back to me?*

She glanced quickly at Hope to assess the black spot on his leg, but he was lying on it. Then her attention was drawn to the front of the house when the doorbell sounded. Hope's aged ears remained oblivious to the musical alarm and he continued his mid-morning siesta.

When Kim opened the door, the delivery man presented her with a bouquet of an assortment of flowers.

"Oh, how beautiful!" Kim exclaimed as she smelled deeply of the fragrance of the bouquet. "Who sent these?"

After dispatching the delivery man, she placed the surprise gift on the dining room table and opened the card. It was a thank you note from her publisher.

"How nice," she said aloud as she realigned several of the stems. "I'll text him a thank you and give Tony a call. As my agent, he'll appreciate the rapport I've built with the publisher."

She fussed with the arrangement briefly before she rescued her cappuccino from an opportunistic dog.

"You don't miss a trick, do you?" she scolded him politely. "Since you're up, we might as well go for a walk. Both of us could stand to lose a couple of pounds."

Kim plucked her cup from the wicker end table and led Hope outside onto the deck. Before they had gone far, Kim heard the phone ring. Her first inclination was to let it ring, then she thought it might be her publisher calling to see if the flowers arrived.

She quickly deserted Hope, rushed into the kitchen, and grabbed the phone on the fourth ring.

"Hello," she announced, expecting to hear the publisher's voice.

"I was hoping you'd be back."

Kim recognized Sheriff Coleman's voice.

"Matt, what a nice surprise! How are you?"

"I'm fine. How's the best selling novelist?"

"Glad to be home again. Twenty cities in eight weeks seems too much like the old days," Kim replied, referring to her full-time search for Graham.

"Never thought of that. You must be exhausted."

"I am a little. I've got another tour in September."

The sheriff hesitated before he spoke again.

"Kim, I've got another note from your boy."

She drew a cautious breath and was about to speak when he continued.

"It's addressed to both of you in care of the paper. Want me to open it or send it?"

"No, open it, please."

She listened intently as he tore open the envelope.

"Here it is. Are you ready?"

"Yes, go ahead."

> *Dear Mom and Mom. I hope one or both of you will meet me this time. I don't know what happened in May. Maybe you didn't get my note in time or maybe something's happened to you. But if you get this in time, please meet me in the lobby of the Grove Park Inn in Asheville, North Carolina on June nineteenth at around nine a.m. I hope we can meet.*
>
> *Love Graham*

She was hyperventilating by the time he finished reading the note.

"Matt, I don't understand. What did he mean by the May reference."

"I thought you knew. I sent his letter to you as soon as it came in."

"What do you mean?"

"Oh, no, Kim. I am so sorry."

"Matt, what are you trying to tell me?"

"You got a note from him around the first week of May."

Kim closed her eyes as she smothered a gasp.

"It was addressed same as always. I sent it to you, figuring you'd copy one to Joyce. I thought I was doing the right thing. When I didn't hear from you, I assumed things were okay. I forgot about your book tour."

"Oh, Matt! Wait! Hold on a minute, will you?"

"Sure, hon."

Kim planted the phone on the table and rushed over to the mountain of correspondence on the sun porch.

When her trembling fingers found the note from Graham, she quickly ripped it open.

Her tear-glazed eyes swarmed over it.

> *Dear Mom, would you and my other Mom meet me at the Hiawassee Dam at around nine in the morning on May tenth? If you can meet me it would be great. I'll wait a half hour. If you can't come, it's okay.*
> *Love, Graham*

Kim clinched her fists as she finished the note. She cried in despair, realizing she had missed an opportunity to see him.

"I was on tour!" she lamented, as she collapsed into one of the kitchen chairs. "Damn it. Damn it. Damn it."

Her anger forced her to sweep the rest of the mail off the wicker table, sending it like paper missiles across the room.

"Oh, Graham, honey. I've let you down."

She kicked angrily at a piece of mail lying next to her. Hope thought her tirade was directed at him so he left the room, deciding not to be the beneficiary of her next kicking spell.

She ran to the phone again and spoke into the receiver.

"Hello, Matt. I'm sorry I left in such a hurry. I had to find that letter."

"That's okay, honey, I understand."

"I found it," she reported as she began to cry. "Matt, he needed me and I wasn't there!"

"Kim, settle down and tell me what this is all about."

She tried her best to compose herself.

"The letter Graham sent me in May ... the one you forwarded to me ... was buried in my correspondence. My parents must have missed it. They didn't say anything about a letter from Graham ... I ... "

"Now, honey, stop right there and take a deep breath."

"I wasn't here to ... "

"Do as I told you before you speak another word."

Kim censored her own uneasy chatter and did as he insisted.

"One more time, slowly now."

Kim swallowed her tension before she spoke.

"I missed a chance to see him, Matt. And because I was gone, Joyce missed seeing him, too. I should have been here. I should have double-checked with my parents. How can I ever tell Joyce?"

"Now, Kim. There's no way you or anybody else could know Graham would write you. "

"I should have had you send the notes to Joyce first, then to me."

"Okay, that's it, young woman. You got your ears on?"

"What?"

"Are you listening?"

"Yes. what are you ... "

"Then stop shoulding on yourself."

"What?"

"Shoulding on yourself. You know, I should of done this ... I should have done that ... "

"What are you talking about, Matt?"

"Just listen to me, honey. Once something happens, it's fact. You weren't there to get Graham's letter. It's part of your past. Sure, we can wish it happened differently. But the fact is, you can't change it. So stop "shoulding" on yourself! It'll only make you feel worse. Instead, let's talk about next time."

"So when I said I should have checked my mail, I should have said ... "

"Ah—you just should on yourself again."

"I did, didn't I?" Kim admitted, laughing at herself.

"So, let's not worry about that old note now. The next time is right now." Matt checked the note again. "He says he can meet you on June nineteenth."

"That's a week from tomorrow."

"You want me to go with you?"

Kim hesitated as she edited her thoughts.

"No. I'll call Joyce. Graham asked for both of us to come. I don't want to scare him off."

"You be careful, now. You hear?"

"We will. Matt, I'm a little frightened. And confused. I wonder if he's left that maniac of a father? Maybe he's trying to come home. Oh, Matt, do you suppose that's it?"

"Could be. But don't get your hopes up."

"Why? He's contacted us for a reason."

"He could be a fourteen-year-old boy in trouble. Maybe he wants something from you. Money. A place to stay."

"Matt, you're sounding like an old sheriff whose lost his faith in people."

"He's sent you three notes, including the one I'm holding. He's never asked for your addresses or phone numbers and he's never picked up any of the mail you've sent here the past five years."

"But Matt, I don't ... "

"Kim, honey, the letter sounds like he only wants to meet you. He doesn't say nothing about coming home."

"Read it again, Matt. Read it again."

He read the note more slowly than he normally would so her emotions would have time to catch up to her objectivity.

"Sounds like he's confused about which one of us to call mother. He's only seen me once."

"That's true."

"He probably wants to come home, but doesn't know where home is. Do you think?"

"I don't know, honey."

"He wants us to help him decide. That's it. Do you suppose that's it?"

"Maybe so."

The sheriff's economy of words was intentional. He could think of any number of scenarios that would explain the notes. Graham could simply want money. He may be a seasoned disciple of Julian's perverted thinking by now and need help. He may be on the run himself. Or he may simply be a frightened fourteen-year-old who wants to come home.

"I'm going to call Joyce now. I'll keep you posted. Okay?"

"As long as you're sure now."

"I'm sure."

"I'll get down to the newspaper and run a fax of this note off to you. Then I'll send you the original."

"To me?"

"I thought we decided that already."

"We did. I just wanted to make sure."

"Kim, honey, you be careful."

"I will."

"From the way his note sounds, I don't think Julian will be there. Sounds like Graham has managed a way to see you two alone. But if you see any sign of Mr. Fergusen, I want you to hightail it outta there. You hear me? You don't know what kind of emotional baggage they're carrying around with them. Remember the woman that was shot five years ago? They may hold that against you two. You never know."

"I never thought about that."

"Well, I did. And I'm not entirely satisfied that you want to go it alone."

"Joyce will be with me."

"Just the same, you don't know what you're walking into."

"That's true. But in a way, I do."

"What do you mean?"

"Graham signed it: Love, Graham."

§　§　§　§　§　§

"He said to meet him here in the lobby at nine a.m." Joyce verified, as she nervously checked her watch. "It's nine-twenty."

"I know," Kim said, frowning her disappointment. "Do you think anything has happened to him?"

"I hope not. Oh, Kim, what are we going to do if we've missed him again?"

"I don't know. I don't even want to think about it. Maybe something's happened to delay his getting here."

"Maybe he's here now, close by, watching us to see if we're alone."

Both of the women visually reconnoitered the plush hotel lobby. Except for a few renovations, the hotel looked the same as it did during Kim's ballroom dancing days. The Heritage Classic continued to be one of the premier dancesport championships in the United States. Kim smiled as she remembered Jim's and her first amateur couple championships in the Grand Ballroom on the sixth floor.

There were plenty of tourists scurrying about, many with children. But none looked Graham's age and all appeared dressed appropriately for vacationing in the mountains of North Carolina. Their last contact with Graham proved he wasn't the kind of youngster who wore shorts and sneakers or short-sleeved, designer knit shirts.

Suddenly, Joyce thought she heard her name.

Kim thought she heard it, too.

Both women froze, too breathless to speak.

"Mrs. Fergusen. Mrs. Julian Fergusen?" a man's voice petitioned. "You have a phone call."

The women sprinted toward the registration desk. One of the hotel employees was holding the phone and looking directly at them.

"I'm Mrs. Fergusen," Joyce said, trying to catch her breath.

"You have a phone call," the assistant manager said politely. "You may take it over there." He pointed to another phone at the end of the counter.

Both women raced over to it, and Joyce jumped on the receiver.

"Hello, This is Joyce. This is Mrs. Julian Fergusen."

"Hi, Mom. This is Graham."

Joyce dropped the phone, but managed to catch it before it slipped from her ear.

"Graham, honey, where are you?"

Kim squeezed her ear next to the receiver so she could hear, too.

Joyce eased the phone away from her ear, to accommodate Kim's ear.

"Graham, we love you," yelled Kim into the receiver.

"I love you, too," came the soft reply.

"Why aren't you ... where are you?" Joyce asked excitedly, trying to complete a sentence.

"I want to see you."

"We want to see you, too." Joyce expressed both of their sentiments.

"Are you alone?"

"Yes, of course. There's just the two of us."

"You and my other mother?"

Kim's heart sank. She was still the other mother.

"That's right. Kim and me. We're the only ones here. Your real mother and me."

Tears moistened Kim's eyes.

"Graham, honey. What's wrong? Are you all right?" Kim interjected, as goose flesh covered her arms.

"Walk to the elevators and go down to the first floor. Go out the service entrance."

"What? Graham, what are you saying?"

"Once you're out back, walk over to the hotel maintenance van parked next to the stone wall. There's a note on the windshield."

They heard a click.

"Graham! Graham! Are you there?"

"He hung up," Kim declared the obvious.

Joyce tossed the receiver across the counter and needed Kim to plant it properly before they scurried through the hotel.

They saw the maintenance van parked out back and rushed up to it.

Kim plucked the envelope from behind the windshield wiper and opened it.

They recognized the handwriting immediately as Graham's:

> *Tie this piece of red ribbon around your*
> *car's antenna and drive back out of the front*
> *entrance of the hotel.*

An unsettling chill knifed through Kim as she crammed the note in her slacks pocket.

"Joyce. I don't like all this secrecy. He must be in trouble."

The women ran toward the back entrance.

"He's certainly being overly cautious for some reason."

"Maybe he's run away from Julian," Joyce guessed, as they entered the hotel. "Or maybe he's hurt."

Kim's heart was beating too fast for her to speak. She was the first to reach the car.

Her attempt to insert the car keys in the door failed and she ended up dropping the keys. She fumbled again with the lock and was about to lose her temper when the key entered the lock.

Joyce's attempt to tie the ribbon onto the antenna didn't go smoothly either, but she was finally able to fasten it securely.

"Slow down, Kim," Joyce warned, as Kim pointed the car out of the parking lot and drove toward the entrance.

"I'm sorry. I'm too nervous and worried to take things slow."

"I know, but if Graham's in trouble you don't want to draw attention to yourself, do you?"

"No, you're right," Kim agreed as she hit the brakes too hard, throwing both of them forward against the dash.

"Kim!"

"Okay, okay. I didn't mean to do that."

When she pulled the car to the entrance, she stopped and both worried mothers panned the area on both sides of the street.

"Which way should I go?" panicked Kim.

"I don't know. Most people go right, so go left ... No ... Look ... Over there."

Kim followed Joyce's finger as she pointed to someone standing next to the curb on the other side of the street. The blonde-haired youth was waving something that looked like a red ribbon.

"It's him!"

"It's Graham!"

Kim jerked the car to the right and drove slightly past the youth. She squealed the tires as she forced the car into a U-turn.

"Kim, that's not Graham."

"What?"

"It's not him. It's a young girl!"

CHAPTER
TWENTY-TWO

Are you Mrs. Fergusen?" asked the young girl, as she placed the red ribbon in her vest pocket.

"I am," replied Joyce. "And this is Graham's real mother, Mrs. Sanborn."

"Where's Graham," Kim challenged. "Is he all right?"

"Yes, he's fine. He wants me to take you to him."

Joyce rolled her eyes toward Kim and then back to the young girl who stood beside the car.

"Okay. Get in," Joyce ordered, as Kim unlocked the back door from the driver's side.

The youth glanced cautiously at the surrounding area, and then ducked quickly into the back seat.

"My name is Lisa Youbou. My father and Graham's father are the leaders of our group."

"What group?" asked Kim, as she glanced at her through the rearview mirror.

"Graham will tell you more about it. But for now, I can tell you it's a paramilitary group called RAC. It stands for Reconstitutionalizing America from Canada."

"A paramilitary group?" Joyce asked in astonishment.

"Reconstitutionalizing America from, where did you say—Canada?" Kim chorused nervously.

Lisa nodded her head.

"Graham's father and my father organized it. Oh, turn here. I'm sorry. I'd better keep my eyes on the road."

Kim made a quick left turn. Luckily no one was coming.

"He's still with Julian then," Joyce guessed.

"You mean Commander Fergusen?" replied Lisa.

"Aw give me a break," Joyce sneered. "Commander my..."

"Joyce!" Kim pruned her sentence.

"I know you don't think much of your husband, Mrs. Fergusen, but Commander Fergusen is a great American patriot."

"Oh, please," Joyce countered sarcastically, "he's about as patriotic as the Russian Mafia. And he's not my husband. I divorced him."

"Turn here please, Mrs. Sanborn." The young girl sounded detached, totally unaffected by Joyce's disdain for Julian.

"Tell us about Graham, Lisa," Kim changed the subject.

"What do you want to know?"

"Is he okay? I mean is he healthy? How does he look?"

"He's very healthy and he's extremely good-looking," Lisa confirmed, giggling her amusement.

Kim thought Lisa sounded a little too cavalier. A quick look at Joyce verified similar sentiments.

"We're an item, you know."

"An item?" clarified Kim.

"Yes, you know, well ... we have feelings for each other. Oh, when you get to the next intersection, turn right and then make a quick right again."

"So you're dating then?" Kim queried, studying the young girl in the rearview mirror.

"I wouldn't call it dating. At least not in the regular sense of the word. Our rooms are right next to each other's, in the same compound, that is. His father and my parents share the same cabin."

"Nice cozy arrangement," Joyce commented, trying not to sound too surprised.

"It's not what you think. Our fathers ... and their families ... stay in the headquarters cabin. And that includes Graham and me. We haven't slept together if you're worried about that."

Surprise flew over both women's faces.

"Not that I haven't tried, mind you," Lisa lamented. "Graham says we have to wait till we're married. Oh, when you get to the bridge up ahead, the one outside the entrance to the Biltmore Estate, turn right."

"My parents and I sleep in our rooms. Commander Fergusen and Graham have their own rooms, too. Like I told you, it's next to mine. Turn left here. The rest of the patriots are bivouacked in tents or other cabins on the outpost."

"How tall is he now?" Kim asked, keeping her eyes on the road.

"Your son? Oh, he's as tall as his dad, maybe a little taller. Sometimes it's hard to tell. His boot size is bigger though. But Commander Fergusen can still beat him in arm wrestling."

Lisa reached into her pocket and pulled out a pack of cigarettes.

"Mind if I smoke?"

"Yes," said Kim and Joyce simultaneously.

Surprised, but obedient, Lisa pushed the nicotine packet back into her pocket, and tried her best to smother a sour look.

"Turn here."

"You seem to be taking us out-of-town," Joyce questioned.

"It's just a little further."

"Are you taking us to the outpost?" Kim queried, hoping she wasn't taking them there.

"Heavens, no! They don't even know Graham's meeting you."

"Is he leaving them? Is that why he called us?"

"That's something he'll have to tell you, Mrs. Sanborn. I'm not at liberty to say."

"Then it's just you two. You and Graham ... meeting us this morning?"

"Yes ma'am. If they knew Graham was seeing anybody, they'd court-martial him ... and me, too."

"Court-martial? Lisa, you're kidding."

"No, ma'am I'm not. There's something real big going on and they wouldn't put up with any kind of breach in security. Not even from the Commander's son."

"What is this big something? Is Graham involved?" stammered Joyce.

"He'll tell you. Slow down now. Pull into that rest stop."

The women grew silent in anticipation.

Kim felt her heart pounding in her throat, and her hands were sweaty, as she pointed the car into the rest area.

"Pull in front of that picnic table. The one at the far end of the picnic area. You know which one I mean?"

Kim nodded and eased the car alongside the curb, blocking the view of the picnic table from the road.

Before the car came to a complete stop, Lisa leaped out and began surveying the area in both directions.

The women exchanged nervous looks, wondering if they were in danger.

Lisa motioned for them to stay in the car, and then she signaled for them to come out.

"Just want to make sure we weren't followed."

"We promised Graham we'd be alone," Kim raised her voice defensively.

"Mrs. Sanborn, you wouldn't have gotten this far if I suspected you. It's not you two we're worried about."

The two of them threw Lisa the most puzzled looks.

"It's the government. Graham will tell you all about it."

Both Kim and Joyce glanced around nervously, unsure of how seriously to take Lisa's comments. The parking lot was almost empty. There were only four cars in the lot and all of them were parked next to the rest room facility.

An older woman was walking her dog in a grassy area under several trees near the rest room facilities. The short-haired canine tugged against the leash while the woman strained to maintain her balance.

At the curb next to the rest rooms, a man was disciplining his recalcitrant son after he yanked him from running into the thoroughfare. The youngster seemed both indignant and impatient as he tried valiantly to free himself from the parent's grasp.

"Mrs. Fergusen, would you untie the ribbon from the antenna, please?"

Joyce obeyed willingly, making short work of her assignment.

"Mrs. Fergusen. Mrs. Sanborn," Lisa announced jubilantly as she pointed toward the woods behind them. "Your son."

The women wheeled around as if their move was choreographed.

"Graham," Kim whispered aloud. "Graham, honey."

Joyce sighed heavily, unable to speak.

He limped toward them cautiously, yet confidently, as he emerged from the shadows of the woods. His gaze broke from theirs momentarily as he scanned the area around them. Then he quickly trained his eyes on them again, smiling his delight.

"Graham, it's really you," Kim exclaimed, as she quickly closed the distance between them. She allowed Joyce to embrace him first and watched admiringly as mother and son locked themselves in a lengthy embrace.

Joyce pulled herself free and reached out to include Kim in Graham's encompassing embrace. The three of them remained huddled, arms overlayed, hearts pounding ferociously, reunited in a tangle of tears of joy.

Unable to control her emotions, Kim felt her nose burn and her lips numb as she buried her head in her son's chest.

Graham lowered his lips and kissed Joyce on the forehead. Then he affectionately kissed the hair on top of Kim's head and breathed in deeply the aroma of her scented hair.

Joyce peeled herself from his resistant grasp and caressed his stubbled cheek as she pulled back. When he reached for her with his free hand, she grabbed it and held the top of his hand to her cheek. Then she tearfully kissed his hand and placed it around Kim, who was still clinging tightly to him.

"Graham, honey, this is your real mother," Joyce announced affectionately, "She loves you so much."

Kim's sobs escalated immediately and her rubbery legs gave way, forcing Graham to cradle her to prevent her from collapsing.

Her uncontrollable sobs were the liquid language of pent-up emotion. They were the tears of a mother reunited with the son who was torn from her so maliciously ten years before.

Graham eased her toward the picnic table, but stopped their advance when Kim started wailing again. He kissed her on the forehead and stood dutifully silent as his mother emptied herself completely.

Neither Joyce nor Lisa could censor their own tears in response to Kim's emotional upheaval.

When it was evident that Kim was close to composing herself, Joyce reunited with the two of them and helped Graham plant Kim on the park bench. Then she handed Kim a box of tissues from the car and lifted some of them as insurance for Lisa and herself.

"You okay?" Joyce asked Kim, touching her shoulder gently.

Kim nodded and then blew her nose before she looked up.

"I'm sorry," Kim apologized. "I thought I'd never see you again."

"Don't be sorry, Mom. You've got nothing to be sorry for. I ... you ... I can't tell you how glad I am to see you ... both of you."

"You seem ... so much older than fourteen."

Graham grasped both of the women's hands. "Well, I've had to grow up sort of fast."

Kim noticed the strength of his grip immediately and his hands were rough, like those of a working man. Although his touch was gentle, there was a bridled explosiveness to it, giving it the feel of coiled energy.

His eyes had not lost their intense blueness and although he was wearing a hat, the women could see that he had a military hair cut. That saddened Kim, who hated to see his blonde hair cropped so closely.

"Did I see you limping slightly as you came out of the woods?" Joyce asked, raising her eyebrows worriedly.

Graham nodded quickly.

"I fell from a mountain face a couple of weeks ago. My knee's still not right."

"Oh, Graham," Kim sympathized, as she ran her hand lightly over his injured knee.

Graham smiled, and glanced at Lisa for a perimeter check.

She gave him a thumbs up sign, indicating she was satisfied they were still cloistered.

"I'm fine, really. It'll be as good as new in a couple of months."

"Did you go to a doctor?" Joyce asked.

"Negative. We've got our own."

Kim let out a few chopped sighs, retailing her anxiety.

"I want you two to realize something. I love you. I love you both. Did you get the notes I sent you?"

The women nodded almost in unison.

Kim explained how they had shared the mementos, and described how she cleaned his soiled cap in the dishwasher to preserve it. Then she nervously confessed why the last meeting had not materialized. "I'm so sorry, Graham. I'd give anything if I could change it. If I'd only known ... "

Graham broke into her confession quickly. "It's okay. We're here now. That's what's important."

He squeezed both of their hands and divided his solemn attention between them. "I've got so much to say and too little time to say it."

"I don't think I like where this is going," said Kim, studying him and pining at the same time.

Graham formed his lips into a tight line and frowned.

"You're not going back with us, are you?" Kim spoke pathetically.

"No. I'm sorry. I can't."

His polite refusal was met with solemn faces from both women.

"Why?" agonized Kim.

Joyce threw him another forlorn look.

"I don't know how much Lisa told you, but we're patriots in a movement founded by my father and Lisa's parents."

"The RAC," Joyce confirmed.

"Yes. You know about us then."

"Only what Lisa told us," Kim clarified.

"I didn't tell them much, Graham. I told them you would tell them," Lisa inserted.

"We are going to reconstitute government in America."

"Oh, Graham, honey," Kim interrupted, "do you know what you're saying?"

"What has he done to you?" Joyce asked, horrified at what she was hearing.

"We know exactly what we are doing," chimed Lisa.

Graham motioned for her to be quiet.

"I've been thinking a lot about both of you. I know you're my real mom," he said as he squeezed Kim's hand, "and I know you're my adoptive mother," he addressed Joyce, looking intently at her. "And I love you both."

"We love you, too, honey," Kim spoke for both of them.

"Ever since I saw you at the cabin, I've wanted to be with you both." One of his eyelids quivered as he looked first at Kim and then at Joyce.

Kim started to cry as Graham continued.

"When, uh, my real father and I were carjacked, when I was little, I didn't really understand what had happened. All I wanted was to be with my family. A part of me knew my father wasn't coming back. I don't remember much—I just have flashes of things—like the blood on my father's head and chest. I remember the terrified look in his eyes before he was shot. And I remember thinking we weren't going to have a happy Christmas."

Tears ran down Kim's cheeks as she closed her eyes. Joyce squeezed her shoulder.

"My father didn't move after he was shot and I knew something bad had happened. Then I remember a black man and woman. The woman was really good to me. I think she wanted to keep me. Then Uncle Ben took me to you," he explained as he looked at Joyce.

All Joyce could do was sigh heavily and make good use of the tissues.

"Mom, he said you and my grandparents were all dead, and that someone was trying to kill him, so he couldn't keep me, either. That's why he wore a funny mustache. I knew it was him, and he said he was hiding from the people that killed all of you. He said he'd take me to a place far away so nobody could hurt me. Now I know he lied to me. He was involved from the beginning, wasn't he?"

"Graham, honey, he masterminded the whole thing."

The tears moistened Kim's face, but she controlled her sobbing as she recounted the whole grievous story up to the cabin incident and the notes he sent to Piney Creek.

"As I said in my letters, I didn't know how to get in touch with you. I didn't know Grandpa and Nanna's real names. I still don't," he admitted to Joyce.

"Mr. and Mrs. McDonald, honey," Joyce said.

"And you've got two sets of natural grandparents who are alive, too. My parents—Mr. and Mrs. Spencer. Pauline and Jerry. And your father's parents—Marie and Gary Sanborn. Oh, Graham, they love you so much."

"I think I kind of remember them. I remember a man who liked golf, and he let me hit balls with a short gold club he sawed off just for me. And a woman who used to sneak me M & M's."

Kim nodded. "That would be Grandma Spencer. She loves those M&M's. She still thinks I don't know she snuck them to you."

"And I remember a giraffe. My father won it for me at the fair."

Kim nodded several times.

"Mom number two." He brightened. "I know you and dad adopted me illegally ... "

"Honey, we're divorced. I divorced Julian two years ago."

"Oh," he said, looking at her sorrowfully. "He never said anything about it."

"He doesn't know. I didn't know where he was to have him served. I'm sure he's probably figured it out by now."

"You haven't asked me anything about him," Graham asserted, catching her off guard.

"I'm not really interested. He left with you and never said a word. When we found you at the cabin, I wanted to kill him."

"He was wounded at the cabin and Rachael was killed there."

"So that's who the young woman was we found in the cave."

Graham nodded. "Dad wanted me to keep up with my schooling. She was a good teacher. He met her at one of our reconstitutionalizing retreats. He liked her a lot. I did, too. I never called her mother, though. She was good to me. She treated me like a son." He looked thoughtfully at Kim. "Whose white dog was at the cabin?"

"Hope? You must mean Hope. He's my dog."

Graham smiled.

"Do you still have him?"

Kim nodded.

"He showed up several months after you were kidnapped. He's been with me ever since. Oh, and he has a black spot on his right hind leg, similar to your birthmark."

"How 'bout that."

Graham pulled his pants leg up to expose the almost perfectly formed star on his right knee.

"Here's my lucky star. It's still there."

"May I?" Kim inquired, as she reached out timidly to touch the birthmark.

"Of course."

Kim ran her trembling fingers over it, remembering the times she had pined over his photos, using them as tactile surrogates for the son she couldn't embrace.

"Oh, Graham, why can't you come home with us?" Kim pleaded.

"I wish I could. I even tried to run away when I was younger. Mom, I remember breaking away from Uncle Ben when he was taking me to Atlanta. Boy, he was mad at me. But I wanted to go back to my room and hide under the giraffe. That stuffed toy was the only family I believed I had left.

"When I saw you two at the cabin, I wanted to leave with you. I was about to sneak out when the shooting started. That's when Rachael was killed. Then one thing led to another. Things happened really fast after that. The commander—Dad—was real upset we left the weapons cache there. But we figured you'd never find it."

"Julian was Commander of the RAC even then?" Joyce asked.

"Oh, no. I guess I'm just used to calling him commander. He organized the RAC two years ago."

"Hope found it," Kim volunteered.

Graham squinted his eyes.

"The cave entrance ... behind the fireplace."

"Hope ... your white dog found it?" Graham stammered.

"He's a very special dog. Somehow I feel he's been a link between us. I've always felt closer to you when Hope was near."

Lisa walked behind Graham and placed her hands on his shoulders.

"We haven't got much time," she cautioned. "I'm sorry, but we're at risk the longer we stay here. And we don't want to jeopardize their safety either."

Both Kim and Joyce threw them worried looks.

"Graham, honey, are you in some kind of trouble?" Kim asked. A momentary panic gripped her, locking her gaze on him.

"Six weeks ago our unit intercepted a weapons transfer between Fort Bragg and Camp LeJeune."

"Graham ... what are you saying?" Kim stuttered.

"We ambushed an army patrol and seized all of their weapons," Lisa chimed in. "They didn't know what hit them."

"Oh, my God, Graham ... You didn't." Kim gasped.

Although Joyce looked concerned, she wasn't surprised. She'd heard Julian plan similar anti-government actions ten years earlier.

"Several soldiers were wounded. One seriously, we think."

Kim closed her eyes.

"I think that was in the news, wasn't it?" Joyce recovered.

"On every front page west of the Atlantic Ocean," Lisa squealed with delight, as she paraphrased her father's characterization of the theft.

"Lisa!" Graham chastised, shaking his head at her.

"That's why I just had to see you. To see you both ... before ... we leave the country."

Both of the women jerked backward simultaneously.

"Leave the country?" Joyce repeated.

"You mean you're going to leave America?" screeched Kim.

Graham nodded.

Lisa amplified his nod with hers.

"We're leaving America, Mrs. Sanborn, so we can re-establish it. The politicians and the greedy super rich have squandered the American dream. America today is not the America the Constitution created two hundred years ago. America is no longer a democracy. It's run by lobbyists and corporations with deep pockets. And the government can't protect us anymore. What happened on 9-11 showed us that. We're going to change all of that."

"Easy," Graham cautioned her.

"Well, it's true, isn't it?" she defended.

"Yes, of course it's true."

"Oh, honey. I can't help but feel you're making a mistake," Kim warned, as she touched his arm.

"Staying here and being arrested would be a mistake. Besides, I believe in what we're doing. America has forgotten its roots. The government is so corrupt and inefficient that it can't possibly be a government of the people. We've become a welfare nation instead of a country that values honest work. We don't take care of our old people or our children. The soul of America is dying."

"Nobody cares about us," Lisa chimed. "My brother lost his retirement and life savings in the Enron collapse. What they did was criminal."

"Do you know what you two are saying?" Kim questioned, sending him a horrified look.

"In the summer of 1776, the men who signed the Declaration of Independence made revolution an instrument that could be used by honorable men for a just cause ... Life, liberty and the pursuit of happiness. Those were the truths they held to be self-evident."

"You're beginning to sound like Julian," Joyce spewed. "Graham, honey, you're a better person than that."

"What's he done to you?" Kim snapped.

"He's made a patriot out of him," defended Lisa. "Out of both of us."

"He's turned you into criminals," blasted Joyce.

"I imagine the King of England had this same conversation a little over two hundred years ago," Graham replied, sounding confident and purposeful. "Except that the criminals he referred to were people like Thomas Jefferson, Benjamin Franklin, John Adams, Richard Henry Lee and John Penn to name a few."

"That was different," shouted Joyce. "They founded America. They were our forefathers."

Graham smiled and then sighed slowly.

"We hold certain truths to be self-evident," he paraphrased the Declaration of Independence, "that whenever any form of government becomes destructive of these ends, it is the right of the people to alter or abolish it, and to institute new government. That's what the

Declaration of Independence says. It's our right, our duty, to throw off such government. Read it. Read the Declaration of Independence. See for yourself."

Kim was too shocked to speak.

Joyce opened her mouth, but nothing came out.

"Tyrants are unfit to rule free people. It says that, too, in the Declaration of Independence," Lisa interjected. "Your son is a great American. A lot of our ancestors who fought for our independence from Britain were no older than Graham. I should think you'd be proud of him."

Kim narrowed her eyes at Lisa, who remained safely behind Graham.

"We are proud of him," she spoke for Joyce and herself. "But we want him home. And we want him to stop all this, this ... "

"Anti-government talk," trailed Joyce, completing Kim's sentence.

"I didn't want to leave without seeing you one more time," Graham replied, pulling the three of them back on track.

The finality in his voice produced tears in both Kim's and Joyce's eyes.

"How can we get in touch with you?" Kim asked dejectedly, realizing she was about to lose him again.

"You can't."

"Oh, Graham. No!" Kim pleaded, trying her best not to lose her temper. "Why?"

"What do you ... where ... where are you going?" Joyce asked as she reached for Kim's hand.

"I can't tell you for your own protection, except to say we'll be in Canada."

"How long?" Joyce asked tearfully, beating Kim to the question.

"I don't know. Maybe two years. Maybe longer."

Kim groaned her disappointment.

"You know what you're doing to us, don't you?" criticized Joyce mournfully.

He sighed.

"You're ripping our hearts out. Do you know what we've been through these past ten years?" Joyce screamed.

"Joyce," Kim spoke softly, pulling her friend close to her. "Joyce, it's okay."

"It's not okay," she thundered. "Graham, you were snatched from this woman ten years ago. She's your real mother. You should be with her. You're only fourteen years old. In heaven's name think what you're doing."

Joyce pulled her hand from his firm grasp and put both her arms around Kim.

"Don't do this to her! Let's all four just leave here right now. Come on," Joyce ordered as she grabbed Kim's arm and turned toward the car. She looked back over her shoulder and shouted, "Come on, Graham ... Lisa ... Let's go."

Lisa fired a nervous look at Graham.

After a slight hesitation he shook his head.

"No, Mom. I'm sorry. I can't. Please understand. It's impossible."

"I can't believe what you're ... "

"Joyce ... No, please," Kim whispered aloud, gently unwrapping Joyce's fingers from her arm. "We can't force him to go with us. He's been under Julian's influence far too long. We must let him go."

Kim retreated a few steps and wrapped her arms tightly around Graham. Then she pulled herself back slightly and cupped his rugged face in her hands.

"I love you, son ... I always will."

He drew her to him and then reached out to include Joyce in his farewell embrace.

"I love you—both of you," he whispered tearfully as he squeezed them.

Resignation pried them apart.

Lisa reached quickly into her pocket.

"Here," she said proudly, extending photos of Graham dressed in his military fatigues, one for each of them.

"Will we ever see you again?" asked Joyce as she wiped away a tear.

"I hope so. That's my intention," assured Graham.

"You can come to our wedding," squealed Lisa, as she grabbed his arm possessively.

Both women were stunned by her unexpected announcement.

"We've talked about it privately," he explained, looking at them sheepishly, "and Lisa knows we can't even begin to think about it until we're at least sixteen."

"Sixteen!" quizzed Kim.

"Well, maybe eighteen," Lisa boasted.

Kim locked her eyes on Graham's face.

"Will you let us know when we can see you again?"

He nodded his intention.

"Is there any chance ... we'll be able to ... can we contact you?" Joyce begged.

He shook his head. "No. I'll have to contact you."

"How? How will you know where to reach us? I don't want to keep meeting like this," Joyce stammered.

"I know. Suppose I give you my business card," Kim proposed. "It's got my home address on it."

"I'll write my address on the back of Kim's card," Joyce chorused.

"No, wait. That won't work. I can't carry anything like that."

"Then how will you reach us?" Kim asked pathetically.

"Okay, look. Write your addresses and phone numbers down. I'll commit them to memory."

"He's got a photographic memory," praised Lisa.

"I'm just good at memorizing things. I wouldn't go so far as to call it a photographic memory."

"You do, too," insisted Lisa.

The women hastily scribbled their addresses and phone numbers and gave them to him.

Kim fumbled with the keepsake heart on her necklace Jim bought for her. It was inscribed with all three of their birthdays and divided into two halves. She quickly separated the two halves and gave one to Graham.

"Keep this next to your heart. Maybe when we meet again, we can join these for good."

"I'll keep it forever, Mom. I love you."

Joyce frantically searched in her purse for a memento to give him. Then she frowned her disappointment. "I don't have anything to give you. I ... "

He embraced her and kissed the top of her head.

"I'll settle for a hug," he said affectionately, as he reached out to her. Then he motioned for Kim to join their tearful embrace.

After a few moments, Kim pulled Lisa into the farewell huddle and the four of them squeezed out every ounce of connection between them.

CHAPTER
TWENTY-THREE

Emotionally drained and despondent, the women decided to stay overnight at Karen's house before they drove to their respective homes. Karen wanted them to stay through the week-end, but neither Kim nor Joyce felt they would be much company. Joyce drove back to Atlanta the next morning. A pesky water pump postponed Kim's return trip until after lunch.

By the time Kim picked Hope up from her parent's house and drove home, it was almost dark. The motion sensitive flood light detected her arrival, providing the light she needed to unlock the front door.

"It's good to be home, old boy," she addressed the aging dog. "I'll give you your walk in a minute."

She tossed her purse on the sofa, but it ricocheted off the cushions and fell to the floor along side her shoes. Kim checked for messages on her hasty march to the kitchen and was glad there were none.

"No one missed us, fella. I could have stayed a few extra days with Karen after all. But then I wouldn't have the pleasure of your company, would I?"

She gave him a quick rub and tailgated him a few steps before she moved around him on her way to the kitchen. After giving Hope the customary attention, Kim waited on herself, allowing the cup of instant cappuccino to moisten her tired lips.

"Ah-h-h. This stuff is addictive, you know," she informed Hope, who tilted his head at her as if he understood.

She retraced her steps into the living room and sat slowly, burying herself in the sofa's plush cushions.

Her gaze drifted to Hope as he sprawled on the carpet beside her.

"I've lost him again, old fella. He's probably in Canada by now. That's where he told your Aunt Joyce and I they went."

Hope raised his head and peered at her momentarily, then lowered it again, sensing she wasn't planning to walk him anytime soon.

"He's going to reconstitute America from Canada. What do you think about that? Think you can find him in Canada? No," she answered her own question. "I don't think we'll even try. Looks like our crusade is over, old boy. He's ... he's not a little boy anymore. Just like you're not a puppy. And he's different. I don't know him and I'm his mother. There's a wall between us. He knows I'm his mother, but I feel an emotional void between us. It's like he's perfectly satisfied knowing I'm there for him. I don't think he needs me for anything more than that. Oh, Hope, what am I going to do now?"

Kim placed her cup on the coaster and plucked her purse from the floor. She extracted Graham's photo from the unzipped pocket and held it in front of her.

He looks too much like an adult, she thought. *That uniform adds ten years to his looks.*

She brushed back a tear that leaked onto her lower eyelid.

Looks like I may have lost my little boy forever this time. I've missed sharing his birthdays with his grandparents ...

introducing him to the tooth fairy ... helping ease the fright of his first day at school ... buying his first bicycle ... reading him nursery rhymes and Winnie the Pooh and taking him to see Disney movies. Mom and Dad missed so many chances to baby sit for me.

She was too tired to cry, but the subconscious artifacts kept coming.

Vaccinations. Even his childhood vaccinations had found a canine substitute. She glanced at Hope thoughtfully. "You didn't like all those shots and examinations you had to have, did you, boy?"

Hope looked at her again, then ritualistically plopped his head back down.

She looked longingly at Graham's photo again.

"You've got an athletic build, honey. A football player's body. Maybe a wrestler's quickness," she fantasized aloud.

"I've lost my little dancer, too," she mourned to herself. "You used to like to watch Jim and me dance. I thought we had another ballroom dance champion in the making."

Kim threw Hope an approving glance.

"He wants to see you, too, old boy. What do you think about that?"

She watched his irregular breathing a few moments and was about to treat herself to another sip of cappuccino when the phone rang. Both she and Hope flinched, mirroring each other's surprise.

She glanced at her watch.

Too late for a salesman to call. Better answer it.

"Hello."

"Hello, Mrs. Sanborn? This is Connie Youbou, Lisa's mother."

Kim could sense the apprehension in Mrs. Youbou's voice.

"Yes, hi, Mrs. Youbou. You've certainly caught me by surprise. I never expected to get a call from you."

Kim could feel her throat tighten.

"Mrs. Sanborn, I don't know how to tell you this," she said weakly, as she started to cry.

"Tell me what?" Kim raised her voice, feeling herself flush with panic.

"They're all dead," she announced pitifully before sobbing uncontrollably.

"Dead? Who's dead, Mrs. Youbou?" Kim screamed. Mrs. Youbou! Talk to me!"

"He's dead, Mrs. Sanborn. Your son, Graham, is dead."

Unable to keep her spinning head from weakening her knees, Kim tried to steady herself as a dizzying wave of nausea swept her off her feet. She collapsed in a heap beside the sofa, paralyzed by what she just heard.

"How ... how did he ... what happened?"

"My husband, Commander Fergusen, and your son are all dead ... and so are four others," she railed, still struggling to get the words out.

"What? How?" Kim repeated, as she stumbled toward coherence. "How do you know?"

"We were ambushed by government agents this afternoon on our way to Beckley ... Beckley, West Virginia."

She surrendered to another outburst of tears before she could continue.

"The government set up a road block ... " she gulped out the words. "Commander Fergusen radioed back to us to wait until ... They decided to plow through the barricade instead of surrender ... They lost control as they crashed through the road block ... " she trailed off.

Kim closed her eyes as she pulled herself up to a kneeling position beside the couch. She was oblivious to the constant licks generated by Hope as he bathed her hands, face, and neck.

"The van rolled down an embankment."

Kim turned as pale as a sheet. Her eyes sagged into narrow slits and her dry mouth locked open as she knelt beside the couch.

"I ... we ... were in the car behind them. We saw it all ...
I ... I could see flames ... the van was on its top ... we stopped
just beyond it. We opened fire on the FBI agents ... so we
could ... We ... we rushed up to the van and tried to get them
out."

Kim breathed in several choppy breaths.

"Graham ... was in the van? You're saying my son was
in the burning van?"

"Mrs. Sanborn, I'm so sorry. His head ... the blood ...
his head was crushed."

Kim lost her grip on the phone and it slid down her onto
her lap before she could catch it. She could vaguely hear
Mrs. Youbou's voice through the receiver. By the time Kim
lifted the receiver to her ear, she knew she had missed some
of Mrs. Youbou's explanation.

"I'm sorry ... didn't ... I didn't hear what you said."

"Our men pulled him ... pulled your son out of the
wreckage. My husband was still in the van. I could see his
arm and head sticking out of the window. The men tried to
drag Commander Fergusen out, too ... it was burning ... they
tried to get them out before it ... exploded. It was awful ... it
was ... awful."

"Do you ... have my son's body?" Kim whispered,
hoping she could at least bury her son.

"No, I'm sorry. We didn't have time. Government
reinforcements were moving in on us. I only had time to pull
my daughter off your son. The Feds were swarming all over
us. A carload of us managed to get away. I don't know how
many of the others got away."

Kim remained on her knees, too shocked to move.

"Mrs. Sanborn, are you there? Mrs. Sanborn?"

"Yes, I'm here."

"Lisa wants to talk to you."

Kim waited catatonically for Lisa's voice.

"I'm so sorry, Mrs. Sanborn," Lisa said, sobbing through her apology. "I know you loved your son. I loved him, too. I can't believe he's dead ... And my daddy. And Commander Fergusen."

Numbed by the terrible news, Kim let the tears blur her eyes as she looked blankly at Hope.

"Lisa, are you all right? Were you or your mother injured?"

"Yes ... no. I'll never be all right again ... I just wanted to tell you ... well ... you know. My mom and I are fine. We weren't injured."

"You take care of your mother, okay?"

"We've got to go now. Mom wants to say something before we go."

Lisa handed the phone to her mother.

"Mrs. Sanborn, you probably won't be hearing from us again. I'm sorry we had to met under these horrible circumstances. Lisa says Graham loved you both. Oh, I almost forgot ... Mrs. Fergusen. I can't ... I won't be able to call her. I'm sorry."

"I'll make sure she knows."

"I thought you'd want to know about ... your son. I ... we didn't want you to read about it in the papers. That's why I called. Lisa told me about your meeting in Asheville. I'm glad you saw him again ... before ... before he died. I wish you the best."

Kim let her silence speak for her.

"Well, then. I guess it's good-bye. God bless you and Mrs. Fergusen."

"God bless you both, too."

Kim eased the phone slowly from her ear, letting it slip purposefully through her fingers to insure herself an uninterrupted cry.

§ § § § § §

The small intimate group of mourners huddled respectfully as Kim placed the photo of Graham into the shallow hole Jerry had dug earlier that evening. It was a copy of the photo Lisa had given the grieving mothers the week before in Asheville.

Kim tossed the first handful of rooting soil into the miniature grave and watched as the others paid similar respects. Her parents sprinkled their share of the soil mix and were followed by Jim's parents, Joyce and her parents, the Lees, Pamela and Karen.

John and Louise sent e-mail condolences along with their regrets from Ireland, where they were celebrating both his sixty-eighth birthday and his Irish heritage. John assured Kim they would conduct a moment of silence out of respect for the family on the day of the funeral.

The Colemans sent a huge bouquet of cut flowers and expressed their sincere regrets. Mary was in the hospital, recovering from a cancer operation and Matt was at her side.

Karen planted an azalea over the buried photo and used her hand to shovel the remaining soil into the miniature grave.

Jerry waited for Karen to complete the interment, then he asked all of them to circle the surrogate grave. The last glimmer of hope of seeing her son alive again faded from her tear-soaked eyes. Kim felt the pressure of her father's hand on hers as he lowered his head to pray.

"Let us pray ... Cherishing memories that are forever sacred, sustained by a faith that is stronger than death, and comforted by the hope of a life that shall endless be, we commit to the earth all that is mortal of our beloved Graham Spencer Sanborn. As he has borne the image of the earth, so shall he bear the image of the heavenly. Into Your hands ... we commend his spirit ... Amen."

§ § § § § §

"Hello, Tony. This is Kim."

"Hi, doll. I'm so sorry to hear about your son. How are you holding up?"

"I'm taking it a day at a time."

"I guess that's all anyone can do. I wish I could wave a magic wand and make everything all right. Is there anything I can do? Anything you need?"

"A sabbatical."

"A what?"

"You heard me ... a sabbatical."

"That's what I thought you said. You want to give me a heart attack?"

"I need to take the summer off. I've got a few things to sort out."

"Does that mean the September book tour is still on?"

"Oh, I see. It's okay for me to grieve, so long as I grieve on cue."

"I didn't mean it that way."

"If I thought that, I'd look for another agent. I don't know if I'll be ready for the September tour. I hope I will."

"You're not planning on making the Palm Springs or Hawaiian writer's conferences then?"

"No, I think not."

"Oh, Kim. I wish you'd ... never mind. Your publisher is not going to ... well, you know how they are. Publishers support novelists who play by the rules, particularly when they've received huge advances."

"Tony, I realize the possible fallout it'll generate, but I need time to heal or I'm not going to be any good to anybody."

"Kim, I can understand that. I really can."

"I heard a but, Tony. I'm sorry you're having difficulty with this. I need a time-out before I can be around people again, especially the media."

"I'll handle things at this end. Don't worry about a thing. You just do what you've got to do. And if there's anything I can do, let me know."

"Thank you, Tony. I know this isn't the kind of launch you expected. I'll be in touch."

"Don't forget. Call me."

"I won't forget. I promise."

"And if you should change your mind ... "

"I won't change my mind, Good-bye, Tony."

"Good-bye."

Kim placed the phone on its plastic cradle, and sighed her relief at making the call to her agent.

I'll give Tony a chance to call the publisher and then I'll call him, she thought. *I believe Mike sees novelists as people, not robots covered with flesh whose only purpose is to provide literary fodder for the publishing mill.*

Kim looked lovingly at Hope, who was lying on the couch facing her.

"Looks like I'm going back into hibernation, doesn't it, boy?"

Hope barked his sentiments.

She deserted her half-empty cup of cappuccino and walked slowly past the bouquet of flowers her publisher had sent her. As she advanced lethargically down the short hallway leading to her bedroom, she patted her hip several times signaling for Hope to follow.

Grief led her to her nest of melancholy. She neglected to turn on the light and didn't stop until she stood in front of the mirror. The half-moons under her eyes and the smeared mascara mocked her beauty. Her disheveled hair fell in blue-black strands across her pale face.

Standing in black from neck to toe, she looked like one of those silent, talented women who play cellos or violins in symphony orchestras. Except in her case, the strings were heart strings and the musical score had flopped, sending her into a tangle of miscues and sour notes.

Wordlessly, she retraced her steps and planted herself on the edge of the bed. Her leaden eyes found the painting of Graham and Hope standing in front of the Christmas tree. Karen had entitled it *Homecoming*, anticipating a happier reunion.

"Good-bye, son. I guess we were just star-crossed in this skin school experience. We never really had a chance to enjoy each other, did we?"

She sighed her depression, but kept her swollen eyes on the painting.

"I wish I could wave a magic wand and start us all over again." She extended her arms outward and waved an imaginary wand. Then she glanced at the boxes filled with memorabilia in her closet and decided to postpone her nostalgic walk through them.

Her eye caught the article she'd clipped from the newspaper earlier in the week. It was the news coverage of the shoot-out, describing the FBI's heroics in aborting the attempt by a renegade paramilitary outfit to transfer stolen armaments.

The report identified the RAC as responsible for the attempted theft. The report did not disclose the names of the suspected anti-government militiamen. The names of the federal agents killed in the daring mid-day raid were released with strong assurances from the White House that the ones responsible for their deaths would be apprehended.

Kim's weary eyes panned back up to the painting.

"I know one militiaman they won't question or apprehend," she confirmed aloud.

I almost wish they could. That would mean you'd still be alive, she grieved silently.

The ensemble of events over the last four days had completely derailed her. She felt strangely robotic, numbed by the turn of events.

The news of Graham's death scoured her clean of hope. She wanted to go on, but she didn't know where she wanted to go. She hadn't realized until now how much of her self-worth was wrapped around the reclamation of her son. Now that he was gone, she felt diminished, incomplete, halved and quartered.

She suppressed an impulse to curl up into a ball of self pity. Heaving herself up to a standing position, Kim shuffled slowly to the mirror and faced her tear-blemished double.

"We're writing another novel, dear. It's about a mother's search for her son. So pull yourself together. We've got work to do."

She forced a frail smile and lingered long enough to turn it into a self-conscious grin.

"If faith moves mountains, it ought to move this one hundred fifteen pound best selling novelist down the hall to her office."

Finding a sudden burst of energy, she pirouetted slowly around and headed toward the hallway.

"Where's that half-empty cup of cappuccino? I can't write without it."

CHAPTER
TWENTY-FOUR

Y ou have what we call retrograde amnesia."

The young man's eyes were riveted on the doctor, who smiled clinically at his patient.

"Retro ... Retro ... grade ... Am ... nesia?"

"Yes. That's right. As you've already begun to suspect, the injuries you sustained nine months ago erased all of your memory."

"No mem ... memor ... ies," he agreed, pointing to his head.

"I'm afraid not. We'll know more when we get your latest test results, but the principle damage was to the connections to your hippocampus, the neural structure responsible for recording new memories. Even if some of your memories survived the accident in some latent biochemical form, they will probably never be available to your conscious mind."

"Never?"

The doctor shook his head.

"Why?"

"That's the question that has kept me in the business for the past twenty years. The human brain seems to be a highly resilient organ. Despite massive injuries, like those of your own, the brain attempts to heal itself. It strives to remain fully functional and begin the memory reacquisition process immediately. As soon as it's deprived of one complete set of memories, it begins to lay down a fresh set."

"Nine months ... new set?"

The doctor nodded.

"That's exactly right. Over the last nine months your brain developed an entirely new neural network. This regeneration takes place automatically. Life goes on, as they say. A new you is emerging. A new narrative of memories."

"Different person?"

"Yes, in your case a totally different person. The post-amnesia brain, following recovery, is usually totally different from the pre-amnesia brain. Biomedically speaking, it's an entirely different neural network. You are wired differently now. If the wiring is repatterned, the self is a different self."

"Quite ... a lot to handle."

"Extraordinarily so. You are essentially a new person. Your body is the same body you inhabited during the pre-amnesia phase of your life, but your brain has absolutely no memory of it."

The doctor pulled up a chair and sat next to his patient.

"I'll try to explain this as clearly as I can so you can understand it."

"I'm young ... but ... I'm not dumb," the young man challenged.

"I'm sorry if I gave you that impression. I wasn't implying that at all. Even older retrograde amnesia patients have expressed difficulty understanding what's happening to them."

"Frighten ... ing."

"Very frightening. In fact, situations like this occur more frequently than most people realize. They're called fugues. Times in their lives when they suddenly forget who they are and find themselves in unfamiliar places among unfamiliar people."

"Like me," the patient repeated himself.

The doctor nodded.

"To the victim of a fugue, it's like they were suddenly born as an adult. They have a basic understanding of language and of the world, but they don't have the slightest idea who they are. However, they eventually recover and go on to lead normal lives."

"You're sure I don't ... have a fugue?"

The doctor frowned, realizing what he was implying.

"I'm sure, son. Unfortunately your memory loss is permanent."

"The real me ... is lost too?" the youngster lamented.

"Well, yes and no. Can you handle something really heavy?" the doctor asked, as he placed his hand on the patient's shoulder.

"Try me."

"Okay. I don't believe you've lost the real you. The real you is sitting across from me this very minute. The real you is hearing me say this right now. The real you is the new you."

The doctor pinched the patient on the arm.

"I just pinched the real you. The real you is the subjective you. In subjective time, you did not experience a gap between your old self and your new self. Are you with me?"

He nodded. His intense gaze was locked on the doctor.

"One instant you were rendered unconscious by the accident. The next instant, according to your conscious mind, was when you regained consciousness in the hospital. In your subjective experience, you lost no time. But from other people's experience of you, there are three you's. There is the pre-accident you, the part of you that was unconscious for five and a half months, and the conscious you who is listening intently to me now."

"Three pieces of me which make the real me?"

"Basically, yes. I believe your real self is composed of all three you's. Unfortunately, you do not have what we call interphase continuity. You don't remember who you were before. The only continuity you have now is the past four and a half months of your life."

"Baby ... in a man's body."

"Actually, no. You have a fully developed brain. That's why we told you to be patient with your new self. You're learning fast. Extremely fast. Soon you'll be able to carry on a conversation like an adult."

"Intelligent ... I hope," the patient added, laughing at himself.

"No doubt, young man. I can already tell you are extremely bright. By the way, they did a phenomenal job on your reconstructive surgery. You are a very fortunate man."

"I know ... I am grateful."

"He certainly looks a lot different than he did nine months ago," confirmed the rehabilitation therapist who joined them.

The patient smiled.

"Lucky ... to be ... alive."

"Has anyone told you how you got to Saint Gabriel's?" the therapist asked.

"No," he replied, straightening himself in his chair.

"We found you lying on the curb outside the Emergency Room entrance. You were in pretty bad shape. Someone looked after your wounds before he dumped you on our doorstep, so to speak. Otherwise, you would have died."

He squinted, trying to organize his thoughts.

"Just ... left me there?"

"You had no identification, no footwear, and no one to explain what happened to you. There is no match for your fingerprints on record with any law enforcement agency. The only things you have from your past are the heart pendant found beside you and this," the doctor said, tapping the patient's knee.

The young man lifted his right trousers leg, exposing the star on his knee.

"We thought that beautiful birthmark would help locate your parents. We sent your picture to every school in Montreal and your handsome face has been in the news all over Canada. Of course, your face reconstruction makes it harder to recognize you. You're quite a celebrity though. And that heart pendant looks like it belongs on a necklace. I feel certain we'll find your girl friend, wife, or folks—or they'll find you."

"By the way, have you decided what you want your name to be?" the doctor asked.

"John Doe," the young patient said proudly.

"John Doe?" the doctor repeated, finding his choice amusing. "You could name yourself anything you want. Why John Doe?"

"That's what we put on his admissions slip," the therapist replied, "and when he saw it, he decided to adopt it for himself."

"John Doe ... perfect name for me. I am no one ... but I am ... everyone."

"Mr. John Doe, I'm amazed at your progress," the doctor praised. "You've had to learn how to speak again, how to think and reason ... "

"How to spell ... how to add ... multiply ... divide," the patient interrupted.

"Well, whoever you were in your past life, Mr. Doe, you've been given a phenomenal set of wiring. You have accelerated through the battery of therapies since you've been here. So I've got some terrific news for you."

"Terrific ... is good."

"First, since we don't know exactly how old you are, we have designated tomorrow March twelfth as your birthday."

"Hurrah ... my birthday!"

"You appear to be about sixteen, maybe seventeen. So how old do you want to be?"

The young John Doe hesitated, considering which direction to take in his future.

"I've lost ... my childhood ... so I want ... to get a head start ... as an adult. I want to be ... seventeen."

"Seventeen it is. But you sound more like a wise old man," admired the doctor.

The therapist nodded her head in agreement.

"We've scheduled your birthday party for three o'clock tomorrow afternoon."

"I'll be there."

"Well, we hope so," the doctor said pleasantly. "Miss DeRose, make sure that cake has seventeen candles on it."

She raised her eyebrows at the smiling patient.

"Now that we know your age and your name, Mr. Doe, it is my great pleasure to inform you that you will not, I repeat, not be going to a state agency."

"Thank you ... thank you ... thank you, Dr. Damien."

"You will continue to be the guest of Saint Gabriel's off and on for at least another nine months to a year."

"That's ... great, Dr. Damien."

"I couldn't wait until your official birthday to tell you. That's the kind of news that shouldn't wait."

"I agree ... a cake can wait ... but not my future."

"There is one catch, however,"

"Oh ... oh."

"You will have to work for me. And I'll expect you to continue your amazing progress."

"Deal!"

§   §   §   §   §   §

"What a deal," said Kim, as she toasted her agent with her cappuccino. "Thank you, Tony."

"You've kept the paperback copyrights. We've protected your electronic, movie, and foreign rights. You'll get five thousand dollars each week your novel is on top of the bestseller's list, not to mention your two million dollar advance. Yes, I'd say it was a pretty fair deal."

"As you know, I always exercise guarded optimism until we have a signed contract and the advance check in my hand."

"Well, the contract is signed and your advance is in the mail as they say. Oh, I should close the deal next week on your TV movie contract for your first novel. If you think your bank can handle it, you've got another million coming."

"Deposits are much more fun than withdrawals," Kim joked. "That check has already been spent."

"Another donation to your child recovery agency?" guessed Tony.

"All of it. I want state of the art everything."

"How many children did you locate last year?"

"Twenty-two, ten and under. Fourteen, ten to sixteen. That's three children each month. But we've still got such a long way to go."

"Kim, I'm so proud of you. You've helped so many families reunite."

"Well, when Graham died, I decided I'd do all I could to keep another mother from having to go through the same heartbreak I did. Each time my agency reunites a mother and child or a family and child, I feel like Graham did not die in vain."

"You couldn't have given it a better name. The Graham Sanborn Child Recovery Institute. What a nice tribute to your son. Sorry we can't attend the celebration tomorrow."

"That's okay - I'll miss seeing you and Maria and the children. Mya is becoming quite beautiful and David is getting so tall. You know, Tony, something occurred to me the other day and I'd like to share it with you."

"Oh? What's that?"

"Graham wanted to reconstitutionalize America. He said it was in danger of forgetting its roots. So it occurred to me on my flight from Toronto last week that he is reconstitutionalizing America posthumously through the agency. We are keeping children with their natural families, their genealogical roots. Keeping families together means building a stronger America."

"I never thought of it that way."

"Every time a child is ripped from its mother, a family is severed. And every time a family's unity is threatened, America's promise to its people for life, liberty, and the pursuit of happiness is compromised."

"Sounds like the makings of a new novel to me."

Kim laughed.

"Perhaps. But there's plenty to do with this one. Which reminds me ... "

"Oh, oh. I don't like the sound of this," Tony teased.

"I'd like you to take a look at the manuscript of a young man I know. His name is Paul Updike. I met him at the Palm Springs Writer's Conference last year. I've seen the first fifty pages or so of his manuscript and it's pretty good."

"Okay. I'm always interested in new talent."

"I'm serious," Kim challenged, annoyed at his cavalier tone.

"I know you are."

"Then don't patronize me. He's been in the slush pile for over two years. He deserves a break and our sluggish industry deserves his fresh approach."

"What's his genre?"

"Suspense. He seems to complement his originality and invention with a new literary terrain I think you'll be interested in. Will you give him a serious read?"

"Okay. Tell him to send the usual package to my attention: query letter, synopsis and first fifty to seventy-five pages. Be sure to tell him to mention your referral, in the first sentence of his query letter. You say you met him at Palm Springs last year?"

"Yes. That's the only time we've actually met."

"I sense there's something else you're not telling me."

"I wasn't going to mention it because I thought you'd take it the wrong way. His authorship really is quite polished and I didn't want my feelings to interfere with his getting his manuscript to you."

"Go on. There's got to be more."

"You're not going to let me by with this, are you?"

"Nope."

"He looks a lot like Graham, although much older, of course."

"Now, Kim ... "

"I knew you'd take it that way."

"I'm taking it the only way I can. You meet a young writer, who happens to look a lot like your deceased son. He approaches you at a writer's workshop like any aspiring writer, sticks his manuscript in your face, and coyly asks if you'd critique a few pages. You melt immediately because he looks like your son."

"I was feeling pretty good about our conversation until now."

"I'm sorry, Kim. I didn't mean to upset you. Look, I'll read the young man's partial manuscript. I've already promised you that. I just want to make it clear that my assessment will be based on the quality of his writing and not his looks. Okay?"

"That's all I'm asking. And I admit that his resemblance to Graham influenced me. That's what made him stand out from the crowd. If I didn't like his writing, though, we wouldn't be having this conversation."

"Okay. I just wanted us both to be sure what the expectations were going into this read. I value our relationship as friends, not just business partners. I hope I haven't upset you."

"You have, but it's okay. I don't expect you to represent him just because he resembles my son in appearance. If his craftsmanship isn't there, or the story turns out to be something you're not interested in, or if you believe it's not marketable, just say so. I'm only asking you to take an honest look at his manuscript."

"And I'll keep my promise. I'll let you know what happens."

"Okay, call me either way."

"Sure. I'm glad we had this talk."

"Me, too."

"Again, congratulations on your contract and on your institute's child recovery performance."

"Thank you, Tony. What a nice thing to say. Are you interested in making another contribution this year?"

"Why do I feel like I've just been set up? How large a donation will you accept from a struggling agent?"

"How much you got?" teased Kim.

"Oh, boy! Now you know how generous I've been in the past."

"You've been very generous. And I love you for it."

"I think I hear a but ... "

Kim laughed heartily, "I'm going to stay to the left of but!" She laughed again. "No buts intended. I'll be happy with any donation you give. Part of my job as director is to raise money from important people."

"So, I'm an important person, am I?"

"Of course and just to show you how important you are, I'm going to let you buy me lunch at Pete's Tavern when I'm in Manhattan next week."

"I think I can handle that. I'll try to reserve O. Henry's booth. You know, the one where he wrote the *Gift of the Magi.*"

"That's a great idea. Maybe sitting in his booth will turn you into a writer, Tony. As a matter of fact, you can write a check, donating some of your hard-earned commission to the Graham Sanborn Child Recovery Institute."

"I was hoping for a less expensive lunch."

"Oh, well, in that case you can donate in advance."

"I'd better get off this phone before I sign over my entire commission to you."

Kim paused thoughtfully, considering his generous suggestion.

"Hey, I was kidding," rallied Tony. "Just kidding."

"I know. Relax. I was just salivating. Please don't think I'm applying undue pressure."

"Somehow a part of me doubts that."

"Me, too. But the other part of me knows how fortunate I am to have friends like you. Your friendship means a lot to me, Tony. I love you. Give Maria and the children a hug and a squeeze for me."

"I will. Love you, too."

"Bye."

"Bye now."

Kim hung up the phone and then glanced at the calendar.

March eleventh, she thought sadly. *He would have been fifteen tomorrow.*

"The Institute is a year old tomorrow," she reminded herself aloud, "and I promised I'd get down there to help out with the last minute preparations."

CHAPTER
TWENTY-FIVE

They were spending the first day of their week-long vacation at Atlantic Beach. Her father bought them a beach front townhouse as a wedding present. This was their first opportunity to have a real honeymoon and they had not wasted anytime shedding their shoes.

They existed only for each other. Wanted only the intimate seclusion with the other. Every thought, word, and action was centered around the wants and needs of the other. So taken were they with one another that they rarely shared more than a few hurried pleasantries with anyone else.

A mere love-stung glance was as heated as a kiss. Every word settled like a thoughtful caress. Each derived enormous pleasure from watching the other occupied in even the simplest, most mundane of activities like eating, studying, and sun-bathing.

They were celebrating his first major art deal. The City of Montreal commissioned him to create ten life-sized bronze sculptures of children to beautify three of the parks that spotted the city.

Broken shells speckled the beach under their bare feet. The sharp edges of partially-submerged shells protruded claw-like out of the moist sand, causing the newly-weds to alter their steps occasionally.

A gull first quickened his step, then stalked away arrogantly as the preoccupied couple approached. Sporting a scallop shell in his powerful beak, the gull glanced back at them over his ruffled feathers, spiteful of their unsanctioned intrusion on his stretch of bleached sand.

"Did you see the look he gave us?" Cindy asked, amused at the gull's territorial obstinance.

"No. I wasn't paying attention. Whose look?"

"That gull," she said, pointing an accusing finger. "He isn't at all happy sharing the beach with us."

"Oh, yes, I see him. Hey, fella, there's enough beach for all of us. We're from Canada. See?" The young sculptor emphasized his heritage by patting the red Canadian maple leaf emblem on his white t-shirt. "So be nice to us."

Her falsetto giggles were attached to squeals of sheer delight as her husband shuffled his feet and put the bill of his cap in his mouth, imitating the antics of the gull. His spontaneous displays of buffoonery always made her laugh. That was what she enjoyed most about him. He refused to take the world too seriously.

Joining hands again, they smiled their way past the upset gull and walked slowly up the beach.

"Well, Mrs. Twain, how does it feel to be married to an almost famous sculptor?"

"Wonderful," she cooed. "But I was happily married to you when you were just a struggling sculptor and rising star ballroom dance champion."

He smiled as he watched their feet make indentions in the wet sand.

"I can't believe how far you've come in such a short time. It's like you were born to dance. You're as good as I am and I've been dancing ballroom for twelve years."

"Must be in my lost genes," he joked. "Maybe my parents were dancers or artists or something."

"I must confess though, I don't think I would have liked being called Mrs. John Doe."

Caught off guard, he could only throw her a surprised look.

"You know how I felt about the name John Doe," she challenged. "It never suited you."

"I know. It was my first attempt at my new self-definition. I felt like a John Doe after losing the first sixteen or seventeen years of my life. It was a transitional label. An attempt by a frightened young man to fit in. I didn't have a past. Or at least I wasn't conscious of one. And no one claimed me. I had absolutely no idea who I was. I don't know what kind of person I was before the accident. I still don't know. I have no idea who my family is, or if I have any brothers or sisters. All I know is I had a shirt and torn jeans on and this," he summarized, pulling the divided heart pendant, fastened to a key chain, from his pocket. "Other than this, I have no personal history except for the last five years."

"You have me."

"Oh, Cindy. I don't know what I'd do without you," he admitted, pulling her to him.

He attended deliberately to her lips, kissing her softly. Then he nibbled across to her cheeks, over her closed eye and finally to her forehead. Lingering there only for a moment, he extended the tease of his moist warm lips to her open mouth again.

"I love you."

"I love you, too," he whispered, caressing her cheek with his hand.

Her hair fanned out like spangled threads of silk as the breeze lifted it, then let it fall before it sent its golden strands flying again.

"These last three years with you have made my recovery so worthwhile. I never want to have to go through something like that again."

Cindy kissed him on the cheek.

"You've never told me why you changed your name to Mark Twain."

Mark raised his eyebrows and laughed a sigh before he spoke.

"Once I got out of the hospital and started living my new life, I no longer felt like a John Doe. I was somebody. I earned my G.E.D., reinstated my Canadian citizenship, rented a five-room crib over-looking the St. Lawrence, started my own art business, got some money in the bank and met you. What more could I ask for, except a real name."

"But why Mark Twain? I admit I like it a whole lot better than John Doe, but Mark Twain? Wasn't that what the American writer and humorist Samuel Clements called himself?"

Mark nodded triumphantly.

"But that's not why I picked it. Clements was an American. I'm Canadian. Besides, many people have the same first and last names. Actually, I decided to use Twain before I even thought about Mark Twain. I picked Twain because it means two, and I've obviously had two lives. One before my accident and this one, my post-accident one."

Mark squinted, momentarily editing his thoughts.

"Besides the obvious connection to the American, I chose Mark because it stands for a standard of quality or measurement. It means distinction or importance, like to make one's mark. And that's what I plan to do, make my mark on society."

"You already have," complimented Cindy, referring to his contract with Montreal Parks and Recreation and their recent gold medal at the LaClassique Du Quebec dance championship.

"I know. Can you believe it? We're the youngest Canadian Rising Star champions. I love ballroom dancing as much as I do sculpting. I also thought about calling myself Peter Pan."

"Oh, Mark! You're not serious!"

"I'm serious. I've lost my childhood. And Peter didn't want to give his up. I'm a little envious of him for that."

Cindy frowned her sympathy. Then her eyes brightened.

"You haven't lost your childhood. You mimicked the gull a little while ago. You're always doing things like that. You help me run my day care center and the children love you. You've taught some of the children to dance. I commissioned you to build the jungle-gyms and sliding boards long before the city made you an offer you couldn't refuse. Remember Jamie, the little autistic youngster last year? You showed him how to finger paint. He crayoned a picture of a white dog, and used an ink pen to put a black star on the dog's leg to match your birthmark."

"Yes. I still have the picture," Mark verified, remembering Jamie's gift.

"Jamie's first words were your star. Remember? He has a vocabulary of over two hundred words now, thanks to you."

Mark smiled as he dug his toes in the sand.

"So you see -- you have a sense of childhood locked inside you. You helped a little autistic boy unlock his childhood. I think you're living your childhood now through others. You have a phenomenal ability to draw the child out in adults as well as connect with the child in children. You convinced my father to appear dressed as a clown in the children's cancer ward at the hospital last Sunday. I've never seen my dad do anything like that. Who would have thought that one of Montreal's wealthiest real estate barons would ever appear in public dressed in a clown's suit? It's like you're building your childhood memories through others."

Mark grinned his embarrassment.

"Someone once said that the child is father of the man. Somehow, you've got both operating simultaneously. You are very much a responsible, mature, decent, talented, caring adult. And you're also in perpetual childhood. Honey, please don't lose those childlike qualities of imagination, wonder, and innocence. The world is your mobile. And I'm glad to be a part of it."

She gave his hand a playful squeeze. And her arms, automatically solicitous, hugged him.

"Your sculptures will help an entire city—no, an entire world—honor childhood. Mark, honey, I think the world is your playground. Mrs. Clinton, the American President's wife, wrote a book called: *It Takes a Village*. It's about raising children, appreciating them as people, loving them, educating them, protecting them, making the world a safer place for them. I think your sculptures will do the same thing."

"Well, I don't know about that, but it's nice of you to think so."

"I know so, Mr. Mark John Doe Peter Pan Twain. I know so."

Feeling much too patronized, Mark turned, heading them up the beach.

The opaline morning mists which blanketed the beach lifted, unveiling bleached stretches of sand and promising another gold-toned day. A rolling cinema of clouds moved wistfully, in fluffy caravans, along the perimeter of the beach, playing dutifully to the natural metronome of the surf.

"Listen," ordered Cindy softly, pulling them to a stop. "Close your eyes and listen."

They stood barefoot inches from the next installment of surf as it gobbled up the sand. They listened to the soothing tones of nautical encores as wave after wave spilled itself onto the bleached sands.

"Listen, Mark, listen. Today it's adagio. Tomorrow, perhaps allegretto," she praised as the shoreline before them disappeared, then reappeared in rhythm with the primordial dance of the spheres.

"Doesn't it just wash civilization off you?" he exclaimed, as he listened to the richness of the oceanic concert.

"Um ... mm. It's so soothing. I just want to stay here all ... year."

"All year?" he questioned, good-naturedly. "You are a dreamer. I've got children to sculpt, remember?"

"I know, silly. I was only kidding."

Cindy followed his lead as he silently slid his arm around her midsection. The faint scent of his aftershave came to her for a brief moment, competing with the gentle breeze which caressed her senses.

She closed her eyes and faced directly into the wind, letting the warm summer breeze whip her long hair into her eyes and then jerk it out again silently, obeying the wispy commands of each small gust of salty air.

They walked slowly, wrapped in each other's arms, only partially distracted by the other tourists who shared Atlantic Beach with them.

Tomorrow they would visit historic Beaufort and the charm of the Outer Banks, from Cape Lookout Light House to Ocracoke where the houses are characterized by their old world irregularity along sandy streets overhung with moss-covered oaks and yaupon. Long believed to be the hangout of Edward Teach, better known as Blackbeard, the Pirate, Ocracoke is filled with the history of a country that moved east to west.

Mark gravitated toward the historical, particularly since his own personal history was so limited. It helped give him a sense of continuity, of kinship, of belonging.

He hoped they would see Bottlenose dolphins further up the coast. Cindy loved to watch dolphins escort sail boats and catamarans along the coastal waters. He admired the playfulness of the sleek mammals as they expertly surfaced dangerously close to boat hulls which churned aqua-marine water into white froth before it reclaimed its Neptunian color.

If his short-term memory served him right, Cape Hatteras Lighthouse, barber-poled and proud, was built in 1870, the year Robert E. Lee died. Both he and Cindy looked forward to standing on the balcony of the renovated lighthouse which overlooked Diamond Shoals, the Graveyard of the Atlantic.

Mark lifted his face toward the golden sphere of sun, flung so majestically in the morning sky, and breathed deeply, letting the salty breeze bathe him in its warmth.

He moved his admiring gaze to the mighty piers, those tenacious wooden peninsulas of sun-bleached planking that brought fishermen and sea together. Stained and weather-beaten, the pilings stood firm against the relentless surf which shoveled tons of sand and water at their obstinate foundations.

His eyes settled on several sandpipers some distance away, as they scurried along the perimeter of the tides foraging for their breakfast. He respected their uncanny ability to stay just out of reach of the aggressive surf as it blanketed the beach, only to pull back again, determined to launch a more lengthy counterattack.

Those stick-legged birds understand decrescendos and ritards, he mused to himself as he watched the sandpipers dodge another series of attempts by the faithful surf. *They would be terrific Viennese waltzers.*

"Look," Cindy exclaimed, pointing at several fishermen who sat on upended buckets or fold-out chairs at the edge of the irregular surf. "See him?"

Mark's sharp eye caught the movement of a lone sandpiper as he weaned his way, unnoticed, under one of the chairs. Then the feathered thief hurriedly retreated, proudly carrying his prize catch in his beak.

"That's very capitalistic of him," Mark commented. "Looks like he's practicing trickle-down economics."

"He's definitely cutting into their profits," Cindy agreed, giggling her amusement.

They watched as another fearless sandpiper sneaked under the fold-out chair and made his withdrawal, as the fishermen swapped stories that nobody believed.

"That's amazing. Those men don't have a clue," Cindy said, amused at their inattention.

"The sandpipers are just trying to make a living," Mark announced.

"They're obviously not going to go hungry," Cindy added, as the couple watched another feathered thief make his approach.

"I'm beginning to get hungry myself," Mark confessed.

Cindy threw him a look of mock astonishment.

"You just had breakfast an hour ago."

"Vacations make me hungry."

"Why don't you follow your feathered friends over there and grab some sushi," Cindy teased, pointing to the sandpiper creeping up on the fishermen.

Mark made a face.

"I'd love to, but I don't have any Tarter Sauce on me. Do you?" he joked, as he began to poke at her waist, tickling her.

"Stop that ... I mean it ... Stop!" Cindy stutter-stepped her way through her protests as he took advantage of her ticklishness.

Unable to restrain his titillating attack, she bolted away from his playful assault and headed laughingly up the beach.

Mark was close behind, allowing her to maintain a slight lead so he could poke at her on the run.

Recognizing the fine line between exhilaration and excess, Mark caught up to her just as he wedged himself expertly between two women who were walking slowly away from them up the beach.

As he caught up to Cindy, he grabbed her around the waist and lifted her off her feet and carried her as he continued to run.

The soft breeze lifted their laughter above the syncopation of the surf, as the honeymooners celebrated the invigoration of the brief chase.

"Ah ... hh, I love you," Cindy whispered. "I think I've just worked up an appetite, too."

"Good," Mark said breathily, still feeling the effects of the short sprint up the beach.

He covered her face and neck with another series of hasty kisses, punctuating his tantalizing play with another abbreviated encroachment on her waist and under arms.

"Mark, that's not fair," she fussed as she fended off his lightning fast jabs.

"Are you sure you're ready for breakfast?"

"Breakfast?"

"Something to eat," he clarified.

"Yes. As long as it's got ocean view seating. How about eating at the restaurant we saw driving in yesterday? The one with the red awnings, the Sandpiper's Eatery."

"Then let's tango."

Mark gently raised her arm and pirouetted her gracefully around a small sand castle tucked in the sand just ahead of them. After circling the hand-made palace a second time, they headed toward the wooden steps that led to the townhouse.

§ § § § § §

"It's a good thing we weren't standing any closer," Pamela commented agitatedly.

"Oh, it's okay. No harm done," Kim said softly as she studied the backs of the two young people who had just sprinted past them. She smiled as they waltzed around the sand castle some fifty or sixty feet ahead of them.

Although she was unable to see their faces, the young man's red Canadian maple leaf on his shirt was very distinctive. Kim could tell by the couple's laughter and the way they touched each other that they were in love.

"It's nice to see young people so happy," Kim stated emphatically. "I hope they'll always find that kind of enjoyment with each other."

Pamela steadied her gaze on them, too, out of consideration for Kim's comment.

"Thanks for making me take some time off this week-end. I've been working entirely too hard these past four months," Kim confessed, as she watched the couple walk hand-in-hand toward the sun-bleached section of wooden steps.

"That's an understatement if I ever heard one. You've just finished another novel, which will probably be another bestseller. You work much too many hours at the Institute. As Director now, I'm tempted to order you on an extended sabbatical. You just returned from a children's aid conference in Paris. And by your own admission, the cup of cappuccino you drank this morning was the first one you've had in three months."

"Three weeks," Kim corrected.

"Okay, three weeks, then," Pamela surrendered, eyeing her suspiciously.

Kim chanced one more backward glance at the young couple who disappeared past a planked spur of sidewalk leading to the cluster of expensive townhouses nestled beyond the grass-spotted dune.

"You managed to get two novelists down here this week-end," praised Kim, smiling thoughtfully.

"Louise needed the rest, too," Pamela affirmed. "Between the two of you, you've written six bestsellers in the past seven years. I'd say that kind of productivity needs a break once in a while."

"You mean an intermission."

"An intermission?"

"I don't want a break. I don't want to break anything or have anything broken."

"All right. An intermission then. You are a stickler for the right words, aren't you?"

"I'm a writer. I pay attention to the power of words."

"How about the power of food?"

Kim checked her watch.

"It is getting about that time, isn't it?"

"If you don't mind, Kim, I'd like to stay at the cottage for lunch and go to the Sandpiper's Eatery for dinner. Is that okay?"

"As long as we eat there before we leave. I want to try their crab cakes and scallops. Your grandparents said they serve the best crab cakes on the Carolina coast. And the restaurant has a great view of the ocean."

"Let's go light on our lunch then, so you'll have plenty of room for your crab cakes. Louise should be back from the grocery store by now. If she's like me, grocery shopping builds appetites and accelerates impulse buying. It's hard to tell what she's come back with, particularly since she didn't have breakfast."

"I'm sure we'll help her consume whatever she bought."

"We're not counting calories this trip, right?"

"That's right. We're calling a moratorium on calories. Nothing tastes as good as thin feels except when you're on vacation." Kim teased, modifying a Weight Watcher's Axiom.

"That sounds like a plan to me," agreed Pamela jubilantly.

The sharp pitch of her applause scattered a half dozen or so sandpipers, sending them scurrying as fast as their thin stick legs could carry them. The winged troubadours of the beach managed to stay just ahead of the women as they advanced up the beach.

Kim watched admiringly as the sandpipers weaved and dodged their way in concert with the ebb and flow of the tides. She was impressed with the sandpipers' consummate ability to stay clear of the next salty installment of inexorable surf.

She threw the industrious birds a smile before she withdrew her attention, redirecting her gaze toward a crowded section of beach ahead of them.

Irregular rows of blue and white striped umbrellas, each an oasis of shade, lined the beach for several hundred yards. Sunbathers baked their bodies on blankets or lounge chairs and children busied themselves chasing wary sandpipers or building sand castles out of moistened sand. The more adventurous vacationers braved the surf by relaxing contentedly on inflated rafts a few yards off shore.

Her nostalgic eye caught the meticulous care of an earnest blond-haired youngster, as he hand-crafted his miniature castle. Aided with buckets and multi-colored plastic molds, he engineered a rather sophisticated maze of terraced estate.

Graham used to love building those, she reminisced. *Jim would serve as both construction superintendent and knight's page as they turned buckets of moist sand into something recognizable.*

A misthrown Frisbee jolted Kim out of her reverie as it knocked her wide-brimmed hat off.

"Are you all right?" asked Pamela, sending the boy who threw it a disapproving look.

"Yes, I think so," Kim recovered, reaching for both the hat and the Frisbee.

By the time she stood, the youth who had thrown the plastic saucer was headed apologetically toward them.

Before he advanced too close, Kim flung the neon-colored projectile over his head, causing him to stumble over his own feet in an attempt to retrieve it.

Both women laughed their delight as he jumped back to his feet and gave them a thumbs up sign, obliging their playful forgiveness.

"That serves him right," said Pamela. "Are you sure you're all right?"

"Yes, I'm fine. But I didn't do it for spite. I surprised myself with that throw. It's been ages since I've thrown a Frisbee."

"Well, you sure aired it out. I was impressed."

"What are you doing July fourth?" Kim asked, purposefully changing the subject.

"I'll probably put in a few hours at the Institute, and work out in the pool. Other than that I expect to be in town. Why?"

"I've decided to throw a star spangled musical tribute at my house to celebrate the Fourth. I've planned music and dancing."

"Are you dancing competitively again?"

"Oh, for heaven's sake no. My competitive days are over."

"But I've seen you dance lately. You're still so elegant. Do you miss it?"

"Dancing? Or competition?"

Pamela nodded "Both."

"Sometimes," Kim replied softly and then grew reflective. "I watch the Ohio Star Ball coverage on PBS.

And as you know, I sponsor two couples. But competing only made sense with Jim. Ballroom championships were our dream. There wasn't any room for anyone else ... except Graham. So, when I lost both of them, I lost interest in ballroom dancing. I buried it when I buried Jim."

"Well, let's bury those memories, too. We're on vacation," Pamela said quickly. "I want to hear more about the Fourth of July celebration."

"It'll be like the one you had several years ago."

"I'll call Blaine and see if he'll provide the music—if he's not playing somewhere else. I'll ask Debbie to sing. What do you think?"

"I think it's a great idea. You want help organizing it?"

"Why do you think I mentioned it?"

"I walked right into that one, didn't I?"

"Like a rich donor attending one of my fund-raisers."

Pamela smiled and then the expression on her face changed.

"Have you thought about what kind of statues you want for the Institute's courtyard yet?"

"Not lately. Have you?"

"I've got a few ideas."

"Oh, yeah?"

"They're on the agenda for Monday. We're vacationing ... remember?"

"You brought it up."

"And I'm shelving it right now."

"You're the boss."

"No. I'm a hungry vacationer."

"That makes two of us," Kim confessed, as she heard her stomach growl.

CHAPTER
TWENTY-SIX

Hello. May I speak to Mr. Mark Twain? This is Kim Sanborn, with the Graham Sanborn Institute in Raleigh, North Carolina."

"Certainly, Ms. Sanborn. One moment, please."

Kim doodled on her notepad while she waited for the sculptor. Her doodling was interrupted when a warm, mellow voice said: "Hello, Ms. Sanborn. This is Mark Twain. How may I help you?"

"Hello, Mr. Twain. I understand you are a sculptor who specializes in children's sculptures."

"Primarily, yes."

"I'm calling because you were referred to me by Dr. Guillaume Nordstrom, who runs a children's clinic in Joliette, Canada."

"Yes, how nice of him to refer me."

"I help run a child recovery center in Raleigh, North Carolina. And I ... "

"I was just down there last month at one of your beautiful beaches. Atlantic Beach. Have you been there?"

"As a matter of fact, I was there last month, as well. What a coincidence."

"Yes, how about that?"

"Mr. Twain, I would like to commission you to do two sculptures. Two children's sculptures. What do I need to do to get the project started?"

"Employ some patience, I'm afraid."

"Oh, what do you mean, Mr. Twain?"

"The City of Montreal has just awarded me quite an extensive two-year contract."

"Oh."

"I've agreed to do ten life-sized pieces of art for them. I'm meeting with them now, hoping to get the approvals I need on my line drawings to start the actual work. As you can see, we've just begun."

"Well, congratulations."

"Thank you. As a young artist I feel very fortunate to have won the city's confidence."

"Then, it looks as if you have a solid two years of work."

"Yes. Isn't it wonderful? I have a half dozen or so current projects that I'm trying to complete. I feel I must honor existing agreements. All but one of the privately-commissioned works are small projects. The one I did for Dr. Nordstrom several years ago was a fairly large and complex piece. Most of the ones I have on my plate are two to three month projects."

"Looks like my timing could have been better," lamented Kim.

"Actually, Mrs. Sanborn, except for the Montreal project, most of my projects are commissioned six to eight months in advance. When did you need the pieces?"

"I was hoping by the end of this year."

"Oh, I see ... "

"Doesn't look as if I'm going to fit into your schedule for at least two years, huh?"

"I'm afraid that's right. My current obligations take precedence. I'm sure you understand."

"Oh, absolutely. But I'd like you to place me on your waiting list."

"I'd be happy to. And if, for some unforeseen reason I can squeeze you in ... Actually, Mrs. Sanborn, I'd better not promise that. I don't want to commit to something I can't deliver. Suppose I refer you to a couple of other sculptors I know? Perhaps they'll be able to help you."

"I'd appreciate that."

"Oh, by the way, how did you happen to meet Dr. Nordstrom?"

"We've been friends for years. We met at a child's advocacy conference and have kept in close contact ever since. He and his wife, Julia, are wonderful people."

"Yes, they are. Oh, here are the two names I promised."

He gave her the demographics of the two sculptors and briefly explained their work, adding a proviso that she should ask them for references. Kim gave him her address and phone number, as well.

"Thank you Mr. Twain. By the way, do you know you're named after a famous American author and humorist?"

"I hear that all the time. I'm getting used to my famous name preceding me."

"Best of luck on your projects. Maybe I'll decide to wait. I really like your bronze statue of the three children and the rescue worker you did for Dr. Nordstrom."

"Thank you. If I get any daylight at all, I'll call."

"Fair enough. Thanks for the referrals. It's been a pleasure speaking with you."

"Same here."

"Bye."

"Good-bye, Mrs. Sanborn."

§   §   §   §   §   §

"Mark, you've got to call her back," Cindy pleaded. "I can't believe you didn't tell me you talked to her in July."

"Why are you suddenly interested in a lady I talked to five months ago? She called to commission a couple of sculptures that I couldn't do then and still can't. I've never seen you so upset. What'd I do? You'd think I turned down an invitation to meet the Queen of England or something."

"She's more important than that."

"You're serious, aren't you?"

"More serious than you think. Mark, darling, I think she might be your mother!"

The most stupefied look covered his face.

"What did you say?"

"I think Kim Sanborn, the author of the novel I'm reading, and the woman who called you five months ago, is your mother."

Locked in a prolonged moment of disbelief, all Mark could do was stare at her. And when he finally attempted to speak his mouth wouldn't work.

"Stay there. Stay right there," Cindy ordered, as she darted toward the bedroom.

I talked to my mother and didn't know it, he whispered to himself.

"If this is true, it's incredible," he shouted after her.

He saw her sprint out of the bedroom, carrying a hard cover book.

"Honey, look," she exclaimed excitedly. "I just started reading this novel. It's by the same woman who called you."

Mark's confused expression fueled her explanation.

"She's writing about a woman whose son was kidnapped when he was four years old. Her husband was killed at the same time her son was abducted on Christmas Eve."

"I don't see what this has to do with me, it's just a novel. Aren't novels fiction?" protested Mark.

"No, it ... I mean yes, novels are fiction, but this one is based partly on her own life. She lost a son in real life."

"Cindy, honey. I'm sure it's a good story, but ... is that the novel you've been reading the past couple of nights and can't put down?"

"Yes, but you don't understand. I ... "

"Oh, but I think I do understand. You're three months pregnant and because it's about a kidnapping, you're ... I think you're over-reacting."

"Babe ... "

"I think you're reading things in that aren't there, that have no bearing on ... "

"He's got a perfect star birthmark on his right knee, just like you," she shouted, pointing to a passage in the novel.

Mark stiffened in amazement.

"Cindy, a lot of people have birthmarks. I don't mean to be difficult but ... "

"Do they have birthmarks in the form of a perfect star — and blonde hair and blue eyes? I don't think we can discount this, Mark. I know it's a shock to you. I'm shocked, too. But I think we'd better check into it. I believe it just might be a link to your past."

"Possible link. It's still only a novel, and I don't think we should over-react based on a story some American novelist wrote."

Cindy was flabbergasted.

"I ... quite agree. But I thought you'd be more interested than you are. Suppose she's your mother? You can find out about your past."

"It's only a book, honey," Mark raised his voice.

"It's a book with at least three coincidences," she shouted angrily, before she settled herself down. She breathed deeply several times as she held her abdomen.

"Honey, are you okay?" Mark asked as he assisted her onto one of the cushioned chairs in the living room.

Cindy waved him off once she was comfortably positioned in her seat.

"Three coincidences so far. It's a book that has at least three things that point to you. A blonde haired ... "

"I know, a blonde-haired, blue-eyed infant with a birthmark like mine."

"That's right. Can't you see? I'm sorry. I said coincidences, didn't I? You don't believe in coincidences. You told me the universe is much too ordered for accidents or coincidences. Isn't that right?"

"Yes. I believe in synchronicity, the term Carl Jung used to describe the causative connecting principle."

"That's it. I couldn't think of it. Synchronicity. So far there are three connections between the book and you. And I've only gotten to the part where he left the two mothers a note in his cap at the cabin."

"Who left the note? What note? What two mothers? Cindy, remember I haven't read the book. I don't ... "

"Oh, Mark, I'm sorry. The boy that was kidnapped left a note. You! You left it if the boy is you and if Graham is your real name."

"Cindy, Mark is my real name!"

"Don't look at me like that. It's not just a book. I feel very strange about the book. Like ... like there's something it's trying to tell me. And Mark is the name you chose. Remember?"

"I don't feel anything about the book, except that I feel concerned for my pregnant wife who needs to calm down."

"A fourth connection is her call. She called you about the sculptures."

"She contacted me through Dr. Nordstrom. That's all that was. Cindy, I'm beginning to ... "

"She's also a director of a child recovery agency in North Carolina. And Dr. Nordstrom is involved in child advocacy of some kind."

Mark nodded several times.

"He runs a children's clinic in Joliette."

"That's right. So that's a fifth connection. They're both helping children. How much synchronicity do you want?"

"I want you to calm down. Is that too much to ask?"

"I'll settle down when you wise up," she said, glaring at him.

"Oh, Cindy!"

"There's another connection. Oh, my God. Hope, the white dog," Cindy exclaimed. She gasped as she covered her mouth with her hands.

"What! What's wrong? Honey, you're really worrying me now."

Mark fronted her on his knees and took her trembling hands in his. His concerned gaze recruited her own tear-filled gaze as their eyes locked on to each other's.

"Remember the picture of the white dog Jamie crayoned for you?"

Mark nodded his recollection.

"He used an ink pen to draw a star on the dog's right leg, remember?"

"You know I do. I had it framed. It's on my studio wall. What ... what are you ... ?"

"There's a white dog in the novel named Hope that looks just like the one Jamie crayoned for you."

Mark winced his bewilderment.

"It's another connection."

"There you go again."

"Mark," she raised her voice, "why did Jamie happen to pick a picture of a dog in the crayon book? And why did he color it white?"

"I don't know, he could have ... "

"And scribble a star on its knee. It's right knee at that."

"Because he saw my birthmark. He wanted to do something nice for me. That's all there was to it."

"Why a picture of a dog? Why not a cat, or goat, or elephant, or ... a jackass," she said accusingly.

Mark grinned and blinked his eyes closed momentarily, before he reestablished eye contact.

"And North Carolina. Why, out of all the places my father could have bought us a townhouse, did he buy one in North Carolina?"

Mark raised his eyebrows, but didn't say anything.

"I think you should call her," Cindy said emphatically.

"Oh, no. I'm not calling her based on what we've just discussed."

"Mark!"

"I'm not going to do it."

"She's your mother."

"We don't know that."

"We don't know that she isn't and we'll never know unless you call."

"Cindy, how's this going to sound. Hello, Mrs. Sanborn. I think I'm you son. My wife read your book and I have a star birthmark on my knee. So can I come home and help you spend all that money? I repeat. How's that going to sound?"

"Like a start. I think your introduction could use some polish, but I think you should make the call."

"I don't believe this," Mark fretted, as he rose to his feet.

"What are you afraid of?" Cindy challenged.

"Afraid? I'm not afraid. What have I got to be afraid of?"

"The truth."

"The truth?" he yelled. "The truth is if she is my mother, she didn't want me."

"That's not what the book says. Oh, oh, oh ... There's another connection. Her husband and her were championship ballroom dancers. And so are we. Don't you see the connections? There are too many of them for them to be coincidences. Listen to the truth."

"The truth is I'm here," he shouted. "I have made a life, a new life, a good life for myself and you. I've gone from nobody to John Doe to who I am now. It doesn't matter who I was in the past. That person is dead. He died in the same accident that claimed my past."

"That's it, isn't it," said Cindy softly. "You're frightened of who you were and what you might have done."

"That's ridiculous," he blasted. "How could I be afraid of a dead young boy?"

"Because whoever that little boy was and whatever he did is part of your history."

"My body's history maybe, but not my psychology, or my emotions or my memory," he interrupted explosively.

"How about your future?"

"What?"

"If you're the same little boy in that book and if she is your mother, you have a future to share as mother and son. Do you want to forfeit that opportunity?"

"But I'm not the same little boy. You're making a false assumption. Don't you remember what Dr. Damien said. I suffered total and incontrovertible memory loss ... basically the total erasure of my old brain. I have a totally different neural network. A new self. The hundred-billion neurons in my brain have managed to turn me into a new person. My future is with you. I have no desire to resurrect someone else's past."

"It's true. For all intents and purposes your brain has created a brand new person inside your body. But your two selves share the same DNA. They're in the same body. Your family and friends would say you look like your pre-accident self because they remember your body. To them, you are your body."

"I know. Dr. Damien said we see and define a particular person by the physical continuity of their bodies."

"That's right."

"But we're not our physical packaging. A book is not its cover. We're something more than that. We're even more than our memories and emotions. We're specks of consciousness in human form. People who have out-of-body experiences confirm that."

Cindy nodded. "I've read documented accounts of people, seriously injured in accidents, describe how they hovered above their own bodies in some sort of conscious pocket of selfhood. Clinically, their physical bodies were dead. There were no brain waves to monitor. Yet they were conscious of themselves. Clinicians refer to it as near-death or out-of-body experiences. Medical science can't explain it. Yet hundreds of thousands of people the world over experience it and live to tell about it. So you owe it to yourself, your present self, that is, and Kim Sanborn to find out whether you're mother and son."

"I'll have to think about it, Babe. I don't want to be pushed into this."

"Pushed into it? You were born into it. Somebody out there is your mother. You don't owe it to your past self. You're right. He's dead. But you are alive and once upon a time you had a history. And that's all the people who love you have. They'll love you Mark, for who you are. Not who you were. You won't know them. But they'll recognize the physical part of you—and the spiritual you. They'll recognize your soul connection."

"They may not," Mark countered.

"What do you mean?"

"My face was reconstructed. Remember?"

"But you've got the same blue eyes and smile. And a possible DNA connection!"

She looked at him sternly.

"Yes, I'm pushing you. You need pushing. You need a swift kick in that cute little tush you've got."

"Cindy, I've never heard you use that kind of language."

"You've never seem me this passionate about what I want you to do. Mark, I can't make you call her. And I'll understand if you decide not to find out who you were. But I'm going to tell you something, Mark. This baby I'm carrying has only one set of grandparents as it stands right now. Wouldn't two sets be nice?"

Mark squinted.

"You won't have to give up who you are. You'll be adding to who you are. Think about it, honey. Okay?"

Mark sighed heavily.

Still uncertain as to his intentions, Cindy cupped his face in her hands. "I've got about a hundred-or-so pages left to read in her book. Maybe we'll find there are no more connections. Maybe there are more. I can tell you this ... If she's the kind of person portrayed in her book, she was a wonderful, loving mother. Why don't we find out. Will you read the rest of it with me?"

"You're not talking about tonight, are you?"

"How long do you want to wait to find out?"

"I'm not sure there's anything to find out. You seem to want to know more than I do."

"I'm asking for all of us. My parents, the child I'm carrying, you and me and a grieving mother in North Carolina. I'm not sure how the story in her book ends. Maybe you're right. Maybe she finds her son. It's possible that I've over-reacted. But it's also possible that her novel really is about you. I'm willing to risk hearing your criticism if you're right. Are you willing to risk losing a chance to find your real mother if you're wrong?"

He studied her for a moment.

"You realize I have absolutely no emotional attachment to my pre-accident past, don't you?"

Cindy nodded cautiously.

"I understand that my body has a past that predates the new me. And it's a past that doesn't matter to me. Can't you see? I am literally not the same person I was four years ago or ten years ago or even five minutes ago. Nobody is!"

Cindy started to speak but he waved her off.

"You're asking me to resurrect a past I consider to be someone else's past. Babe, I have no desire to do that. I'm being as honest with you as I can be. Part of my resistance to finding out who I was, if that fictional account you're reading has any value at all, is this. What if that person did something terrible? What if he killed somebody, or robbed a bank, or bombed a federal building? I don't want to jeopardize our future by finding my past. I'm not going to take a chance on ruining our future. Our baby is going to have something I never remember having—a father."

"Oh, Mark."

"Cindy," he cautioned, glaring at her, "I'll agreed for us to finish the book together. That's all I'm committing to. I'm not going to let a silly novel ruin our future. Have I made myself clear?"

"Crystal clear. As clear as fear."

Mark threw her a disgusted look.

"Give me half an hour to straighten up my studio. Then I'll let you read to me."

"That's all I ask. Honey, I'm sorry if I've upset you."

He smiled reprovingly, then wheeled around as if pulled by an invisible cord and headed down the hallway.

Cindy followed his angry retreat until he disappeared through the doorway at the other end of the hall.

She had only seen him this upset one other time. He had labored over a stone sculpture for months, trying to get every cut just right, expertly striking the balance between dynamic tension and rest. Unsatisfied with the look of the insubordinate rock, he made several more critical cuts which compromised the final result. Although the client loved the piece, Mark considered the piece defective and refused to sell it to him. After considerable negotiation, the client happily hauled the piece away. Mark donated the remainder of his commission to an orphanage, refusing to accept money for shoddy work, as he referred to it.

Sometimes your sense of what's right is maddening, she mourned for him silently. *I hope I'm not running into a stone wall on this. Lord above, help this man become whole again. Please give him the strength and courage he needs to rediscover who he was. If her book is about him, help him reach out to her, not erase her.*

CHAPTER
TWENTY-SEVEN

Unable to control her emotions, Cindy almost shouted into the phone.

"Hello, Mrs. Sanborn? This is Cindy Twain and I've got something important to discuss with you."

"You've reached the Sanborn residence, but I'm not she."

"Oh," Cindy responded. She was both surprised and deflated.

"I'm Pamela Justice, her associate. Mrs. Sanborn isn't home at the present. May I take a message?"

"Yes, thank you ... No. That's not the way we wanted this to go. When will she return?"

"Who did you say this is?" challenged Pamela.

"Cindy Twain. Mark Twain's wife."

"Okay. That does it! Whoever you are, I want you to know I don't appreciate crank calls like this. Mark Twain died almost ninety years ago. I'm going to hang up now. Good-bye!"

Pamela placed the phone back on its cradle and shook her head as she walked back to her post at the partially decorated Christmas tree.

"Mark Twain. She's crazy as a fruit cake," Pamela mused aloud as she renewed her efforts to cover the tree with tinsel.

When the phone rang again, she decided not to answer it, but reconsidered, believing it might be Kim.

"Hello, Kim Sanborn.com."

"Miss Justice, please don't hang up. I called just a moment ago."

"You again! Look you little prankster. There's a law against prank calls."

"No, please! Wait. Please. This isn't a prank call. Please. Don't hang up."

"Then what is it?" Pamela questioned suspiciously.

"We've got to speak to Mrs. Sanborn. It's urgent."

"I told you she's not here. It's two days before Christmas. She's shopping." Pamela was intentionally vague.

"Will she be home later tonight? I mean can we call her then?"

"I suppose so. However, I think you'd better leave a detailed message with me first. Mrs. Sanborn is a busy lady."

"And she's also a mother," Cindy inserted before she realized what she said.

Pamela pulled the receiver away from her ear, intending to hang up the phone, but fury compelled her to launch an angry protest.

"I don't know what kind of game you're playing, you common, insensitive jerk, but if I could get my hands on you right now, I'd wring your neck. Mrs. Sanborn's son died five years ago. How can you be so cruel?"

"Miss Justice, her son is not dead. He's here with me. He's a man now. He's my husband."

Pamela staggered, trying to find purchase amidst the open boxes that cluttered the floor beneath her feet. Before she could catch her balance, she tripped over one of the end tables and landed hard against the side of the sofa, sending Christmas ornaments in all directions.

"Miss Justice. Hello? Are you all right?"

Pamela snatched the phone from off the floor and raised it to her ear. She was too shocked to attempt to stand, so she used the sofa as a backrest and straightened herself to a sitting position.

"Yes, I'm okay. I fell."

"Oh, my goodness. Are you sure you're all right?"

"A little shaken, but otherwise I think I'm fine."

"Thank God. This is not at all like we hoped it would go."

Pamela noticed the small cut on her hand but decided it didn't need immediate attention.

"Perhaps you should start from the beginning and tell me why you called tonight. Is the 'we' you refer to her son, Graham?"

"Yes, I believe my husband is Mrs. Sanborn's son. Please don't hang up. This is not a crank call. It's the most important call we've ever made in our lives."

"All right, I won't hang up. As long as you're legitimate, that is. Let's start with your claim that Kim's son is alive."

"Oh, Miss Justice. He is alive. And we can prove it. Several months ago, in July to be exact, Mrs. Sanborn spoke with my husband. She wanted to commission him for two sculptures."

"Oh, of course. Mark Twain. Now I remember. The Canadian sculptor."

"That's right. His name really is Mark Twain."

"Forgive me for being so rude earlier! Mrs. Sanborn and I talked about your husband's famous American name after she spoke to him in July. I had forgotten all about it. But having recently spoken with your husband doesn't qualify him as a relative."

"I know. I understand. But please hear me out. Mark, ah, I mean ... my husband didn't mention his conversation with his mother, ah ..." Cindy faltered, trying her best to remain objective, "... with Mrs. Sanborn until two weeks ago. He didn't know then she was his mother, of course. Oh, dear, I think I'm really botching this up!"

Pamela closed her eyes and took a couple of deep breaths to slow her breathing. "You're doing fine. Keep talking ... I'm listening. Please understand my confusion — and my sincere desire not to upset Kim unnecessarily. "

"I don't blame you for being suspicious. I know this is a shock. Let me try to say this right. I was reading Mrs. Sanborn's novel, *Twist of Fate* and was really amazed at some of the things in it. There were several references that sounded like possible links to Mark's childhood. Then, when I discovered he talked to her and hadn't even mentioned it to me, I couldn't believe it. Of course, at the time he didn't know the connection. His mother ... I mean, Mrs. Sanborn ... didn't either. There was no reason for either of them to see it. To Mark it was just a customer placing an order for a sculpture. To Mrs. Sanborn, it was only a phone call to a well-known sculptor in Montreal."

"And just what makes *you* think he's her son?"

"Oh, Miss Justice, I *know* Mark's her son."

"But I don't."

"Oh, please forgive me. Of course you don't. Well, let's see ... as I was saying, there appear to be too many coincidences in the book to discount them. Oops, sorry, not coincidences. We don't believe in coincidences," she corrected herself with a nervous giggle. "Mark just reminded me of that."

"Go on," Pamela prodded, pressing the receiver tightly against her ear.

"There are so many connections, but I think the one you'll be most interested in is the star-shaped birthmark on his right knee. It's still there."

Pamela gasped and eased herself onto the edge of the couch.

"The star!"

"Yes, It's still there," Cindy repeated. "It's just like the one in the book."

"Okay, you've got my attention. He has a birthmark like her son's, but you'll have to excuse my skepticism. You could have read the book, produced the birthmark and incorporated any number of coincidences into your story. You'll have to do better than this."

"I ... you ... " Cindy stammered. "The birthmark is real."

"So you say. You could have tattooed it on, or even if he has one similar to Graham's, that doesn't make him Kim's son."

"Bur, Ms. Justice ... " Cindy started, then hesitated.

"Ms. Justice. This is Mark. I'm as skeptical as you are. My wife believes I'm Mrs. Sanborn's son. There are many things in Mrs. Sanborn's book that seem to suggest I might be her lost son. Believe me, I'm as unsure about this as you are, but my wife is beginning to make sense. You've got to give us a chance to see if I really am her son."

"Please, Ms. Justice," Cindy pleaded.

"What do you propose to do?" Pamela asked cautiously.

"Do you have a few more minutes now?" Cindy replied. "We've got more to say. Then, if you think we're legit, we can discuss next steps. Believe us, we would never do anything to harm Mrs. Sanborn. She's been through enough. But I know Mark is her son, Graham. And I would love to see a happy ending to her story and all of our stories."

When Pamela hesitated, Mark chimed in, fearing she might decide to terminate the call.

"Ms. Justice, both Mrs. Sanborn's and my future as mother and son is worth a few more minutes, isn't it?"

"Yes, I suppose so. You two do know the gravity of what you are proposing, don't you?"

"Yes," Cindy exclaimed. "Her book was her final good-bye to her son. She had come to terms with losing both Graham and her husband."

"That's right. And I won't allow her to be hurt again. Do you understand?"

"Believe me, we understand," Mark agreed. "It's been extremely difficult for me to even consider going back into my past. I've wanted to keep it buried. So, you see, Cindy is asking both Mrs. Sanborn and me to reconsider what each of us believes is the buried past. She's beginning to make a believer out of me."

"I'm not selling false hope, Ms. Justice," Cindy chorused. "I honestly believe we've got to get these two together. Mark is her lost son. I'd stake my life on it."

"Mark ..." Pamela said as she repositioned herself more comfortably on the couch, anticipating a lengthy continuation of this unorthodox call.

"Yes?"

"I'd like to believe your wife. Perhaps we'd better give her some rein here. What do you think?"

"I'm ready."

"Me, too." Pamela took a deep breath and released it noisily. "Okay, Mrs. Cindy Twain, tell me what you know."

Cindy described the connections between Mark and Graham as suggested in the novel. She explained the similarity of physical features like the blonde hair and blue eyes each had in common. She recounted their surprise about the crayoned picture of a white dog which Jamie colored for Mark and the painting presented to Kim by Pamela's sister, Karen.

Pamela gasped at the uncanny coincidence of that connection.

Cindy indicated their surprise when they discovered Mark's correct age as proposed in the novel.

Pamela assured them that if Mark was indeed Graham, he was nineteen now and not twenty-one. Then she jumped in with a question of her own.

"But what I don't understand is why he hasn't contacted Kim before now? And why is he using another name?"

Mark described his irreversible retrograde amnesia and his three-year struggle toward recovery. He briefly explained his identity crisis and subsequent election to use the name, Mark Twain.

When Cindy told her more about Mark's irreversible condition, and his struggle in coming to terms with his new identity, Pamela wept. Both Mark, who was on the extension phone, and Cindy got their chance to grieve when Pamela tearfully described Kim's fifteen-year crusade to find her son, which ended with the news of his death.

"Miss Justice, I remember the torn jeans I was wearing when they found me lying on the sidewalk outside the emergency room entrance. The only other material possessions I had on me was a pendant, a small fourteen-karat gold heart, half a heart, and the name Graham scribbled on a piece of paper."

Pamela shrieked her surprise.

"A what? You've got a half of a keepsake heart?"

"That's what sealed it for us," chimed Cindy. "It's like the one in the book."

Pamela's heart jumped to her throat, making it difficult for her to speak.

"Would you describe the heart?"

Mark read her the broken series of numbers etched on his half of the pendant. Pamela shrieked again, and was hyperventilating by the time she forced herself to speak.

"Those ... those are ... " she stammered, "those are half of the ... those numbers are half of the birth dates for Kim, her husband, and her son ... They weren't mentioned in her book ... Oh my God, it's really you. Graham ... I can't ... it's ... I don't know what to say. I'm beside myself."

Cindy tried unsuccessfully to control her sniffles.

Mark was the first to speak.

"I know what that feels like. Being beside yourself. I've been beside myself for the past five years. Literally. My new self has been living next to my old self."

Although both women saw the comedic link, neither could muster the slightest hint of a smile.

"Oh, Ms. Justice, does Mrs. Sanborn still dance?"

"No. Well, very rarely. Why do you ask?"

"She mentioned it in her book. I didn't know if she and her husband were ballroom dancers or not."

"Yes, they were ... they were the United States Ten Dance Champions when Jim died."

"We've got one more connection for you, then," Cindy exclaimed, hardly able to contain herself.

"'Oh?"

"This coming February, we are defending our Canadian National Championship. We're ballroom dancers, too."

Chills flashed up Pamela's spine, causing her to shiver.

"That's ... that's absolutely incredible."

"Mark learned to dance so fast, Ms. Justice. It must be in his genes."

"Oh, wow! Kim will be so thrilled. Graham, sorry, Mark. Fifteen years ago she and Jim dreamed of you following in their footsteps. And now ... you ... you two are the Canadian National Champions."

"Our goal is Blackpool two years from now," Mark boasted.

"Ah, kids, Kim will be ecstatic. This is unbelievable. No ... No ... It's believable. It's so wonderfully believable."

"When can we see her? When can I see my mother?" Mark asked, recognizing the obvious next step.

Both women renewed their sobs, with Pamela being the one to regain her composure enough to reply.

"As soon as you want, dear. When can you see her? Oh, Graham—or should I call you Mark—oh, it doesn't matter. This is wonderful!"

"We decided yesterday that if this call turned out to be what we thought it would, we'd fly down immediately," Mark announced calmly.

Pamela broke down again, unable to bridle her joy. She quickly collected herself, sniffling as she spoke into the phone.

"I'm sorry, kids," Pamela apologized as she wiped her runny nose. "It's just that ... this is going to be such a ... a tearfully wonderful Christmas."

Her nervousness erupted into a brief spell of laughter mixed with sobs of joy.

"Miss Justice ... " Cindy said, hesitating nervously.

"Cindy, please call me Pamela. I think this forty minute conversation has earned you that."

"Pamela, we've told my parents about the book and about Mark's possible parentage, but we've asked them to wait until we've met Mrs. Sanborn. I wanted to tell you that so you would know we have their full support. We think Mark needs to see her first ... to have time with her. Before ... you know what I mean?"

"I know exactly what you mean."

"And we haven't called the Joyce Dole from Atlanta in your book because we guessed that probably wasn't her real name or city address. We want to see her, too," Mark announced.

"The first name is right. Her name is Joyce, and she does live in Atlanta.

"Wonderful!" Cindy cooed.

"Are you driving or flying to Raleigh?"

"Flying in sometime tomorrow if we can get tickets this late," Mark confirmed.

Pamela coughed uncontrollably before she could slip into the kitchen and draw a glass of water from the spigot. She took a few sips and forced out a weak sentence.

"Tomorrow's ... tomorrow's Christmas Eve."

"Oh, that's right. Should we wait till ... " Mark cut himself off, unsure what to say.

"No! No! Good heavens no!" Pamela found her voice. "Tomorrow's perfect. She lost you on Christmas Eve. And now, fifteen years later, you're coming back to her on Christmas Eve. Kids, this is going to sound rather strange, but bear with me, okay?"

"Okay."

"Sure."

"I want you to call our office number. You know the one for the Institute. Do you still have it?"

"Yes, it's right here. We called it first before we realized the offices were closed."

"Leave a message for me. My extension is 511 and this will put you into my voice mail. Let me know when your flight arrives and I'll pick you up at the airport. I hope you can get a flight. It's the Raleigh-Durham Airport—RDU."

"Okay."

"Bring anything you think is necessary to help your mother understand who you are. You've sold me already. And I don't think you'll have any trouble convincing your mother. But any little thing will help."

"We'll bring the pendant."

"And Jamie's crayon picture," chorused Cindy. "And I'm sure she'll recognize Mark. He's got the same boyish face he did when I met him."

"Perfect."

"And we'll have to bring someone else," Cindy inserted, intentionally adding a tone of intrigue.

"I thought you said we weren't ... Oh," Mark recovered, sending a short chuckle over the phone.

"What is it? Who ... ?" Pamela stuttered her confusion.

"I'm ... we're pregnant," Cindy said proudly.

"Three months," added Mark.

Pamela gasped with delight.

"Oh, my, you two. Kim will be so excited. She is going to be a mother and a grandmother after all these years of being alone."

"We'll call you with the flight number and time as soon as we know," Mark reaffirmed.

"Great. Oh, can you stay a few days? Cindy, I hate for you to spend Christmas Day away from your parents, but ..."

"We're planning to stay there for a couple of days, maybe more. Then I'd like to come back again in January for a few days. I'm not exactly sure how to handle our reunion," Mark said.

"We'll figure all of that out later. Dress in layers. It's not as cold down here as it up there. You're in Montreal as I recall."

"Yes, and it's fairly mild here as well. Although we've already had several snowfalls."

"Oooo ... keep it there. Cindy, I apologize for the grilling I put you through at first and for hanging up in your ear. That is so uncharacteristic of me."

"Oh, Pamela, that's okay. We understand your wanting to protect Mrs. Sanborn."

"Does she look like her picture?" Mark asked, referring to Kim's picture on the back cover of her novel.

"It doesn't nearly do her justice. She's much more beautiful. I'm not going to tell you more than that, though," Pamela teased. "You two are already a couple of surprises up on her."

"Thank you for allowing us to explain."

"Cindy, dear, it's I who should offer the thanksgiving. God bless you both and God speed."

"We'll see you tomorrow. Oh, how will we know you?" Mark asked, realizing they had never met.

"It won't be hard at all. I'll be the silly woman dressed in a Mrs. Claus costume holding a sign that reads WELCOME HOME."

"You're kidding!"

"I'm as serious as an elf. It's Christmas, and Mrs. Claus and I are delivering a special gift package this year."

"Merry Christmas, then. We can't wait to get there."

"Merry Christmas, kids. I'm looking forward to meeting you."

When she hung up the phone, Pamela raced into the bathroom to freshen herself. She didn't want Kim to see that she had been crying. After she did a proper job on her face, Pamela straightened up the mess she caused from her fall earlier.

By the time she resumed her tree-trimming duties, she had composed herself outwardly, but her thoughts worked rapidly as she filtered through the logistics, considering whom to call about the reunion and when to notify them.

"Graham is alive! Graham is alive! And he'll be here tomorrow. Kim's son is alive and coming home!" she repeated the mantra to herself.

She grabbed a handful of tinsel from the bag on the chair and tossed a few strands of the shimmering strips on the lightly-trimmed branches of Kim's magnificent artificial tree.

Before she knew it, she found herself humming a few verses from the song, *I'll be Home for Christmas.*

§   §   §   §   §   §

Kim was sipping cappuccino in her favorite high-backed chair when Pamela came into the room.

"Are you still dressed in that Santa costume?" Kim asked, amused at her friend's levity.

"It's a Mrs. Claus outfit and I have a surprise gift package for you. I thought I'd deliver it tonight ... on Christmas Eve."

"Now you know we agreed not to exchange gifts. And why are you looking at me that way?" Kim asked, growing suspicious of her empty-handed friend who couldn't keep a straight face.

"Oh, I'm not exchanging gifts with you. I'm simply delivering them."

"From whom?"

"From God," Pamela bantered thoughtfully. "They're definitely from God."

"What are you talking about?"

"Remember that sculptor from Canada? The one who couldn't start the work for our courtyard?"

"Yes. The young man from Montreal. The one Dr. Nordstrom recommended."

Pamela nodded jubilantly, trying her best not to betray herself.

"But what does that have to do with ... Oh, Pamela! Has he decided to do the work?"

Pamela shook her head.

"Nope. He's decided to do something better than that!"

"Oh," Kim pretended she understood.

"Kim, darling, I think you'd better put that cup of coffee down. I've got something to tell you."

Pamela started bouncing on her feet, unable to channel the sudden rush of adrenaline which coursed through her body.

"Before I present you with the gift package, I want you to know that I have thoroughly checked everything out. Everything's on the up and up."

"What are you up to? Has Tony put you up to something?" Kim guessed, suspecting her agent was in collusion with Pamela.

"Listen to me. Did you hear what I said?"

"Yes. You've checked it out. Everything's on the up and up, as you say."

"Okay. Good. You heard that. It's important that you understand and believe that, because I don't want anything to interfere with the joy you are about to experience."

Kim squinted at her, confused as to where Pamela was headed.

"You must accept what is about to happen at face value, because a miracle has happened and I want you to give yourself to it completely. Do not doubt your eyes or your heart."

"Pamela, you've got me both confused and excited."

"Do not doubt what you are about to see. The sculptor and his beautiful young wife, Cindy, are here to see you."

Kim threw her a questioning look and then switched to a surprised one when the couple stepped from behind Pamela into the room.

Kim rose to greet them, but found it difficult to move her feet right away. Then she started toward them and extended her hand, expecting a handshake.

Cindy rushed to her and embraced Kim, who threw Pamela the most surprised look. Uncertain as to what to do, Kim allowed her hands to migrate up to the other woman's shoulders so she could reciprocate the young woman's surprise embrace.

Cindy pulled away slightly and looked Kim directly in her puzzled eyes.

"This is my husband," Cindy announced proudly as she pulled him closer to her, "and your long lost son."

Surprise flung Kim's mouth open as she struggled to maintain her balance. Her bewilderment immobilized her for a moment. Her eyes shot around the room, from Cindy to Mark to Pamela and back to Mark.

"He didn't die in the accident, Kim," reported Pamela tearfully.

Cindy was beaming.

Kim riveted her gaze on Mark, studying him through blurred lenses. A coagulation of thoughts rushed through her head, sending her into a jumble of stupification.

Mark reached into his pocket and held up the pendant.

Kim's eyes fell upon it's glistening surface immediately. "The heart pendant," she whispered, dividing her look of astonishment between Mark and the pendant.

Just as her legs started to buckle, Kim reached for Mark.

"It's really you," Kim sobbed. "You've come home!"

Still wordless, Mark embraced his mother, holding her tightly. He wished he could feel more, remember more. But he could feel her love in the way she clutched at him. Her sobs were genuine. He knew that much.

He could see the look of recognition in her eyes and feel the unmistakable pounding of a mother's heart as it recorded the long-awaited encounter with her son. He was surprised to find a tear slip down his cheek as he held his mother tightly.

With her head still buried in Mark's chest Kim reached for Cindy and pulled her into Mark's accommodating embrace.

Unable to stop the flow of tears, Kim held both Mark and Cindy in the intense nostalgic merger of mother and child.

The three of them held their tangled embrace until Kim broke the spell, pulling herself back slightly to allow for some space between them, but not permitting a complete separation.

Kim sensed a slight hesitance in Mark's touch. But her maternal instinct understood. Both of them, all of them, were in unchartered emotional territory. She was unsure what to do next. But she was certain of one thing. Her son was home, and he brought a wife with him.

"What shall I call you? Mark or Graham? Oh, I'm sorry, forgive me, we don't, we don't have to talk about that now," Kim corrected herself.

Before Mark could reply, Cindy spoke. "You can call me pregnant."

Kim's mouth flung open.

"You're ... "

"Pregnant," Cindy repeated, beaming with the news.

"I have a grandchild on the way? I ... we've ... " Kim trailed off, unable to hold back the tears.

Hope came sauntering into the living room, wagging his tail.

A sudden rush of emotion caught up to Mark when he realized the old dog was the same animal in the crayoned picture he brought with him. He threw himself on his knees in front of Kim and grabbed her around the waist.

"Mother," he said, sobbing apologetically. "I believe I am your son."

Kim held his face in her palms.

"I know, you look like your father. It's ... it's like having both of you back again."

Kim lifted her head and looked at the other two women.

"I ... I can't believe it. He's really here. My son has come back home to me."

Both women smiled, but remained standing where they were.

"We have fifteen years to catch up on and you have people to meet. Special people," Kim said affectionately.

Hope circled behind Mark and planted his front paws on Mark's shoulders. The old dog punctuated his climb with a bark, and then followed it with a flurry of hasty licks to the back of Mark's head and neck.

"You recognize him, too, don't you, boy?" Kim whispered aloud.

Hope answered her with another collaborative bark.

Kim closed her moist eyelids and held Mark's head tightly against her stomach.

Jim, darling, he's back. She addressed her dead husband in her thoughts. *Our son has come back to us. And he still has your eyes.*

Mark raised himself to his feet and kissed his mother on her forehead.

"This feels too right to be a dream," he whispered to Kim.

She tightened her lips and nodded radiantly.

"Pamela, get the phone, please," Kim instructed as she squeezed Mark's arm.

With one of her arms wrapped in Mark's, Kim used her free hand to speed dial a phone number.

The puzzled looks of the others followed her ear to the phone.

"Oh, good, you're home," Kim said. "Joyce, I hope you're sitting down, because you're not going to believe what I have to tell you ... "

About the Author

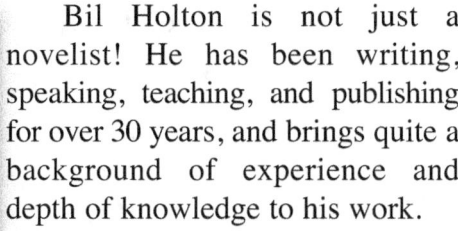

Bil Holton is not just a novelist! He has been writing, speaking, teaching, and publishing for over 30 years, and brings quite a background of experience and depth of knowledge to his work.

In 1984, he and his wife, Cher, founded The Holton Consulting Group, Inc., which is still alive and well today! They work with clients in the U.S., Canada, Germany, England, and South America, with a mission of creating extraordinary leaders and engaged employees. Their impressive client list includes Fortune 100 companies, healthcare facilities, universities, associations, and government agencies.

In addition to Bil's novels, Bil and Cher have authored and co-cuthored over 50 titles, including business books such as *The Manager's Short Course to a Long Career*, which was selected by SoundView Executive Summaries as one of their Top 30 Business Books, and spiritual books including *New Metaphysical Versions of Matthew, Mark, Luke, John,* and *Revelation* – the first ever verse-by-verse metaphysical interpretations of these books.

When he isn't involved in work and research, Bil enjoys golf, travel, jigsaw puzzles, the theatre, and landscaping. The Holtons like to push the envelop and maintain their zest for life by taking what they call "Indiana Jones Adventures," such as white-water rafting, sky diving, and fire walking. American-style ballroom dancing is also in their DNA. Although they have retired their competitive dance shoes, Bil and Cher love to perform ballroom showcases and exhibitions. Their two sons, beautiful daughters-in-law, and incredible grandchildren all live nearby. Their visits are always joyful.

To learn more about Bil, order books, and contact him for speaking appearances and book signings, visit Bil's novelist site, BilHolton.com

---

Other novels by Bil Holton

Silent Echoes

Ultimate Betrayal

Coming Soon:
Déja Vu All Over Again
(the exciting sequel to *Silent Echoes*)